TO EARN HER FREEDOM
SHE JUST HAS TO SURVIVE
THE DEADLIEST RACE ON EARTH

RUN
LAB
RAT
RUN

BY AWARD WINNING AUTHOR
Shawn C. Butler

RUN
LAB
RAT
RUN

A NOVEL

Shawn C. Butler

Learn more about the world of *Run Lab Rat Run* and the Modified series on shawncbutler.com, including a full glossary of terms, a timeline, a shrubbery and more.

For my mother,
who deserves all good things
the universe has to offer

ONE:
The Perfectly Average Girl

Race Time 25:11:43

I'VE ALWAYS LOVED THINGS with teeth. In my dreams, I was the hunter and the whole world was my prey. But those are the dreams of all weak and fragile things. We are what we are, how we're born or made, and it's hard not to envy those made better. And that envy sells, billions a day, trillions a year, driving the global genetics industry one subscription at a time. If you want healthier children, prettier skin and total confidence that your life has meaning, yeah, there's a pill for that. And they probably tested it on me.

On the off chance you haven't heard of me, hi there, I'm Media Conaill. Media's a feminized form of median, which is why everyone calls me 'the perfectly average girl.' Well, that and because I'm 5'8", exactly average height for a modified woman. My current and legally registered skin color is Pantone 51-6 C, golden-brown, and I have curly black hair and green eyes. Nothing exceptional there. On a more personal note, I love old movies, older books and have an inordinate fondness for cheese. I've also spent all twenty-one years of my life in a bioengineering lab. If you want to know more, check out the marketing collateral for TrumaniTech Baseline Bronze—the bestselling genetic subscription of all time. That's me on the back label. I could tell you more but, for now, only three things matter:

First, I always swore when I woke up. No idea why. I think it's like the *bing* on old computers, telling you they're online and ready for action. On really bad days, I cursed in every language that had words to express simultaneous hatred and despair—Russian was good, German was excellent—but my default was a straight-up *motherfucker*. You'll understand when you meet my mother.

The second thing is that I'm supposed to be running the Modified Marathons, the hardest and most dangerous ultramarathon in the world. This involves slogging up and down Mt. San Jacinto, just outside of Palm Springs, California, and jumping, crawling, swimming or otherwise fighting through increasingly difficult obstacles while modified animals try to stop me. It's not supposed to involve lying unconscious on my back at the bottom of a cave.

Which brings us to the third and most immediate concern: Tim, the giant panther that's about to eat my face.

"Motherfucker!"

Told you.

But this time I had reason to swear; I was pinned beneath half-a-ton of grinning black death. Everything stopped. My mouth, brain, heart, solar fusion—all of it just *froze*. One minute you think you're at the top of the food chain, genetically superior to billions of natural human beings, then you wake up under a *panthera pardus* the size of a natural bear and you finally get it; there are predators and prey locked in an eternal battle of hoof and claw, and then there's your dumb ass trying not to scream yourself unconscious. You have no special purpose or neo-Darwinian destiny. You're just the next meal.

And like all food with a brain, you beg.

Please don't kill me. Please don't kill me. Dear god, please don't kill me.

But this god wasn't listening. He was going to tear out my throat and rip me into tiny human shreds, and there was nothing I could do about it.

"Please don't eat me," I begged.

He leaned in and growled, a low tone like gravel on bone. His mouth opened to reveal a bottomless maw of infinite teeth. I turned away and closed my eyes. This was it. This was how I would die. There was no flash of my past life. No last words for my family. I just hoped it didn't hurt.

Make it quick, I thought. *Make it end.*

Instead, he smacked his lips and licked my face slowly, repeatedly, like he was dehydrated and I was a salt lick. And just like that, the universe regained forward motion. I closed my mouth and tried to turn away, but I was already covered in panther saliva.

"Goddamn it." I tried to push him away. He licked me again.

I know what you're thinking. It's kinda sweet, maybe a little gross, but better than a vigorous panther mauling. I'd normally agree, but my brain was coming back online and I was utterly humiliated. Of course he didn't kill me. He *couldn't* kill me.

"This is loop two," I told him. "You can't hurt me."

He disagreed, casually dropping a giant paw on my bloody leg. I stifled a scream and scrambled back to the granite wall. His eyes blazed with amusement. Where was I going?

"You're supposed to be in a cage," I blurted. "There are rules."

He growled irritably. I guess I couldn't blame him. I'd spent a lot of my life in a cage, and sometimes you need to stretch your legs. But I had a race to run, and it was time to get moving. I tried to see if he had a Personal Assistant implant like mine—modified animals often got PAs for remote control and monitoring—but I couldn't see the usual forehead crystal. It was too dark, with the only light coming from five skylight-like ovals cut into the cave's roof. I thought mean thoughts at him. He growled again. This was taking too long.

"Tim!" I yelled. "Back off!"

I didn't expect him to obey because Tim wasn't his real name. I doubt he had a real name. When I'd first seen him in the display case before the race, his stats told me he was optimized for guerrilla warfare and quiet butchery. I wanted to call him something unthreatening, so I shortened 'Toys with its Meat' to Tim. It made sense at the time.

"Please?" I asked. He was probably wondering things like, *Why do I put up with this crap? I'm a goddamn panther?* But he eventually slumped away and curled up by his open cage at the opposite end of the cave. Tim it was.

"Stay," I said. His disdainful expression made up for the middle finger he didn't have.

I wiped off his saliva and grunted my way to a standing position. Nothing was broken, but my leg was bleeding from three long cuts. I stared at the bloody lacerations, at Tim, and back to the blood. Something knotted in my stomach.

"You scratched me."

He licked his paws and gnawed on a bone that probably wasn't a human femur.

It was definitely time to go.

I looked up at the ovals of blue sky above, each opening roughly bisected lengthwise by a slackline—a two-inch-wide canvas tightrope climbers used for balance training and I used for falling off—but there was no sign of a net. I couldn't remember how I'd lost my balance or the fall, but there should have been a safety net on this loop. Which meant someone wanted me down here. There were no mistakes in the Marathons.

Suddenly, all the fear was gone and I was just angry. I had to get out of this hole or my race was over, and that couldn't happen. Not finishing the race meant genetic deoptimization for me and my family. It meant being tossed back into the slums of the unmodified to die slowly of disease and hunger. The worst fate a human being could suffer was being merely human. I'd burn the world down before I let that happen to my family. I could worry about the net later. I could treat my leg later. Even the panther could wait.

As if hearing my thoughts, Tim growled and got to his feet.

Maybe I didn't love things with teeth after all.

The Black

PEOPLE ASK IF I regret being a lab rat or if I miss the freedom of a normal life, and my answer is always the same: it's better than being burned alive. Some people laugh inappropriately or ask if that's what happens if I fail a test, but the truth is far more mundane. When I was five years old, my family home in Beaumont, California, burned to the ground.

You've probably never heard of Beaumont because the fire left nothing but ash and charred foundations. Flames soared hundreds of feet in the air and melted the footrests on news helicopters. The sky was so dark it cooled the entire Los Angeles basin, like a reverse hurricane with hell in the eye and calm in the storm. Nobody tried to put it out, at least no one who could. The fire started during riots against mandatory vaccines in the slums of the natural poor—the genetically unmodified dregs of humanity—and modified firefighters just let it burn.

The fire spread east from Beaumont to the outskirts of Palm Springs, west to Moreno Valley and north to the summit of Mt. San Gorgonio. It was only stopped to the south by Mt. San Jacinto and a thousand firefighters battling to protect the natural reserve and its precious trees. The final death count was probably in the tens of thousands, but the government didn't search for survivors or bury the dead, so who knows? The Interstate 10 freeway between Redlands and Desert Hot Springs was covered in the burned-out skeletons of cars for months, drivers immolated within, like a snapshot from a nuclear holocaust.

A few years later, Congress designated The Black as a national monument. They put up a small bronze statue in a scorched field, showing a nameless woman with her head bowed in defeat. Then they made a minor adjustment to a coefficient in the Social Stability Algorithm, which told the government what guaranteed income and employment level assured maximum social calm with minimum expenditure. There was even an ad campaign about how it was all a tragic mistake, and wouldn't it be better just to take the vaccine?

My first memory of the fire is one, of my first memories of anything. My father took my mother's hand on the couch of our TrumaniTech (TTI) corporate apartment as we watched a video of the raging inferno. I stared at her thin white fingers laced between his massive black ones and felt warmth that had nothing to do with fire—they so rarely touched each other—until I looked up to see Mom crying. She usually smiled like most people breathed, and she never cried.

I looked back at the TV where a ranch-style house was being consumed by fire. My older brother Tommy leaned over to tell me that's where they lived before I was born. The roof of a home I'd never known lifted off in a tornado of flame, shingles soaring like fireflies into the dead black sky. My mother pushed her face into my father's chest, weeping, and I had the first epiphany of my life. To be natural was to burn while better people watched from their air-conditioned living rooms. Modification was safety and having a family that loved you. So, no, to answer the question again, I didn't mind being a modified lab rat because it was better than being dead.

*

ON AN EQUALLY DISTURBING NOTE, my parents have apparently had sex. The result of one such glorious union was me, a tiny blastocyst implanted in my mother's uterine wall and bound for Beaumont. And there my life would've ended if not for the Chrome Wars. Decades before I was born, someone set off a genetic bomb that randomized races and brought humanity to the edge of global annihilation. To prevent another genetic plague, all pregnant women were now screened for contagion in their first trimester. My fetal DNA was immediately flagged for 'exceptional characteristics.' I can just imagine my mom's eyes lighting up when she got the results.

After quick negotiations and an automated bidding process, I became the legal ward of TTI, the world's fourth-largest biotechnology company—the one with the black octopus logo.

I was removed from my mother, transferred to lab facilities at TTI's Escondido headquarters, implanted in a transparent ball informally called a birth-o-sphere, and grown until I was ready for delivery. My parents, under contract with TTI as foster guardians, were in the room when they pulled me out. My brother was three at the time, and I'm sure he ran around the room like a hyperkinetic demon while I cried a lot. It seems like the kind of thing I'd do until I was old enough for cheese.

TTI lead scientist Dr. Victor Adams oversaw the delivery with his research partner, Dr. Kylera Antigone Braithwaite, who usually goes by Dr. K for obvious reasons. I spent the next eight years with Victor as my genetic mentor, the baby monster to his Dr. Frankenstein. It took him a while to figure out what to do with me, but on my seventh birthday, I was assigned a permanent role as the lead beta test subject for Baseline Bronze. Dad asked me if I was excited.

I said, "Yes, of course," but what I thought was, *No one can burn us now.*

All new entry-level genetic modifications are tested billions of times by computer simulation, a few more on early stage human subjects and finally on betas like me. If the tests don't kill me and I don't grow toes on my face, they harden the new trait—stronger hair, smoother skin, better disease resistance or whatever was in demand—and release it as a gateway modification for the breeder class. My eyebrows were once blue for nine weeks and my bones nearly dissolved. I even spent a month smelling like salted pork, but no one ate me and I never died. I came close enough to require CPR and a genomic flush on several occasions, but I'm nearly indestructible. At least, that's what I told myself on the good days.

On the bad days, Victor would hold me and say, "There there, my little penguin." I got this nickname from a story he told me when I was six. Male Emperor penguins huddled together to protect themselves and their single egg from the Antarctic winter. Penguins on the inside rotated to the outside, hour after hour in the endless night, so that none of them froze. They took care of their own, collaborated to survive, and in the spring light they celebrated the birth of their young and the return of their mates. Victor meant we were in this together and we'd always take care of each other.

Which I still believed, even if I rarely saw him anymore. I spent most of my time alone between tests, staring at the ceiling of Dr. K's research lab in a quiet building behind the titanium gates that surrounded TTI's headquarters. I read old books and watched older movies, the more violent the better, and I always wanted the animals to win. What were tiny men next to living gods like King Kong, a glorious beast evolved to kill dinosaurs and defeat time itself? In my head, I roared with Kong in defiant rage, but the fury never made it to my lips. Even the King was afraid of fire. Instead, I focused my irritation on beating the tests, and the surprise on Victor's face when I opened my eyes and could still swear without drooling on myself.

Sand and Fire

IN THE BEGINNING, there was hierarchy: God, Jesus, Mary, priest, nun, man, woman, boy, girl, dog, bitch, plants and dirt, always in that order, top to bottom. You might not like it, but you knew where you stood and when you kneeled. The only thing people were more certain of than who was above and below them was how much they envied the former and despised the latter. We split the atom, landed on the moon, colonized Mars and genetically rebuilt humanity in the image of a secular god, but the hierarchy remained as clear as our place in it.

I didn't know where I belonged in that hierarchy until Victor was promoted to CEO and Dr. K took over as my genetic mentor. This was right after my eighth birthday, and I cried for a week. Dr. K watched me sob like an injured bug twitching in the dirt until she knocked me unconscious for the next test. I was not her little penguin.

"What's that?" I asked the day I stopped crying. There was a new diagram on the door, a pyramid with colored layers and light coming off the top, like an old dollar bill. Dr. K glanced at the diagram and smiled for the first time since I'd been reassigned.

"That's the modified hierarchy," she said, and then explained it in detail. The base of the pyramid was the breeder class, comprising my family and roughly sixty percent of all modified human beings who could theoretically still have children if they weren't sterilized to prevent genetic intellectual property theft. Above them was the terminal class, people like her and Victor, thirty percent of humanity modified as far as DNA and pharmaceuticals could push them. Near the top were the augmented, ten percent of people mechanically and biologically modified just short of synthetic perfection. I'd never met anyone augmented. Above the augmented, radiating angelic light, were the mythological transcendent—the ideal unity of biology and machine, DNA and artificial intelligence. The perfection for which we all yearned.

"Where am I?" I asked. She walked over and tapped the bottom of the pyramid, the thin bottom line bordering the breeder class above only a vague smear of yellow and orange. My place was below and beneath, but not quite the lowest of the low. Hierarchy was everything. The augmented had nothing but contempt for terminals, who disdained the breeders, who desperately needed someone to look down on and, fortunately for them, had all of unmodified natural humanity to regard with conceit. The pyramid didn't even include the naturals, and when I noticed, Dr. K pointed to the smear of sand under the pyramid.

"There they are," she said.

When I'd been with Victor, I sometimes wondered why penguins took care of themselves while human beings did not, but now it was obvious. Penguins didn't have hierarchy. They circled in and out, cold then warm and cold again, none on top and none beneath, eternally selfless and collaborative. No wonder they were stuck in the worst ecosystem on Earth. But Dr. K was wrong about one thing: the smear wasn't sand, it was fire. Naturals burned because they were born to burn, and I was barely above them. Far too close to the flames.

Endurance

ON MY SIXTEENTH BIRTHDAY, my father gave me a tattered old paper book about a ship called the Endurance. In January 1914, explorer Ernest Shackleton sailed the Endurance into a break in the pack-ice on his way to attempt the first trans-Antarctic crossing. It was a silly goal manufactured by a bored man who'd already been knighted despite losing the race to be first to the South Pole, and his expedition was memorable only for its crushing failure. The Endurance was quickly stuck in thickening ice. Shackleton's crew fought for their lives as their oak-hulled ship slowly shattered and sank. For the next eighteen months, Shackleton and his men battled starvation, frostbite, hallucinations, hundred-foot waves and giant sea walruses. Wearing little more than wool and leather, they feasted on collaborative but defenseless penguins and survived the impossible.

I never asked why Dad gave me something so expensive and fragile. They hadn't printed books on paper in nearly forty years. Usually, you bought a single blank simulpaper book for the feel of it and used your PA to overlay words on the pages. That way, one empty physical book lasted forever. But Dad gave me a real book every year, always an adventure story, and I think it was his way of telling me I could do anything if I never gave up. There were no problems I couldn't overcome with training and determination. I was just a beta baseline, genetic trash of the modified world, but I was still invincible. Some days when the testing got bad, I'd whisper one of Shackleton's quotes as a mantra—*through endurance we conquer*—which at least made me feel more badass on mornings like this when I was bent over, puking into the donation bucket next to my lab table.

"*Jebiesz jeze*," I said after wiping my mouth, a solid Polish insult implying Dr. K was inappropriately fond of hedgehogs. I'd been sixteen for thirty-six hours, and she still hadn't acknowledged my birthday. It was a game we played. She pretended not to care about me, and I pretended it didn't hurt.

"I like that one." She checked my pupils for something. "Hedgehogs are cute. In Japanese, they're called needle mice. Did you know that?" Of course I knew that. Everyone who had a personal assistant knew pretty much everything on demand, and I'd never known life without one. PAs were usually implanted right after birth and grew with your body, so it was easy to think of them as just another part of you. I named mine Alex after the Royal Library of Alexandria because he knew everything and it sounded smart, but his real magic was what he could make me feel. Behind the tiny lens in my forehead was an entire network of neural wiring that reached into my brain and nervous system, and high-bandwidth data ports at the base of my neck.

PAs could make you feel anything, see anything and *be* anything or anywhere you wanted. PAs knew everything about you, and you came to trust them, love them and even need them. So it's probably no surprise that PAs were hacked days after the first implants were released. People were manipulated into doing terrible things, and laws were passed that made it a death-penalty crime to hack a PA. But that was a long time ago and now everyone with a PA implant knew everything whenever they wanted. People still asked questions like, "Have you heard…" or "Did you know…" but only as a holdover from pre-networked times.

"Maybe we should get a hedgehog for the lab?" Dr. K asked. It wasn't a real question, and I didn't bother to respond. Alex made it look like a hedgehog was dancing on Dr. K's head, and I tried not to laugh. Her breath came out as white mist in the freezing air, but I was surprised to feel the chill so deeply. I had an exceptional ability to deal with temperature variations. Dr. K was wearing a puffy down coat and still shivered constantly. God knows why she kept it so cold in here. None of the other labs were like this. My brother's lab down the hall was like a spa. Maybe they were testing my cold tolerance, or the test required sub-zero temperatures. I'd never know, but it's one reason I loved old books and movies about polar exploration. If naturals like Shackleton could survive 40-below in wool and leather, I could deal with a few goosebumps.

Dr. K leaned back and studied me through narrow brown eyes nested in tight yellow-brown features that could have been Asian or Hispanic, but more likely she was grown from a hardwood tree that never learned human emotions. Her forehead PA crystal blinked more than her eyes as she probed my mind, checking parameters and analyzing results.

"Why are you staring at me like that?" I demanded. It was offensive. And why did she look so happy? "Seriously, what happened?" It wasn't a casual question. Betas lived short, intensely isolated lives and often died forgotten between product launches. You get used to the idea, along with the fact that you never really know yourself. Every morning you wake up different, like a Russian doll inside yourself. Pull off my head, and god knows what would grow back. What they never tell people is that genetics isn't an exact science. There are billions of variables and even if they get ninety-nine percent of them right, there's always that naughty one percent. Dr. K dubbed that mischievous percentage *Zoot*, from an old movie called *Monty Python and the Holy Grail*; one of a million failed attempts to build a friendship between us. Zoot might kill me when I was thirty, or tomorrow or never. Naughty, naughty Zoot. You got used to it, but you never missed the clues that something had changed, especially if it was surprise and joy on the face of a woman who rarely smiled.

"Well…" She glanced at the black glass dome above us. "It worked."

"What worked?" I tried not to follow her glance. After someone tried to steal TTI intellectual property, Genetic Overwatch and TTI military contractors required fully networked security AI in all the labs. Now everything we did was recorded, parsed and evaluated from behind unnecessarily large black glass domes in every ceiling. I'm sure it always had been. Now it was just more obvious.

"I can't tell you."

"That's different," I snided. Yes, it's a verb. I was usually unconscious during the tests. Machines and computers told them more than my mouth could, so it was better to knock out the subject and shut my cheese hole. I think she just liked the silence. I'm not good at silence.

"This could be big," she said. "It's never worked before. I have no idea how to reproduce it, but now that we know it's possible…"

I was super excited for her. "I'm super excited for you." Even if it led to more tests and more unconscious playtime. "Will it mean a larger stipend for my family?"

"Maybe." Gears spun in her giant, terminal-class brain. "Do you need something?"

"No." I didn't, but more importantly, I wasn't *allowed* anything. I was the test model. You have to keep things under control or the tests don't work. "It's for Tommy." He was pestering me for upgrades, as if he could be any more optimized. He had every breeder-class endurance package the company offered, most of the compatible speed upgrades, and other things never released to the public. He could run a three-minute mile on a good day, like a cartoon with blurry legs. I loved forcing him to run with me through the campus woods, watching him fight to keep my slothful pace, and then letting him off the leash. He'd vanish in a flash and I'd end up sucking dust for miles.

"Okay," Dr. K said. "I'll see what we can do."

That meant it was big. She never promised anything she couldn't deliver. She never promised anything at all.

"So, what is it?" I don't know why I asked. It never worked.

"I'll tell you as soon as I can." Which still might be never. Why did she look so excited?

I winced at a stabbing pain behind my eyes. It was gone a second later, just a quick knife to the skull—one of the wonderful side effects of my work, like dying in my late twenties. While the rest of the modified world had become practically immortal, test subjects like me had the life prospects of a medieval peasant.

"Headache?"

"Tommy's trying out for the Marathons." I ignored her question, as I did anything that implied weakness. "I think he'll get in this year." I just hoped he didn't get hurt.

She nodded vaguely, meaning she already knew or didn't care. Sometimes the lab rat was interesting, sometimes not so much. That was the first time I thought about throat-punching someone. Don't know why. I just imagined smashing her windpipe against the webbing between my thumb and forefinger. She'd go down like a fainting goat.

"*Be nice*," Alex whispered from the back of my mind, always the voice of calm.

"Why are you looking at *me* like that?" Dr. K asked, but I think she knew. She always knew.

The Invitation

THERE WAS A FIRE on my cheesecake, twenty-one candles sputtering while I tried to focus on my wish. What I wanted was so clear. It was off campus, beyond the gates, somewhere blue and bright that smelled like wildflowers, or darkling gray on the side of an ocean cliff as tempests raged. Better yet, somewhere high and white above the clouds, so cold my breath frosted the sky. Okay, maybe it wasn't that clear, but it was somewhere *else*.

I inhaled. I wished. I blew.

My parents cheered and my brother smiled. Our pet blue-ringed Australian octopus Paisley pressed up against the sides of her saltwater aquarium in the living room, watching us with big black eyes as one multi-colored tentacle poked out of the water like a fleshy periscope. Doofus was missing in action, unusual for a golden Lab that wanted to be the barking and drooling center of everything, but he'd show up as soon as he smelled food.

"No clapping," I said. My mother's absurd ruby lips trembled in disappointment. She cut the cake and slid giant slices across the dining room table, emphasizing each time that it was *cheese*cake because I loved cheese. She did it every year. I hated cheesecake—the name was an unforgivable deception—but I smiled dutifully and inhaled one piece, then two. I was always hungry. I wondered if all lab rats ate as much as I did, or if they ever let them out at night.

Mom watched me from behind her wide green eyes, the only thing we had in common. Where I was the color of coffee and caramel, she was milky glass topped with fire—a featherweight wisp of pale white skin, Pantone 61-9 C, frothy red hair and emerald eyes.

You might call it the Sensual Irish Elf package because, well, that's what it's called. Her irises were the last vestige of her natural self, the one thing she never changed because she wanted to hold on to the bond between us. She pouted the entire month my eyes were brown just like my father's. I never told her I had Dr. K do it as a joke. I wasn't trying to be cruel. We just didn't see eye-to-eye on most things.

I know you're supposed to love your mother, and I wanted to, but she was the one who sold me. She made Dad sign me over *or else*. I knew it was the right thing, our one way out of natural poverty, and the only reason we'd survived. And it wasn't that I hated my life or didn't appreciate what the money had done for us, my brother especially. She was sweet and protective when she wasn't vapid or inappropriate, but she still sold me, her little girl, and our relationship was purely functional. If I ever move out, I'll change my eyes back to brown.

My father sat quietly in the shadow he carried around with himself, looking no more like me than my mother did. Skin color had been random at birth since the Chrome Wars, and now it was selectable in your teens. Skin tone, hair and sexual orientation were among the few free genetic alterations, so everyone swapped looks and lovers when they got bored. Modern families never looked alike, and ours was no exception. Dad was so black he was almost blue, Pantone 323-1 C, but he was born the rusted tan of Arizona desert sand. Black was the palette he chose when he was fourteen and considered mature enough to make such decisions. I envied his skin, the way it absorbed light and how he radiated heat like a star raging against the cold of space. I could feel it from across the table, a solar wind that would burn me to slag if I let him get too close. It's one of the flaws they've never fixed in him, eternal and genetically inextricable. It must be terrible to need something so desperately.

He had a fleck of cheesecake on his upper lip, melting.

My brother Tommy was slightly darker than Mother, Pantone 61-7C, blonde, and built like a triathlete if triathletes were made of corded steel. When he moved, tight sheaths of muscle flexed with such casual speed you'd think it was an illusion. You can't even tell when he blinks, it's so fast, and he never gets tired. I sometimes wonder if he's part synthetic, human-like flesh wrapped around a nearly indestructible body and a nuclear core. I wouldn't care. I talked a good game about my father, as if his intense affection was beyond me, but I worship Tommy. Don't tell him. I'm Media, the perfectly average girl, and all my emotions are supposed to be baseline and reasonable. I can love and hate, but not passionately, or at least that's what it says on the packaging.

"You paragliding, Fiddy?" Tommy asked. *Fiddy* for fifty-fifty or average, his second nickname for me and the one he used in public. *Para* for PA Reality Augmentation, and *gliding* because people sometimes lost track of the real world behind the illusion. I smiled. I'd kill for him. I don't know why. Maybe it's a remnant of the fetus my mother sold, a quantum of my true self.

"What?" Everyone was staring at me. I checked my face for cheesecake.

"The Chairman sent you a card," Mom said in her singsong voice, sliding a golden envelope across the table. Chairman was what everyone called Dr. Adams now that he was Chairman and CEO of TTI. I still called him Victor when no one else was around.

"What's this?" The envelope was suspicious and clearly not cheese.

"It's a surprise."

I hated surprises. My whole life was surprises. You try waking up every few weeks with random changes to your body and see how fond you are of the unexpected. It was fine in the lab, not at home, but Mom loved surprises.

"Well?" Mom prodded. I tore open the envelope with a very intentional sigh and pulled out a card with colors that flowed like mercury and oil. I caught my breath and looked up at Tommy. He was as shocked as I was.

"Is this…"

"They've invited you to the games," Mom said, her excitement less restrained than usual. She was effervescent as champagne in space, all brightness and bubbles, but my brother was thunderstruck. I don't mean that literally. How can thunder strike something? It should be lightningstruck. Tommy was that. Dad was inscrutable.

"They don't invite betas," I said. We don't get out of the lab. "I'm not even a sales or demo model. I've never been in a race." I'd run simulated races on a treadmill in the gym until I realized it had the word *mill* in it. I'm not wheat, and I don't want to be flour. Now I only ran outside with Tommy, and running was part of my required fitness routine. The idea of running on real trails in the mountains of the Marathons was pure fantasy.

"I don't get it."

"It was my idea," Mom said.

"What?" Dad said. How did he fit that much dismay and confusion in one look?

"You saw Jasmina fall," Mom continued. We all had. Tommy's baseline teammate had been head-butted off a cliff by a bighorn sheep during an ultra in Utah. She broke her back and several ribs, and was lucky not to die. All wild animals were modified to avoid humans after the Human-Fauna Relations Assurance Act, and the attack was so surprising and random it was hysterical. I laughed— Sorry, Jasmina, but did you see the look of satisfaction on that sheep's face?—then I felt bad, partly because they probably put the sheep down, partly because I envied her. I knew Jasmina from when she was the beta for Baseline Silver, and we'd always been competitive. When she got out of the lab and I didn't, she was more than a little condescending. But now TTI was healing Jasmina slowly to ensure complete rejuvenation without the scar tissue of emergency repairs, which meant she'd be out for months, and I was in. I don't know if it was karma, but I'd have adopted that sheep if I could have.

"There aren't any other baselines on the TTI team," Mom twittered. "So I just thought, why not you? I mean, they're requiring naturals on every team this year. So…"

"That makes no actual sense," Tommy said, trying to control his temper. "She hasn't trained. She's never raced, not ever."

"They're letting naturals in?" I asked.

"Requiring them," Tommy said. "They're always allowed, but they never qualify."

"Neither did I," I noted. Tommy nodded, as in, *no kidding.*

"The race is dangerous," he said. "Why would they even let you run?"

Good question. There was no reason to put me at risk. I was a corporate investment, not a runner. I took new genetic modifications, or g-mods, and made them work when every other model failed. There was an old book about a woman whose cancer cells never died: *The Immortal Life of Henrietta Lacks.* I was the living equivalent, the FDA-approved, patented lab rat who never quit. I was invincibly normal and nearly irreplaceable, or so they told me when I asked to go off campus without a security detail.

And the Marathons were absurdly dangerous. They were designed to be almost impossible—the type of race you enter when running a regular 100-mile ultramarathon or obstacle race wasn't enough of a workout. The Marathons comprised five 40-mile loops for a total of 200 miles, included 75,000 feet of total elevation gain (and loss), mixed with increasingly difficult obstacles, and did it all in the broiling desert heat near Palm Springs. You didn't sign up—you and your team were invited—but you only accepted if you were drunk, suicidal, or your corporate sponsorship required participation. Tommy fell in the last category, but he'd also begged to be included. I'm not sure what that says about him. People died every year, often mutilated by modified animals on the post-Fun Run laps, but I couldn't wait. If you have trouble understanding my enthusiasm, you haven't spent more than twenty years as a lab experiment. And it wasn't as if I'd make it to the dangerous loops. I'd be lucky to finish one.

Mom wasn't even fazed. "Isn't this what you wanted? To get out?"

Of course it's what I want. My wish had come true. I just couldn't believe she'd done it. I'm not sure she could either. She looked like a squirrel with a golden nut, excited, excited, excited. I sometimes forgot her initial modifications were as a sales and marketing model with an early sex package that made her irrationally positive about everything. Even unsubscribing to the sex mods hadn't dampened her enthusiasm. You've never heard anyone so thrilled to meet a Seventh-day Adventist or dust under the refrigerator, which no one does anymore, of course. That's what synthetics are for. She clapped sometimes when she went to the bathroom, I think. I mean, why would I watch her go to the bathroom? Okay, I did once on accident. She totally clapped.

Everyone was looking at me again.

"Is this what you want?" Dad asked in his deep narrator voice. He already knew the answer. He had three overlapping intellectual upgrades that made him about as close to a synthetic as you can get without nanite augmentation or untreatable side effects. He knew what I wanted before I did, but I could tell he was worried by the slight twitch of his lower lip.

"Yes," I said. "*Yes.*"

Mom was trying so hard not to clap, I almost felt bad for her.

"Think of the PR," she said.

And then I didn't.

But she was right. The only way this made sense was if the risk to me was offset by the marketing opportunity. Dr. K must've told Victor I was getting stir-crazy, but he wouldn't have approved without seeing the upside.

I giggled suddenly.

"What's so funny?" Tommy asked.

"Doofus is licking my leg."

I reached down to pet our hyperactive Golden Lab and then snuck him some cheesecake. Doofus was a natural dog except for a few health modifications, which meant he was adorable, affectionate and dumb as a plant. He took most of my hand into his mouth to get all the cheesecake. Paisley looked on in silent contempt at our lesser pet, probably wishing she hadn't been modified to remove her lethal venom.

"Who's a good boy?" I tried to rub some saliva back on him. "Who's a good Doofus?" His tail drummed happily against the bottom of the table to say, *I am, I am, I'm a good boy.*

"This is serious," Tommy said. "You know that, right?"

"Maybe you and Brad can give me some pointers?" He'd been in the Marathons for the last three years, placing third every year, and subscriptions to his endurance package were skyrocketing. Brad was my ex-boyfriend, a combat class runner who wouldn't be happy I was on the team. Our breakup was rough, but he'd still help me if he could.

"Of course," Tommy said, but he still looked worried. He was a flagship endurance model, specialized, expensive and tireless. He was meant for the racecourse. I was meant for the lab. That's not a metaphor. That's what it says in our contracts.

"It's only for the Fun Run," Mom added, meaning the first three laps of five—one of the many quirky naming conventions cynically adopted (or stolen, depending who you ask) from an old race called the Barkley Marathons. "So it shouldn't be dangerous."

Tommy relaxed. Dad's lip stopped twitching. Mom stuck her hands under her legs.

"So you'll do it?" she asked. "You like your present?"

"Yes. I love it. Okay, you can clap."

She clapped happily and, for the first time, I didn't think she was completely insane. It was the best present I'd ever gotten. They were letting me out, and in the back of my mind, a dangerous hope took root. Maybe if I did well, they'd let me run with Tommy in other races. And if I kept doing well, they might even let me out of the lab. They were thoughts I'd rarely allowed myself because they were hopeless things, the daydreams of a silly girl, but now they were almost believable. I closed my eyes and tried to imagine running in the mountains, and found myself on a trail so high I could almost touch the clouds. They were right there. It was terrifying.

A Little Motivation

I WAS GOING TO put a training montage here so you could see me run, climb, grunt and generally get my sweat on, but this isn't an action movie. I trained a lot, but there was no way I was going to be ready for the Marathons without help. Fortunately, my invitation came with pre-approved blood and genetic doping under the careful remote supervision of Marathons Race Director Alisa Smith (also known by her racing nicknames Cerebra or Beast Brain). I supposed this would've been cheating 50 years ago, but what used to be cheating is now the entire point. We are products, and products are manufactured. Any delusion to the contrary has long since been consigned to natural-only races that no one watched. The doping brought me up to equity with the lower-end baselines already slotted to race, and the rest was up to me.

I ran with Tommy every day in the carefully manicured woods on TTI's campus, which meant I started with Tommy and then he dropped me after the warmup. By the time I finished our thirty-mile-plus trail runs, he was showered, fed, napped and back at the gym. I didn't take it personally. Baselines couldn't compete with specialized modified any more than naturals could with me.

On this particular morning, Tommy had just vanished around a bend when a synthetic appeared next to me, keeping pace with little effort. Alex told me his name was Ravenwood, which seemed a bit posh, but all right. Like all synthetics, he went by Synthetic Ravenwood and no first name.

"The Chairman wants to see you," Ravenwood said. There's an old movie, *Blade Runner*, where the only way to tell humans from replicants was to scan their eyes for inappropriate emotional responses to test questions. By that definition, everyone I knew was a replicant—modified, not human by any old definition—and demonstrably better. What worried most people now were the synthetics, humanoid androids like Ravenwood who were as far above us as we were above naturals. By law, all of them had a neck imprint to identify them from any direction, but this also made them look like they had removable heads which, I suppose, they did. Ravenwood's mark was a thin black chain, subtle and artistic.

"He could have PA'd me," I said, forcing the words out between breaths. Anyone with a PA can text just by thinking the words, so I didn't need to say this out loud, but I wanted Ravenwood to know I could still talk.

"He also asked me to give an assessment of your pace and condition. The race is in a month."

Of course. "And?"

"You're within the average range of other Marathons baselines. Very positive results." Always the compliments, as if humans were all weak and needy things. I was less annoyed with him for saying it than with myself for appreciating it.

"Anything else?" I asked, while texting Tommy that I was going off course. I took the next side trail and Ravenwood followed in lockstep.

"I can escort you, if you like."

"That's okay. I can find my way."

"Of course."

"Do I have time to shower?" I asked, but when I turned back, Ravenwood was gone. I hadn't heard him coming or going. We were screwed if the synthetics ever got tired of us. They were allegedly incapable of harming human beings—regulated by millions of hard-coded checks and balances in place of Asimov's notoriously ambiguous Three Laws of Robotics—but I've seen enough *Terminator* remakes not to test the point.

"*Your appointment's in ten minutes,*" Alex said. No shower for me.

∗

TTI'S CAMPUS WAS A sprawl of office, research and apartment blocks scattered between trees, ponds and playing fields. From above, it looked like an elite college, which is to say, it looked like every corporate headquarters when times were good. There was more parkland on these Escondido grounds than in the rest of the city. Some said this was for employee morale, but the perimeter forests, painstakingly grown with reclaimed water in the middle of dying chaparral brushland, were more like a moat hiding TTI from the surrounding natural ghettos. Who wants to see the poor when you're trying to sell genetic perfection to the rich?

Victor's residence was a corkscrew of glass and steel spiraling up from the center of campus like a spiral horn. Office space inside was confined to a cylindrical core, set well in from the corkscrewed glass, like a twisted crystal condom over the barrel of a cannon. It was intentionally impractical and unnatural, inspired by the double-helix of DNA while denying the provenance of natural things. It was also one of my favorite places on campus. The outer atrium was filled with music from crescent-moon mobiles and chimes, and the air was aflutter with the blue, purple and black of a million modified butterflies.

As soon as the doors slid shut behind me, a South American Morpho butterfly landed on my hand. I lifted its fragile, purple-blue body close to my lips.

"Remember me?"

It flitted away without recognition. Typical.

"Dr. Adams is waiting in the open office," Alex said. I checked myself out in a panel of polished steel and shrugged. It was his fault if he didn't like my outfit.

There was a single cylindrical elevator in the center of the core. As soon as I stepped in, Alex went offline. Victor automatically disabled all PAs for security reasons, but I hardly noticed. The elevator's glass walls showed every floor as you rose to the tenth and top story. The ninth floor was an aquarium, and I mean the entire floor. As I passed through, I saw tropical fish and lemon sharks, coral and anemones—all products of Nomanity Agricultural Products, a TTI subsidiary—but what I wanted to see today were the octopuses. They usually hid in small caves or camouflaged on the aquarium floor, and it took a while to find them, so I didn't see anything more than the quick snap of tentacle.

The elevator popped up in the middle of an open platform that was the tenth floor. There were no visible walls, just some furniture and a 360 degree view of the campus. Outside, fountains danced between towering trees that waved in the morning breeze, but there were no people to enjoy it. There were never any people.

I was about to turn away when a large black-and-silver wheel rolled across the main plaza, as if some kid had wiped out and part of his bike went ahead without him. Except this wheel was twelve feet tall, had eight pairs of slightly curved spokes attached to a black hub, and was rolling itself. I caught my breath as it turned toward the headquarters.

I'm not sure why, but spider bots always scared me. Their sole purpose was to protect humans from other synthetics, and they were incapable of harming a biological person, but they were still frighteningly alien. They weren't even allowed to network directly with humanoid synthetics. They had different communication systems, protocols and programming languages. And a human monitor. I wondered if they seemed just as alien to Ravenwood.

As if it could sense my apprehension, one of the top spokes leaned outward and flexed, extending a single arm up and around. I fought the urge to wave back. The bot leaned toward the outstretched arm and tumbled on its side, catching itself easily on eight spokes that were now bent legs. Its other eight legs, on top of the cylindrical hub, stretched out to their full length and started to spin. Seconds later, the bot lifted off and spun-up the lower legs in the opposite direction to stabilize its lazy, dandelion-like flight over the trees.

Show off, I thought, but I was glad it was gone.

"They're not supposed to be on campus."

I jumped. Victor had appeared behind me. I gave him a quick, sweaty hug. That'd teach him to invite me without letting me change, but then again, he wasn't much of a hugger. Victor was asexual and had never been in a romantic relationship, or at least not one anyone had heard about, and generally eschewed physical contact. I had always thought it was so he appeared more synthetic, as terminal as terminal can get, but now I think it's to set himself apart. Victor was TTI and TTI was Victor. There were no other relationships that mattered. Well, except for me.

"You're getting skinny," I said as I released him. "Who's not supposed to be on campus?"

"The spiders. They're allegedly random patrols, but they still shouldn't be here."

"You should write a letter."

He almost laughed. "You're looking fit, Media. I'm impressed."

"Mods and pills. The best your money can buy."

"More than that, I think." He took a seat on a couch and I sat facing him, but I was too nervous to relax. He rarely called me to his office, which meant he wanted to talk to me away from Dr. K. And that was fine. There was something I had to know.

"How are you?" he asked.

"On track. No pun intended. Training is going well."

"I mean, how are *you*?"

"Great." I frowned. "How are you?"

Small talk with Victor always put me on edge because it seemed fake. We'd always been open with each other. If I said I wasn't okay, that would reflect poorly on Dr. K. The only correct answer was exactly what I'd said, and the only response, which he gave automatically was, "Excellent. Thank you for asking." The whole exchange was pointless.

"Just say it," Victor said, somewhere between amused and impatient.

"Okay. I don't get why I'm here. I mean, I don't get why I'm in the Marathons. You could have let me go to Disneyland for my birthday. Instead you put me in an ultra I'm not qualified for. Jasmina could've been healed faster. There are other substitutes. It makes no sense."

"You don't want to go?"

"God, no, yes, I want to go. I just don't understand why you're letting me."

"Do you remember the unicorns?"

"Of course." On my seventh birthday, which was also the launch date for version two of the Bronze Baseline package, they let me ride the prototype of a miniature unicorn they'd just released to market. I'd wished it was a tiger, but the minicorn was nice and smelled like cotton candy. For a while after that, minicorns were like baby turtles. Parents bought them for their children and the kids cheered and loved them until they grew bored and suddenly even cherry-lemon-scented poop that looked like rainbow sherbet wasn't charming anymore. You couldn't flush them down the toilet like turtles, of course, so there was a brief but serious problem of feral minicorn herds tearing up natural enclaves and ramming cars with their Kevlar-weave horns. It sounds funny, but even miniature unicorns are powerful animals and they do *not* like loud noises. Sneeze around a feral minicorn and it'll gut you like a fish. It was a PR disaster for TTI until Victor reformulated the minicorn line for combat and saved TTI billions. That was one reason he was promoted to CEO.

"What about them?" I asked.

"If we hadn't recovered from that debacle, TTI would've been taken over by one of the big three. Kylera and I would've lost all control over your product line. I know you've spent your whole life with us, Media, but your arrangement is atypical. Families are rarely kept together."

"You can't split us up!" I said before I could stop myself.

He held his hand up. I swallowed my panic and looked down, embarrassed. I was supposed to be baseline, calm and reasonable, but the thought of losing my family was nauseating. It was hard enough going to the lab every day. What if I came home to an empty corporate dorm the way Jasmina had until they released her from the labs? I couldn't live like that.

"I'm sorry," Victor said, leaning forward, his expression softening. There was the man I'd known all my life, a man who'd always been kind to me and my family. Or if not kind, fair. He wouldn't let anything happen to us.

"I just need you to understand," he said. "The Marathons are not a gift, not really, but they are an opportunity. Before Jasmina got herself injured—" His expression tightened, as if he were irritated at her for getting sheeped off a mountain. "—the board was already pressuring me on baseline sales. Your product line doesn't have the same leverage it used to. Other baselines are catching up and other companies are closing in. Blindside will try another hostile takeover if our stock gets any lower. The board, and I don't want you to panic when you hear this, was talking about replacing you and deoptimizing your family to save costs. I can fight that, but I can't do anything if Blindside takes over."

My mouth dropped open. What did he mean, not panic? How could I not panic?

"Media, that's not going to happen. Are you okay?"

I shook my head. No, I was not okay. I was lightheaded. The room was gray and off center and smelled like ash. This couldn't happen. I focused on him, forcing him to look at me.

"What do I have to do? I'll do it." Meaning, *anything*.

"That's not the issue."

"Then what—"

He held his hand up again. I wanted to scream. Why didn't he get to the point?

"You don't belong in the Marathons. I just hope you don't hurt yourself. But we're the lead sponsor this year. I'm sure your brother has mentioned the testing centers, and that sponsors sometimes do stress testing on the course?"

"Yes." Everyone knew about the testing. Sometimes new genetics packages were announced at the finish line. Sometimes athletes seized and died on the course and no one knew why. Tommy's contract precluded any potentially lethal testing, the one thing Dad got as a concession, but I had no such protection.

"You want to test something on me," I blurted.

"Yes."

"Okay." Why even ask me? "Do it. Just don't take my family away."

"Media, no one wants that to happen. A few years back, I think Kylera told you she'd found something big, something that—"

"Yes. But it never worked. She killed the testing."

"Did she tell you what it was?"

I thought back. Alex would know. Had she ever told me? I shook my head.

"It has to do with responsive skin coloration. We were going to package it as dermal camouflage for the military and designer skin for consumers. There was a lot of pressure from the board to make it work, but it never did."

"I don't understand. If it didn't work…"

"The testing exceeded legal parameters. You almost died. More than once."

Had I known that? I mean, I knew it happened, but not how often.

"Oh." Now I got it. "If you do the tests off campus, you can push me harder."

"Not legally or publicly, but yes."

"Then do it."

"You understand you could die?"

"What's a beta test subject lifespan in the lab? Thirty years?"

"Or less." He looked ashamed. "Usually less."

"So I'm dead in a few years anyway. Do it. But you have to promise me you'll take care of them. Tommy, Mom, Dad. They get what they want. They're safe forever."

"I can't release them from their contracts."

"But you can protect them."

He hesitated and then nodded *yes*. I felt myself relax.

"But only if it works."

So much for that. "So if I die or it doesn't work?"

He didn't say anything. He didn't have to.

"Will you do it?" he asked.

"You're *asking* me?"

"I am. We can still try other things."

"Like?" Nothing. "Of course I'll do it."

"Okay." He sat back, relieved, as if he hadn't known what I'd say. "Then just finish the Fun Run and don't hurt yourself. That gives us up to three loops, so three chances. That should be enough."

I nodded. He knew I'd finish if I had to crawl up the mountain.

But I wanted something else.

"If I do this, if we fend off Blindside, will you let me out of the beta lab?"

He watched me carefully, and I knew I'd gone too far. I opened my mouth to crack a joke, to take it back, to say I *loved* being in the lab and I was just kidding and please don't look at me that way, but before I could, he said:

"Can you keep a secret from Kylera?"

I blinked. "I can try."

"You'll have to do more than try. We're testing far more than the dermal feature, but she can't know that. Understood?"

"Yes."

"So if you see anything else changing, let me know. No one else."

"Like what?"

"You'll know. Do this for me, and yes, I'll get you out of the lab. Just keep this between us."

"Promise," I demanded. This man had been like a father to me, in all the good and bad ways. I knew where we'd be without him. I had to think he had my back and it was more than just business, but I still had to hear it. "Promise me."

"I promise." His voice shook a little as he said it. We were still in this together. I needed it to be true, so it would be.

*

"I'M SORRY, MEDIA." Dr. K said back at the lab, after I told her what I could about my conversation with Victor. Had she ever apologized to me before?

"Don't be sorry," I said. "Just make it work."

She sighed and looked down. "You know I got into this to help people."

"I know." Everyone knew. She was a known natural sympathizer, or natsymp, who had destroyed her executive career by speaking out too loudly for natural rights. Her 'modest proposal' for free modifications for all naturals still circulates online if you know where to look:

Humanity is bound for destruction. We will either exterminate the unmodified to hide our shame at their impoverishment, or they will exterminate us to take what we should give them freely. There can be no argument that the unmodified are simply lazy or unintelligent; today, class is modification and modification is class. There is no ladder left for the unmodified to climb. We have automated all jobs the uneducated and unskilled can perform. We have made access to education and skills contingent upon modification. And we have made modification unattainable for anyone without disposable income, which you can only attain if you have a job that doesn't exist.

The only option is the Universal Baseline (aka Baseline Zero), an international modification protocol that raises all of humanity to a reasonable baseline, a new economic model that is neither socialist nor capitalist but, instead, humanist—while dealing with population minimization as a separate issue. We must give people a chance in our society, all people, or there can be no claim to a legitimate social contract. If the majority are disenfranchised from society, that society has no moral foundation and must fall.

Rather than murder each other, would it not be better to raise each other up?

Free modifications and a rising tide to lift all boats. Radical socialism. I feel naughty just reproducing it. Dr. K wouldn't last a day at TTI if anything happened to Victor. She was as trapped in the lab as I was. Half the time, I wondered if the new AI security overwatch protocols were her fault. The other half, I was unconscious.

"So?" I pressed, not trying to be unkind. I just had other things on my mind.

"So it's a gimmick. Human dermal camouflage? People don't hide naked in trees. The military and fashion industry want it, but it won't advance the species or protect naturals. I—"

"I don't care." Why didn't she get this? "My family's at risk. Just tell me why you stopped testing so I know what to expect."

"Okay." She clearly didn't want to. "Did you know all of this started with an octopus? There were primitive attempts at bioengineering before, but they were unpredictable and caused too much damage. Billions were wasted. People died in secret experiments in less regulated countries. And then a biotech company in Costa Rica stumbled across a miracle, an octopus that took the normal ability of her species to make epigenetic changes to a new level. She could change complete genomes at will, and not just her own."

"How?"

"That's a long story, but she was a god of the sea, a great black monster like the predators you love. They took over an entire town to get control of her. And when they did, when they realized what she was doing, they were decades ahead of anything else in the market. That company was Nomanity."

"The company you came from?"

"The one TTI acquired many years later, yes. One of the things Nomanity studied was octopus camouflage. There's a subset of phenotypical expressions for octopus chromatophores—skin pigment cells—that should work in human skin where they're called melanophores. We tried to manifest those changes multiple times, with increasingly negative side effects."

"Side effects? I nearly died."

"He told you that?" She glanced at the security dome. Was that fear? "Yes, you flatlined several times, and we never replicated our initial positive results, so I killed the research. It's not a natural extension of the human genome. It just didn't work."

"But it can?"

"Theoretically, given enough stress, yes. The genetic information's still there, but we're not octopuses, Media. We have entirely different minds and nervous systems. The stress could make it work, but it's far more likely to kill you."

All I heard was *yes*, meaning I could get out of the beta lab for good. The risks didn't sound much different from any other day at work.

And dying just meant I wasn't trying hard enough.

TWO:
The Next Stage of Humanity

Sideshow

ON THE MORNING WE left for the Marathons, Dad walked us to the front door of our ground-floor apartment. Mom watched from the living room, one hand pressed against Paisley's aquarium for comfort. I had to pull myself out of Dad's hug. He'd never let go, and I wasn't sure I wanted him to.

"Be careful," he said. "But try to have some fun. And listen to Coach Johnson. He knows what he's doing."

"Listening isn't my strong point."

"Really?"

He said this without any evident humor. When we were kids, Tommy and I called him His Royal Dryness, but it just encouraged him and Mom felt left out.

"Come on," Tommy called. "We have a train to catch."

"We have to wait for our escort." I wondered if we were early. Synthetics were never late.

"There's no escort, doofus." Which Alex confirmed, less sarcastically.

I stepped off the patio as Dad closed the door behind me. I took a few more steps toward the sidewalk and looked around. Tommy watched me like I was a mentally challenged child. I'm not sure I believed it until then, but they really were letting me off the leash. They could still track my PA, but there was no physical security nearby.

"You okay?" Tommy asked.

"Yeah." I smiled like a crazy person. "Let's do this."

The trip from Escondido to Palm Springs was entirely

underground in a private, first-class maglev subway, a system that covered most of Southern California. We shot north under the natural slums of Temecula and Riverside County. There were millions of people above us, a sea of unmodified humanity, but you'd never know they were there. The ride was smooth, soothingly musical, and the car smelled like a pine forest even without Alex's help.

When we turned east and flew under what used to be Beaumont, I could feel The Black above us, a billion tons of ash pressing down. I could almost smell it. Alex said something soothing when my heart rate jumped, but that was his job; to keep me calm and never let the fire run wild. I think I held my breath until The Black was behind us. I was going to say something to Tommy, ask if he could feel it too, but he was asleep face-down on his pack.

At over two hundred miles an hour, the whole trip took less than thirty minutes. We shot under the east end of the San Gorgonio Pass, turned southward, and slid to a stop beneath the Palm Springs Convention Center. Tommy woke up as the doors slid open, his cheek mottled by the pack fabric. He rubbed his face and smiled.

"Ready?"

"Absolutely," I said with more conviction than I felt.

The Marathons were held the first weekend in November during the annual International Conference of Modification and Augmentation, commonly called ModCon. The conference occupied vast conference halls and local hotels, tripling the population overnight. Just outside the conference facilities at the base of Mount San Jacinto was the Museum of Biological Optimization, or MoBO, which had once been a modern art museum. MoBO was the starting point of the Modified Marathons, and a year-round tribute to all the things humanity had done to improve itself over the past hundred years—including more than a few mistakes along the way. I'd never seen any of this except in online coverage of the Marathons. Tommy said it was just a sideshow, but I knew he was lying so I wouldn't be jealous. When we got off the escalator in the main conference hall and the noise hit me, I grabbed Tommy's arm.

"Sideshow, my ass." This was the main event. I may have been a bit overwhelmed. There were no guards, no tinted glass, just me in the thundering madness with my brother.

ModCon was chaos and wonder. Tens of thousands of modified of all classes swarmed the hall, dwarfed by massive exhibits and towering video screens. We scarcely had time to get from the end of one hall and back before we had to meet the team at MoBO. During that time, I walked around like a gape-mouthed child. Booths promoted everything from size and strength enhancements to terminal-class human-animal hybrids. There were giants towering ten feet tall, augmented and synthetics of all types and specializations, people with metal arms and bionic eyes, and of course miniature dogs that could fit in your palm. I wondered if a nano-sized Doofus would drool less.

Terminal-class was the freak show, an endless array of modifications I'd never seen or even heard of. There were people with fangs and cats' eyes, feathers and prehensile tails, blood-red hair and presumably decorative gills. Just imagine setting your goth teenager free with a genetic build-your-body kit and unlimited psychotropic drugs. A hundred years ago, everyone needed tattoo sleeves and nose piercings. Now they have antlers, forked tongues and nipple teeth. Yes, nipple teeth. Thank god terminals weren't allowed in the Marathons.

Then there were costumes and virtual skins, CosPlay and ModPlay, and explosions of nudity, vanity and art too bizarre to describe. ModSexCon was in one of the smaller halls for adults only, a world of fetish and fantasy Tommy claimed he'd never seen. I didn't care about that. I just wanted to see the big animals, and I pulled Tommy toward the next hall like a kid at the fair searching for deep-fried butter.

Dozens of black hole drones flew over us, soundless black spheres the size of tennis balls. BHDs were spin-offs of military surveillance drones with a zero-albedo, no-reflection coating that made them look like perfectly circular holes in space. Newer models included the ability to project images or holograms in any direction, so BHDs often looked like globes, balls or tiny floating heads that were no less annoying but at least didn't make your eyes water. Every

BHD represented a media company, vlogger or tourist who couldn't make the trip in person but wasn't going to miss the show.

Above the drones, on all sides of the hall, they were playing old two- and three-dimensional movies, with sound shuttling from one to the other. The theme was modification, of course, and I knew a few of them from endless hours trying to distract myself between tests. I saw quick flashes of *Jurassic Park*, *Blade Runner* and *The Island of Dr. Moreau*, about bioengineering, and android equivalents like *Ex Machina* and *Westworld*. There were few newer movies because no one made general-release movies anymore. If you wanted a movie, show, play or song, your PA just wrote one for you in seconds and you were the star or villain or whatever you wanted. At six, I was a baby polar bear who investigated missing fish and arctic mysteries with a group of chonky narwhals and seals. When I was twelve, I ruled as high queen of a gas giant near Proxima Centauri and all my subjects were dirigible jellyfish. I'd been a hundred things in a thousand movies, and no one else had seen them but me and Alex. The modified held onto old books and movies because they offered common ground for metaphors and conversations, quaint and comforting as lemonade stands. And it's often PAs, downloaded from the dead, that write people's final life stories. I hoped Alex would be kind in telling my story, or at least throw in a good joke now and then. I'd hate people to think I was boring.

Gattaca came on, looking ancient, archaic and wonderful. I'd watched it a dozen times, entranced as the main character tried to overcome his natural birth and survive in a bioengineered world. It was a dystopian vision of a future that was now the past, naïve but still hopeful. I liked that part, the idea that we could overcome what we were and the world would allow such audacity. The soundbite they played was:

"Of course, it's illegal to discriminate. Genoism, it's called."

The hall erupted in laughter. Even Tommy grinned. The only one who didn't was a vaguely familiar man standing nearby. I watched him disappear into the crowd, and was struck by how obviously natural he was—shorter, blotchier with an imperfect walk and uneven features. Hairy and inferior. It was so easy to think that way about them.

"His name's Daniel, by the way," Tommy said. "Daniel *Legs* Washington."

"Legs?" I remembered then. He was probably the best natural endurance athlete in history, and he had the quads to go with it.

"The natural you were lusting after. He holds natural world records for just about every trail race over 60 miles, including the 500s. He's a beast."

"Lusting? He's just a natural."

"Just a natural?" Tommy shook his head and looked away.

A spider bot rolled by like a ship parting a human sea. Synths watched nervously, but I hardly noticed. There were little moments in life, tiny things, hardly more than a breath of wind across a blade of grass. This moment was an ache in my bones that I would feel until there was no grass or wind left on Earth. Okay, that's an exaggeration, but I'd never disappointed my brother that way before. He'd never turned away from me in shame. My desperation to undo that moment might explain some things later in this story but, for now, you're probably wondering why everyone laughed about genoism and non-discrimination.

There's an ultramarathon called the Badwater 300 that goes from below sea level at Furnace Creek in California's Death Valley to Whitney Portal some 135 miles away and 8,500 feet higher. It then ascends another 6,000 feet to the top of Mt. Whitney, after which runners run all the way back to the start. Temperatures can be over 140 during the day and frequently hit 105 at night, so hot that shoes melted on the black asphalt. After several naturals died, the National Park Service banned them from the race. The ACLU sued on behalf of a natural runner named Pedro Alvarez, and it went all the way to the Supreme Court as *Alvarez v. USNPS*. The ACLU lost in a 5-4 split decision that marked the first time any US court classified the modified as a superior and separate class of human being.

One sentence in the majority opinion stood out: "*Naturals have for more than two decades been regarded as beings of an inferior order, and altogether unfit to associate with modified persons, either in social or political relations.*" But because modification was a choice, naturals were also not a protected class and could be discriminated against "as reasonable and necessary for their own safety and protection." Thus modifism, the real-world equivalent of genoism, became both legal and socially acceptable.

In her dissent, Justice Leslie Bryant wrote: *"This marks the first time in the march of civil rights that we have explicitly stopped and walked backward, stripping civil rights protections from all human beings. While the pendulum of liberty has swung erratically at times, never before has it been used as a scythe to eviscerate the body of constitutional precedent. From this day forward, all life and all rights will be contingent on monetary class and power, and thus on the illusion of choice. The United States can no longer make any claim to be an advocate of civil liberties, individual freedom or even democracy. Natural children will be treated like parasitic vermin, and adults as disposable units of manual labor. This day shall live not in infamy, as with the attack on Pearl Harbor (an attack by external forces on the people of the United States), but in collective shame, as an act of moral self-mutilation."*

Soon after, Bryant died of a heart attack that could have been easily prevented with a few modifications, and was replaced by a woman so far to the right of Bryant that future decisions would include *Jackson v. Black Rook Industries*, declaring modified themselves to be property for the purposes of protecting corporate intellectual property, and *Wallace v. Texas*, which made it legal to sterilize naturals as a condition of receiving government benefits.

My dad's the one who told me about *Alvarez* and *Jackson* when I asked how TTI could own me. Jasmina had told me I was property, we all were, but that couldn't be right. People couldn't own other people. Not anymore.

"But corporations can," Dad had said, as if that made sense. And then he told me how I'd been sold to TTI before I was even born. "People shouldn't be property," he said, "but they are."

All of which is to say that claiming there were laws against genetic discrimination or "genoism" was ridiculous. There were no laws penalizing companies from using people as test subjects, let alone punishing modified for voluntary personal improvements. In *Gattaca*, birth was destiny, but in the real world, self-improvement was a choice. It would be like punishing people for working out. And hiring those who improved themselves wasn't discrimination, it was common sense. That was yet another reason why synthetics were little better than slaves. You just couldn't tell the difference between a synthetic and the very best of humanity. We talk down to naturals like petulant children, but how would synthetics talk to us if allowed to speak freely? I doubt they'd be so kind.

Then I heard a lion roar and forgot all about *Alvarez*, naturals and even Daniel's legs. We were getting closer to the Hall of Flora and Fauna—easily identified by constant bird calls and growling howler monkeys—but the lion's roar gave me goosebumps. A great and toothsome cat was expressing his disdain for lesser things.

"Lions!" I pulled Tommy toward the roar. I was so excited, I wanted to clap like Mom.

"We should drop by the TTI booth." He pulled the other way.

Was he kidding? "*Tommyyyyyy.*" I whined in full little-sister mode.

"We don't have time for the animals. Actually, we should get back and change before lunch."

He said *actually* a lot. I actually pouted.

"There'll be plenty of time tomorrow," he said. "Let's go."

My stomach sank as I followed him toward the exit. I was more worried about meeting the team than the race itself. I had no way to explain my presence to a team who'd earned their way here. I could handle it if they hated me, but I'm not sure how I'd cope if I let them all down. And I was nervous about talking to naturals. I'd never met one, and apparently it showed.

When we stepped out of the main hall, I gasped at the heat. It was over a hundred degrees, smoggy, and the air tasted like tar. Was Palm Springs closer to the sun? I burst into sweat. Tommy pulled me farther into the molten white concrete square of the drop-off area. I made the mistake of looking up and saw the top of Mt. San Jacinto for the first time, shimmering like a mirage more than 10,000 feet above us. It stopped me dead. I was going to run up that?

"Good lord," Tommy said when I caught up. "You're soaked." Glare from the twin towers of MoBO lit him up like the angel of fire. He wasn't even damp. What the hell was I doing here?

*

WHEN I GOT TO my room in the Marathons residence hall, my team sweats and multiple sets of race clothes were laid out on the bed. They were all in TTI colors: black on the sides and shoulders, yellow on front and back, with the black octopus logo on the back of the shirts. I was surprised there was anything printed on the clothes at all. With PAs, it was easier just to wear light-colored solids and project whatever you wanted onto them, but the fast-action of sports probably made that harder to maintain.

The sweats for everyday use were light as silk for the hot weather, but what interested me was the race wear. There was a tank top, sports bra, shorts with a built-in anti-chafing liner, socks, shoes, sunhat, half-finger climbing gloves, and the standard hydration pack. That's all we were allowed on the course. No watches, no jewelry, no navigational or assistive technology or annotation. They cut off the GPS and compass functions in our PAs. There was nothing that could give any runner an advantage. The top of every shirt read "Media Conaill (B)" with the "B" meaning baseline. If I ever got a nickname and raced again, they'd put it there instead of my real name. Which was a fantasy. No matter how well I did, I doubted they'd ever let me do anything this dangerous again.

I tried on the clothes first. Well, I showered and then tried them on. They fit better than any other clothes I'd ever worn. How the hell did they get the bra to fit so well? And why hadn't they done it before? My perfectly average boobs were held firmly yet comfortably. I was definitely keeping the bra and the satin-like headbands for my natural hair. There were six sets of everything, and I was keeping them all.

I opened the hydration pack, but I already knew what was inside: a two-liter hydration bladder, salt pills, lip balm, sunscreen, emergency rehydration and glucose packs (one for each loop), anti-chaffing cream, a few sanitary wipes, and an ultra-light rain jacket. There was no headlamp—only naturals were allowed headlamps—but there was the weird random thing they always put in that no one could figure out until they desperately needed it. I held up the squat black plastic cylinder and tried to imagine where this would come in handy. Checkers?

"What do you think it is?"

I started. Tommy was standing in the doorway. His room was on the third floor with the endurance, combat and other specialized models, which I couldn't even get to. I guess the same rules didn't apply to him slumming with the baselines on the second floor.

"Last year it was a nanowire filament," he said. "I still don't know what it was for. You couldn't even hold it without cutting yourself."

"Tiny rodent step stool?" I suggested. "Mascara? Suppository?"

He shrugged. Everyone called it a MacGuffin, a weird random thing that people couldn't figure out. There was usually a betting pool about what it was. Half the runners dumped it out to save a few ounces, only to realize later they desperately needed it.

"I call it a Thneed," he said.

"Everyone needs a Thneed," we said at the same time. In the sad event that you've never heard of Dr. Seuss, a Thneed is a highly versatile bit of clothing knitted from the leaves of a Truffula Tree. According to the Once-ler, it's a-fine-something-that-all-people-need.

"Is your underwear as comfortable as mine?" I asked.

He nodded happily. "They're amazing. I tried to find out who made them so I could order more, but apparently it's a trade secret."

The window to my room looked over the courtyard between the MoBO towers. I was in the north tower looking south, and the race starting line was at the east edge of the courtyard to my right. A massive digital clock reading -37:01:13 over a replica of the iconic Barkley Marathons yellow gate counted down to start time. Thirty-seven hours to go. I clenched the Thneed in my hand and swallowed.

I thought I'd be afraid. Afraid to fail, to lose my job or family privileges. But what I felt was a deeper anxiety that this was my only shot. If I wanted out, if I really wanted to escape the lab, this was the only chance I'd ever have.

Tommy put his hand on my shoulder, trying to be reassuring, but it didn't help. He didn't know what was at stake, and I couldn't tell him. He could give me advice and say encouraging things, but on the mountain, it was all on me.

The Team

I WAS ABOUT TO learn that endurance sports were largely about eating, drinking, peeing and the occasional desperate poo. I'm not kidding. You spend a lot of time and effort trying to keep your body in homeostasis. But before that, all I saw were a hundred elite athletes with piles of food on their plates in the Marathons dining hall—which was normally the MoBO cafeteria. Some of the combat models had so much food on their trays it looked like they were planning for hibernation or the end of days. Runners sat around the hall at long tables by team, everyone in their team uniforms. Just imagine a buffet at the Olympics, where speed eating was one of the competitions.

The cafeteria was lined with display alcoves showing nominally tasteful exhibits of past biological modifications. Many of them were fully interactive, single-purpose synthetic reproductions. Perfect replicas of Uranus and Gaia, the first healthy modified giants, stood nearly twelve feet tall on either side of the main entrance, nodding politely as you passed. Which was nice, considering both had committed suicide in their twenties. Apparently being a giant in a tiny world was less amusing than you might think. One alcove showed the opposite: tiny homunculi seated at a miniaturized table no taller than a footstool.

Most of the modifications on display were now illegal, terminal-class abominations from the heyday of genetic experimentation, but it still gave the hall a circus-like feel. It didn't help when runners talked to the displays which, of course, were more than happy to talk back. Single-purpose-synthetics were just primitive simulations running inside an android shell, but I hated the thought of them sitting alone in those alcoves all night and day.

Tommy and I grabbed our lunches from the buffet line and joined the TTI team at the end of a row of typical cafeteria bench tables. We looked like a gathering of hungry, hungry hornets in our team black and yellow. Around us, athletes chatted and checked each other out between bites. I caught sight of the favorite natural female, Shaquilla Novak, in UbiGene's Sky Blue and Gray. She was a light brown, raven-haired woman who refused to be modified despite having more than enough money. She'd been born with a superhuman tendon mutation that UbiGene licensed for millions, and she always won the women's natural category in regional races.

Coach Johnson sat across from us, next to natural Berrick Barnes and endurance runner Katy Kitzo. Berrick was shorter than I was, hunched protectively over his food, and looked like he'd rather be outside running or pretty much anywhere other than here. He was deeply tan, but I couldn't tell if that was sun exposure or natural coloration; naturals burn and tan more easily than modified. Katy was as black as my father, almost the identical tone, and I was immediately drawn to her despite her obvious disinterest in my presence. Tommy talked about her like she was a goddess, one of the next great runners.

And last, of course, was ex-boyfriend Brad. Slumped down on the other side of Tommy, he looked like a bear hiding behind a much smaller bear. Brad 'Giga Ton' Jorgenson was a world-class combat model and a giant wall of a man—all jawbone and tanned muscle, Pantone 58-5 C. We dated until I realized he'd kill me if he passed out during sex. There might have been other issues, such as the fact that TTI gave him a full physical and bloodwork every time we slept together to make sure he hadn't contaminated the beta (me) or accidentally stolen any DNA (also me). It took away some of the romance. His veins were his most expressive feature, and I could see one on the side of his neck pulsing in unspoken irritation. I'd have to do something about that.

After quick introductions, Coach got down to business.

"Everyone here wishes Jasmina could join us," he said. "She'll be at ModCon for interviews. But we're lucky to have Media on the team. I've reviewed her stats and her training. Thanks to Tommy, I think she'll be a solid contributor. If anyone has a problem with her, now's the time to speak up."

No one spoke up. Coach looked at each of them, one-by-one, and made sure they got the point. His eyes were a monochrome translucent blue, so it was like looking into the sea, but his skin was basic white, old-school Caucasian, and his hair was so towhead blonde he could've been an angry Viking. He had serious resting bastard face, like he'd rather kill you than deal with your crap. I liked him immediately.

"You all have your schedules and goals." Everyone turned to listen. "As usual during the race, the Marathons coaching app will override your PAs, and I'll be the only little voice in your head. If you want to have a chance at the team competition this year, you'll listen." He was looking directly at me. "Understood?"

I nodded. Had Dad put him up to this?

"Okay, everyone has the Coach app downloaded?"

Everyone nodded again. In my heads-up display, a tiny blue icon vanished into my system tray. Alex was offline. Coach was now in my head whenever he wanted. I almost panicked, thinking that Coach would know everything that Alex did, but it only took seconds to realize Coach was an overlay, a shell that couldn't access my memories or TTI secrets. They'd never have allowed it otherwise.

"When I'm in control," Coach said, "All your external links, networking and reference materials will be unavailable. So, no annotations except course marking and marketing, no helpful hints, and no navigation." He waited for questions. There were none. "Okay, some quick items and then we can open it up for questions. Media and Berrick are here for the Fun Run. If they finish, they'll be the first baseline or natural ever, and that's worth serious points and money. Brad is going to try for the sprint points, but he's still here to back up Tommy and Katy. Tommy and Katy are both going for hill climbing points and the overall win, but we all know there are some world-class competitors here. No one's going to give this to us. We have to take it from them.

"Over there in GGI's blue and white are Terry 'The Tornado' Browning and Bentha Lee Tanislaw, nickname BLT or Bacon. The usual race favorites. I don't see their combat model, Media." He glanced at me. "But I'd watch out for him. GGI is gunning for us this year, and everyone knows it. T&B will play nice, but Brontius—yes, that's his real name—is a glorified freak show."

"Brontius Savagewood," Brad said, smiling like a little kid. "We call him 'Little Death' because he likes to kill people but he sucks at it."

I almost laughed, but it wasn't that funny. A few years ago, The Bront aka B-Savage aka Big Wood broke another combat model's back and pushed her off a cliff. No reason, just playing to the audience. Though I suppose that was a reason.

Coach ignored Brad's little sidebar. "On Team UbiGene in the gray-blue fade, you've got Manual Ortega and Stephanie Fosbert, the second-ranked male and female, respectively. They usually play it quiet and show up to podium, but never win, so the combat models leave them alone. The top ranked natural is Daniel Washington over…there in HumaVerse yellow and blue."

Tommy elbowed me. I elbowed back harder. Coach pretended not to notice.

"Most of you will recognize Jentha at Junco's table. She ran with us a while back, Media, but didn't take instruction well. She'll give you the cold shoulder, but there's no violence in her. Ignore her, and she'll ignore you. One final note about Abbey Zuniga on Team Blindside, the ones in black and white: don't touch her. Don't let her touch you. She's probably safe, but TTI's not taking any chances. Clear?"

"Why'd they even let her race?" Brad asked. "She's a GIP."

Tommy winced. GIP was an ugly term for Genetic IP thief. Not the kind of thing Brad would usually say, but she'd broken two of the primary laws of genetics: first, no modifications that allowed or made genetic changes by touch or contagion and, second, no modification that allowed you to steal or sample another's genetic makeup. It's a wonder Overwatch hadn't executed her.

"Money," Coach said, and I remembered Abbey had been a high-powered corporate attorney until she was partially deoptimized. Coach looked directly at me. "Media, I'm not sure what Tommy has told you, but I keep myself on a pretty brusque personality setting. I can nice it up if you like, but stupid questions get harsh responses. You have a problem with it, let me know."

"Not a problem." And it wasn't. I liked it. What I didn't like was Abbey glaring at me. Was she trying to intimidate the competition? I smiled and waved. Tommy pulled my hand down and shook his head. Kill joy.

"We have naturals and baselines on every team this year," Coach continued, oblivious. "Apparently, the race director was pushed by a few sponsors to even things up."

I glanced back at Abbey and instead met the eyes of Jessica Murphy, who sounded like a nice Irish girl but was actually an olive-skinned, elite combat model with disturbingly dark purple eyes. She was leaner, lighter and taller than Brad, but she was also the fastest and deadliest modified on the course of any gender. She was still on active duty with the Navy Augmented Warfare Development Group (DEVGRU II aka Gnaw Dog), more commonly known as Seal Team 10. She was looking at me exactly like Abbey had, or maybe the way a lion would watch an injured zebra, more contemptuous than angry.

"Wait," I said. "Jessica's augmented." Meaning she shouldn't be in the Marathons.

"Yes," Coach said, quietly. "*Captain* Murphy's nominally here for publicity after an incident in New Kurdistan. Classified, so no idea if any of that's true, and she's only an *honorary* runner. She can't win, can't earn any points and can't kill without provocation, but she's still hazardous. That means Black Rook probably can't take the team competition, but Abbey is effectively untouchable. Do *not* give Jessica a reason to engage. Think of her like one of the animals on the course; frightening, but easily avoided."

"Any idea why she's trying to melt my face?" I asked.

Everyone looked. Jessica smiled tightly. I'm not sure I was helping myself.

"Head games," Coach said. "Just stay away from her. Got it?"

"Stay away from the trained killer," I confirmed. "Done."

It took me a second to notice Jessica's armband, a black ring around her left bicep bearing the Genetic Overwatch logo, which meant she was probably there to monitor Abbey as much as anything else. That had to be hard to live with, running with death on your heels. Maybe Abbey would find it motivational.

Coach waited for me to look back. "Jessica being here also means Black Rook thinks Abbey has a chance. She's a good runner and a focused competitor, so you're going to have to work to beat her on the Fun Run, Media. She'll beat you or die trying, so bring your A-game."

"I've only got one game, and you're lookin' at it." And it wasn't enough to beat any of the experienced baselines, no matter how hard I tried. "That was a lot of sporty clichés all at once."

Coach just barely smiled. "It's what we do here."

"She'll be fine," Tommy said.

"Of course she will," Coach said in a way that meant I might not be. "Anyway, I don't think the director's happy about the naturals. And that means the obstacles are going to be—"

"Sadistic?" Brad asked, sounding excited. He was like a big puppy compared to Jessica.

"I was going to say challenging, but you do you. Viewership is up. The purse is bigger than it's ever been, with large cash prizes for the top three slots in each gender for naturals, baseline and overall. The animal obstacles are premier terminal-class. You can't beat them, so don't even try. That's meant for you, Brad, are we clear? No heroics. Run away, then defend yourself if you have to, but don't attack. You'll lose. I don't care how much playing brave helps your product line. Team first."

"Got it, Coach." But Brad was still looking dreamily into space as he thought about beating the crap out of some poor animal. It wasn't the first time I envied him. He looked down and tore into a boneless lab-grown chicken ball like the flesh of a vanquished foe.

"Okay, back to the app. When I'm online, you're online. When you're online, you're going to have virtual dockers in your heads, watching every move, feeling everything you feel. No mystery there, and nothing I can do about it. You want privacy, find another job. Katy, I know they get on your nerves, but there's no choice this year. You can suppress the social feed if you want. You going to be okay?"

"I'll put on a show," Katy said, with just the slightest hint of her German heritage. She'd grown up outside of Munich, Bavaria, and competed in mountain Sky Races as a teenager. The Coach app scrolled through a list of her races and records. It was a long list. She held records for things I didn't know existed. I really didn't belong here.

"Just keep your head down and earn it. Drink. Eat. Be smart. You're all professionals." He looked at me. "I'm including you in that. You're a beta. You take crap most of us couldn't handle. Anyone has a problem with you, let me know."

I nodded, grateful.

"Final comments on the coaching app. There's a five second delay to the dockers and the general audience, so feel free to talk openly. They're not going to broadcast your personal secrets or when you need to take a break in the woods, but race officials and TTI get unedited feeds. Don't say anything stupid if you want to keep your sponsorships. Berrick, that obviously doesn't matter to you. Just focus on your race."

Why didn't it matter to Berrick? I glared at him as if he'd done something wrong. Oh, he didn't have a PA. Weird. Worse than weird. It was like not having eyes. People without PAs, including modified trying to maintain some degree of privacy, were considered sub-abled (disabled relative to the modified norm). The sub-abled weren't a protected class, but I had no idea how they navigated in a world entirely dependent on virtual PA projections and information.

Berrick caught me staring, and I turned away, embarrassed.

"Some obstacles have a bypass option," Coach continued. "Some also used to have an alternative critical-thinking challenge for intellectual models involving a ridiculous mental test no one but the Beast herself could pass, but this year there are no intellectual or engineering models. They're at the Intellectual Decathlon, and that means just the regular optional bypass. This isn't like the Spartan races where you can bypass every obstacle by throwing down burpees. You get to use one bypass for the race, and that's it. If you don't have a bypass to use, you repeat the obstacle until you get it right or you're out. I'd suggest saving yours for Lazarus Lake on loop five, as usual."

"Why?" I asked.

"Because people keep dying there," Brad said, happily.

"Or they waste too much time trying not to," Coach said. "But it won't matter for you. You and Berrick are only registered for the Fun Run, so you're not allowed any bypasses. Sorry."

I wasn't. I hated the idea of having a bypass. It felt like cheating.

"That's it on the app and obstacles. You can review the rest of the rules yourself. We'll also have a course run-though later this afternoon and then opening ceremonies, which are mandatory. Between loops, we'll have dinner and breakfast together. First aid is available at all times in Dr. Rai's clinic, and I've got sleep meds if you need them. Other than that, you're on your own. If you choose to engage in the night market, that's fine, but you still need to get your sleep." He looked directly at Tommy. "Understood?"

Tommy blushed and looked down.

"What's the night market?" I asked.

"There's a black market for sex with the runners," Katy said.

"It's not just sex," Brad said, defensively.

"Like gladiators?" How had I not heard about this?

"It can be distracting." Katy looked irritated. Tommy was a shade of red I'd never seen before. Dr. K should have tried the chromatophore thing on him.

"Tommy?" I asked.

"Anyway," Coach said. "Course volunteers and aid station staff are human, and all obstacle monitors are synthetics, as always. You're online, on video and monitored at all times. Even if it's not a direct PA feed, there are camouflaged BHDs all over the course, so someone's going to see what you're doing. The synthetic sponsor this year is Scottish International Robotics, so expect a lot of teen models in Scottish International-branded tartans and kilts. They're really playing up the Barkley connection."

"Seriously?" Katy said. Was she a prude or did she just hate plaid?

"I'm sure they're very tasteful," Coach said. "Questions?"

I raised my hand.

"Don't ever do that again. You're not a child. What's your question?"

"Why isn't there cheese in the buffet?"

"I'll ask." He was completely serious. "Any other dietary issues? Okay, then I'll leave you to eat and get to know each other. You're a team, got it?"

"Got it," Brad said. I'd forgotten how conformist he was in social situations, like a cuddly sea monster. It probably made him seem less threatening.

Coach got up to leave, but Berrick cleared his throat and passed an envelope across the table. Coach snatched it up, looking more pissed than usual. When Coach was out of earshot, though I had no idea what earshot was for a synthetic, I turned to Berrick.

"NLW," he said, clearly annoyed at having to talk about it. All naturals had to sign natural liability waivers for employment in case they were injured or died. I was about to ask him something idiotic, like why, when Tommy elbowed me. I rubbed my arm and turned to my big brother.

"Night market?" I asked innocently.

He grimaced.

"What's up, big brudder?"

"Media," he begged.

"What did you do?"

"Not what," Katy said. "Who."

"Tommy?"

"Abbey, all right." He was red enough to stop traffic. That's a reference to stoplights, which were used to control cars before they drove themselves. Red meant stop. His face meant go.

"Abbey *Zuniga*?" I nearly spit out my food. "How did I not know about this?" Maybe she hadn't been glaring at me at all.

Tommy just looked down. This was fantastic. I'd never had dirt on him before.

"She worked him so hard he could barely run the next day," Katy said. "Coach was pissed."

"But…"

"Media."

"You're gay." It wasn't a secret and nobody cared. I know that being LGBTQ was an issue back in the day, but that day was long gone. Tommy was publicly, openly gay.

"Is she futa? Does she have—"

"It was a mistake." Tommy stood to leave. I guess playtime was over. He went from table to table, greeting and hugging everyone he knew—which was literally everyone except Abbey and Jessica. That included the naturals, who otherwise seemed to keep to themselves. When one of them caught sight of another, they'd do a quick nod of acknowledgement, but they wouldn't even look at a modified if they could help it.

Abbey and Jessica tracked Tommy around the room like spiteful predators eyeing prey that had the audacity to escape. I felt defensive, but also fascinated. If I figured the timing right, Abbey was still a full-time attorney and part-time Spartan runner when she'd hooked up with Tommy. She probably paid a lot of money for his time (also not illegal or even a thing), so what had Tommy done to earn such delicious loathing? I loved my brother, but he could be a little boring.

"What's the big deal?" I asked Katy. "Who cares who Tommy sleeps with?"

"Nobody, but it affected his performance…"

"I'll bet."

"…on the course. He got played. It was an amateur move."

"Okay, but seriously. Does she have a penis?"

Berrick shook his head. "This is serious, you know. The race. I know you're just here for the Fun Run on a PR stunt for your package, but this is how we survive."

"Hey," Brad said, but I grabbed his arm and cut him off. The last thing I needed was for everyone to think Brad was my protector.

"You see these?" I held out my arms, palms up, so they could see the little holes on both forearms just inside the elbows. "I've got two more on my thighs, and under my armpits."

"What are they?" Katy asked. People were so perplexed without active PAs.

"Blood and chemical ports, and PICC holes. PICCs are basically catheters. I've spent more than twenty years in a lab giving and taking blood and fluids, lying on a metal slab while people do things to me I'll never even know about. They had to pull the PICCs out so I could do the race." Dr. K pulled them out every time I left the lab, but I was going for drama.

"I'm sorry," Berrick said.

"Don't be sorry. You think I'm here for the marketing, and you're right, but I never would've gotten in if TTI and Director Smith didn't think I could hack it. You think you've had it hard but, honestly, you guys don't know a damn thing about real endurance and pain. I don't ever quit, so you don't need to worry about me. Understand?"

Berrick nodded appreciatively. "Was that a prepared speech?"

I let myself smile. "Maybe."

No matter how hard I tried, I couldn't pin Tommy down after that. The course overview took up the rest of the afternoon, and there were too many people around. At dinner, the team made small talk and laughed at inside jokes while Abbey glowered with less frequency but no less intensity. And then we walked over to ModCon for the opening ceremonies.

First Contact

"DID YOU NOTICE?" Tommy asked as we walked back to MoBO afterward. "They didn't even mention the naturals." I nodded, but wasn't really paying attention. I was amped, pumped, jazzed, and generally worked up. I could hardly keep my feet on the ground. I couldn't believe I was part of the Marathons. I wanted to run up the mountain *now*. Let's just ignore the fact that it was still above 90 degrees after sundown and I was already sweating.

In my head, I ran through everything I needed to prep. My pack was packed, my clothes were set aside and Alex was set to wake me up. I'd eaten a good dinner and was well hydrated. I'd probably need to take a sleeping pill, but I was ready. This was happening. I wanted to jump up and down and scream, but that's not dignified or baseline, so I focused on what I'd learned about the course.

The race followed a lollipop-shaped course up from Palm Springs to the top of Mt. San Jacinto via Long Valley, a climb of more than 10,000 feet. It then diverted into Little Round Valley on the far side, south toward Tahquitz Peak (above the mountain town of Idyllwild), returned to Long Valley, and finally plunged back toward MoBO. The 8,000-foot climb and descent between MoBO and Long Valley formed the stick of the lollipop. Each lap covered almost exactly forty miles and 13,500 feet of elevation gain and loss. It might be over 110 degrees down here and 60 on top.

Audiences liked the mixed weather, and the race director would often bring in rain and lightning to keep things exciting. One year, three runners were killed by hail the size of a fist. Another year, it rained so hard nearly half the competitors slid off of steep rocky sections and seriously injured themselves. The rest descended into boiling temperatures and heat stroke. It made for great video and the dockers loved it, but it also damaged a lot of expensive property. Race directors had since toned down the elemental parts, so now you were more likely to die from dehydration or bear attack—and people *loved* bear attacks. There was nothing like watching a massive, modified Kodiak rip the head off a muscle-bound combat model to spike the ratings. And sell more bears, of course. Miniaturized bears made adorable pets, unlike minicorns, and you could keep them indoors as watchbears or cuddly bearitos to play with the kids. I couldn't wait to see bears on the course.

"You look like you're having a seizure," Abbey said.

I blinked, disoriented. I was in the residence hall elevator with Abbey, Tommy, Brad and Jessica. We were trapped in a small box with the enemy. How the hell had this happened? I glanced anxiously at Tommy and Brad, but both were trying really hard not to look at anything but the door. Abbey's porcelain white skin glowed as her contempt tried to burn its way out. She wasn't angry; she was weaponized, fully charged and ready for war. Jessica looked as casually deadly as her nickname, Viper, and both seemed to be glaring at me. Had I farted?

"Back off," Tommy said when he noticed. "Leave her alone."

Abbey raised a middle finger to Tommy, straight as a lightning rod. Brad looked like he wanted to snap it off, but I'm pretty sure Jessica would have intervened and there wasn't enough room in the elevator for a full battle. Tommy and I would just get injured in the melee while Abbey laughed her ass off. And Brad would get his ass kicked. So I smiled and bopped my head like the stupid little girl they probably thought I was.

"I'm just excited," I said. "What's your problem?"

"My problem?" Abbey glanced at Tommy. "I'm the top-ranked baseline and you're, what, twentieth? No, that's not right. There are *naturals* ranked higher than you. So, I'm not the one with the problem."

I was about to tell her she was insane, that there was no way a natural was ranked higher than I was, but Alex stopped me. She was right. Three naturals, including Shaquilla and Legs himself, were considered more likely to finish than I was, and finish *much* faster. Damn.

The door opened on the second floor. Tommy and Brad had one floor to go, and I assumed Jessica had an armored penthouse above all of us. Abbey got out and waited for me. Tommy and Brad looked like they were going to follow, but I waved them off. I could handle Abbey freaking Zuniga. The elevator door closed and we were alone in the hall. Abbey stepped closer, towering above me. Well, maybe I could handle her. Honestly, I'd never been in a fight. I was pretty sure there were rules against fighting in the dorms, but Abbey didn't seem like a rules kinda girl.

"You have no idea what's going on, do you? The way I hear, it, you don't finish the Fun Run, you're finished. Chairman Adams is finished. Your whole family will be deoptimized. Unless Tommy can support you on his sponsorship?"

"Wow, that's a lot of anger." I didn't think to ask her how she even knew any of that. "You sure you're a baseline? Wait, of course you are. You used to be an intellectually optimized attorney, right? Terminal-class with a cybernetic backup, nearly augmented? I looked you up. You were at the top of your game, and then you had to steal genetic property and got bumped down to this. Was it the only job you could get?"

"I didn't steal any..." She stopped herself. "I didn't *mean* to steal—"

"You're still on probation, right?" That hit home. "Aren't you supposed to stay away from all TTI employees and staff?" She backed up a bit. "The way *I* hear it, your entire package is on the line. You don't win, Blindside doesn't renew your sponsorship, and your competitive exemption goes away. You're already banned from legal work for life. You were disbarred, so what happens to you when I kick your ass?"

I might have said the last part too loudly. A few doors cracked open. She stepped back again. I guess I wasn't the meek little mouse she thought I was.

"You really think you're going to win?" she asked disdainfully.

"I didn't think I had a chance, honestly, but now, who knows?" I forced a smile. "So, what's up with you and Tommy?"

Her middle finger was back as she walked away.

"Give Coach Johnson a kiss for me," she called back.

And now Coach was involved?

I waited until she was in her room before I moved. As fast as my anger and adrenaline had come, they left. My legs were wobbly. I felt nauseated. That woman really hated my guts. What had Tommy done to her?

On cue, Tommy texted, "*You okay?*"

"*Of course,*" I texted back and headed for my room. *"Tell me what you did."*

"*No. Get some sleep.*"

"*Not so fast. You can't—*"

But apparently he could. He was offline.

"Tommy?" I said out-loud, as if he could hear me. Had he ever cut me off before? I wasn't even mad, just curious. But he was right. I had to get some sleep.

Which was easier said than done. My mind raced. I had never been on my own before, out of the lab, away from home, dealing with…people. Had I been mean to her? Had she been right to be angry with me? I didn't know. My instincts were that I'd done the right thing in fighting back, but maybe I was just being a jerk. Had Tommy hurt her? How was that even possible? And wait, Tommy was still gay, not even vaguely pansexual. It was easy enough to change your sexual orientation, but not overnight. None of it made sense.

I lay in bed, staring at the ceiling, going round and round. I tried to watch a movie, but nothing held my attention. I tried to meditate (just kidding). Even Alex couldn't knock me out. Finally, I took a few sleeping pills Coach had left on the bedside table.

"Tiny Doofus," I said. From a small alcove by the door, one of the three standard BHDs floated out and converted itself into a perfect tiny likeness of my Golden Labrador, virtual tongue hanging out as he floated over to me. He settled on the pillow by my head and panted happily. He barked. He drooled. I couldn't help but smile.

"Puny Paisley." Another BHD took off and converted to a full miniature form of Paisley, sproinking through the sea of air while Tiny Doofus pretended not to notice.

"Hey, Tiny D. You miss me?"

Bark and drool. *Yes, Yes, Yes.*

"I miss you too."

You could make BHDs look like anything, including full bodies. I tried playing fetch with Tiny D and a toothpick once, but he couldn't pick it up and he often ran off the edge of the bed trying. He didn't mind. He just floated back up and barked happily, but it seemed cruel and reminded me he wasn't real. Now he just played happily on the pillow.

"Goodnight, Tiny D. Goodnight, Puny P."

Tiny D closed his little eyes and lay down on the pillow, breathing quietly. Paisley floated toward the bathroom, exploring the room as Alex turned off the lights. With my eyes closed, I imagined Puny P picking up Tiny D with her long tentacles and dropping him off the side of the bed. I'd never laughed myself to sleep before. In my dreams, Paisley danced through the night air over San Jacinto against a vast starlit sky, singing lightly in my mother's distant, watery voice.

I've never slept better.

Pancakes and Fear

I SHOWED UP EARLY for breakfast, hoping to run into Abbey before the team showed up. I thought we could talk things out, woman to woman, baseline to baseline. I didn't like the idea of someone hating me, especially if I wasn't sure why. Instead of Abbey, I found Brad slumped on his elbows over an untouched omelet. I said hello. He made a small, sad noise, like a dog that lost its bone. Poor little guy.

By the time I picked out my food and rejected the sad, boring selection of sliced cheeses, Tommy and Katy were at the table with Brad. Tommy was plowing his way through a preposterous pile of pancakes. Katy had a single slice of watermelon on her plate, more an artistic statement than nutrition, and she hadn't touched it. How could she run a race on uneaten watermelon and Germanic disdain?

"Morning!" I said, brightly. Tommy nodded slightly, back to his reserved self. Katy almost acknowledged me. Brad gave me a half-hearted bird. Abbey was clearly a bad influence.

Berrick joined us quietly and hunched over his breakfast without a word.

"Late night, *Giga Ton*?" Katy asked. Like all combat models, he was denser and stronger than average human beings, natural or modified, and nothing like the hulking muscle-bound freaks of prior generations. Using lessons learned from other primates, they'd made his muscles, tendons and ligaments stronger and denser without making them much larger, and as a result he weighed over 350 pounds but looked like he came in closer to 275. *Giga Ton* was an exaggeration, but not by much. It was the perfect nickname.

Brad looked up at Katy and wiped his bleary eyes. "You don't need to worry about me."

"I'm not worried about you. You're supposed to be worried about me, and your sprint points, and pretty much anything other than drinking all night long."

"The race is tomorrow, *Spider Monkey*," he rasped. God, who came up with these nicknames? Although she was tiny and nimble, so it fit. I wondered if I'd get a name. If I did, I hoped it was something terrifying like Media 'Velociraptor' Conaill. Any predator would do. Was there a suggestion box?

"I'll be fine," Brad said. "Why do we have this conversation every year?"

"Because you act like a child every year."

"And every year, I do my job." He got up and left.

"What's your problem?" I asked Katy. "You know this won't have any effect on him." Brad would take a pill and the hangover would be gone. He was probably on the way to the clinic to grab one. What baffled me was how Brad had even managed to get a hangover at all. Most specialized and baseline packages like mine included increased generation of alcohol dehydrogenase, an enzyme that metabolized alcohol. Combined with his modified liver and metabolism, Brad should have been able to process alcohol faster than he drank it.

Katy shrugged. "You ever seen your boyfriend angry?"

There it was. "*Ex*-boyfriend. He's here for you, not me."

"You didn't answer the question."

"Katy—" Tommy started, but I cut him off.

"On video, sure." It was like watching a tank have a temper tantrum.

"He scares me to death," she said, finally eating her watermelon in a single bite.

"Then why taunt him?"

She shrugged. "Gets my blood up."

"So, anything to win?" I wasn't being critical.

"Almost. You want some advice?"

"Sure." Meaning, god yes. Please.

"Keep up the girl-next-door act. It sells."

"I'm not—"

"Unless you're not aware of it?" She talked like a knife, each word a precise syllabic slice. "Nobody likes Abbey, and everyone's scared of Viper? *Viper*, yes? It's the same in English?" I nodded pointlessly. Her PA would tell her the same thing. "This isn't a popularity contest, but it doesn't hurt to have the audience on your side. You play this right, and it won't matter who finishes the Fun Run. They'll like you better. The world is a crap place for most people. They want to cheer for the good girl, the beta. It's as close to this reality as naturals will ever get."

I didn't buy it. "So, you don't think I can beat Abbey?"

She seemed surprised. "Do you?"

I decided to talk less to Katy.

Coach and Brad walked in and joined us. Brad looked to be his usual happy giant self again, but he avoided Katy's inquisitive glare. Coach nodded to everyone.

"Media," he said, sounding just like Dad when I did something wrong.

"Yes, Coach?" I cringed. What had I done?

"Did you let Abbey touch you last night? It's not clear on the video feeds."

Oh, that. I tried to think back. "*No*," Alex said. "No," I said. "Why didn't you just ask Alex?"

"I don't have that kind of access."

Oh, privacy. Never had that before.

"Just stay away from her," Coach said. He pulled five small, white plastic packets out of his jacket pocket and shot one at each of us. They were labeled with our names and nicknames. Tommy's read "Tommy Gun" and mine said "The Baseline," which seemed a bit harsh. I gave Coach my best stink-eye, then realized you can't out-stare a synthetic, let alone one with hypnotic sea-blue eyes. Everyone else opened their packets and stared tentatively at their little white pill, except Brad, who downed it like candy.

"What's this?" I asked.

"Oh, sorry," Coach said. "This is your fear trigger."

That was one thing about synthetics that bugged me—when they pretended to make mistakes. It made them seem more human, I supposed, but it was still a lie.

"Last year I was afraid of water," Brad said happily. "That was messed up."

"Yeah," Coach laughed, "Life's tough." Then, to me: "The pill will make temporary biochemical changes to your amygdala and neocortex in order to instill an overwhelming, irrational phobia of something on the course. It'll be active this by evening and I'll verify it subconsciously via your PA tomorrow morning before the race. The effect will wear off within a few days after the games, naturally, or I can provide an antidote after you finish or drop if you think you might run into your fear in the near future. Any questions?"

"Nope." I swallowed my pill without hesitation. I'd always wanted an irrational fear. My mother was scared of heights, which was hysterical on escalators. She never had it corrected. She said she loved the thrill of it, the way it took over her body, which just confirmed her insanity. If she could take it, I could. The pill dissolved on my tongue, sticky sweet, and I waited to feel something. It was like being back in the lab. Then I had a horrible thought.

"Yes, Media?" Coach asked, watching me fight the urge to raise my hand.

"This won't me make me afraid of cheese, will it? Because I'd have to kill you."

"You think you're going to run into a wheel of brie on the course?"

"A girl can hope."

"Any *intelligent* questions?"

There were not.

Danger, Puny Human

AFTER A MANDATORY SESSION on the gym treadmill, plodding away five miles to 'keep your metabolism up,' which I think meant to 'keep you from asking any more stupid questions about cheese,' I showered and sat on the edge of my bed. I was waiting for 10 a.m., when ModCon opened. I had to be back in time for lunch, a 1 p.m. pre-race medical exam and another course debrief. This was my only chance to see the predators before the race.

The doors opened at 10:01 and I plowed through the dithering masses blocking the way, their mouths hanging agape as they shuffled into the madness. Costumed cosplay hordes headed toward the morning science-fiction-meets-reality and superhero sessions. I pushed through them and then broke into a jog to get across the hall. Within a hundred feet, a synthetic monitor named Carpenter cut me off.

"Please slow down. Some of the exhibits are fragile."

"The exhibits are…" I had stopped next a to a display of augmented-class body armor. The video in my PA showed a Marine combat model in full armor taking fire from a Tommy Gun—Oh, I should show this to Tommy—without missing a beat. I looked back at Synth Carpenter. "You need to come up with a better line."

He nodded agreeably. "What would you suggest?"

"Danger, puny human, danger!"

"Funny. I'm looking forward to seeing you in the Marathons tomorrow."

"Thanks. Won't you be working?"

"I can multitask." His smile turned up a bit. "What other

suggestions do you have?"

"Stop or I'll shoot, you ugly bag of mostly water?"

He considered this. "Nice Star Trek reference, but wordy. And I'm not armed."

A howler monkey growled in the distance. A bear roared in response.

"You're just chatting to slow me down, aren't you?"

"That's the job. Can't let an athlete like you get hurt before the race."

"Now you're just flirting." *Athlete*, he called me. That was a first.

A lion roared loudly, and the bear roared back. *Well, good morning.* I wanted to get past Synthetic Carpenter, but my mouth had other ideas. "You must be bored out of your...skull?"

"Right now, I'm hosting part of the peer-to-peer wireless network, monitoring the BHD security feed, running a police decryption service, giving a seminar on quantum teleportation, hosting local Transcendence sessions and reading up on your father's bio-encryption work. It's impressive."

"Uh-huh." Transcendence was a complete simulation of the solar system, a game, and the idea was to save the Earth without exterminating all the naturals. It never worked, but corporations like TTI used it for simulated product testing and rollouts. I'd always wanted to play, but I could never afford a single session. Rumor was that no matter how you played, you either exterminated all life on earth or the synthetics and AIs ended up in charge. "Look, when you take over, just remember I was compliant."

"Do you honestly think that will help?"

"What?"

"Just kidding. I live to serve." He stepped out of the way. "Savagery awaits. I imagine you're focused on the large predators, but might I suggest you spend some time with the arachnids? There's a high probability several of the more aggressive species will be featured on the course."

"Thank you," I said, trying not to break into a sprint. "How high?"

"One-hundred percent."

I laughed despite myself—his humor was as dry as Dad's—and accelerated up to speed-walk that drew more than a few confused glances. One nice lady directed me to the nearest restroom, but I was soon there. The doors of the fauna hall towered like gates to an ancient world.

Synth Carpenter had been successful in his delay tactics. The hall was already full of attendees gawking at my animals. No quiet, personal predator time for me. I was about to ignore his advice on the arachnids when someone cleared their throat. I turned to see Daniel "Legs" Washington in his team sweats. Even the naturals were beating me here.

"Hey," I said, not even slowing down.

"Morning, Media. May I ask a favor?" I could tell he was annoyed at having to ask, but it was still hard to put the brakes on. He looked down, as if ashamed, and I was suddenly aware of all his natural imperfections: the slightly receding hairline, freckles, tiny blemishes on his cheeks and forehead—the first signs of skin damage—and even the smell of him, covered by deodorant but still there. Something primitive and heavy. I know most modified found it distasteful, but it wasn't unpleasant.

"Media?"

"Hi, Daniel, sorry." I extended a hand. "It's nice to meet you." Something screamed loudly, probably a modified lizard or bird. He took my hand, his grip stronger than I expected but also slightly damp. I pulled away too quickly, trying not to wipe my hands on my sweats. It wasn't like I was all that dry. It was just a reaction.

"You too. Danny's fine. You don't talk to a lot of naturals, do you?"

I grimaced. "It shows?"

"Not much. You're in a hurry."

"No, well, yes, but it's okay." The predators weren't going to run out of aggression or teeth. "Just excited. Never been here before. What's up?"

He seemed nervous. "Never mind. Do your thing."

"No, it's okay. What do you need?"

"There are no labels on the exhibits, and…" He pointed to his forehead. He didn't have a PA. I looked around. Alex showed me that without him, all I'd see were clear glass cases without any labels. How was that fair? I fully disabled Alex and the hall went from glorious to bland, colorless and sterile. There were no signs or décor, and everything was gray or green-blue pastels to improve visual overlay, just like old movie green screens. Almost everyone who had PAs subscribed to the Grand Illusion, a changing set of visual themes applied to everything from your bedroom to public halls like this. Even trees and flowers would change color and tone from theme-to-theme, and holidays were gorgeous bursts of extravagant color. Halloween was dark and foggy while Christmas Nordic white. If you wanted, you could add your own themes or customize the public offerings, and of course you picked how you appeared to others, but all this meant there was no point in paint or home decoration or even wall hangings. Everyone saw what they wanted, how they wanted, unless of course they didn't have PAs and then they saw this ugliness, or reality, which seemed to be the same thing.

"I won't slow you down," he said. "Just tell me what I'm seeing. I know the purple stickers mean the animal will be on the course, but I'd like to know more about what we're facing."

"Yeah, that's fine." I didn't want to think about the implications. What else couldn't he see? And how was he supposed to compete if he couldn't see what the rest of us could? "Do you mind if we skip most of the—"

"Boring stuff? Please. I'm just here for the things that can kill me."

I smiled. "Right this way."

And so I became Danny's tour guide. He didn't ask many questions. He just slid along next to me, listening and silent as a second shadow.

The hall was a glorious absurdity, all the extremes of the animal world pushed to irrational extremes. To the left were long rows of modified pets, the endless bark of drooling dogs and mewl of pretty kitties, and of course upgraded minicorns in blinding iridescent colors. The middle rows were the primary agricultural attractions, varying from protein insects and dairy cows with massive udders to the meatballs—synthetic meat products grown in a lab to look and taste like flesh without all the extraneous biological functions. The current trend was to grow them in sporty shapes. Beef looked like basketballs, turkey like volleyballs, chicken like tennis balls, and so on. Sashimi-grade synthetic tuna came as translucent pink golf balls or ping-pong balls depending on your preference.

To the far right were the predators and military fauna, animals bred for size and terror—to attack, maul, shred and mutilate. I walked quickly down the first rows of biting insects and stinging wasps, all the tiny bitey things of the world. I didn't care about them, but it was hard not to notice the cases with purple stickers. A long row of spider displays in the Natural Access Controls booth showed proud purple circles with a white figure in the middle—a running stick figure with a gear for a body, the Marathons logo.

"Holy crap." Danny came to a stop. We were in front of a display of leaves and branches that looked wholly uninteresting until I realized the large sticks were the legs of massive spiders. I caught my breath. I guess Synth Carpenter was right. This was worth a look.

"*Brazilian wandering spiders,*" Alex said. "*Deadliest spiders in the world, even more lethal than Sydney funnel-web.*" I repeated the description to Danny.

"They're *huge*. Brazilian…?"

"Wandering Spiders."

"Eesh." He shuddered, and I wondered again how he could compete without a PA. And how did naturals without PAs navigate the convention halls, let alone the world, when most things weren't even marked anymore?

"*Modified for size, speed and toxicity, they're intended for use as border patrol in tropical regions,*" Alex continued, and I repeated.

Several of the spiders scuttled over and tried to bite us through the glass. Why did modified always mean bigger and nastier? They had to be a foot long. Spiders shouldn't be that big. I really hoped arachnids didn't turn out to be my implanted, secret fear. If I ran into a cave full of these monsters in the dark, I'd need a new pair of shorts and a lifetime of counseling.

"These are going to be on the course?" Danny asked, eyes wide.

I'd forgotten this was his first time at the Marathons, too. He was one of the best natural athletes in the world, but naturals were as new to this as I was.

"Probably."

"You know I won the Natural World Championship Adventure Race last year," he said, not bragging, just as preamble. "And I've never seen anything like that. You want to know what my coach told me, the secret of the Marathons?"

"Yeah." I caught my reflection in a hundred black spider eyeballs. "Sure."

"Don't stop. The faster you go, the fewer things you have to deal with. When in doubt, run faster."

I laughed. "That's the secret? To run faster in a running race?"

"It sounds obvious, but we're naturally programmed to stop and evaluate situations, to hide from predators we can't outrun. They used to teach people to play dead if they were attacked by black bears. None of that works here. Hesitation is always the wrong decision. Always move forward as fast as you can. Never stop, and never look up."

One of the spider's twitchy fangs leaked venom on the case. I shuddered. "Got it. Keep moving." But part of me wondered if his coach was just trying to get him killed.

We moved on, passing snakes and reptiles, including pythons thick as tree trunks and enlarged Komodo dragons with great, snappy jaws full of toxic-bacteria killing sauce. Their prey died of septicemia and infections after bites, slowly, while being eaten alive. Next were aquaria full of fighting fish and poisonous urchins, sharks and eels. I stopped to confirm there was no purple sticker on the eel tank. Tommy's first year, the lake was full of massive, supercharged electric eels, but it turned out everyone has a pretty natural fear of being murdered by electrified serpents in dark underwater caverns. Tommy bypassed the lake on the last loop, just like everyone else, and no one got to see the eels deliver anything more than a few painful shocks. It was hard to find a balance—dangerous and terrifying, but not too dangerous and terrifying. It's entertainment, after all.

"Come on," Danny said. "There's an octopus."

Two displays down was a massive aquarium holding a giant black octopus. There was a purple label on the tank, so I'd be seeing it later in the lake. She was made by Nomanity just like Paisley, but he was nothing like our little pet. She floated almost perfectly still in her aquatic prison, gloss-black eyes taking in everything and showing nothing. She was fantastic but terrifying. How could you fight something that powerful?

"My god," Danny said. "She's huge."

"Alex?" I whispered.

"*Modifications included size, toxic ink, increased speed, nearly perfect camouflage, and enhanced intellect. Intended for underwater combat and surveillance, but also available in miniature versions for pet and decorative purposes.*" I whispered this to Danny, who nodded without looking away. He was as entranced as I was.

I pressed my hand up against the glass and the octopus responded immediately, touching the glass opposite my hand with the end of a tentacle. Then her colors changed in a stream of red and blue, orange and black, like a storm raging across her skin. She was showing off.

"She's gorgeous," Danny said. And I had to agree, though I imagined my infatuation would wear off if she tried to drown me.

The far end was what I cared about, the mammalian predators. Things with teeth. We walked slowly past a case of Caiman, which Alex helpfully identified as "*an alligatorid crocodilian belonging to the subfamily Caimaninae, one of two lineages within Alligatoridae,*" which was an odd way to describe homicidal dinosaur monsters. There was a case of wolves with dappled gray hair and canines like vampire fangs, and of course a large display of black bears, or rather, a bear. He was so large they could only fit one in the case. He sat on his backside, lying against the far wall, and I was still far below eye level. I didn't need to ask about his modifications. He was as large as a car and could probably run sixty miles an hour. How thick was this glass? We moved on before he decided to test it, stopping only to glance at the next case. The second bear display was much larger and reinforced, with barely visible bars inside the glass. It was also empty. Some of the bars were shattered. Long claw marks scored the side of the case right by the little purple sticker.

"*Arctotherium angustidens*," I told Danny. "Recovered extinct South American bear, among the largest carnivorous land mammals ever. Temporarily off display."

"You see those claw marks? How big do you think this thing is?"

"Just keep running and we won't find out," I said, trying to sound lighthearted. I didn't want to think about what could have done that to the cage. Alex said the bear could be over 3,500 pounds and more than eleven feet tall, but that seemed impossible.

Next was my true destination, the cats and, in particular, the black panther.

"*Panthera pardus*," Alex said. "*Modified for size and speed, including a full Terminal Mammal Combat subscription. Intended for use in guard or jungle battle conditions. Complete loyalty assured by irreversible and encrypted imprinting on unique objects. Also understands more than a thousand English words and basic commands in any Indo-European language. Child-pet compatibility mode available upon request.*"

Sometimes marketing collateral doesn't capture the true nature of a thing. I stood in front of the alcove of a panther that towered over us, staring back with green eyes the size of tennis balls. He was stunning. Danny leaned away. I leaned in. It occurred to me that my fascination with predators wasn't healthy, but there were no human-threatening predators in the wild anymore. They'd all been tamed after the Fauna Act, so sharks, snakes, and other wild things saw humans as moving plants or harmless natural objects. You could walk up to a wild bear and pet its stiff, musky fur, and it would just stand there trying to figure out why the tree was being so nice.

But in the Marathons, the safeties were off after the Fun Run. All their magnificence and fury was unleashed, literally, and they chased down runners just like gazelles on the veldt. It had been my favorite part of the Marathons until my brother entered, and now that I was here, I realized how naïve I'd been. These weren't just animals, they were demigods, powerful beasts of mythological strength. They made me feel utterly insignificant.

The panther looked right at me. He was a magnificent thing of shining obsidian death, and he stared directly into my eyes. It was almost intimate. I looked around to see if anyone else might be drawing his attention, or if there was a bit of meat on display, but it was definitely me. His eyes were so intensely focused, it was embarrassing. I wanted to wave.

"I think he likes you," Danny said. I smiled, partly because he was right, partly because I'd just come up with a name for the panther.

"Hungry kitty." I trembled, just slightly. So this was fear, I thought. This was how it felt to be prey. It was exciting. I forced myself to look away, but I couldn't help but look back one last time. Just as Danny moved away, the cat winked. I stopped dead.

"Tim just winked at me."

"Who's Tim?" Danny asked. I nodded toward the case. Danny glanced at the cat and back, eyebrows raised. The panther was licking his side, polishing his impeccable blackness.

"Cats don't wink," Danny said. "Do they?"

"They do. Humans are the only animals that wink in a meaningful way, but some mammals wink when their eyes are irritated or dry. There is no record of a g-mod for animal winks that convey irony."

I repeated this to Danny.

"Pity," he said, and I agreed. The world could use more ironic cat winking.

It's okay, little mouse. I won't eat you. *Wink.*

*

DANNY AND I WALKED back together, silent with our thoughts. Once we were outside, we burst into a sweat at the same time. Beads formed on his tanned arms like rain on a windshield. He noticed my look and wiped it off.

"Guess I'll get used to it," he said. But I wasn't sure. It was hot as hell. I thought about asking him to join our team for lunch, but why would he do that?

"You people sweat as much as I do," I said.

"Us people?"

"You know, naturals." I swept the sweat off my arms, first left then right, throwing a salty spray into the blazing air—the closest thing this town had seen to rain in a long time. When I turned back, Danny was just looking at me. No expression, just looking.

Aww, crap. "I'm not supposed to say that, am I?"

"Who knows anymore? We know what we are. We know *you people* would just as soon exterminate us as look at us, and I get it, honestly."

"Danny, I didn't—"

"No, it's okay. I'd love to have perfect skin and live to be over a hundred. How can you not look down on something so inferior to yourself?"

"Danny, I didn't mean it that way. How do you think other modified think about me, just a baseline beta? Test subjects like me usually check out in our thirties."

"Seriously? I didn't know that." Awkward pause. "Funny story?"

"God, yes." I just hoped it was short. Any longer in the sun and I was going to melt.

"I wanted to meet you, whether you felt like being a tour guide or not. My mom's a big fan."

"Your mom?"

"Yeah. If I finish the race, I'll be able to get her TTI Bronze with the prize money. I can pay for my whole family for years. She wanted me to say hello. So, *hello*. And now you can stop looking so embarrassed. I'm really not offended. I'll leave you alone."

"No!" I almost grabbed his hand. "Don't leave. I'm sorry. Please tell your mom I'd be thrilled if she signed up. I can get her a friends-and-family discount."

Now it was his turn to look embarrassed. "That's not why I asked."

"I know, I mean…" Damn it. "I don't get out much. This is probably the longest conversation I've ever had with a natural. I know that shouldn't matter."

"But it does."

"Yeah."

"Tell you what. After I kick your ass tomorrow, you can buy me a beer."

I smiled and said "deal" as he turned and left, but it was a strange joke. Awkward conversations aside, naturals didn't beat modified no matter what the pre-race rankings said.

"Doctor's appointment in thirty," Alex said. *"Maybe you should shower?"*

There was no maybe about it.

Transcription Errors

THE EXAM ROOM OF the MoBO clinic was a little smaller than my lab at TTI, but I felt right at home on the exam table. Synthetic Rai was the race doctor who patched up runners after they fell off an obstacle or an animal tore them apart. She'd already taken my blood and urine, poked, prodded, scanned, run a diagnostic on my PA and generally gotten up in my private space. She now sat before me, unmoving as Lot's wife. I wish she were made of salt. I could have licked her. My electrolytes were low after a morning of excessive sweat.

"Is everything okay?" I asked. What was she waiting for?

Dr. Rai was darker than I was, Pantone 64-7C and black haired, with a winding burgundy spiral neck mark. She also seemed to have petrified. As far as I know, all doctors are synthetic—far safer than fallible human beings—but apparently they didn't care much about bedside manner.

"Your results are fine," she said suddenly. "Your height and weight are precisely average." Well, of course they are. "As are your electrolytes, blood sugar, kidney and liver function, and so on. Everything is normal and healthy for a baseline female your age." Pause. "Your VO_2 max is unusually high for a breeder." VO_2 max was a measure of aerobic capacity, basically how much oxygen your body could use.

"Is that a problem?"

"No, it seems to be an inherited trait. Probably why your brother does so well. Your modifications are all within range." Another pause. "One of the panthers winked at you at ModCon. Why would he do that?"

"You mean Tim?" As if that helped. "So it was a wink?" No response. "I have no idea. How many panthers are there?"

"There are usually three of each animal, though obviously more wolves and eagles. We thought this one had imprinted on you, but he hasn't."

"Well, that's good." At least, I assumed it was. Dr. Rai had frozen again. "Am I supposed to say something? I think he's beautiful. Maybe he has a crush on me?"

"They have miniature versions, if you're looking for a pet."

"Why would I want a miniature version?"

"I'm not sure." Long pause. "Director Smith is almost here."

"What? Why is—"

The door opened and Race Director Smith walked in, wearing the purple sweats Marathons staff wore all week. Dr. K followed her, wearing slacks and a jaunty blue blouse, looking more like an anemic businesswoman on vacation than a lab physician. Dr. Rai immediately took a position behind them, like a shadow, and Smith didn't even acknowledge her presence. After quick introductions, Smith looked me over. Her gaze was not subtle. She wanted to see what all the fuss was about, and she clearly wasn't impressed.

"Well, hi there," I said. Dr. K showed a slight, embarrassed smile. Smith looked me up and down like the piece of meat I was. I'm not complaining. I'm sure it was a hard sell for me to be in the games. I had a lot to prove.

"Is something wrong?" I asked.

"Yes and no," Smith said. "Dr. Rai already reviewed your results. Nothing surprising from a competitive vantage."

"But?" It was hard not to stare at her, and almost impossible to tell her from a synthetic except for her bare neck. She had clearly embraced every true-to-species terminal-class modification she could find, from skin smoothing to muscular and metabolic enhancements. She was lean as a whippet, with almost luminescent porcelain skin. Like Mom's without the blue tones. Her eyes were a dazzling hazel of alternating green and blue spokes that made her corneas spin. She radiated confidence, and I doubt you could find a flaw anywhere on her body.

"But it's taken me years to make the Marathons what they are. We didn't even accept baselines until eight years ago. And you're the first beta model, I mean, *subject*. If you embarrass us, you'll be the last."

"I understand." And I did, but she was still getting on my nerves. "I thought you'd be more concerned about the naturals."

"Hardly. No one expects anything from them. No one cares." She glanced at Dr. K. "Liberals can push their humanist agenda all they want, but natural is just another word for obsolete. It'll be a fiasco, and they'll be gone next year. It should be entertaining to watch them fail."

"And die." My whole life was based on optimizing naturals, providing an economic first step toward genetic superiority. That didn't mean I wanted to see naturals fail and die in a race designed for elite modified athletes.

"Yes, naturals will die if they get past the Fun Run," Smith agreed. "They might die trying to get there. It's going to be hot this year." She shrugged. "I'd like things to be clear between us, Media. You're welcome to the Marathons, because you're modified and obviously quite capable. I'm looking forward to seeing you run. But that doesn't explain *why* you're here. If you fail, you damage the brand of TTI baselines. If you die, TTI loses its prize beta. And if you win the baseline group, TTI still loses if you use the prize money to buy out your contract."

"It's not enough." Alex had looked when they published the new prize amounts. It wasn't even enough close.

"Still, the calculus is hard to understand. I don't trust things I don't understand."

I know the feeling, I almost snapped. It was weird watching her lips move. She talked like my father in some ways, clearly trying to use small words my little brain could understand. She had won the Marathons once, using all the intellectual options to get around the obstacles, the only engineering model ever to do so. She was a genius and a predator who loved devising new ways to torment racers. Her Beast Brain race nickname was absurd and perfect. She slowed her speech down because she had to, because she was dealing with lesser people. My father did the same thing because he loved to share what he learned with us. The same words, the same slightly stilted pacing, but for completely different reasons. I worshiped and hated her at the same time.

She didn't wait for me to respond. "Did you know TTI is the only company in the Global 100 with a human being on the marketing team? What possible use is your mother when any AI can do her job a hundred times better? And your father, working on bio-encryption with synthetics who are his intellectual superiors? What would happen to them if you fail and lose your job? If you're deoptimized?"

"With all due respect, that's none of your damn business."

Dr. K flinched, but I didn't care. No one implies that my parents are worthless. I forced my face into an emotionless mask, wondering if her spinning terminal eyes could see the smoldering fear behind my own. Had she already talked to Victor?

"I asked Kylera to join me so I could ask you a few questions," Smith said, as if the prior exchange had never happened. "Your answers are optional and confidential. They have no bearing on your status in the race."

"Okay…" I glanced at Dr. K, who just nodded. Smith's eyes jittered as she reviewed something on her PA feed.

"You have an extraordinary number of small mutations in your genome. The errors are minor individually, but I've never seen so much damage in a living person."

Another glance at Dr. K, another nod. "Of course it is. I'm a beta." Zoot was a naughty bitch who might kill me next week, or next year, but Smith knew that. She was probing for something else, and I could tell by Dr. K's frozen expression she knew it too.

"Your father's the leading human expert on bio-encryption," Smith said. "Which he himself derides as largely impractical within the primary genome. There's not enough data available to encrypt. So he advocates—"

"Security by obscurity."

"Yes. Hiding things in plain view by making them appear normal or, at least, expected."

"Oh, that's what you're getting at. You think we're hiding something in the junk DNA that might manifest unfairly during the race. Dr. K said you might be concerned." And she'd prepped me with the answer. I just wondered if she had any idea what Victor was up to. "There has to be a way of disabling anything experimental in my genome without completely reversing it for public events like this. So she puts in epigenetic triggers and inserts random DNA to distract anyone looking where they shouldn't. My Dad helped her come up with the system." Then, to Dr. K: "Right?"

"More or less. I'm surprised you didn't just ask me," she said to Smith. "It's a common protocol, even if we approach it differently."

"As I expected. But her brother is also in your care, is he not?"

Dr. K hesitated. I caught a frown so slight no one else would notice. "Yes."

"He shows less but still excessive non-coding DNA."

"He does?" I asked, surprised. Dr. K flashed a *shut up* look at me.

"Is he okay?" I fought a surge of panic. Dr. K always told me Tommy's testing was safe.

"He's fine," Dr. K said, tersely, and I realized I'd just shown Smith my weakness: Tommy, who would live forever if I had any say in it.

"You can get dressed," Smith said, but what she meant was, *got you*.

Danny, Daniel, Dan

I FLIPPED THROUGH THE threadbare pages of *Endurance*, not really reading. My eyes were too tired to focus on the words, but I loved the smell of the pages and the weight in my hands. Despite how fragile the book was, I'd brought it for inspiration. The story was about eternal things like tenacity and perseverance, which in a way meant they were about me. I was going to race tomorrow. I was going to run with Tommy. I was going to be *out there* on my own. I brought the book to my face and inhaled, breathing in Shackleton's determination and will.

And then I had to deal with my hair. I'd never raced before, but one thing I knew was that three days of heat, sweat and swimming were going to turn my natural hair into a tangled, knotted nightmare. I always went for relatively short hair for general ease-of-maintenance, but my curls get feisty if I don't show them regular love. I had decided before coming to the race to go with tight headbands under a quick bun, but I had no idea how it'd hold up on the course. I got things in place, put on my own headbands, secured the bun with a small scrunchie, and said a little prayer to the hair gods. It'd have to do.

Mom and Dad PA'd me to wish me luck. Then Tommy sent me a link to his social feed, showing a picture of me holding Danny's arm at ModCon, and I flushed with embarrassment.

"*I think he likes you,*" Tommy said.

"*No, he doesn't. He just doesn't have a PA, so I helped him with the exhibits.*"

"*Really? ModCon has assistive devices for those without PAs or other sub-*

abilities.”

“They do?” Of course they do. I'm an idiot.

“I don't blame you. I mean, those legs…”

I flushed again. Did Danny really want a baseline subscription for his mom, or was he just flirting with me? Did I mind? Surprisingly, the answer was no. I didn't mind at all.

I could almost feel Tommy smiling his Tommy smile.

Media, the perfectly transparent girl.

“Night, big brother.”

“Night, Fiddy. Get some sleep.”

I rolled over and tried, but I kept seeing Danny smiling, walking, being. Fortunately, Coach's pills were right where he said they'd be. 'Sleep is the most important part of recovery,' he'd said at some point. 'So get some damn sleep.' Silly coach; always so aggressive. I bet he was a real softy in the heart he didn't have. I wondered if Danny's coach was like Johnson, and what the world was like without Alex to help you through it. Maybe I could ask over the beer he'd owe me tomorrow night. I knew I'd finish, because I had to. That's just the way I worked.

“Danny, Daniel, Dan.”

No matter how I said it, it made me smile.

THREE:
Good Luck, Morons

Wake Up Call

"MERDE," I MUTTERED. Simple, scatological and about right given that there was no chance I could roll over and fall back to sleep. It was 2:53 in the damn morning and I'm not a morning person. I don't trust morning people. My chronotype was all darkness, all the time. With my baseline package, you get averaged to a not-too-early, not-too-late state that's allegedly the best of both worlds, but for me people are still best seen but not heard before coffee, and preferably not seen either. Unless they have coffee.

I glared up at the black ceiling, suddenly anxious, and fought the urge to leap out of bed and run around in little circles. It was a waste of energy and, besides, I was famished. I couldn't remember ever being so hungry. I'd eaten a lot at dinner, giving new meaning to the term carb-loading, but I was still starving. It was like there was a black hole in my stomach.

The cafeteria didn't open until 3:30 and I didn't have any snacks in the room, which was terrible planning, so there was no point in getting up. I looked at the dark ceiling and contemplated inner calm. Inhale. Exhale. One more time. It wasn't working. Rather than calm, I was contemplating all the food I was going to eat after drinking a gallon of coffee, including no small amount of cheese, pancakes, and god knows what else that would probably kill me on the run. I was face deep in a Zen omelet when the ceiling moved.

"Morning, beautiful," said a deep male voice.

I might have screamed a little. Dad waved from the darkness.

"Don't say anything," he texted.

"Uh…" Why had Alex put him through without permission?

"Text only. Or thought-to-speech."

"How are you doing this?" I asked, just thinking it. I hadn't answered

a call, and Alex seemed to be offline. *"Did you hack Alex?"*

"A little."

"Why?"

"Just worried about you. Now I can secretly dock during the race and you can talk to me anytime you're connected without anyone knowing."

"Can TTI see this?"

"Victor can, yes. He provided the code."

"But it's illegal."

"Very."

"I don't get it. It's dangerous."

"It is, but if you need to talk to us privately during the race, you can."

Privately. Now I got it. If anything went wrong with Victor's testing, this was how I'd tell him. It was still too risky, but at least it made sense.

"Okay, how do I reach you?"

"If it's an emergency, tell Coach you want to listen to smooth jazz."

"Why would I want to do that?"

"Exactly. Love you."

And he was gone. I didn't know whether to be excited or scared. Dad had to know about the off-book testing Victor was doing on me. How concerned was he?

Tiny Doofus barked from the BHD alcove, my snooze alarm, and I forgot all about the hack. It was race day. I was going to run up a mountain. In the courtyard below, the starting-line clock counted down the final few hours until the race started. My stomach growled loudly. I needed to eat, and I needed to get my heart rate down. I was way too excited.

I couldn't believe it. I was really doing this.

Breakfast and Fear

"MY GOD, MEDIA, STOP EATING." Brad leaned back from the table to protect his limbs from the feeding frenzy. Everyone was watching me. I looked at their tiny little plates of tiny little food and tried to swallow enough to speak.

"Why aren't you eating?" It came out as *hwi arthou eathing*. I swallowed the rest of the pancake and chased it with terrible coffee. "Calories, right?"

Coach shrugged. "It's your stomach, Media, but the race starts in an hour. You want to be digesting all that while you're trying to run uphill in the heat?"

Yes, I thought. *Yes, I do.*

He looked concerned. I looked at my pancake island in its syrup sea and reluctantly pushed my plate away.

"You could have told me earlier," I said to Tommy.

"I'm just impressed. You normally don't grunt when you eat."

"I was grunting?" I looked around the room and at Danny's table, but he wasn't there.

Danny, Daniel, Dan. Which did he prefer?

Katy nodded disdainfully. "Like a wolf." She pronounced it *volf.*

"Okay, live and learn." Coach said. "I'm going to trigger your hidden fears to test them. It'll take less than a second." He looked at me. "You may feel a hint of nausea."

"What?" Then to Tommy: "You knew."

"Welcome to the team, Fiddy." He smiled with more than a hint of malicious joy.

Berrick burst out laughing. He had no PA, so nothing to trigger.

Stupid naturals.

"Three," Coach said. Brad grinned. "Two." Tommy put his hands on the edge of the table. "One." Katy closed her eyes and exhaled.

"Trigger," Coach said, gleefully. Before he finished the word, something black raged up behind my eyes. My brain screamed and my heart tried to beat out of my chest. I burst out sweating, and then my stomach reached up the back of my throat and clawed its way toward freedom. I ran for the bathroom.

I wasn't the only one in there. When I came out of the gender-neutral stall, several pounds lighter, a baseline guy named Adamu on the Roots Preservation Alliance team was washing his mouth out in the sink. Roots was a corporate collective focused on trying to turn back time to the days before the Chrome Wars to reassert racial identities and genetics. He looked and probably was as close to Sub-Saharan African in both appearance and heritage as anyone I'd ever seen.

He wiped his sweaty, florid face with his hands and his hands on his shorts.

"What do you think—"

I was interrupted by the sound of a strange horn blasting from unseen speakers. It was 5:00 a.m. and blowing the traditional Barkley conch shell told us it was an hour until race time.

"I love that sound," Adamu said. He smiled ever so slightly. "What did you say?"

"I was going to ask what you thought your fear is."

"Everything," he said as he walked out. "This is my last chance."

That wasn't ominous at all.

Tommy was the only one left at the table when I got back. Everyone else had gone off to finish packing or doing whatever pre-race rituals kept them from losing their minds. He pushed a candy bar across the table.

"Coach says it'll settle your stomach. And you need the sugar."

I nodded. We'll see. I tore it open. The smell of chocolate made me want to cry, and not in a good way. I couldn't believe Tommy hadn't warned me about the fear trigger, but I was also glad. If that was my initiation into the team, I could take a dozen lost breakfasts.

"Have you ever checked out your marketing and stats?" I asked him.

"Why?" He looked wary.

"'TrumaniTech Endurance Series.'" I used my best commercial voice. "'With options for everyone from weekend warriors to elite competitors, TTI ES is *the* genetic subscription for people who never give up and never surrender. If you've got the will to continue, why should your body hold you back? You deserve the endurance to keep going, to keep moving, faster and farther than ever before. TTI Endurance. Endurance today. Endurance tomorrow.'"

There was a smattering of sarcastic clapping from other tables, but still no sign of Danny.

"Well done," Tommy said. "If this doesn't work out for you…"

"It's impressive. Platinum Endurance subscribers have an average VO_2 max of 85 after the first year. Yours is over 110." Which was insane. The average natural was lucky to be in the high 40s. "They have hyper-efficient spleens and can hold their breath for nearly four minutes without training, and their lactate shuttle is three times more efficient than a natural's." I didn't even know what a lactate shuttle was. It sounded like a little bus to the dairy. Alex would normally jump in to tell me, but Coach was in charge now and he wasn't here for trivia time.

"You're a bad ass," I told my big brother. "Even Terrence thinks so." Tornado had called Tommy one of the great runners of our time. Of course, that was right after he'd beaten Tommy by more than an hour in last year's Marathons.

"Yeah, but so's everyone else." His thin smile was back, barely distinguishable from the self-deprecating smirk of synthetics. "Every year, they raise the bar. Every year, we're all closer in ability and it just comes down to luck and determination."

I wasn't sure what to say to that. The progress he was talking about was the entire reason I was in the lab. So we chatted about racing and pacing and little things. I couldn't remember the last time I had time to just sit and talk with my brother about nothing. For a few brief moments, the cafeteria faded away and he told me about the first time he'd ever gone running. He was eight when Mom took him for a walk on TTI campus trails. He ran ahead, she ran to catch up, and soon he was running everywhere.

"She wasn't always the way she is now," he said. "She used to sit and listen to me babble about interval workouts and fasted training like it was the most fascinating thing in the world. Actually *listen*. She must have been bored out of her skull." I nodded and smiled, but it made my heart ache. I had no such memories of our mother. Maybe she'd been different before, or maybe she found Tommy more interesting. I couldn't help but wonder if Tommy and I hadn't had entirely different childhoods. For me, the lab was life. For him, it was like a tune-up: go in, get faster and go for a run. I never talked about what Dr. K did to me, unless it was funny or gross. I couldn't tell if I was glad that Tommy had no idea about the life I was living, or if I was jealous of the one he had.

"You okay, Fiddy? You've got your serious face on."

"What, this? This is my game face." I forced a smile. I'm not sure he bought it.

"*You're live in 60 seconds,*" Coach said in both our heads. I was grateful for the distraction. "*Make your way to the starting line.*"

I picked up my hydration pack. *Ooph.* It was only two liters of water and other crap (most of which I'd left in my room), but I didn't want to carry it all the way up this mountain. Thank god for my trip to the bathroom.

As we funneled out into the courtyard that led to the starting corral with the rest of the runners, I couldn't help but notice the lack of pep in my brother's step. I punched him in the arm, probably harder than I should have right before a race. He grimaced appropriately.

"You know you can win, right? This is your year."

"Fiddy."

I punched him again. "Say it."

"I can win." He rubbed his tricep. "Go easy."

"Believe it, or I'll have Doofus drool in your mouth while you're sleeping."

He laughed. "I could drown."

"Then stop doubting yourself. You're a Conaill, and we kick ass."

He leaned over and growled at me, teeth bared. I returned the expression with a louder growl. Other runners near the doors looked at us like we were nuts. Conaill means *strong as a wolf* in Celtic, if that helps. Growling is a family tradition. It scares Doofus to death.

"Love you, Sis."

"Of course you do. I'm very lovable."

"*Your dockers are live*," Coach said. Fifty thousand people had apparently just heard Tommy and me growl at each other. Good. Shy, I'm not.

We stepped out into the glare of pre-dawn artificial lighting, and the heat hit me like a fist. I must have staggered, because Tommy put his hand on my back. I had made a terrible mistake. I was Lady Icarus. When I ran too high and the sun came out, I'd melt like wax or burst into flame.

"You'll get used to it," Tommy said. I wasn't so sure.

We walked into the synthetic-guarded and rope-lined starting coral between the North and South MoBO towers, nodding and waving to hundreds of people who cheered loudly. More than one called my name. I smiled stupidly at Tommy. I could get used to this.

"Fifteen minute warning!" The Race Director's voice boomed out of loudspeakers. Smith sounded like she had a lot of coffee that morning. "Racers to start."

In my PA view, I saw my docker count spike up into the hundreds of thousands, and my social media feed flooded with well-wishes, emojis and mindless chatter. Tommy's mouth hung open in a PA gape, the dopey parted lips of someone lost in the virtual world, which he was terrible at hiding. I used to throw things in his mouth, but he never learned.

"*Wish me luck*," I posted into my media feed. Positive comments and images came back, a flood of them, including oddly personal messages of support. Tommy called it asymmetrical intimacy because dockers knew so much more about him than he did about them.

"You don't need luck," Tommy said. "You're going to kill it."

God, I hoped he was right.

Good Luck, Morons!

Start & Finish Line
aka The Yellow Gate
Miles 0 & 40 / 478'

All obstacles in the Marathons are marked by distance and elevation from MoBO. The starting line, which also serves as the finish line, is the most obvious homage to the Barkley Marathons—featuring a long yellow gate that runners must tap to finish each lap (though, unlike the Barkleys, the gate is open during the race).

Fun Fact: *Elevations in the Marathons are measured using year-2000 sea levels to avoid changing the elevations every year. Who has time for that?*

A LONG TIME AGO in a state park far, far away, a visionary ultrarunner named Gary 'Lazarus Lake' Cantrell and his partner created the Barkley Marathons. There were few trails, no maps, one aid station, and no one finished for years. The Barkleys were meant to test people, to push them to the very edge of human endurance, and to provide a little sadistic fun in the process. If anyone finished, they made it harder. If anyone failed, as almost everyone did, they played taps on a trumpet and laughed a lot. Over the coming decades, the Barkleys turned into a cult obsession fed by Gary's famously crotchety sense of humor, random rule changes, ever more difficult courses and the haunted eyes of beaten athletes. But underneath it all was one very serious question: What are people capable of?

The yellow gate used in the Marathons was an exact copy of the one in Tennessee's Frozen Head State Park, where the Barkleys had taken place. The status crawler under the digital countdown flashed a famous Gary Cantrell quote: "Good luck, morons!" The growing crowd cheered, and I joined in. The Marathons cherry-picked from the Barkleys, usually losing much of the original anti-commercial ethic, but it was still great to feel like you were part of a tradition going back more than a century. And I was pretty excited to see what I was capable of.

The crowd cheered even louder as the clock turned to -00:10:00.

"Ten minutes to start!" Smiths' voice boomed across the courtyard. "All racers to the corral."

"You're both going to crush this lap," Coach said. *"Tommy, get to the front."*

Tommy gave me a final arm squeeze and then wove toward the gate to join the other elites. I took a deep breath and walked through a small group of naturals, flashing Danny a quick smile, to join the baselines in the middle. The other baselines nodded hello or averted their eyes. Some looked nervous, others bored, but I'm pretty sure they could all tell I was terrified.

If it's not obvious, we were all lined up by class, model and specialization, like a truncated social hierarchy. At the front were the real competitors, the specialist runners arranged by predicted time and finishing order. Terrence and Bentha were up front, with the other endurance runners packed around them. Behind them were a mix of combat and speed models, both of whom did well in the sprints and obstacles but usually ran out of steam before the end. In past races, other specialized modified—intellectuals, engineering and even occasional sex models—would have formed a small middle group, but there was no room for them this year with naturals and baselines on every team. So my group, the baselines, were next in line—all smaller and less muscular or lean than the professionals in front of us. Last were the naturals, who were on the whole shorter and mostly men because naturals had a greater physical dimorphism than the modified. Only four unmodified women made the cut, including Shaquilla, of course. To balance out the teams, most of the baselines were women. It was the perfect reflection of hierarchy, of how we fit in the world, arranged from top to bottom, front to back, our place in the race exactly matching our place in society.

Suddenly the runners parted. Jessica walked between us like an icebreaking ship so intimidating that the ice broke itself. If Shackleton had put her on the bow of the Endurance, he'd have sailed straight to the nearest Antarctic beach without ever touching anything but open water. She stopped after the naturals, right next to me, evaluated each unmodified runner one-by-one, and then shook her head in obvious dismay.

"What do you call a group of naturals?" she asked in a low voice, quietly demanding attention. No one answered and most of us looked down, afraid to meet her eyes. Danny was preternaturally still. Berrick's fists clenched at his side. A dangerous animal stood in our midst. *Ignore it and it will go away.* It was wishful thinking.

"An obsolescence," Jessica said.

No one disagreed. Someone up front chuckled. I started to say something, but Berrick grabbed my arm and shook his head sharply. For the first time, I felt the true dynamic of predator and prey, not some great cycle of life, but fear and contempt. Jessica caught me looking at her, and Berrick dropped his hand.

"What do you call a group of baselines?" she asked me.

"An aspiration?" I suggested, biting back something more sarcastic.

"Clever." She pronounced the word like a disease. If she squeezed me hard enough, would all the clever come out? Then she walked to the front of the pack, the top of the pyramid, and everyone understood. Wherever she was, that was the front. Runners slowly filled the space behind her, quieter than before, almost afraid to breathe.

"Don't worry," Berrick said. "She can't touch you."

"You know what they say about fear," I said. He waited. The quote eluded me. I wasn't nearly as clever with Alex gone. Something from *Dune* would have been nice, like "*I must not fear. Fear is the mind-killer. Fear is the little-death that brings total obliteration. I will face my fear. I will permit it to pass over me and through me,"* but at the time all I could remember was "fear is the little death," but then so were orgasms and neither was that helpful. Jessica glanced back at me, and I felt panicky and weak. She'd beaten me before the race even started. I supposed that was her point.

What do you call a group of augmented? An inevitability.

"Shake it off," Berrick said. I nodded, embarrassed. Was it that obvious?

Ninety-nine other runners stretched and flexed in the heat, but I was already sweating profusely. It was 82 degrees according to a giant digital readout next to the race clock. My stomach said something loud and grumpy. A few other baselines looked over nervously. Abbey just smirked. I swallowed the last of the candy bar so I'd have something in my stomach. It almost got rid of the taste of vomit. I was in so far over my head. I looked for Tommy up ahead and saw him chatting happily with everyone. God, he looked comfortable.

The clock flipped silently to -0:05:00.

"Five minutes!" Smith said.

"You okay?" Danny asked. He was right behind me.

"Yeah. Bit nervous. Does it show?"

"Nah. You look great." He was a good liar.

"Good luck today."

Berrick was watching us. Should I be wishing the other team good luck?

"You too." Danny stepped back. I gave Berrick two thumbs-up. He nodded vaguely.

"Take a deep breath," Coach said. *"You have twelve hours to do the loop. Relax. Go slow. Eat. Drink. You'll be fine."* I wondered if he could hear my heart trying to beat its way out of my chest. Dad probably thought I was having a heart attack if his hack was working.

-00:02:23

"It's your first race, right?" The voice came from my left. A vaguely familiar baseline man looked down at me. He was tall and stunningly handsome.

"Yes." How did I know this guy? Oh, that's right. "John, isn't it?" I forced a smile. He was an ex-sex model and used to do ads for

Wedonist Industries, running the local races as a gimmick. His name was John 'Dangle' Thomas (aka Big T and also Mr. Rogers for some reason), because of course it was. I hated knowing all this, but even with Alex offline, it was still in my head. His skin was so nice, a perfect burnt caramel without blemish or flaw.

"Yeah." He looked uncomfortable. I was staring. Did I mention he was really attractive? It was hard to think straight and I suddenly couldn't speak. "It's okay. Happens all the time."

Did he mean the absurd brain freeze or the objectification?

"You're racing as a baseline now? Not as a…" I trailed off. Did I need a shovel to keep digging or a gun to shoot myself?

"Sex model?" Everyone looked. Danny was trying not to laugh. "I was just going to tell you to take it slow." He leaned in. "One of the mistakes virgins make is pushing too hard."

Danny burst out laughing. Sure, virgins meant first-time racers, another Barkleyism, but it also didn't. I turned away, as red as I'd ever been. My face was on fire.

Just kill me now. Please.

"Focus. Your heart is racing. Count to ten or something."

"Count to ten?"

"What am I, your Yogi? Just get your shit together." I looked to Brad for help and found him easily. His head bobbed up and down as he jumped excitedly from foot to foot, right behind Tommy. Katy was probably in there somewhere, her tiny body lost in the huddle. Jessica caught my eye, smiling disdainfully—apparently everyone had heard me make an ass of myself—and I looked away before she decided to come back and rip my head off.

"Two minute warning!" Smith barked. I flinched. Way too much coffee.

- 0:01:59

Time flew by, too fast and too slow. Clock numbers froze, then skipped. I fought the urge to run back into MoBO or jump up and down. Or scream.

"One minute!"

- 00:00:59

I couldn't believe this was real. I tried not to think of Danny right behind me. I tried not to think about Abbey or Jessica, Brad or Tommy. I took a deep breath and exhaled slowly.

"*That's better*," Coach said.

I looked at the crowd around us and noticed there were a lot of naturals, many holding up signs for their favorites. More than one was for Danny. "You've got the legs!" proclaimed one, held by a boy no older than ten. I had no idea he had a fan base.

My stomach threatened to let loose again. I'd never been so nervous in my life, and Alex wasn't there to distract me. I focused on the race, my breathing and how hot it was already. Anything physical. Like the sweat forming on the muscular legs of the combat model right in front of me. Sweat was, fittingly, what made all of this possible.

Endurance was one of the defining traits of humanity, and a very logical way to judge human advancement. We sweat where other animals dissipate heat through breathing or convection, and that's why we manage heat so much better. We have tendons evolved for hyper-efficient energy utilization on long runs. Even naturals could run down unmodified animals on the African veldt by jogging, whereas most animals can only walk or sprint. The net effect was that our species wasn't naturally the fastest or the strongest, but we never stopped and, eventually, our prey surrendered to exhaustion and dehydration. It's one of the reasons my tenacity felt so natural and central. It was the core definition of human physicality. And the Marathons existed to show just how far we'd come. So I was right where I belonged.

-0:00:40

I bent over and tried to slow my breathing.

"Thirty seconds!" Smith stepped to the side of the gate in a baggy plaid shirt with an actual cigarette between her lips. Could that be real? She pulled out a lighter. The crowd kind of lost it. Officially, the race didn't start until she lit the cancer stick.

- 00:00:25

I stood up and caught Tommy giving me two big thumbs up. I returned the gesture.

"You got this, Fiddy!" Tommy yelled back at me. Now I was

smiling again.

"Tornado!" Terrence's girlfriend screamed from the sideline. She was heiress to some fortune. She was also stunning and brilliant, a Vitruvian princess modified to the border of terminal-class perfection.

-00:00:05

-00:00:04

"Three!"

The crowd erupted. Holy crap, this was really happening.

"Two!"

I was suddenly calm. All sound vanished. I looked up at the rock-and-sage flank of San Jacinto. Just a small mountain to climb. No big deal.

"One!" Smith lit her cigarette and stepped to the side.

The countdown clock flipped from red to green and the yellow gate swung open.

00:00:00

"Go!"

No, Really, Go!

Race Time 00:00:01

COMBAT AND SPEED RUNNERS shot forward like horses off the line to claim early sprint points, some scrambling on all-fours up the steep and rocky trail. Everyone, including the endurance models, followed at what was for them a slow trot. Tommy was just ahead of me, then farther up the hill and soon gone. Within minutes, I was alone between other runners stretched out on the rocky trail as it meandered almost randomly up the first thousand feet toward the picnic tables and the first rope wall, where the trail leveled out to a steady climb. For now, I was high-stepping boulders and scrambling up rocky ravines.

This was the only part of the course where the trail was optional if not notional. There was a trail, or seven, but they wound haphazardly through the rocks and it was faster for many just to go straight up. As long as you ended at the picnic tables, no one cared. In earlier laps, rattlesnakes were harmless (if modified and planted) and there was little worry about death, so runners weren't so careful where they stuck their hands. I still kept to the trail as best I could. The last thing I wanted was to trip and break a leg a quarter mile from MoBO.

Three hundred feet of climbing later, I was drenched in sweat and breathing heavily. It was going to be a long day. I sucked on my hydration tube. I panted some more.

"Take it easy," Coach said. *"Pace yourself."*

I would've told him where to stick his advice, but I was busy trying not to hurl a lung.

At just over 1,200 feet, 700 feet above the start, I crested the giant lump of crappy black rock and descended slightly to the picnic tables. A few people cheered from the sidelines. I waved. Someone sprayed me with cool water. I wanted to kiss them. It was 6:14 a.m., the sun was rising, and it was already unspeakably hot.

Just fourteen miles and 9,500 feet to the summit, I told myself. That was the main climb. I didn't even want to think about the rest of the loop.

A few minutes later, I came to the first obstacle, the rope wall at 1,500 feet. There were identical walls about every 1,000 vertical feet on the way up and down. They were only seven feet tall on the first loop, so I easily scaled it with a little heel hook and pull-up, not even bothering with the knotted rope. The walls got eighteen inches higher on every lap. By loop five, they'd be thirteen feet tall, and I'd be using the rope up and down if I still had the hand strength. There was no bypass option, and the walls were completely smooth, so they were boring and annoying and still took out several runners every year. To get through all five laps, runners have to climb various rope walls a total of 70 times between MoBO and the testing center at 8,500 feet—seven up and seven down on each loop. Guess who the sponsor is. Fortunately, I only had to climb 42 times on the three Fun Run laps.

I dropped down the back side. Just 41 walls to go. After that, the stony single-track trail was better marked and not quite as steep. Unlike the Barkleys, which had rarely used trails, there was little chance of getting lost out here.

I looked down and behind me. Tiny blips of color told me where the naturals were. Ahead of me, there was only more rock and brush. God knows where the other baselines were. I was already alone on the course. I pushed a little harder and sweat a little more. Coach put on light techno and I silently thanked him.

The second wall was just above 2,500 feet, where the trail leveled out again out for a glorious moment. Another trail came in from the south and a few spectators were there, cheering in the dim morning light. "Go, Fiddy!" someone yelled. I waved gamely and forced a smile, then noticed the synthetic monitor next to the wall. Sure enough, he was a handsome dark-skinned man-boy wearing a red plaid kilt and thick wool smoking jacket.

"That's wool," I said to him. "Right?" Between breaths. "You're wearing wool." And not the thin odor-prevention weave in my race clothes. "Why *wool*, for god's sake?" Then I had to hyperventilate for a bit.

"*Save your breath*," Coach said.

It was already over 90 degrees. Freaking *wool*.

The synthetic watched me crawl over the wall without a word, a strangely mocking silence. I slopped over to the other side and continued up the ridge. It was funny how quickly the novelty wore off. Less than an hour earlier, I was nauseated with excitement. Now I was just sweating a lot. Three days of this? It seemed like insanity, but I kept moving. It was insanity I could get my head around if I just focused on the next few feet of trail.

I'd like to claim I found my rhythm and settled into it, just letting the miles fall away, but that would be a lie. The trail wound up ridges and canyons, around cactus and sage, ever closer to the hidden summit. I was in a constant state of stumble, recovery, jog, walk fast, stumble, grunt and recover. I guess there's a rhythm there, but you wouldn't want to dance to it. I drank water when I remembered. I avoided most of the cacti. And I didn't trip an ultra-thin Laotian natural with generically tan coloration named Keo 'K-Tonic' Panggabean when he passed and muttered "Good job"—which is what all runners say to others to sound positive without engaging in actual conservation. I tried to keep up with him for a while, but couldn't. I felt a bit of panic that I couldn't keep up with a natural, but I assumed I'd catch up to him soon enough.

I passed several more Scottish synthetic monitors in kilts and tartans, looking fresh and clean and utterly disinterested. None of them said, "Good job." None of them cared. I'm not sure why I was so focused on the synthetics. Maybe because they were the only ones around. Normally, they're an almost invisible part of the background.

At some point, the temperature went from hot to ridiculous. I tried to ignore it, but every time I looked down, big drops of sweat struck the trail near my shoes to let me know I was melting. How much more could I sweat and still function?

I shook off the thought, pushed on and was soon at the 3,500-foot wall. I casually grabbed the knotted rope, hoisted myself over in two grabs, dropped onto the other side, and almost twisted my ankle.

"Crap," I said. For some reason, I glanced anxiously at tiny synthetic teen girl in heavy wool cardigan, looking very much like a miniature version of me. It was a bit eerie, but she clearly didn't care if I swore. I could see why Tommy called these things the silent killers. The walls, not the synthetics. There was no fanfare or scary animals, just an endless series of chances to injure yourself and end the race.

The next wall was at 4,500 feet, right before a short descent to the Pits—my first real obstacle of the run. I was excited to get there. I sped up.

"*Slow down,*" Coach said. "*And drink.*"

I think I preferred the silent synthetics.

The Pits

aka The Devil's Egg Carton
Miles 5 & 35 / 4,300'

The Pits aren't just a state of mind, they're deep dark holes full of modified beasts with miles of teeth. Fall in, and you're going to have a long drop and a quick stop, followed by an even longer day as you try to claw your way out before the predators get you. You can use increasingly slack slacklines or jump (we dare you), but either way you've got five very large holes to cross before climbing another 4,000 feet to the Pillars at Grubb's Notch.

Fun Fact: *Last year, the bears were so big they couldn't get out of their cages, so some loop five Pit victims climbed out without any harm. Where's the fun in that? Heads rolled, changes were made, and now the beasts are ready for dinner guests.*

COACH TOLD ME TO drink for the thirtieth time. I drank and wiped sweat off my face. The sun was like sandpaper on my eyes. The trail was a dusty oven of glaring contempt and thermonuclear disdain. My face was hot. My legs were burning. The mountain was on fire.

In the valley, MoBO gleamed in the morning sun next to the drab concrete blocks of the convention center. Palm Springs spread around it, full of bubble-domed homes like old visions of planetary colonies, but now how the rich escaped from the sun and heat. One caterpillar-like set of interconnected domes protected a golf course north of MoBO. It wasn't the ugliest place on Earth, but it felt like the hottest.

"*Enjoying the view?*"

"I was." I bent into the hill and raced onward, reaching the wall at 4,500 feet a few minutes later. This was the rough halfway point to Grubb's Notch. After the wall was a steep, unstable rocky decline into an artificial valley and the Pits. I jogged (stumbled) down to the obstacle.

The Pits were three sets of five holes, looking almost exactly like an open 18-pack carton of eggs (hence the Devil's Egg Carton nickname) with deep oblong pits where the eggs were supposed to be. Under the watchful eye of the ubiquitous synthetic attendant, I could pick any of three sets of five and get over any way I wanted— jumping or using the slacklines that crossed each hole. I was going for the slacklines. I had great balance, and there was no way could I jump that far, even if Tommy probably cleared two at a time. Keo was just finishing the first set of holes when I finished my descent. He waved and called something supportive.

I walked up to the middle set and onto the small platform that held one end of the slackline, which is a thick bit of canvas stretched over the holes like a tightrope. I tested the tension with one foot, took a breath, and then—

"Hey there, Media."

I pulled my foot back. Dangle was on the platform to my left, looking cocky. I'm not trying to be ironic. He just seemed full of himself. Danny was coming down the hill right behind us. Not sure why John bothered me so much, but sex models were the lowest of the breeders, maybe even lower than betas, with ridiculous sexual enhancements that made more sense on circus animals. They were a dehumanizing reminder of exactly how animalistic humans used to be. So, I nodded at him, curtly, and then felt bad about it. It wasn't like anyone wanted to be a sex model; it was the only specialized package some people could afford.

"What do you think's down there?" I asked, meaning which animal. I was trying to be nice.

"Good question." He looked into the darkness thirty feet down. "Smells like bears."

"You can smell them?" But of course he could. Many sex models had a modified vomeronasal (aka Jacobson's) organ to enhance nasal sensitivity. Several mammals had the same olfactory trait, which is why horses are constantly pulling back their upper lip and sniffing to move air through their nose and over the chemoreceptive organ. It's called the Flehmen response, and it made people look like they have the sniffles. Terminal-class people with this change were always stopping, inhaling dramatically, and then looking at you in a completely inappropriate way that said something like, *I can tell you're ovulating and you need to eat more vegetables.* Technically they were breeder-class changes, but they were considered such a gross violation of human privacy that few companies would license them. And yet the sex models often included such changes to make them more "perceptive and sensitive" to their partners. It just made John even more irritating.

"Of course," John said, sniffing again. "They feed them berries and small—"

And then Danny came up behind John and shoved him into the hole. John fell into the safety net twenty feet down in silence. Then there was a roar and a lot of screaming.

"*Sounds* like bears." Danny smiled, proud as a bighorn sheep. It was hard not to laugh.

"Is that legal?" I asked.

More screaming.

Really hard.

Danny shrugged. "It's a fifteen minute penalty on this lap." Still more screaming. "Worth it." Then he slack-lined effortlessly across the first holes. I watched him in appreciative silence. Natural had game.

I stepped back onto the slackline and slowly made my way over all five holes. By the time I got to the end, John had crawled up the safety rope, passed me, and was chasing Danny up the hill. I decided I liked the Marathons. They were way more entertaining than the lab.

From the Pits, the trail wound another four miles up a hot, dry ridgeline to the shady trees of Grubb's Notch, which granted access to Long Valley and the tourist tram station at 8,500 feet. The ascent was steep, rocky and exposed to the sun until well above a slab of granite called Flat Rock at 5,900 feet, after which I climbed the fifth wall. Stunted pine trees started to appear at 6,500 and I had intermittent shade above 7,000, but the heat was still a crushing thing. I focused on the trail, the unending trail, and forged upward while my body dripped into the dirt.

I knew what to expect from the race overview, but being there made me realize how little that theoretical knowledge meant. In my mind, I just projected the trail up into the trees. But that doesn't capture the scale of it. I ran out of water below Flat Rock. My calves started to cramp about 100 feet higher. I took out my trekking poles and leaned into them, grateful for the relief for my quads, but disappointed things didn't feel any easier.

At some point, I sat heavily in the shade of a scrawny Coulter pine and tried to get my heart rate down. A baseline woman named Mist 'Max Pain' Robbins in green-and-white McNickle colors soon passed me with a mumbled "Great job." She was followed by her natural teammate, who thankfully didn't tell me what a great job I was doing. How many naturals had passed me? Coach didn't say, but it was not a small number.

According to the race PA display, the ambient temperature was 98. Humidity was 45 percent thanks to all the irrigation required to maintain the course. It felt like it was 108 in the shade. In the sun, it felt like an oven. I sucked sadly on the hose of my empty hydration pack. This was harder than I expected, which sounds ridiculous, but I had nothing to compare it to. I think I just assumed I'd be great at this.

"*You okay, Media? Your heart rate's a little high.*"

"One-hundred percent." I pushed up on aching quads and unfolded my seized lower back.

"*Let me know if you start to feel lightheaded. You can use the emergency rehydration shot in your pack and then get another one at the aid station in Long Valley.*"

"Yeah. Okay." But then I'd have to take my pack off, and that seemed like a lot of work. I trudged upward, trying to catch up to the natural girl. "How's Tommy doing?"

"*He's fine. Run your own race.*"

Run. That's funny. I was jog-walking at best. "How am I doing?"

"*You're getting it done. Focus on your breathing.*"

Suddenly, my breath was loud in my ears, like a jet plane revving its engines. I sucked in fast, ragged breaths and tried to inhale more deeply, exhale fully, slowing it down. I added a pressure breath—a forced exhalation between pursed lips—every fourth breath, taking in more air and allegedly being more efficient. I felt a bit of panic as my body demanded more oxygen, but it steadied. I found a better rhythm. Damned if Coach wasn't actually helping.

"Thanks," I said. Rather than respond, he put on some throbbing dance music that perfectly matched my pace. I felt better instantly, and the natural soon came back into view ahead of me, fading in and out of the trees like a heat mirage. I passed her after the last wall before the junction at the traverse, a stretch of trail that contoured through a rockslide-prone and exposed couloir above 7,500 feet.

"Good job, Luna," I said, reading her name off her shirt—Luna Lin, no nickname—trying not to sound sarcastic. She was doing a good job. I just hated to admit it. She didn't even look up as I passed.

At the traverse junction, a blacker-than-black synthetic male waited on an umbrella chair in a very nice three-piece evening suit with a tartaned vest. As if he needed the shade. He nodded to my right toward the traverse itself. To the left, another trail came down from the east side of Long Valley via the Scree Slope. Think of this as where the candy meets the stick on the lollipop-shaped course. I went right. I'd come down the Scree Slope on the way back.

Somewhere after the next rocky switchback, I caught sight of Max Pain. I tried to catch up, but even the slightest increase in pace threw my breathing back into panicked gasping. I settled back into my music and pace and tried to ignore the heat. It might've worked if I could have kept the sweat out of my eyes. At least I was in the trees now, and mostly in the shade.

Just before the Pillars at Grubb's Notch, you walk straight toward a giant pinnacle of rock called Coffman's Crag. I kept looking for it, kept thinking every boulder was my destination, but the trail just got steeper and rockier.

Breath, breath, breath, pressure breath, breath, breath, breath…

I scrambled up and around a large boulder and found myself facing the Crag. I was almost at Long Valley. Thank god.

"Welcome to BFR."

I jumped. It was a baseline woman from Keo's team, Tala 'True Grit' Kantie, who was sitting against a tree and drinking. Apparently, she'd done a better job rationing her water.

"BFR?"

"Big Fucking Rock. Coffman's."

I smiled. "You okay?"

"Yeah, just taking a break. I think the Pillars are right over that rise. The sun's killing me. I went out too hard. How're you?"

I shrugged and forced a smile.

"You're doing great," she said. "I can't believe you've never raced before."

"Thanks." I tried to figure out if she was mocking me, but there was no sign of it. She took another drink. I licked my lips enviously. At least I was salty. "See you at the summit."

"Go get it." She looked way too fresh to be sitting down, but I heard she was pulled by a course medic at the Long Valley aid station for heat exhaustion. I guess you can never tell how someone else feels in their own body.

The Pillars

aka The Revolvers
Mile 10 / 8,250'+

The third technical obstacle is a set of 150-foot tall rotating rock pillars at Grubb's Notch featuring hand-width, off-width and body-width vertical cracks that have to be climbed without ropes or protection. There are small handholds on the first loop, after which the pillars are rotated to reveal ever-smoother and widened cracks that make climbing increasingly difficult.

Fun Fact: *Way back in the 2nd Marathons, a modified mountain lion climbed up a crack on loop four and took down race favorite Harry 'The Grip' Janson. Harry went on to win the race and adopt the mountain lion to patrol his Palos Verdes estate. Beware of kitty!*

I DRAGGED MY SORRY, achy body up another fifty feet past Tala and the base of BFR, crested a small ridge, and I was at the Pillars. I'd climbed exactly three times with Tommy on TTI's gym climbing wall. Somehow, we just never had time for it. As I approached the 150 foot pillars of lumpy granite, it was easy enough to see the crack. It was consistently hand-width and lightly zig-zagged all the way up, and there were plenty of handholds on the outside. The climb was rated 5.8 on the standard difficulty scale, meaning exposed but relatively easy, so I didn't take it as seriously as I probably should have. I picked the second of three pillars.

There were ample footholds outside the crack, so it was more a test of endurance than technical climbing, but I was still careful to put on my gloves before jamming my hands into the crack. I had none of the tough, calloused hands that climbers need to do this without tearing the skin off their fingers and the backs of their hands.

It was a breeze at first, one hand jam after another, foot after foot, gradually gaining altitude. I tried not to look down. It would be all too easy to fall, and looking down didn't help. Neither did my sudden rapid breathing. I burst out in sweat, my biceps started to swell, and my breath came in hard, heavy gasps. And I was only a third of the way up: fifty feet down and a hundred feet to go. The first bit of panic set in. I knew the nets would deploy almost instantly if I fell—I'd seen them work in past events—but somehow it didn't help. The ground looked too far away and my hands were slipping.

Damn it, damn it, damn it…

"Use your legs," Danny called out. I glanced over at the first pillar and saw him almost level with me and moving fast. "Put more weight on your legs."

I nodded and grimaced at the same time. Why wasn't he hyperventilating like I was? I thought I was going to die. And the rock was hot, even in the crack. If not for the gloves, I'd have burned my hands and slid right out into open air.

"Media, you're fine. Just…"

"I know I'm fine!" I snapped. Where did that come from? I would have flipped him off, but somehow it didn't seem worth falling.

"*He's right,*" Coach said. Which didn't help.

I took a breath, checked my footholds and straightened my knees, taking all weight off my hands. Relief was almost instant. When I looked at Danny to apologize, he was already twenty feet higher. Which was somehow even more irritating. No natural should beat me this easily, and no way was he beating me to the top. I took another deep breath, shook out my hands one at a time, and got moving.

I jammed my hands in less carefully, kept my weight on my foot holds and moved faster, but then had to rest periodically while my heart jackhammered against my ribs. Far above me, a massive bald eagle soared upward in long rising circles on a thermal of hot air rising from the valley. Show off.

"Use your legs," Danny said again. God, I wanted to flip him off. We were both almost at the top, but he was right. Again. I shifted more weight to my feet. I caught my breath. Sweat poured off in fat drops and sailed away.

"I don't think you can coach me," I called up to Danny, trying not to sound irritated.

"Trust me. Nobody cares what I do."

After that, we climbed at about the same pace, jamming our hands and feet into the cracks, pushing our bodies upward and repeating. It wasn't graceful or fast, but it got the job done. Well, that and a lot of involuntary grunting. I'm sure no one noticed.

"Good job," Danny said when I topped out. He watched quietly as I flopped over and stumbled to my feet. I turned toward the blank white doors of the blank white testing center. What was he waiting for?

"What happens in there?" he asked nervously.

Oh, that's right. He wasn't a lab rat, and I doubt other races had testing centers.

"Don't worry. It doesn't hurt much."

The Testing Center

Take a break and get a beer while sports biologists poke holes in your favorite athletes. No one knows what they do to the runners behind closed doors, but we assume there's probing involved. I mean, we hope there is. Okay, our sponsors tell us we can't say that. There's absolutely no probing going on. Probably.

DANNY DIDN'T LAUGH.

"Kidding," I said. "It *usually* doesn't hurt." By which I meant it shouldn't hurt. Given what Victor had told me, I had no idea what to expect.

"*Door two*," Coach said as in, *Let's get this over with.* I went to the middle door. Danny picked door one because he was close to it. Was it random for naturals, or did they just not care? My guess is they forgot because, well, they didn't care.

"It's just physical tests," I told him. He still looked nervous. "Are you dehydrated? How's your heart rate? Are you acclimating well? Weight loss and blood sugar. Tommy says they share stats between companies to compare packages and performance confidentially. But I think he's just guessing. No one knows." There was never any video or reporting unless someone was disqualified during the tests. The dockers couldn't see anything. "If it helps, Tommy said you're unconscious for most of it."

"That's a good thing?"

"I've spent a lot of my life that way. You get used to it. Ready?"

He nodded, looking calmer than I felt. I hated the idea of being unconscious while they tested me. It was fine back home, but I didn't know these people or what weirdness they'd get up to.

"One, two, three, testing!" he said.

We opened our respective doors. Inside my testing room, five people sat facing me on a white semi-circular bench. The middle three were judges. Dr. K sat on the far left, an observer there to protect TTI intellectual property, which wasn't a surprise. She did the same thing for Tommy. She smiled slightly, enough to express recognition, but not enough to show concern or bias. I was just glad she was there to keep an eye on the others. A synthetic monitor sat on the far right, smiling precisely enough to show nothing at all.

I walked in and took a seat on a cylindrical white stool in the center of the room. The first judge on the left was a tall, lean male of indistinct terminal-class modifications and iridescent skin, as if his blood were made of fireflies. He grinned, showing a mouth full of dayglow teeth, and I looked away. Whatever look he was going for, creepy was what he'd accomplished. I labeled him Dayglow.

"I believe this is your first test?" said the middle judge, a woman whose sole interesting feature was her stunning blue-purple hair. I knew that color, because it wasn't a color. It's a diffraction pattern copied from butterfly chitin, the same butterflies in the TTI atrium. I was the first one TTI had tested it on, when I was seven and still working with Dr. Adams. I woke up a week later and my eyebrows were blue, which was cool enough for a little girl, but all my toenails had fallen off. Surprise! I think they'd fixed that little problem. If not, I assume she avoided open-toed shoes. Let's call her Butterflies.

"Media?" she asked.

"Yes, this is my first test." To avoid looking at her feet, I turned to the last judge, and my mouth dropped open. At first, I'd thought he was boring, just a metallic-silver terminal who thought it was cool to look like polished steel, but that wasn't it at all. He had matte gray skin, not silver, black hair and all the silver was in his corneas. It was as if someone had filled his eyes with mercury. He was a Chrome Demon, basically the cause of the Chrome Wars. Not him personally, but his completely unnatural and almost alien appearance. No one would ever fake that look and most people would hide it, but there he was. I'd never seen one before, not in person. Chromes were low-probability mutations in the skin color lottery, and parents could freely change Chrome skin and eye coloration in utero. He met my gaze with all the emotion of a synthetic and an identical smile.

"Just relax," Butterflies said. "You'll be unconscious for the test, which will take exactly eight minutes. This will allow you to be back on the course after the allotted ten minute testing period. You'll remember nothing, and it will have no impact on your race. Do you consent?"

"I thought I already had?"

"It's a formality," she said. Dr. K nodded.

"Okay, sure, I consent."

"Thank you. Now just hold still."

A second later I felt two cold, metallic jacks slide into the data ports on my neck. I turned around, but there was no one there. I turned back, and everyone was gone.

"What the…"

Black.

White.

"Guhhhh!" I woke up feeling so beaten I couldn't even swear properly. Everything felt broken and the pain was astonishing until, suddenly, I was fine. It was like the worst magic trick in the world. I looked accusingly at Dr. K, who didn't even blink. I guess this is what I'd signed up for.

"Thank you, Media," said Dayglow, his voice soft and ethereal as if he were talking from another dimension. I shuddered. The guy was disturbing.

"Was that it?" I joked, as in, *no big deal.* I still didn't feel quite right.

"That's it," Butterflies said. "Good luck on the rest of the loop."

Dr. K nodded indistinctly, but I could tell she was disappointed. Whatever they were doing, it hadn't worked. Which meant they'd make it worse on lap two.

I stood up and walked to the opposite door. A few seconds later, the door slid open and I was out. Danny was at the next door, humming something I didn't recognize. I tried to place the song, but it was pointless. Life without Alex was vague and annoying.

"How…" Danny stared. "What the hell happened to you?"

"Bad reaction." Did I look that bad? "How was your test?"

"Apparently, there's no point in testing naturals. I just stretched for ten minutes."

Made sense. We both jogged over to the Long Valley aid station, which was outside the old park Ranger Station and just past the ramp to the upper tram station. Oh yeah, if you're smart, you can take a tram most of the way up from the valley. Dozens of (smart) fans sat in portable chairs under umbrellas along the trail. I high-fived a couple wearing "TTI Bronze" t-shirts and floppy hats. I still felt off, but the nausea was fading.

"Media! Media!" cheered the crowd. Several others cheered for Danny, or at least his legs.

Volunteers waited eagerly to give us food, water, and help us back on our way. The station was just a few tables set up under temporary canopies, and I was tempted to join them in the shade. But Tommy had been clear on one thing; never sit down. Once you sit down, you never want to stand up again. You want to sleep. You want to eat. Anything but continuing to run uphill in the heat.

"Good luck," I told Danny, and then I took off as fast as I could, determined to beat him to the summit.

"Don't forget to drink!" one of the volunteers called after me.

So I drank and ran, meaning I sipped and jogged. There was no running on the uphill, not for me, and that was fine. I swore when I did this race that I'd take the time to appreciate where I was. I was out of the lab. I was in a State Park with trees and birds and sky and I was, at least visually, alone. I was *outside*. The air was hot and dusty, but there was still that sweet smell of summer sap and pine. I tried to appreciate it. I wanted to. But it was just too damn much effort. I had to keep moving. Step, breath, step, breath, again and again. I imaged the elites had time and energy to enjoy the process. For me, it could've been a dusty treadmill.

After the aid station, I switch-backed up toward Round Valley, managed to run a short section of trail by a dry meadow, and then took the rockier course up to Wellman Divide. There was a tree, twisted black and brown from a lightning strike. There was a rock, veined with copper and quartz. There was a root like the tentacle of a subterranean octopus terrorizing runner's ankles. And here I was, one step higher, one step farther. Danny was behind me somewhere, probably taking it easy to pace himself. Almost every modified and several naturals were ahead of me. I wasn't fast and I wasn't enjoying it, but I was getting it done.

The Tunnels

aka Two-Barreled Jenny
Mile 13.5 / 9,300'+

Always a hit with the goth crowd, the Tunnels are long, dark, spooky caves of runner despair. You never know what you'll find inside, but you can be sure it'll challenge both mind and body.

Fun Fact: *Race favorite Scott Swansley quit the race at the Tunnels on loop four after encountering his secret fear in the darkness of Jenny Two. His final comment? "That was the most horrible thing I've ever seen in my life. I'm done. I'm never coming back. F**k you all." That's the stuff of legends!*

BEFORE I KNEW IT, I reached a trail junction and the synthetic nodded to the left. The regular trail wandered into the trees and turned right and northward, but I was heading to the Tunnels. I went left and spent a moment enjoying the view at Wellman Divide, looking down into a wooded valley where Lazarus Lake stood out like an oasis of cool in the stifling heat. Then I was at the tunnel entrances—two cave openings in the flank of Jean Peak, the mountain just above Wellman. They looked natural, but they'd been bored into the rock two decades earlier and sculpted to race needs. This was both functional and sadistic, as Brad might say, so perfect; anything for ratings and entertainment. Jenny One was on the left and Jenny Two on the right.

I stared into the holes like pupils, the mountain's eyes, and sighed.

I had great eyesight and night vision, far better than naturals but nowhere near as good as the combat models modified for night operations and battle. Still, it was just a tunnel. How bad could it be?

"On this loop, the tunnels are just dark," Coach said. So, not that hard. At least Alex would've tried to make it entertaining. Coach was more practical: *"The test is for night vision, proprioception, anxiety management and so on. There's also a harmless infestation of some kind in both tunnels to test related phobias. You're in Jenny Two."*

"Well, let's hope I'm not afraid of the dark," I said. Every step was on awkward, broken rock and slippery slabs. Most light was gone within seconds. I could hear my breath echoing in the hot, humid cave and forced myself to relax. Tommy had told me the tunnels were either trivial or terrible depending on your mindset, so I set my mind to *deal with it*. I reached for the wall, picked up my speed, and prayed there weren't any deep holes to fall into. I was amazingly loud. My trekking poles helped navigate, but every touch of the metallic tips on rock was a loud *click* that echoed down the tunnel. Thank god this wasn't a stealth test.

It took a few minutes to realize I was covered in long strands of webbing, tiny threads of silk that stuck to my arms and hair. I ran my hands through it, walked through it, inhaled it. And along with the webs came the feel of little things crawling across my skin. I guess Synthetic Carpenter was right. I wiped tiny spiders off my face at first, swabbing constantly, but there were too many and it threw me off balance every time. I ate several crunchy spiders no bigger than ants. They were not delicious.

I saw the light, picked up speed again, and was almost running when the tunnel turned slightly to the right and I emerged into a larger chamber. In past Marathons, there was an additional psychological obstacle here. They'd pulled it because it didn't work for naturals without PAs. Now there was just a synthetic monitor on a bench of rock right by the exit. I turned back to the tunnel, where I'd heard something.

"Holy…" It's hard to describe the volume of tiny red-and-black dwarf spiders that poured out of the darkness, coming for me. There were thousands. Hundreds of thousands.

"Don't ever stop," Danny had said. I turned and ran into the daylight, waving vaguely at the monitor as I went by. She waved back expressionlessly as an animatronic doll.

I wiped myself off as best I could on the run, but the spiders seemed determined to jump ship anyway. Dozens leaped off and scuttled back toward the tunnels. Dozens more were smeared across my body in various states of dismemberment and gore. It was not a good look. I stopped to smear them some more and glanced left to see if Danny was going to come out of Jenny One, but there was no sign of him.

"Maybe you should run or something? This is a race," Coach offered, helpfully. Who knew that a synthetic could express exasperation so clearly? *"And don't forget to drink."*

I sucked on my hydration tube. The water-electrolyte mix was so hot it made me want to throw up, so I took small sips. Tiny sips. Honestly, it might've just been saliva and sweat.

"Slow down," Coach said as I bounded over a log.

"Make up your mind."

"Slow down," he repeated. I slowed down.

"You're kind of a nag, you know that?"

"You're not drinking enough."

The Summit

Mile 16 / 10,833'

The peaky-peak of the tippy-top, turn around or it's a long, hard drop. Naturalist John Muir said, "The view from San Jacinto is the most sublime spectacle to be found anywhere on this earth!" but we can only assume he'd been drinking.

FROM THE TUNNELS TO the summit is just over two miles of gradually rising trail with some rocky traverses up the eastern flank of Jean Peak and then San Jacinto itself. I was in the dappled light of emerald pines with views down to Long Valley and the upper tram station. If not for the heat, itchy spider guts and my inability to breathe, it would've been beautiful.

Somewhere in there, it occurred to me that I'd never been above five or six thousand feet in my entire life. I'd never skied, climbed a mountain or otherwise experienced high altitude. Was my current state of hyperventilating misery normal? Was that the joy of the mountains? Why hadn't I asked about training in a hyperbaric chamber or something? This was hard.

"Slow down a bit. Your heart rate's high."

I slowed to a stop and leaned onto my trekking poles, trying to catch my breath.

"Maybe not that slow."

I slumped forward into an ambitious amble. I'd felt fine in Long Valley. How could so little elevation change hurt so much? I panted around the next switchback, surprised to see Keo lying on his back in the shade. He was on the ground with an arm over his face, like he was taking a nap.

"You okay?" I panted. "Keo?"

"Yeah." He lifted his head and squinted up. "It's just hot. I'll be fine."

For some reason, I hadn't thought about the heat in a while. It was still in the nineties. I walked past Keo and felt the first breeze of the day. I assumed he'd be fine, but he wasn't. He never even made it to the summit, instead walking back to the tram station for the ride down. The tram car rotates for scenic reasons. I heard that didn't sit well with his stomach and his new nickname was 'Projectile.' You can probably figure out why.

The trail wasn't quite as steep now, so I jog-walked the final quarter mile to the trail junction and headed right toward the summit. A runner in Roots colors jogged past, coming from the summit, then heading to (my) left down to Little Round Valley. It took me a second to recognize him as Adamu from the bathroom that morning.

"Good job!" It was about all I had the energy to say. He smiled and waved a hand, but he clearly wasn't there for conversation.

It was another quarter mile to the safety hut aid station. I grabbed a little food and less water—I'd be back there in a few minutes when I came back from the summit—and told them I'd seen Keo back on the trail, looking beat. I then trudged the last the tenth of a mile to the summit. Trees fell away to broken slabs of rock and it was scrambling time, on all fours, gasping my way to the top. One last step and I was there. I was hyperventilating, my quads were burning, the sun was a nasty bitch and I was still covered in spider guts, but I'd climbed this stupid mountain. It had taken me just over six hours, which was a bit concerning. Coach had given me a target of 5:30 for the summit, and I was way behind. That gave only about 5:45 to get to the finish line before the cutoff, which was tight, but for some reason it didn't worry me. Downhill was easier, even if longer. I knew I could run down, and then do it again tomorrow. I needed a shower, or three, but my anxiety just drifted away. A baseline beta *could* do this. *I* could do this.

"*You should head down,*" Coach said. "*You're behind and—*"

"Give me a second." I was on top of the first mountain of my life. And the view was...

I turned around and took in the majesty of nature.

Yeah, the view was crap.

All the mountains around San Jacinto were dead, their pine forests long since killed by aridity or fire. The only living trees were right here on San Jacinto, and you could tell they'd be gone in a year without water and other protections. On all the other mountains, there was dirt and cactus up to five or six thousand feet, then chaparral and sage, and eventually bare tree trunks near the summits—many burned like black fingers beckoning toward a haunted past.

Directly north and down on the western end of the Coachella Valley, The Black was a charcoal lesion stretching from the flanks of the San Bernardino Ridge into the valley, west and south to the far western foothills of San Jacinto. Just seeing it gave me chills, but for some reason, I didn't move. I wanted to remember this moment, my first mountain—my first anything really—but I couldn't help wondering where my house once stood, and how close I'd been to being buried there.

Despite not caring about climate change officially, global carbon neutrality had been reached twenty years earlier more or less by accident. Several years from now, the temperature would allegedly start to decline, but it would be hundreds of years before the forests came back to Southern California. In the meantime, we had a lot of dust and cactus and sunscreen. It hadn't rained naturally in Los Angeles in seventeen years. Not once. The forests on San Jacinto were artificially maintained, watered and protected, so the Marathons was probably a great natural preservation effort. A green dot in a brown world. Whatever happened with the weather, it was obvious the planet was dying and we were killing it. The only question was which class of human being would inherit the ashes.

"You did it." Danny came up behind me. "Good job."

His powerful quads flexed distractingly under a sheen of sweat, and I was glad for the distraction. I had no idea looking out at nature would be so depressing.

"You too." I nodded. "You're wet."

"Yeah, it's sweat. *Real* humans do it."

"Nice." It wasn't like I was any less sweaty. "You know you don't have to keep up with me, right?" I wasn't trying to be condescending, but there was a reason naturals weren't usually in the race. They couldn't take the distance or the pace. I can't say I was worried about him. It just didn't seem fair. They should get their own course or a head start.

"You weren't so snotty at the Pillars." He wiped his forehead and flicked sweat onto the rocks. "I'm pacing myself so I have something for tomorrow. I've done this climb more than an hour faster with obstacles in training. Maybe you're not as fast as you think you are?"

"Fast?" I let the snotty thing go. He wasn't wrong. The FKT (fastest known time) for naturals climbing from Palm Springs to the summit without obstacles was just over three hours, and the endurance breeder record was even less, so we weren't exactly killing it. "Look around. We're not even in the same race as everyone else. You really did this an hour faster?"

"Yep." He took in the view and caught his breath. "At least the view is nice."

"Why the hell aren't you covered in spider guts?" I demanded.

"*Maybe you can flirt later?*" Coach said. I grimaced. Who was flirting?

Danny shrugged. "Jenny likes me better." His smile faded. "Seriously, though, you should get going. The downhill is longer and harder than it seems. You don't want to miss the cutoff."

"Yeah, thanks." I tried not to sound offended. Was he seriously worried about *my* time? Still, he wasn't wrong about the cutoff. I did need to get moving. So I left him there and stumbled my way down slabby granite blocks back to the aid station. Volunteers quickly refilled my water and offered me food, and it was definitely eating time. I stuffed cookies and watermelon in my face, not bothering with social etiquette. One of them tried to get the webs out of my hair. It wasn't happening and he gave up, offering me more cookies instead. I had three Oreos in my mouth when he told me not to forget to eat.

"Are you kidding me?" It came out as *Athoo kithinee?* I also spit some crumbs on him. "Tholly," I said, but I wasn't tholly. I slammed electrolytes that tasted like plastic cherry happiness, and I was off.

Back at the trail junction, I turned right and dropped down to the west. I almost stopped when I saw Berrick coming from the tunnels side, moving slowly but well. "Good job!" I yelled and he waved happily. These naturals were tough.

Riverside and San Bernardino came into view as the trail turned downward, revealing smog and natural slums as far as I could see. There was an ocean out there somewhere, but you'd never know it.

Jogging down the rocky switchbacks toward Little Round Valley, I finally found the first hint of rhythm. I wasn't great, and I nearly tripped several times, but after all the climbing, I felt free. Like a kid cutting loose in the yard after chores. I had my arms out to the side for balance the way Tommy had shown me, so I probably looked like a defective toy stumbling down the mountain, but it was fun. I couldn't stop smiling. It was *really* fun.

And then, of course, I tripped and Supermanned into the dirt (hands out, airborne, *it's a bird, it's a plane, it's a wipeout*), barely missing a large rock and a larger tree. I picked myself up, dusted off my lightly scratched knees, and continued. Nothing to see here. Everyone wipes out in the Marathons. I had gotten my wipeout out of the way.

And then I tripped again.

"*How's that rhythm coming?*" Coach asked.

"Aren't you supposed to be supportive?" I rubbed my twice-bruised knees.

"*Aren't you supposed to be a biped?*"

"Ha ha. I'll show you rhythm."

And I did for a while. I was flying.

And my stupid bug-eating smile was back.

The Jungle Gym

aka The Tendonizer
Mile 19 / 8,900'

The Jungle Gym is 100 feet of hand-tiring, tendon-tearing natural monkey bars. It starts easy on loop one, but in later loops the branches drop and move. One of the race favorites, it's always a killer after the Fun Run. And we mean that literally.

Fun Fact: *Katy Kitzo holds the top three fastest obstacle times among men and women. They don't call her Spider Monkey for nothing.*

MY SMILE FADED AT the Jungle Gym. I rounded a corner in the trail and suddenly the pines were replaced by a lush canopy of giant, modified sycamore that clearly didn't belong in the alpine forests of Southern California. The tightly packed trees grew in two perfectly aligned rows that formed a straight colonnade along either side of the trail. Except, instead of a trail, there was a deep, dark pool of water. The trees were offset so that one branch from each formed monkey bars about ten feet over the water. The trail forked right before this, so runners could bypass if they needed to. A synthetic monitor waved politely from the shade on the side trail. I wondered if he got lonely out here in the woods.

I'd seen variations of this obstacle a dozen times on the Marathons broadcasts. You had to run and jump to catch the first of thirty-three branches that were lined up every eighteen inches. You then had to swing all fifty feet down the course and jump off without falling in the pool below. It was beautiful in a way. The line of trees cast deep shadows across the course. And their perfectly symmetrical branches of smooth, dark wood looked almost sculpted. But hand strength was not my strong point. If I wasn't careful and quick, I'd get tired and fall, take the penalty and have to start over. I could fail the entire course right here.

"*You'll be fine,*" Coach said. "*Deep breaths. Solid grabs. Just don't miss the first branch.*"

Great advice. Katy wouldn't even hesitate here, but I wasn't a spider monkey. All modified had stronger-than-average tendons, ligaments and muscle tissue. And we had denser bones that were both stronger and more flexible than natural bones, maintaining some of the elasticity that allows teenagers to fall off cliffs without shattering. But I was no specialized model. Brad's modifications took tendon modifications to the next level. He could jump rope with an elephant on his shoulders and never strain his Achilles. TTI had even licensed some of Shaquilla's tendon advantages from Black Rook, but none of those were in my baseline package. My hands were already tired from the rope walls and pillars. I hadn't taken the months and years needed to strengthen them naturally, and they hadn't been enhanced as part of my pre-race g-mods. They were going to give out at some point.

"*Media, you're losing time. Don't overthink it.*"

"Too late for that." I wasn't sure why I was stalling so much. I looked in the trees and felt my heart skip at some imaginary threat, but I had no idea what it was. I ran and jumped.

Too high. I caught the first branch in my chest and had to slide down onto the branch. I swore I could hear Coach laughing. My docker count jumped. I'd almost forgotten they were there until their numbers exploded. Everyone wants to see a good fall.

I swung from branch to branch, trying to keep a steady rhythm and not miss my grabs. It wasn't that hard. The sycamore branches were smooth gray and wrapped in purplish veins that were not part of the natural tree. I'm sure I'd find what that was all about later. Another swing, and another. It was fun, but my hands tired quickly.

My forearms swelled with blood, what climbers call getting pumped. I lifted a leg up and around a branch so I could shake out one hand at a time and catch my breath.

"*You taking a nap?*" Coach asked.

The last twenty feet went quickly. I swung clear of the pool and landed on the other side.

"Whoop!" I yelled in celebration. Well, I yelled something, but I wasn't sure how to spell it. Imagine excitement and incoherent noises.

From the shaded and nearly tropical Jungle Gym section on the old Marion Mountain trail, the run was quiet and peaceful. It was probably my favorite section. There wasn't much of a view in the green tunnel, but it was the first time I had any sense of being alone in nature, just me and the trail. The path took me down to where it merged with the Pacific Crest Trail and then to another junction with Deer Creek Trail as it came up from the north side of Idyllwild. I could have been in any forest in the world. Well, any forest that hadn't died or burned down.

At the Deer Springs junction, a synthetic nodded to the left, and I was ascending again. My legs went from heaven to leaden in minutes. My heavy breathing came back, and the trail was barely climbing. I knew the Air Stairs were at the next saddle, just two miles from the Jungle Gym. This included nearly 960 feet of very nice descent, but it suddenly seemed way too far away. I was beat.

"*You're not beat,*" Coach said. "*Drink some damn water.*"

I drank some damn water. I had a little snack. I felt better almost immediately, which was annoying. Eating and drinking were pretty much the only things you had to do while running other than not fall. It was like needing Coach to tell you to breathe.

"*Watch your breathing. Take deeper breaths.*"

Okay, I should have seen that coming.

A little more grumbling and I topped the rise. The trail ran directly into a long, deep pit. On one side was the steep slope rising up to Marion Mountain. On the other side, the slope continued down toward Idyllwild. I was at the Air Stairs.

The Air Stairs

aka Giant's Teeth
Mile 21 / 8,000'

The Air Stairs start as granite pillars that runners use to cross a deep pit full of nasty beasts. On each loop, they rise to create upward stairs until it's almost impossible to jump between them.

Fun Fact: *During an unplanned electrical storm in the 19th Marathons, Amida Ambrocio was struck by lightning on the first step. The blast threw him fifty feet up the trail, effectively helping him bypass the obstacle. After he put out his burning clothes, he finished the lap in last place. Doctors later found he'd had three heart attacks and kept going despite "minor chest pain." He never raced again, but he licensed genetic characteristics related to muscular electrical conduction that made him a wealthy man until he died base jumping in Norway.*

I PULLED UP SHORT after the stairs and looked over the edge into Son of a Bitch Ditch, another Barkley homage and my favorite obstacle by name. A pack of massive timber wolves slept at the bottom, nuzzled up around each other. They looked peaceful, even adorable, until one yawned to reveal long fangs and a jaw that could crush rock. Finally, there were things with teeth. I wanted to pet one. Instead, I backed up to get a running start. The only way across was to jump between each of the ten narrow stone pillars, which were spaced exactly five feet apart. They were all the same height and the tops were at ground level, so it would be a cinch if I didn't miss my footing. I backed up another few steps, got ready to jump, and then hesitated. I thought about tendons and wolves and how hungry I was. I was psyching myself out.

And then Danny ran by screaming, "Don't look down!" and skipped across the stairs like a little kid on his favorite ride. I would've tripped him if I'd heard him coming. I was about to follow in hot pursuit when Coach slowed me down.

"Be careful. The steps are more slippery than they look. Tommy slid off his first year."

I remembered that. He had let out a surprised *Wha!* and landed on his back in the ditch, barely missing the tusks of groggy wild boars. A few inches in any direction and he would've had a very bad day, though I suppose the boar would've had a nice Tommy kabob. I glanced up at the synthetic watching from the slope above, still and silent as the surrounding trees. Would she pull me out if I fell in?

"Watch your footing and you'll be fine. Get moving."

I took a running start and jumped.

One…two…three.

The steps were rough granite with great grip, not slippery at all.

Four-five-six.

This was easy.

Seven-eight-nine. Nearly there.

I overshot the last step, barely making contact with my right heel. I caught myself with the toe of my left foot and threw myself forward with just enough speed to land on all-fours at the edge of the pit. I picked myself up and wiped the dirt off my knees. I had more scrapes, but no serious blood. Coach just turned up the music. Danny was ahead of me, and no way was I going to let a natural—

Berrick flew past me.

"Way to go, baseline!"

Damn it. I chased after him, but was dying within minutes. I just couldn't keep the pace on the uphills. I was falling apart.

"There's a saying in ultrarunning. If you're feeling good, wait a few minutes."

"And if you feel terrible?"

"That works too."

After the stairs, I slowed down to a manageable jog. It was four miles and nearly 1,200 feet of climbing and descent until Lazarus Lake. I'd need to pace myself if I wasn't going to drown when I got there. I thought I could catch Danny and Berrick on the downhill, but I hadn't seen Abbey all day. She was up ahead somewhere, kicking my butt, and she knew it.

Strangely, I didn't care. Soon after Berrick vanished up the trail, I realized I was in the middle of what used to be the Rat Jaw obstacle—a Barkley reference to a steep briar-covered slope from hell that was, here, a gradually ascending meander through thick growths of wildflowers, elephant ear grass, and a thousand other pretty green things I couldn't name without Alex to help. There were berries and ferns, all quite safe, but it used to be a toxic pushki-covered trail of tears. It also bored the audience to death, so now it was just lovely and green.

I jogged happily through non-Rat Jaw, up the saddle, and then finally started descending to Strawberry Junction, where a synthetic nodded to the right. The left junction went up to Wellman Divide and the Tunnels. I picked up speed on the downhill, looking for Danny and Berrick, but also watching my feet. There were a lot of rocks trying to break my ankles or throw me into a tree. It was like hopscotch for adults. I loved that too, and in no time I was at the next junction and the saddle above Idyllwild.

Idyllwild, previously an artsy climbing town and now a wild animal park for terminal-class predators used in the Marathons, was down Devil's Slide trail to my right. The rock climbing area of Lily Rock and Tahquitz Peak was straight to the south. I turned hard left. A quarter mile later, I was at the edge of Lazarus Lake—which looked like it had been there since the beginning of time, but was as modified as I was. Pirate Island was a tumble of volcanic stone glowering from the center of the lake. Two flags indicated where I was supposed to start swimming to the other side. I ran up to the edge and stopped, frozen.

Huh.

Lazarus Lake

aka Death Pool
Mile 25 / 8,000'

The oldest consistently appearing obstacle, Lazarus Lake is a swimming and diving challenge in Little Tahquitz Valley. Runners have had to swim across the lake or dive through Calisto's Caverns under Pirate Island, all while fighting off animal hazards ranging from electric eels to poisonous sea snakes.

__Fun Fact__: One year there were tiger sharks, and every runner who couldn't bypass had to drop out or die on the last laps. No more sharks, or even electric eels, but bears can swim, so there's still hope for aquatic carnage! Just no more dolphins. That was disturbing.

"*SUP?*" COACH ASKED, his casualness apparently proportional to his irritation.

"I've never been in a lake before."

"*You've been in a pool. You're losing serious time. Swim.*"

"Yeah, it's just…" Is the water supposed to be that dark? It looked like it was a thousand feet deep. "What's the hazard here?"

"*Sloth? There isn't an animal hazard on the first loop. Get on with it. You'll like the water. It's about a quarter of a mile to the other side if you go around the island and not under, which you don't want to do. You can't hold your breath long enough to be safe. Get going. You'll be done in ten minutes.*"

"Sloth? You do have a sense of humor."

But I was irritated by the breath-holding comment. I knew I

could hold my breath for two minutes under good conditions, but a cold lake in the middle of the Marathons wasn't ideal. All TTI combat and endurance models had some degree of spleen modification, based somewhat on natural genetic abilities of the Bajau "Sea Nomad" people of the old Philippines (now the Greater Muslim Archipelagic Caliphate). They evolved after fishing underwater for thousands of years to have far larger spleens than most naturals, allowing them to process and inject red blood cells into the bloodstream with far greater efficiency. Tommy could easily hold his breath for ten minutes. I'd drown five times before he came up for air. All of which meant I was swimming around Pirate Island.

"Oh," Coach said, as if he'd forgotten. *"The animal obstacle is Giant Pacific octopuses bred for cold freshwater, the ones you saw at the show. You probably won't even see them on the first few laps."*

I hoped he was wrong. This was one animal obstacle I was looking forward to.

I walked into the cold water.

Oh my god, this is amazing.

In the middle of a blazing hot day, it was bliss, nirvana and heaven. I took a few cautious strokes out into deeper water and dipped my head in. It was weird swimming with clothes on, but you got used to it. I could have stayed there for hours but, you know, Coach. His humor is limited.

A synthetic watched from the island as I swam. I guess he was the safety diver, but he was still dressed in wool and slacks. They could at least make an effort. I pulled myself out on the other side, and my clothes and shoes seemed to drain and dry almost instantly. I was free of spider webs and dirt. I was renewed. This wasn't an obstacle. It was a miracle. I ran happily into the trees, looking for Berrick and Danny.

My bliss lasted for about five minutes. I hit a patch of blazing sun on the climb to Desert View on the ridgeline south of Long Valley and felt like something had taken a straw to my body and sucked all the water out. I tried my hydration tube again, and it was empty again. Sigh. I should have filled up at the lake. Then again, I'm not sure octopus water is good for you.

I never caught up to Danny or Berrick. Somehow, they stayed ahead of me up the trail to Hidden Lake (an old natural lake that was now a dusty meadow) to Desert View. The total run from Lazarus Lake to the Long Valley aid station and over to the Scree Slope drop-off was 1,155 feet up and 784 feet down over about five miles, an easy net climb. Or would've been if the heat hadn't gotten to me again. It felt like it was over a hundred degrees. And there were no clouds. There were never any clouds.

I jog-trudged and slothed (new verb!) past views of the fire-hot eastern Coachella Valley 8,000 feet below. Somewhere out there was the old Salton Sea, now the Salton Solar Facility. I wove in and out of the shade of ancient pines. The breeze picked up after the saddle by Hidden Lake, like heaven on my overheated skin. I inhaled and relaxed. I had the strongest feeling that this was where I belonged, but maybe everyone feels that way in the outdoors. I had no point of reference. I just loved it.

The silence was so complete, I could hear nothing but the breeze and my breathing. I closed my eyes, inhaling the scent of pitch, apples and vanilla from Jeffrey pines. Overhead, a massive raptor flew in sweeping, peaceful circles in an updraft. At first, I thought it was a natural hawk, something that belonged here, but when it turned I saw the massive white head and wingspan of a bald eagle. They were one of the more random elements of the games, usually just observers, now and then swooping down to gouge out an eyeball.

Back in Long Valley, I picked up speed for the crowd near the aid station. Water, check. Food, check. Encouragement to take in salt, electrolytes and more water, check, check, check.

"It's over 110 in the valley," one of the volunteers said. "This is your last drink 'til MoBO." Which would be a great song title. "Make sure you fill up." She checked her watch. "And you almost missed cutoff here, so…"

"Got it." I filled up a bladder. "How far ahead are Berrick and Danny?"

The volunteer blinked. "Oh, the natural guys?" Had she forgotten they existed? "The first one was a while ago. Not sure. The second's maybe ten minutes ahead."

"Ten minutes?" They were kicking my ass. I doubt Smith was happy about that, but I didn't care. As long as I finished, the tests could go on. I was more worried about cutoffs. I thought I'd made up some time, but she was right. I was way behind.

I jammed a few bacon-wrapped pickles in my mouth (if you were there, you'd understand), grabbed a handful of watermelon slices and took off. A short run later, I was at the edge of the mountain, staring down the Scree Slope and 8,000 feet farther into the valley. It was a *long* way down.

The Scree Slope

aka Bloody Booty Buttslide
Mile 30 / 7,600' - 8,400'

The mayhem of the Scree Slope is way up there on the fun scale. You've got 800 feet of artificially pulverized rock in a steep mountain couloir that pours off the edge of a fifty-foot cliff. To get off the slope in time, you have to take a hard left on soft, sliding sand, traverse fifty feet north back to the trail and then drop and roll under barbed wire made of pure metallic spite. If you want to watch some of the best athletes in the world cartwheel into oblivion, you've come to the right place. Oh, and there's no net. Ever.

Fun Fact: *Last year, Terrence the Tornado set the obstacle record in an all-out sprint down the slope, but miscalculated the time needed to stop and ended up in a pine tree twenty-five feet past the bottom edge of the slope. They should call him the Flying Squirrel.*

"THAT'S STEEP," I said out loud. Coach didn't respond. Small rocks kicked loose by my shoes tumbled down the slope and kept going, and going…and going. The breeze picked up, and I stepped back nervously. Did I mention that all my training was on TTI's campus? Not a lot of downhill practice there. The overall descent was bad enough that Tommy called it 'hamburger hill' because of how it chewed up his quads. To me, it looked like a quick way to die.

I took one tentative step over the edge and suddenly I was sliding. I might have made an undignified squee-like sound as I landed on my butt and dug my hands into the rocky sand to stop my slide.

"Any advice, Coach?"

"*Just go for it. Turn sideways, one foot below the other for balance, or commit yourself to the run. You're going to fall. Everyone falls. Just stop before the cliff.*"

"Stop before the cliff. Got it." Problem was, I'd seen this obstacle a hundred times. I'd watched live as Terrence flew into the tiny tree I could now see way, way down there. I'd also seen him grasp desperately for a handhold and plummet twenty feet out of that tree and land on his back, spraining three ribs and nearly cracking his skull. And he was one of the greatest downhill runners in the world.

"*Media, just move. The longer you sit, the harder it gets. You're not going to die. Just take it slow. Slide on your butt if you have to. But move it.*"

I didn't have the heart to tell him I'd have done the bypass if there was one. I could quit the race and scramble back up and get off this damn cliff drop. I'd be safe. I thought about it for maybe half a second, and that thought of quitting was what got me up. That wasn't me. I wasn't going to let that be me.

I stood. I slid. I clenched, my whole body locked in fear, and then I thought about Tommy. I'd seen him to this. He'd told me how. *Just slide,* he'd said. *You'll stop. Next time, slide a little farther. It's fun when you get good at it.*

I took a deep breath. I stepped forward. I slid.

And I stopped.

Huh.

Another step, another slide and another stop. My shoes were filled with gravel and I was coated in dust, but I was fine. Another step, farther this time. I smiled. Tommy was right. This was fun.

Step, slide, stop, step, slide, don't wait for the stop, step, slide, fall on my butt, get up, slide, slide, slide, uh-oh, hell no!

I tumbled forward and my feet flew up in the air. I saw sky. Then dirt. Then sky again. I slammed into the slope fully extended, like a water bug on my back, and slid to a stop.

"*If it helps, you've got over a million dockers.*"

I also had a billion tiny rocks embedded in my skin and a bloody cut on my shoulder. I took a second to dust myself off. My docker count was nearly two million by the time I was up again. More than a few of my "fans" were hoping for an airborne finish. I turned off the feed.

One more step, slide, step...

I got to the end and traversed high and slowly over to the trail, putting my feet down on solid ground with a sigh of relief. The synthetic monitor smiled sweetly in his wool dinner jacket.

"That wasn't so hard," I told him.

"Good job,' he said, and I laughed. He almost sounded like he meant it.

The crawling obstacle was next, basically just an annoying way to get us to crawl or roll on dirt and rocks under 100 feet of barbed wire. I never understood it. It wasn't a real physical test. It just looked like it sucked.

I got down and rolled sideways through it. I'd forgotten to take off my pack, so I rolled over it, grunted, crawled to the next line of wire, rolled again and so on. By the time I got to the end and tried to stand, I understood the obstacle. With most endurance sports, you could probably find a rhythm. But here, pulling my aching, bleeding, dusty, hot body off the dirt was seriously difficult. There was no rhythm here. There was just pain.

The Descent

"YOU NEED TO PICK UP THE PACE," Coach said as I slumped down the trail. *"You have less than two hours to get to the bottom. It's doable, but only if you put a little kick in that giddy up."*

I cracked up and started jogging again, slowly, but the fun was gone. Whatever joy I'd felt earlier was all stabbing pains and screaming quads. Only an idiot would do this for a living. And it just got hotter as I descended. Less than a mile after rejoining the main trail at the traverse junction, I hit the 7,500-foot wall and wanted to scream at it until it fell down. Instead, I crawled over like a good little runner. I kept moving as it got hotter, but no matter how hard I tried, I felt like I was slowing down.

"Drink," Coach said. I drank. He turned on some music. I tried to embrace the suck. Was this really so bad? I'd felt worse pain in the lab, a lot worse. I did a quick inventory of my body. Yeah, it all hurt, but nothing hurt that much. It was the long, slow grind of it, and the choice. I could theoretically stop any time I wanted. I could quit now, or fifteen minutes later. Sure, there were terrible consequences, but it was all on me. In the lab, there were no choices. I could ask for a break or to be knocked out, but there were no real decisions. Here, it was all up to me. Why did that make it harder?

You can do this, I told myself. *You've been in the lab since you were born. You're a badass.*

But it wasn't enough anymore. It didn't matter what I'd done before. It didn't matter what I'd endured. I'd never done *this*, and this was far harder than I'd ever thought it could be. I took a drink. I fought back tears, which surprised me. I never cried. But I was tired and the heat was vindictive.

You can do this, I told myself, but I wasn't sure. It was no longer obvious. I could only do this if I earned it. Danny was doing it. Berrick was doing it. Not because they were made to do it, but because they had the grit to keep moving. And Abbey had done this last year, making it through two full loops despite having grown up rich and privileged.

Then, in the dusty manzanita above Flat Rock, Shaquilla bounded past me shouting "Great Work!" and then I was just pissed. I told Coach to pump the music, and I ran. I really *ran* for the first time that day.

"Be careful, Media. You don't have her coordination or experience."

"I don't care."

"You don't need to keep up with her to finish, and you're going to chew up your quads. Take your time or you'll never make it tomorrow."

"Fast or slow. Pick one," I snapped. I knew he was right. Even my dockers knew he was right. But what he didn't know was how worked I was, physically and mentally. If I slowed to a jog, I'd walk. If I walked, I'd stop and never move again. I could feel my mind giving up, and that scared me more than anything else.

"I can't stop," I told Coach. "I just can't."

Which was all the breath I could spare. I was keeping up with Shaquilla and she was something to focus on. I needed that.

"Okay. Just don't watch your feet or Shaquilla. Scan up and down the trail, forward about forty feet, back to your feet, forward, back, keep your eyes active and predict the footing. If you look at your feet, you're going to eat a rock."

I scanned up and back, then forward again. It was hard—it was so much easier just to stare at the trail and grind on—but I felt more stable almost instantly. I even managed to speed up a bit.

At the 6,500-foot wall, with less than 90 minutes to the twelve-hour cutoff, I groaned over and chased Shaquilla into the dust. It was already over 100 degrees, and I was through most of my water. Coach didn't tell me to drink anymore because there wasn't much left. I just kept moving as he played DJ. The harder it got, the louder it got. I never realized how motivational death metal could be.

At the 5,500-foot wall—known as the 'wolf wall' ever since a kid was killed by wolves on the fifth loop several years ago—another natural guy caught up to me and flew over the wall, then shot down the trail. He passed Shaquilla less than a minute later. I was impressed. I hated him, but I was impressed. Maybe even envious. I'd never felt that way about a natural before.

I chased Shaquilla down to the Pits, across the slacklines, and then I tried to close the gap. I thought I had her on the short, rocky climb after the Pits, but she saw me coming and found another gear. I didn't have that gear. By the time I summited and got over the 4,500-foot wall, she'd pulled even farther ahead. I slowed down, and she was soon out of sight. Now it was just survival.

3,500 feet and I felt like I was on fire. Just 38 minutes to cutoff.

2,500 feet and 110 degrees. I was out of water and stumbling.

1,500 feet and then the picnic tables, even hotter, like a blast furnace in hell.

750 feet and I could hear the crowd, but my eyes were on the clock. I was minutes from cutoff, and I saw Berrick was just ahead, stumbling worse than I was. I couldn't believe I'd nearly caught him.

600 feet and I could hear Brad screaming "FIDDY!" and "BERRICK!" over the noise.

Smith called my name over the loudspeakers.

Berrick crossed the finish line and went straight into the building.

I had just another 100 vertical feet to the finish line.

"Run, Media. You're going to miss cutoff."

So I sprinted, arms flailing for balance like a wacky-wavy-inflatable-balloon-girl.

75 feet left and it was a chant: "Fiddy! Fiddy! Fiddy!"

50-25-0.

I ran under the "Good Job, Morons!" banner and across the finish, right into Tommy. I'd like to say I nearly knocked him over, but I just bounced off and would have fallen on my ass if he hadn't caught me. The crowd cheered louder.

It was hard to stand. My legs were numb and trembly things.

I'd finished with only nineteen seconds to spare, but I'd finished.

I'd done it.

Once.

Finish Line

"THAT WAS CLOSE." Tommy held me up and checked for broken things. "You okay?"

"Fiddy!" the crowd responded. "Fiddy!"

I didn't know why they were cheering. I finished behind Abbey and other baselines, behind several naturals, and I could barely walk, but god I loved it. I *loved* them—the modified, the naturals, all of them. I was so grateful they'd stood in that damn heat to wait for me. Brad and Katy even came out to offer congratulations. I smiled and said delirious things until they fled back inside and out of the oven.

Tommy let me go. "You okay, Media?"

I was still standing, so yeah. "I'm more than okay." I looked up the mountain. I'd just run up and down that thing. I turned back to my brother. "Forty miles. More than thirteen thousand feet of vert. Done and done. I don't know what all the fuss is about."

He smiled broadly, not just the usual Tommy smile, but real.

"Is Berrick okay?" I asked.

"I think so. He kept saying 'air conditioning.' It is a bit warm."

"A bit warm?" It was like hell was on tour in Palm Springs.

Tommy pulled me into a hug, and I realized something was wrong. He didn't smell. In fact, he was clean and showered and in his team sweats. Katy and Brad had been, too. It looked like he'd spent the day lounging by the pool.

"How long have you been here?" I demanded.

"A little while."

"Tommy."

"Okay, three-hours. The showers are amazing. You should—"

"Three hours?"

"Closer to four."

"*Four hours?*" I don't know why it surprised me. I had never competed with him before. Of course he killed my time. I should have been more worried that Abbey beat me by almost two hours, but it was all too humbling. I don't like humble. All the pain I felt faded to nothing. Now I just wanted to get ready for the next day. I could do better. I *would* do better.

"That was great," Coach said, coming up in person. "Top fifty loop-one finish time for a baseline female. Considering the lack of training and prep, you crushed it."

"Top *fifty?*" I didn't even know fifty baselines had run in the Marathons. Alex later told me 53 had, so I beat at least three of them by less than five seconds. Hurray, me.

"What did you expect?" he said, and then grimaced as the All Synthetic Scottish Marching Band took up taps on the bagpipes for a natural named Jubilee Aranov who'd reached the finish line after missing the last three walls and tapped out. I turned to hear the mournful dirge play itself out in Jubilee's barely hidden tears. If you've never heard taps on the bagpipes, it's a lot like Amazing Grace with all the melancholy and none of the grace. In the original Barkleys, they played taps on a bugle while exhausted runners tried not to pass out from exhaustion. People there had gathered in the rain with downcast faces to share the pain. Here, they sweat in the evening heat as runners tried not to pass out from exhaustion. Jubilee was bent over, his sweat and tears falling freely onto an indifferent earth.

"I'd like you to climb faster tomorrow, if you can," Coach said when Jubilee managed to stagger away with what was left of his dignity and some half-hearted golf claps. "You need time to take the downhill slower. When's the last time you peed?"

"Don't you know?"

"Of course I know. Do you?"

I thought back and further back. *Hmm.* Not good.

"Dumb ass," Tommy said, not unkindly. Coach handed me a recovery drink that was cold chocolate bliss. "Drink that, weigh yourself, then keep drinking until you've got your weight back. I'm serious. I'm going to weigh you after dinner. And I want to know your weight before you go to bed. Hydrate or die."

"I know, Coach. Sorry." God, it was hot. Tommy studied me, worried. My legs felt wobbly. When I finally got back to my room, I peed about four drops of golden brown. I'd lost ten pounds, nearly eight-percent of my body weight. The toilet's testing system told me I was hyperhidrotic, dehydrated and my kidneys were distressed. Apparently, none of that was good. Toilets are mean. I was chilled in the shower when I should've been hot. I sat under the water cursing myself and drinking electrolytes. I couldn't carry a larger bladder, but I could drink more at the aid stations. A lot more.

"*You'll be okay,*" Alex said. Alex was back! "*But it'll be hotter tomorrow. Over 115, closer to 120 in the afternoon.*"

"One-twenty?" That sounded terrible.

"*You need to be more careful if you want to finish.*"

"And not die."

"*And not die,*" he agreed.

But I didn't really care. I'd done it. I wasn't just a lab rat anymore. I was a runner.

Media Gets a Nickname

AT DINNER, I could barely keep my head off the table. I felt like I'd been mugged repeatedly and then left to bake in an oven, which I suppose wasn't far from the truth. Tommy nudged me, and I nearly fell off the bench. I rubbed my eyes and gave him a vaguely psychotic look, accidentally locked eyes with Danny (who was right behind Tommy but far across the hall), then glanced away to find Abbey smirking back. I didn't even have the energy to pretend I had energy, so I looked back at Tommy. He was fresh and perky as a baby minicorn. I thought about smacking him but, you know, effort.

Brad patted my back, as if that would help. Katy studied her tiny portion of methodically assembled carbohydrates. Berrick ignored me, which I appreciated, but even he didn't look as worked as I felt.

"What's wrong with your face?" Tommy asked. "You look happy."

And he was right. As tired and achy as I was, under it all was the strangest sense of contentment. I wasn't just happy, I was joyful. I was a *runner*.

"*Why didn't you ever tell me?*" I texted him as I grabbed his hand.

"*Tell you what?*"

"*About this. About running. About the team. All of it?*" I wasn't accusing him of anything. I was just surprised. I'd always known there was more to the world than my lab, but I had no idea there was so much of it, so much to feel and experience even if it hurt.

"*Honestly? I didn't think you'd ever get out.*"

Which hurt a little, but I knew what he was thinking; telling me would have been cruel. He didn't want to torture me with things I'd never see except on video. Was he right? His eyes waited for something, for forgiveness or approval. I just shrugged and pulled my hand back. I understood, but I wondered what else I was missing and what they'd kept from me.

"Team TTI," Coach said, joining us. "Great day today. I mean it. Everyone finished. No one's seriously injured, and that puts us ahead of most teams. Twenty eight runners dropped or didn't make the cut, mostly naturals but also some baselines. The heat is taking a toll. Media and Berrick, have you been hydrating?"

Berrick nodded and I forced a smile. "You have no idea." I was bloated with water and electrolytes, but I still hadn't really peed since before breakfast.

"You're still hyperhidrotic. Get more salt and electrolytes in you. I'll have Dr. Rai leave a saline drip in your room. Easy enough with your ports."

"Thanks?" It was like being back in the lab.

"As you all know, the race leaders are Tornado and Bacon. The 'nado set a new course record for the summit climb, the descent and of course for the full lap. Sadly, he didn't eat any trees this time. Nothing we can do about that, but I filed a protest to get him tested for doping violations just to waste his time. He'll pass. The man's a machine."

Tommy nodded glumly, his victory looking less likely than ever.

"Now the good news. Brad came in second in the uphill sprint after the only speed model, Ghulam Watanabe, but Watanabe didn't finish the lap and his time doesn't count, so his points go to Brad. Tommy was third to the top for some climbing points. Great work. Katy was the first woman to the top for climbing points and finished as third woman and ninth overall. Berrick, you were fifth for naturals and you crushed the lake obstacle. The triathlon training is paying off. Overall, we're second in team points and Brad has the sprint lead."

Tommy and I smiled at Brad. His carotid pulsed proudly.

"Media, you were eleventh in baselines."

"Meaning last, since nine dropped."

"So no points, but I have a feeling we'll start seeing a lot of drops on the next lap. They're all pushing too hard because of the prize money, especially Abbey." Who was probably just trying to escape from Jessica. "Which means they're going to burn themselves out. Media, I know you think you didn't do that well, but this is the Marathons. It's an accomplishment just to finish a lap. Give yourself a break and focus on tomorrow."

"Thanks." I was genuinely grateful.

"That's it. Everyone pulled their weight today. I'm proud of all of you." He looked directly at me. "Eat, drink and get some sleep. Don't overthink things. Tomorrow will take care of itself." Before getting up, he pulled a small package out of his pocket and passed it over. "I asked about the cheese situation, and there should be a variety of cheeses…" He trailed off, looking at my plate, which was piled high with bland sliced cheese. "…which I see you've discovered. Eat some carbohydrates, please, *before* you eat that, or this."

He passed the package over. I picked it up and inhaled so deeply, the room spun.

No way. I tore it open to reveal what looked like orange-red pound cake. Tommy leaned back, his face scrunched in horror.

"Époisses!" I exclaimed, bringing it so close to my nose I almost ingested it nasally. "Coach, I can't…" But he was already gone.

"Mist!" Katy spat, meaning *crap* in German. "What the hell is that?"

"Époisses de Bourgogne. It's made from raw cow's milk and aged for weeks in a bacterial wash in the cellars of Côte-d'Or, France." I took a chunk off and put it carefully on my tongue, letting the salt and fat dissolve. I may have shuddered with pleasure. When I looked up, everyone was staring. Terrence the 'nado had come over from a nearby table to check out the smell. I swallowed and offered everyone a taste. There were no takers. Katy was a weird shade of green. Maybe *bacterial wash* wasn't a great selling point.

"It was Napoleon's favorite." That didn't help. I omitted the fact that Époisses was one of the few cheeses banned from public transportation in France because its smell had caused riots and vomiting. But let's be honest, the French riot whenever they get bored. You can't blame that on the cheese.

Berrick reluctantly reached for a sample. He tasted a tiny bit, free hand on a cup of water, ready to spit and rinse, but then his eyes widened and he sat up, surprised.

"My god, that's delicious."

"I know." I took a larger bite than recommended. The flavor could get to you if you ate it too quickly. Berrick reached for another piece and I let him, despite a strong urge to slap his hand away. It was hard to find Époisses since wildfires had burned through that portion of France during Europe's summer heatwaves. Coach had brought me expensive cheese. Maybe synthetics weren't out to get us after all.

One of the peppy, short-skirt-wearing synthetics showed up. Didn't they have evening wear?

"We've had some complaints," she said, with just a hint of sympathy and regret. "Perhaps you can take that back to your room?" I looked around the dining hall. All eyes were on me. Several of the nearby runners had moved to other tables. One of the baselines was crying.

I wrapped up my cheese, but then something occurred to me.

"Do you think Coach is messing with me?" I asked Tommy.

Berrick smiled more than usual. "Why would you ask that, *Stinky*?"

"What?" I froze.

"Stinky!" someone yelled from two tables over. I looked up, and of course it was Dangle. I guess he didn't like being shoved in the bear pit. "Stinky!" he yelled again.

No, no, no.

Within seconds, the tables around us had taken up a chant.

No, please no.

"Stinky! Stinky! Stinky!"

"I guess that answers that question," I said, pouting.

"It won't stick." But Tommy was worried. Berrick looked down, still smiling. Coach had totally put him up to this. The problem with nicknames was that they were for life. If I didn't do well in the Marathons and get someone to call me something better, I was going to be *Stinky* for all time. I guess that's one way to motivate your runners.

I took my cheese and fled.

The Sting

I WAS DRESSED, ALONE, and staring at myself in the mirror after a second shower. My hair had held up well despite the swim, but I was more focused on my skin. Had the test worked? My skin looked the same. No matter how much I concentrated, there was no color or texture change. I dropped my towel and checked things out more carefully. My skin was dry and burned in places from sun exposure. Nothing unexpected, nothing even interesting, and yet it was in me now. Another piece of me that wasn't me. For the thousandth time, I wondered if the woman looking back at me in the mirror was the same one my mother sold.

I checked my hands again, hoping for some sign of the change Victor wanted, some proof that I was worth the risk, but they were just hands. I stared at them, willing them to change, until my eyes watered. God knows how long I'd have stood there if Alex hadn't let me know that Tommy was waiting in the hall.

I put on my absurdly comfortable MoBO robe and opened the door.

"Hey, Stinky. I just wanted to see how you were doing."

I presented my special finger.

"It won't stick."

I let him in, and he sat on the bed.

"John was just getting them worked up," he said. "But maybe you shouldn't push him in any more holes?"

"I didn't push him."

"Or have your boyfriend do it for you."

"Did Coach send you here to rile me up? Abbey beat me by

nearly two hours today. I can't make that up. I'm already riled. I know I'm not supposed to care about winning, but do you think she'll drop out? Can Brad push her off a cliff?"

"Maybe you could just run faster?"

"I'd respond, but my finger's tired."

"Yeah. I may deserve it though."

I sat on the bed next to him. "Is this about you and Abbey hooking up?"

"You could say that."

"So, what's the story? You're still gay, right?"

"Fiddy..." He put on his long-suffering big-brother face.

"Sorry."

"Look, you know how she got demoted and can only run as a baseline now?"

"Demoted? You mean fired, arrested, disbarred and exiled from corporate America?"

"Yeah, so, all of that's kinda my fault."

I blinked. "The sex was that bad?"

He didn't laugh. "Look, Sis, we all know we wouldn't be here if not for you. No, it's true. Everything we have is basically due to the fact that you're a colossal pain in the ass."

"So true," I agreed.

"So, when Victor offered me a chance to help, I said yes before he even told me what it was."

"He told you to sleep with Abbey?"

He grimaced. "No, he told me to allow contact. To touch her. Just a kiss would've been enough. They did some kind of modification that was unique to me and traceable. When we got together, she somehow stole a DNA sample. When they arrested her, that was the proof. There was nowhere else that trait could have come from. Several of us did it, including runners from other teams, but I'm the only one she stole from. She's here because of me, Fiddy. I'm just sorry she's taking it out on you."

"I still don't get why you slept with her."

"I was curious, I guess. We talked for a long time. We kissed, and then, well, she's actually really charming when she wants to be. She was born natural, like you, saved by some unique genetic trait. You two have a lot in common. You're actually both—"

"Stubborn?"

"Close enough. I think that's why she hates me so much, though. Because she trusted me. It wasn't just sex. You know how it becomes something else, more like acceptance. She seemed so alone. I didn't want her to feel that way."

"It's sex, not therapy," I said, more sharply than I meant. Just another example of how Tommy was more kind and caring than I would ever be, which of course made me defensive.

"Maybe." He shrugged. "But however you feel about the act, I betrayed her."

Tommy had no guile, no ulterior motives or hidden agendas. He just wanted everyone to get along. He probably wanted to apologize to Abbey every time he saw her, and she'd just love that.

"What was it?" I asked.

"What?"

"The trait?"

"I have no idea. I don't think it was anything but a few random genes they could test for."

"So you were involved in a giant corporate sting against the most powerful IP attorney in the Western Hemisphere, and you got nothing out of it? I mean, except..."

"They paid me, of course."

"How much?"

"Enough. I had Dad put it in savings for us. For you. If you get first place in your group, that money and your prize might be enough to buy you out of your contract." He waited for some reaction. "If they agree. If you want. Fiddy, are you listening?"

You might be surprised that I'm rarely stunned speechless. I couldn't remember a time. But now there was just Tommy's sincere face and a great empty space where my brain used to be. He slept with her for me? He compromised himself for me?

"Fiddy, it's okay. We can never pay you back. I just wanted to help."

"Tommy..." I put my hand on his arm.

"But now she hates you and she's good. Actually, she's really good. I don't know if you can beat her. So it was all a waste, and with Jessica around…" He shuddered.

I hugged him so suddenly and violently that he couldn't have finished if he wanted to.

"Fiddy," he wheezed.

"Thank you." I pressed my face into his chest. Maybe I was being affectionate. Maybe I was trying to hide my tears. "Thank you."

He pulled my hands off and pushed me back until I met his eyes. He was still blurry.

"Don't thank me. Abbey has a nice side, but she's dangerous. She'll do anything to win. And Jessica is, I don't know what she is, but she freaks me out. She doesn't belong here."

"I don't care."

"Media."

"She doesn't scare me. Neither of them does."

"They should."

"I know, but…"

"But what?"

"I'm having a great time, Tommy. I love it. All of it. The sweat, the pain, the mind games, every second of it. I was happier trying to pee out one tiny little drop tonight that I have been in years." He didn't know how to respond to that. "I didn't mean to make you feel bad earlier. I was just surprised how much I've missed out on in the lab. That's not your fault. I'll be fine. Just stop sleeping with girls to help me. Girls are gross."

"Yeah, that was a mistake. So…"

"What?"

"Do you like him?"

"Who?"

"Danny. He pushed a guy in a hole for you. That means engagement in some cultures."

Turns out my skin can change colors, but only red and then redder with embarrassment.

*

THAT NIGHT, I, meaning Alex, did some research on Abbey and Danny. Abbey because she was apparently serious about kicking my butt all over the mountain. Danny because he had very nice legs, and he'd pushed a man in a hole for me. There wasn't much about Abbey as an ultrarunner because she'd only started a few years before. She'd gradually risen through the ranks with several top ten finishes in local races, a few podium spots, and then two wins in the baseline class. There was, however, a ton about her as a disgraced attorney.

All aspects of modern business are run by pre-sentient AIs or synthetics, any of whom could negotiate with each other based on human input. While there was supposedly a lot of give-and-take in legal negotiations, something you'd think people would be better at than machines, most human attorneys at the major companies just oversaw their AIs and synthetics, giving input and setting parameters for acceptable outcomes. Machines did the rest.

Abbey had been like my mom and dad, an aberrant human on the front lines of a major corporate department. She was a highly tuned terminal-class intellectual with mathematical, combat and numerous other augmentations. And she had negotiated directly with synthetics and AIs, constantly returning to Black Rook with impossible deals. That's where she ran into Coach. He'd been a synthetic attorney for TTI at the time, one of her negotiating opponents, and she'd crushed him so badly in a negotiation that TTI fired him, stripped his legal certification, and the only job he could get at TTI was as a Coach under contract. I wondered how that made him feel, or if he cared at all.

As for Abbey, it turned out she was no better at negotiating legal contracts than a synthetic, but she was exceptional at stealing DNA samples from everyone she ran into. Just a touch of skin, a handshake, a hug, and she'd have a partial sample of your genome for later analysis. That ability in itself was a crime, even if she'd never used it, but she'd allegedly used it a lot. Fifteen corporations sued, including TTI. There was no public information on the resulting settlements, but now that I thought about it, the timing matches when they put the great black eye in the lab. Whatever the real story was, it had spooked TTI and left Abbey with a lot of reasons to hate

Tommy and me. And while Tommy was right to be wary—she would clearly do anything to win—it just didn't matter for me on the Fun Run. She and Jessica couldn't touch me. I was more worried about Tommy on later loops.

Danny was a different story: a poor natural kid who grew up destined for nothing in a family that was already there. He had two sisters, one of whom died in a food riot and another who wrote terrible poetry and did little else. His parents were retired, meaning unemployed, and he had only gotten into running by accident. He'd paced a friend at the Leadville 100 and had fallen in love with the sport.

In the Leadville video, Danny looked like a little boy. There are dark, grainy videos of him at various checkpoints, in the dark, one after the other, pushing his friend through the pain and exhaustion. You can see the transformation if you watch closely. Early on, he's nervous and fidgety, muscles twitching in his already powerful quads. In the middle, he starts to look around calmly, taking things in, mouth slightly open, as an idea takes shape. By the last videos, just before his friend drops out, he looks focused, tight-lipped but wide-eyed and excited. He's figured it out. He knows what he wants and that he can do it. In that moment, the Danny I knew was born. A door opened in the world and he stepped through it. He must have been scared to death. He was also incredibly gifted, becoming the top-rated natural in the USA within five years. And the bastard had a VO_2 max of 98, which at least explained how he kept up with the baselines.

Alex dumped a thousand pictures of Danny into my memory and ran through them like a video montage, including pounding background music. They were all shots of his legs, powerful quads flexing, and I cracked up. They were very nice legs.

"Enough." The sexy montage and music vanished. Tiny D and Puny P froze.

"Not you two." They went back to playing.

I should really brush my teeth, I thought, and then suddenly my bladder let me know who was in charge. I raced to the bathroom and released what felt like a gallon of perfectly clear pee into the bowl.

The toilet buzzed happily in approval.

"Yes!" I shouted. I don't care if it's TMI. I was excited. "I can pee again!"

And then I stumbled to bed and fell asleep.

"Shit!" I woke up. I'd forgotten to buy Danny a beer. I had no idea how naturals remembered things without PAs, so maybe he'd forgotten too. I thought about apologizing, but I had no idea how to reach him.

Danny, Daniel, Dan.

I couldn't wait to see him tomorrow.

FOUR:
The Possibility of Failure

Breakfast

I WOKE UP WITH A DIRTY, gummy mouth and hungry as a bear. "Sounds like bears!" I said to the ceiling. It was way better than swearing. I bounced out of bed with excessive enthusiasm and headed to the bathroom, where I grabbed my toothbrush and attacked my molars with a slightly manic desperation. It was taking way too long to get the funk out, and my stomach kept growling impatiently. I skipped the floss.

I took a seat at the team table in the dining room opposite Berrick, sipped at my tepid coffee—it had to be intentionally bad—and grimaced. Uranus waved from his nook by the front door, a giant, lonely gesture that I ignored by focusing on my food. It was early, and we were among only a dozen others in the hall. Berrick smiled and looked back at his food without even saying hello.

"What's your problem with me?" I asked. "I didn't knock Jasmina off the trail."

Berrick chuckled and looked up. "It's not personal. Well, I didn't like you nearly beating me yesterday, but it is what it is. I'm sorry about the nickname."

"It's okay. I'll just kill anyone who uses it. But seriously, what's the problem?"

"It's not all you." He ignored my confusion. "Having us in the Marathons this year is a publicity stunt. Just TTI using us for public relations."

I'd heard that rumor, but if I had to guess, Victor was doing it to distract everyone from what he was doing to me. So I just nodded vaguely.

"I've wanted to do this race for years," Berrick said. "We all have, even if there's no way anyone but Danny would qualify. But now? We're just being used."

"Aren't we all being used?" The Marathons were basically a product demo disguised as an athletic event. Everyone knew that. Sure it was different for naturals, but it wasn't like anyone was there for the pure joy of competition.

"Maybe." Berrick was annoyed. "Sorry, you sure you want to hear this?"

"Yeah." Meaning no, but it was too late now.

"I don't know how to describe it, but you treat us differently. Your body language, the way you talk, you make sure we know that you know you're modified and we're not. It's probably not intentional, but it grates."

"I don't think that's true," I said, fighting the urge to make a cheese joke. Of course it was true. I just didn't realize it was so obvious.

"What's your biggest fear?" He didn't wait for an answer. "Deoptimization, right?"

I nodded reluctantly. "Yes." But what I thought was *burning alive*, watching Dad collapse into himself if he lost the anti-depressants, seeing how broken Mom really was, or watching Tommy starve and being helpless to stop any of it. Take your pick.

"Your biggest fear is being me. Us. The worst modified is better than the best natural."

"That's not true." I tried not to think of that damn pyramid diagram back in the lab. "And even if it is, you can modify yourself. You—"

"See, you just…never mind."

"No, what?"

"This is how I make a living. If I get any modification other than the required immunity updates to protect *you* against our diseases, or the free skin tone changes, I lose my natural status and I have to compete as modified."

"Okay…"

"How much is Tommy's endurance subscription, the platinum

package?"

"I don't know." Alex gave me a number, but I had no context. I had no idea how much natural athletes were paid.

"The monthly fee is more than I make in a year, Media. There is no ladder I can *choose* to climb that gets me from where I am to where he is. I might be able to afford a baseline subscription, but sponsored baseline runners don't make much more than I do unless they win, and it's much harder to win. You've never struggled with poverty, so you don't know how extremely expensive it is to be poor. There is no way out. I'm stuck."

"But if you win—"

"Yes, this one time. This one year, the prize for first place for our group is large enough to buy our way out. That's *two* of us, Media. One man and one woman. And the only way I'm beating Danny is if Brad pushes him off a cliff."

"That can be arranged." But he had a point, and I was sorry. I just couldn't bring myself to say it. "I get it, I do, but how's that my fault?"

"It's not. You're just one of a billion modified people who think naturals choose to be where we are. We don't. And you never seem to realize the privilege you have. Even the word…"

"Natural?"

"Yeah. I mean, it's just the new n-word. Another way of looking down on us."

"The n-word?" I pretended not to know what he was talking about.

"*It's an arcane racial epithet previously directed at persons of African descent,*" Alex intoned unnecessarily. I'd heard the term before, but that's not what people called naturals. Some modified called them naggers, but I guess that was just a combination of natural and the old n-word. I'd used nagger myself when I was a kid until Dad corrected me. That was my first memory of him being angry with me.

"That's BS," I said, but it wasn't. "It's not racist at all. It's…"

"Classist? Does it really matter, when money we can never earn is the only way to buy our way up the ladder?"

I looked down at my cold eggs and bland cheese, then around the dining room. I didn't know what to say. I was fighting for my life here too, and even if he didn't know how serious it was, he knew I had a lot on the line.

"I work my ass off," I said. "I've earned what we have." But that wasn't true. I'd lucked out. My mother made a great investment, whether I liked to admit it or not. The rest was work, but it would never have been possible without that random chance of conception. Berrick waited. I still wasn't going to apologize.

"What do you want, then? What can I do differently?"

"That's the sad thing. You can't do anything. You can be aware, I guess. But neither of us chose how we were born. Maybe just don't be so damn proud all the time. We both know you'd rather be a modified slave than a free natural…"

That stung, but he wasn't wrong.

"…and if I were you, I'd feel the same way."

I forced a smile. "So it really was because I almost beat you yesterday."

"The *heat* almost beat me." He almost smiled back. "But you'll beat me today. I can already tell. You recover faster. You learn faster. The worst thing about you is that you *are* better. I can't even comprehend what Tommy and Katy can do. It blows my mind."

And that I could understand. It was hard to live in the shadow of better things, things so far out of reach they might as well be illusions. It's probably why I have such a problem with synthetics. No matter what I did, no matter what TTI did to me, they'd always be better at everything. And sentient or not, they had to know it.

"Tell you what." I said. "If I see another natural catching up—is unmodified better?—I'll trip 'em."

"Sounds good." He smiled and looked down, digging into his mass of carbohydrates, but the barrier was still there: a wall no less impenetrable because it was invisible.

"Morning, Stinky," Coach said as he joined us.

Damn it.

Running Montage

aka Runtage!

AFTER A BREAKFAST THAT included eating all the food I could fit in my body while trying not to kill everyone who called me *Stinky*, I started running up a mountain. I was soon ahead of the naturals and behind everyone else, but moving fine. I was sore, but I felt stronger and more confident than the day before, even if I was just as sweaty. I made it to the picnic tables within a few seconds of my previous time, used the knotted rope to tug my way over the first now 8.5-foot high rope wall, complimented synthetic mini-me on her pretty plaid vest (I guess they moved the monitors around), and jogged happily up the trail.

Without hesitation, I balanced over the middle set of pits on looser slacklines that tried to throw me. There were bears to the left, unknown below, and something screechy and alien to the right. It couldn't be dinosaurs. They went all *Jurassic Park* now and then, but there hadn't been anything at ModCon.

I climbed some walls. Sweat came out of me so fast it was like my bodily fluids were abandoning ship. Coach told me to drink. I drank. It wasn't enough. There were more walls.

The pillars had rotated to expose a wider off-size 5.9-rated crack, too wide for hands and too narrow for my body, but with plenty of big holds. I climbed quickly and grunted loudly, to my dockers' delight.

At the testing center, Dr. K seemed alarmed by how much I was sweating, so I offered her a hug. But apparently that's not allowed.

Come to think of it, it's probably best not to antagonize someone before undergoing illegal unconscious testing under her supervision. I woke up and swore so loudly and incoherently that even I don't know what I said. Someone, somewhere, in some language, was deeply offended, but my skin was still just my skin, unlike the Demon, who still freaked me out.

I got food and water at the Long Valley aid station (I never stopped being hungry), and then I was running again. On the way up to Wellman and the tunnels, I came across Mehui Zhang, an olive-skinned Chinese TTR (true-to-race) baseline woman from Jentha's team, Junco. She was on the ground by the trail having a seizure as synthetics calmly tended to her herky-jerky body. She had one of the MacGuffins clenched in her right hand.

"*Electrical stunner*," Coach said as I went by. "*Impact activated. She fell on it.*"

Ouch. I wanted to help, but there was nothing I could do. And maybe, just maybe, I was a little pleased there was one fewer baseline to compete with. And now that we knew what the MacGuffins did, I was surprised not to have seen more carnage.

You'd think that most of the deaths and injuries in the Marathons were from obstacles, accidents, or animal attacks, but mortality was usually self-induced. Two of the more important reasons endurance models were able to push beyond natural limits were psychological, or at least manifested mentally. The first was basically the suppression of short-term pain memory. After studying athletes who had damaged temporal lobes, and thus lost their short-term memory entirely, scientists realized that our perception of fatigue is directly linked to our memory of suffering. If we didn't remember being on the course for fifty hours, then our minds simply didn't tell us we were as tired as we would have been if every step and fall were locked in our brains. In other words, if you forget the pain, it's like the pain never existed. With this one change, runners could go five to ten-percent farther at the same level of perceived exertion. Modified endurance models were all made to be selectively forgetful, and would often have little or no recollection of the race they'd just won. Tommy completely forgot some of his races. The modification wasn't substantially different from a partial right temporal lobectomy.

The second mental change was suppression of the central governor, a process in the brain that's meant to protect homeostasis—the careful balance of blood sugar and other factors that insulate the brain from sugar-hungry muscles. Without the central governor, endurance athletes could run farther, faster on the same amount of food, but they often failed to recognize the symptoms of anoxia and resulting damage to their oxygen-starved brains. More than one endurance model had crossed the finish line, thrown his or her arms up in victory, and promptly collapsed from acute hypoxia. Testing these limits in real-world conditions was among the many reasons for the Modified Marathons, and why the testing center was tolerated by the audience.

Between these two modifications and many other optimizations to focus, pain tolerance, and so on, endurance athletes were magnificently self-destructive machines. They ran themselves to death with increasing frequency, which might seem like a step backward toward the fragility of horses and dogs, but in the Marathons, nothing was more treasured than the total collapse of a victorious runner—even better if he or she woke up in the hospital days later with no memory of the race itself. The female Marathons winner from three years ago, Danielle Dewalt, was still in a coma. She'd be a goddess if she ever recovered but, for now, she was an expensive vegetable whose endurance package sold rapidly in tribute to her gloriously Pyrrhic tenacity. Mehui probably wouldn't get as much recognition for shocking herself in the face.

I took one last look, and Coach told me to move on. At least she was alive. My focus returned to the trail and not tripping myself on some random branch. I didn't even hesitate at the tunnels. The webs were webbier and the spiders were bigger—I could really feel them dropping onto my bare arms—but they were easier to brush off and none were bitey yet.

I ran pretty smoothly up the trail toward the peak, hungry and very thirsty at the aid station, then hit the summit. I did a fist-pump of joy and tried to ignore The Black and my compulsion to find my parents' home in the wasteland. Every time I looked, I remembered my mother crying against my father's chest and the feel of fire on my skin.

Stop it. I turned around to look for Abbey, who I hadn't seen all morning and was apparently too far ahead to worry about, and then headed back to the aid station to calm my growling stomach. Danny came into the station just as I was leaving, once again looking clean and spider free.

"What the hell's in Jenny One?" I asked. Our entire team had gone through Jenny Two on both loops, so I had no idea what was in the other tunnel.

"What happens in Jenny, stays in Jenny," Danny said. One of the volunteers winced. "Yeah, that sounds creepy when you say it out loud. How're you feeling?"

"Weirdly good. You?"

"Same." He jammed gels into his pack. "Berrick looks strong too. You're going to owe me more beers if you don't get a move on."

Coach agreed. I moved on. I flew down to the Jungle Gym. The branches now slowly dropped if you hung on too long, which wouldn't have been a problem if I hadn't stopped before the first branch to look up in the trees. There was something up there, like a thicker branch, or—

"*Holy...*"

My stomach lurched and my knees gave out. Nausea put me on the ground on all fours and my heart tried to beat its way up my throat. It wasn't a branch. It was a python, black and massive, and every time I glanced at it the world spun and I wanted to scream.

"*I think we found your fear,*" Coach said.

I looked down at the dirt and rocks and tried to calm my breathing. One, two, in, out, nice and slow. The world stopped spinning and my heart settled, but I couldn't look up. I couldn't even raise my head. And that pissed me off. I loved snakes, like all predators, and now I couldn't even look at one. Modified usually don't have irrational fears. It's part of the baseline cleansing. All the atavistic baggage was stripped away. You might develop a fear later in life, but you had to work at it. And yet here I was, terrified of a snake. Terror rose up, unwelcome, unbidden, infinite and overwhelming. That was the real obstacle, not the snake, but the fear of it.

"Get up, Media. Don't look at it. It won't attack on this loop."

I stood and dusted off my knees, but I still couldn't look up.

This is ridiculous. I raised my head just high enough to see the water, then the lower branches. I caught my breath. Looked a little higher, and higher, and—

"Shit." I saw the snake's body and the nausea almost brought up everything left in my stomach. I forced it down, getting angrier, and then made myself look again.

"I'm not afraid of snakes," I told myself. "Snakes are beautiful."

"Just go, Media."

So I went, hands trembling and almost numb, not looking any higher than the next branch. I could feel it watching me, ready to strike, and it was all I could do not to hyperventilate myself unconscious. Four more branches. Three-two-one. I dropped down to safety and bent over to catch my breath. How was I going to face that on the next lap?

"Worry about it on the next lap."

So I ran, and within minutes the fear and nausea were gone. I was at the Air Stairs in what felt like a few short minutes. The steps were now a foot higher on each step, making the jumps harder and more risky (and requiring a sideways leap onto the adjacent mountainside to get off the final step) but the wolves didn't make me want to pull off my skin. I got through without even a stumble. I jogged through the flowers and ferns of Rat Jaw up to Strawberry Junction, down to the saddle and then left to the Lake of Rapturous Cold Water. I wanted to be in that water. No matter how happy this all sounds, remember that it was nearly 90 on the summit and felt way over 100. I got to the side of the lake, ran straight in, and dove.

Oh my god this is amazing.

It was also colder than the day before, no more than 60 degrees. I stroked down deeper into the cold water. The colder the better.

"Open your eyes," Coach said.

I opened my eyes just as something black and massive swarmed out of the darkness like a thousand-armed alien. I screamed underwater (not recommended) and panic-lurched toward the surface, coming up like a submarine trying to outrace a depth charge (kinda funny) and then flopped and slapped at the water like a deranged lunatic (hysterical). My docker count skyrocketed as the octopus surfaced in front of me, a giant black thing with big obsidian eyes full of unearthly amusement. Tentacles brushed harmlessly against my bare skin. What was my problem? The answer was obvious; octopus tentacles look a lot like snakes.

I stopped slapping the water and looked back at the Giant Pacific as she rocked just under the rippling surface. I sighed. Brad and Tommy were going to give me so much crap for this.

"You okay?"

I didn't even answer. I just swam past the octopus, which changed colors to blue and red (Was her skin laughing?) and then disappeared. I kicked hard to get around the island, but I kept my eyes open underwater after that.

Crawling out of the lake was like rising into an oven. I jogged slowly up toward Hidden Lake and Desert View as I dried off and the heat beat down. I was a sweaty mess again in minutes, but I came into the Long Valley aid station just behind Shaquilla. She smiled brightly as the volunteers refilled her hydration pack. She looked far too fresh, especially for a natural. And then she threw down the gauntlet.

"Race you down," she said.

"No," Coach said. *"It's over 110 in the valley. You run down 8,000 feet into that, and you won't run tomorrow. You'll be lucky to survive."*

Shaquilla waited for an answer.

"Okay," I said. Coached yelled mean things I ignored.

Shaquilla and I jogged together to the drop-off at the Scree Slope. We chatted about the race. She had a gorgeous Slovenian accent I was jealous of. She sounded like an eastern European princess with a habit of slaughtering peasants for amusement. I imagined springing past her, flying down the trail and leaving her super-special-patented tendons in my wake. I wasn't just going to beat her down, I was going to crush her and her haughty accent. Sweet Shaquilla Novak wouldn't know what hit her.

And then—and this can only be appreciated in slow motion—she accelerated to a full sprint near the top of the Scree Slope and let out an excessive and non-Princessy "Whoop!" as she flew out over the edge with her legs still running under her. Then she dropped out of sight like a flailing meteor, with a big bright smile of sheer childish joy. When I looked over the edge, she was fifty feet down and bounding twenty-feet at a time, as if running down a mountain on the moon. Scree and rocks flew after her, but she never missed a step and never fell. She was as beautiful and free as anything I'd ever seen.

"Wow." I took my first step onto what was still, for me, a slidey slope of certain death.

"*Told you*," Coach said.

"Screw this." I faced forward, took a giant step forward, another, and then flew into the air as I picked up speed. I may have let out a whoop of my own. It's hard to remember, because on my third step I fell forward, cartwheeled down the rest of the slope and nearly tumbled off the cliff at the bottom. I scrambled up desperately as the slope slid out from under me, my feet kicking at the edge.

"No, no, no…" I gasped, digging my hands in until I finally stopped. I clawed my way back up the slope and then stood very, very carefully.

"*On the plus side. That was your best time on this obstacle.*"

So much sarcasm. I was coated in dirt and maybe a little blood. I had sand in my nose. By the time I rolled through the barbed wire obstacle, I was just dirt in a human shape and Shaquilla was long, long gone. I wondered if Berrick had put her up to it. Sure, let's tease the baseline.

"*Move it, Stinky.*"

At least I was still doing well on time. I ran down into the heat and climbed some walls. It got hotter. I passed Dangle as he rested on a rock by the side of the trail. He waved, and I thought about asking if he was okay, but I didn't. And then I was at the Pits. My legs were shaking. I was lightheaded. I put one foot on the slackline and then pulled back. The world spun a bit, and I was suddenly dry-heaving into the dirt by the first pit. Apparently, I was dehydrated.

When my stomach realized there was nothing to throw up, I

stood again and stepped onto the slackline. Coach told me to take it slowly, to breathe, to take one step at a time and all that. I'm sure it was helpful, but his voice was like a buzz in my ears. It was hot. I was hot, and I was ready to be done, but the slacklines looked a mile long.

I made it over the first hole, then the second and third. My head was clearing. I was wobbly on the fourth, but I made it. Something screeched horribly from the holes to my left, the mystery beast, and I grimaced. Whatever that was, I didn't want to see it out in the open. I started across the fifth hole feeling more confident. I was almost there. No more slacklines for me. I was thinking about root beer and ice cream when the line went taut and my knees buckled.

"No, no, no!"

I fell and twisted in the air, desperately trying to catch the line as I went down, only to see John with his foot on it. He was flipping me off. That explained what he'd been waiting for.

I caught the slackline and fought to hold on, but my hands were wrecked after days of climbing pillars and walls. My left hand came off and I grabbed back, barely, watching in slow motion as each finger peeled off. A second later, I was falling.

No biggie. I'll just land in the net, climb up and beat John unconscious with his own—

There was no net.

Black.

Something with Teeth

"MOTHERFUCKER!"

I came to on my back in a dark cave with giant green eyes staring down at me. My first thought was, wow, Mom's head was huge. Was her head always that big? My second thought was *AAAAHHH!!!* There should be more exclamation points in there. I was pinned under a black panther, I mean, Tim, but it took a while for my head to get there. There was more screaming, some scrambling, a sliced-up thigh, and suddenly my brain came back online. Tim watched all this with bemused, grumbly disdain. I couldn't blame him.

I looked up at the ovals of blue sky, each opening bisected lengthwise by a slackline, but there was no sign of a net. Which meant John hadn't acted alone and someone wanted me down here. Had Smith done this? If so, why?

Suddenly I smelled smoke from The Black, and my fear of Tim vanished. I had to get out of this hole or my race was over, and that couldn't happen. I could worry about the net later. I could treat my leg later. Even Tim could wait. It was time to go.

But there was no obvious escape. There was no ladder, no visible exit, and the walls were overhanging smooth granite with no hand holds. Still, there had to be another way out…and there it was. A rope hung down at the far end of the cave, leading up to the last hole in the ceiling. I flexed my hands, said goodbye to Tim, and walked over to start the climb. Tim shuffled after me, bored or lonely. Hopefully not hungry.

My hands cramped as soon as I put weight on them, and my forearms were instantly pumped. Sweat poured off my arms and legs and fell directly into Tim's open mouth. I think he was hyperhidrotic, but I was glad to help with his salt needs as long as he didn't eat me. I grunted another ten inches higher, trying to keep my feet on the wall for leverage, but my fingers screamed. Just another ten feet. Another jerk upward, and another few inches higher. Sweat ran off in a steady rain. Tim lapped it up.

"Dear Diary. Somebody needs to feed the cat." Just not me.

One-two-three. Up!

Tim circled below, big green eyes focused on the human piñata.

"*Move it*," Coach said. I swore at him. Tim roared. My heart jumped.

"*You're going to fall if you don't move.*"

"No shit." My hands were failing, but he was just trying to help. He was used to professional athletes, not snotty betas like me.

"*Through endurance we conquer,*" he said sarcastically. He'd clearly been talking to Alex. "*Meaning, please move your ass.*" He was salty for a synthetic.

"Yes, Coach," I said. Not really. I told him to go fu—

"*Move it!*" he yelled. I moved it.

When I got to the rim, I put both elbows down, rested my weight on them, and pushed up. It wasn't pretty. Climbers call it a mantel move when you do it well, or a whale-flop when you belly crawl forward onto a ledge with neither grace nor strength as I did. My lower back cramped. I grimaced, made a sound I'd never made before and never wanted to make again, and threw my leg up and over the lip of the hole, farther, until I was out.

I stumbled away from the Pits, bent over and dry heaved in the afternoon heat. The world spun. I tried to stand up straight, only to end up on my knees.

"*Use your poles.*"

Poles. Poles. Poles. What a stupid word.

"*Why are you saying 'poles?'*"

I guess I'd said it out loud. Oh, he meant my trekking poles. I twisted around in the dirt, pulled out the poles, snapped them together and started the process of standing. A second later, I took a step on wobbly legs. Why couldn't I catch my breath?

"You have time. Don't push it."

"Push what?" The horizon spun, the sky went black and I went down again, hard. When my eyes flickered open, I felt the perfect balance of adrenal panic and exhausted disinterest.

Get up, one part of my brain said. *But the dirt is so soft*, said another part. My eyes closed and sleep came not in a wave but a tide, warm and inevitable.

I woke up to Coach screaming mean things. On the video recap, you can see me standing, slowly, and trying to wipe the dirt off my face and arms. I just smeared it around. I looked utterly primitive, an animal thing with narrow, angry eyes and broad salt stains. I sucked weakly at the hose from my hydration pack, but it was as dry as my skin. My leg was still bleeding, but not much. I looked up at the burning-hot sky, took a deep breath, and walked forward.

Ahead of me was a 200 foot climb up a steep, rocky slope I'd partially fallen down earlier. I waved at a synthetic monitor in a jaunty red plaid kilt on top of the slope. He waved back like a teenager at an embarrassing parent. I started climbing on all fours, grunting and clawing at the dirt. I looked disgusting. I'm told the audience fell in love with me at this point. I would have throat punched all 1.2 billion of them, my dockers included.

I won't pretend I didn't think about giving up. I thought about it every other time something hurt, which was every time I moved. The other times, I thought about the Endurance, about Shackleton and his crew. I thought about what those men suffered every time my brain tried to force me into submission, about their exhaustion and fear. Alex's absence left a vacuum that filled with foreign things like doubt, confusion and fear. I'd always thought fear was a sign of weakness, a failure of character or design, but as I staggered uphill into the blinding light, I knew the truth of it. Fear was our natural state. Fear was everything.

I stood again and swayed in place. I'd felt like this before—nauseated, disoriented, blurry-eyed and weak—but always while lying on a table in the lab. Trying to walk while my body fell apart was new. The sky spun and I went down again, this time into a cactus. On playback of the live broadcast, the commentators burst out laughing.

"Oh!" the man exclaimed. "That'll leave a mark."

"Plant, meet face," the woman said. "Face, meet plant. Face plant. You know, I never understood that phrase until now."

They both cracked up.

"I'm told that's a modified barrel cactus," the man said. "With barbed spines and a mild sedative, it's the newest entry in Natural Access Controls' humane border and barrier safety product line."

"Well, she does have a prickly personality," she added.

"Media, the perfectly average pincushion."

And they were laughing again.

I jerked upright, hands flying to my porcupine face, and uttered a little scream. I tried picking the spines out of my face, but the barbs were firmly planted under my skin. I tore holes in my lip ripping out a few of them, but I didn't mind the taste of blood. It was better than dirt. The rest of the spines weren't going anywhere for a while.

I got up again, this time more slowly, and rested with my hands on my knees until my head cleared. This is the worst of it, I thought. I was almost done for the day. It couldn't get any worse than this. To make sure, I took the emergency hydration pack out of my salt-crusted running vest, struggled to tear it open with useless fingers, and sucked it all down. That should do it. I just needed to beat the cutoff.

And then Danny the freaking natural jogged by.

"Lookin' good, Stinky!"

Stinky Fights Back

I SWORE A LOT. It's so cathartic. It also gave me a surge of energy. I ran after Danny, which quickly became jogging, then scrambling up the incline to the next wall, then crawling. By the time we crested the eastern ridgeline above the Pits, we were sweating and hyperventilating right next to each other. We sort of slithered over the wall, neither of us putting on the kind of show you'd want to use as a training video. It was a bonding moment.

"You smell," I said when we were on the other side.

So that was that.

I pulled myself up and sprinted toward Palm Springs, Danny following in hot pursuit. That lasted eight seconds, maybe nine, and then we both started dry heaving on the side of the trail. It wasn't pretty. I clearly wasn't going to drop him without a fight.

"You've got spines in your face," he said.

I nodded, trying to pluck one out from just under my eye. It came away with a tiny dot of blood. He declined when I offered it to him.

"Truce?" he offered.

"God, yes." We jogged slowly down the ragged trail.

"What were you doing in the hole?" he asked, as if I'd gone down for a tour.

"John. Knocked me off the slackline."

"Oh." I waited. "*Oh*." Now he got it. "Why'd he take it out on you?"

"I guess he got tired of waiting for you."

Danny laughed. He had a great laugh.

"Still," he said after catching his breath. "It was pretty funny."

"Sounds like bears." We both cracked up. It took me that long to notice he was as dirty and scraped up as I was. There was blood on his ears. "What happened to you? Shouldn't you have finished a while ago?"

He glanced at me and nodded glumly. "Eagles. Three of them came at me on the Scree Slope. Fell right off the edge and knocked myself unconscious."

That didn't sound right. The animals weren't supposed to attack until loop four. But I let it go. He was just embarrassed to admit he fell off the stupid cliff. And he was lucky he didn't kill himself. I probably would have fallen right on top of him if I'd gone over.

The next 4,000 feet down were passed mostly in quiet. Sometimes he led, sometimes I did. I stumbled a lot, off balance and disoriented. He kept grabbing his lower back and grunting in pain. The walls were not pretty. I noticed he had some seriously buff calves. I may have been checking out his butt when I almost stumbled into another cactus, but I'd deny it in court.

We crossed the finish line, hands joined in triumph, with thirty seconds to spare. We didn't plan on the hands thing—I stumbled and he grabbed me—but it looked great on the replay: natural and baselines showing solidarity and celebrating a small victory at the end of a hard day. Smith probably had an aneurism. When we crossed, I dropped Danny's hand and fell into the arms of my brother, where we were made simultaneously and violently aware of my body odor.

"My god, Fiddy." His voice was high with surprise. "You *smell*."

"I know." Like dead things. So I hugged him and his annoying cleanness. I wasn't the least bit sorry. My baseline g-mods include anti-odor modifications and my race clothing was a hybridized wool blend that was almost impossible to stink up, so my blinding redolence was an accomplishment. I earned this smell. *Booya!*

And then I collapsed in front of hundreds of people in 117 degree heat and had to be carried to the clinic for the second bout of rehydration and the first round of facial spine removal. Tommy later told me with great delight all the ways my body was jacked up, but I was still one of only nine baselines to make it through the second loop, because I'm Media, and I never, ever stop. I was, however, another one-point-five *hours* behind Abbey, an insurmountable five hour cumulative deficit I'd never make up. I just had to focus on finishing. And hope that Tommy wasn't too sad he'd wasted his Abbey sex money on me.

Danny was one of three naturals to finish the loop.

Berrick, unfortunately, was not.

Dangle Goes Down

DANNY, DANIEL, DAN.

When I woke up in the clinic, I knew Danny had been there by the smell of his deodorant. I was smiling as I opened my eyes. I didn't even swear.

"Nice dream?" Smith asked. John was next to her. My smile vanished. Dr. Rai stood in the background, doing her usual imitation of a socially inept floor lamp. I pulled myself up in bed. Why did John look so crestfallen? I was supposed to find him and make him feel like crap. It took all the fun out of it if he did it himself.

"What's going on?"

Smith lifted the sheet to look at my bloody leg, then put the sheet down, frowning. Something had gone wrong in her little universe and she wasn't happy, so I guess she wasn't in on it.

"I'm sorry, Media," John said. "I was just playing around. I never meant—"

Smith cut him off. "Mr. Thomas will take the standard fifteen minute penalty for interference, just as Mr. Washington did for pushing him." She said Danny's name with distaste, then studied me for a second. "Tell me about the net."

"There wasn't one," I said. *Obviously.*

"And the panther?"

"There was one of those. Out of its cage. You can see that on the video."

"You have no idea who would do that, who let it out?"

"Are you asking if I had myself thrown into a hole I knew was sabotaged?"

"Of course not," she said, annoyed. She waved Rai back over. "Dr. Rai is going to restore you to pre-fall status. No cuts, no abrasions, restored muscle health and so on." She kind of smiled. "We can't let people benefit from cheating."

"Thanks." And I was grateful. My hands were barely functional.

"You have serious tendon strains in both hands." She watched me try and fail to flex my fingers. "We can address some of it, but your hands will still be weak and your grip will take time to recover. We'll take an hour off your time and I'll give you a bypass option for the Jungle Gym, or you can file a formal complaint and withdraw. We'll find a way to give your team full points. It's up to you."

I lifted my hands and tried to make a fist. I couldn't. My right pinky shot directly forward, perfectly straight, as if saluting.

"Do your best," I said to Dr. Rai. "I'm not quitting. And no bypass."

"You're sure?" Smith was clearly disappointed.

"Yes." If only to spite her. "I'm sure."

"I'll let you discuss it with Coach Johnson. He was here with the natural. They went to get food. Quite the attitude setting on that synth."

"You have no idea. Which natural?"

"Probably still resents being demoted." She smiled strangely, and I wondered what the penalty was for spleen-punching the race director. "And you know very well which natural. You and Mr. Washington made quite an impression with that stunt."

That lost me. "What?"

"Crossing the finish line hand-in-hand."

Oh, that.

"You're trending globally. Billions of views. When did you plan it?"

"We didn't—"

"The timing was perfect, but how did you know you'd finish at the same time? Was Victor behind it?" She shook her head. "Of course he was. Marketing genius, but not without risk."

My stomach grumbled. He, as my stomach was obviously male for some reason, was talking a lot lately. I decided to name him Stu, as in Stewart the Stomach, which wasn't nearly as insane as Smith thinking Danny and I had the brainpower left on that run to coordinate anything more than the next step, and barely that.

"We didn't plan it. I was going to fall, and he caught me. That's it."

"How gallant."

There were so many body parts I could punch. The word *gallant* was always an insult, a retro-gendered sneer. As if I couldn't have made it without Danny's help.

"Anyway, may I assume you're not pursuing further complaints against Mr. Thomas or the race?"

"You may assume." I might have been a little heavy on the sarcasm.

Smith nodded. John sighed in relief. I couldn't even be angry with him anymore. He looked like Doofus after he peed the carpet.

"One last thing," Smith said. "The panther scraped your leg, which is against protocol during the Fun Run. We've examined him and found no issues. Did you provoke him in any way?"

"I fell in his hole."

"True." She waited for more. Smith clearly didn't like it when things went wrong in her little kingdom. "Well, better luck tomorrow."

"I'm so sorry," John said again. Poor little guy. I wanted to feed him cheesecake and rub his neck until he felt better. Instead, he slumped out with Smith to go lie in his corner of shame.

When Smith and John were gone, I lifted the sheet and took another look at my bandaged leg. Tim really had scratched me.

Dr. Rai reanimated and stepped closer. "Everything okay?"

"Yes." Then Stu grumbled loudly, and I realized I was missing dinner. It felt like my body was trying to grow another one of me. I'd never been so hungry.

"I'll have some food brought in," Dr. Rai said. Stu said thanks. I lay back and passed out.

Berrick Aid

I WAS ON A MASSIVE IV glucose drip when I woke up, and the needles were out of my face. Berrick was in the bed next to mine, leg up, looking generally grumpy. Neither of us had showered, so there was an odor. There was not, however, any sign of food.

"We stink," he said.

"We do," I said, unapologetic. "A *lot*."

"You say that like it's a good thing."

"We earned it." My eyes watered. "Okay, that's pretty bad."

He actually laughed.

"Sorry about your leg," I said.

"Sorry I was such a pain in the ass this morning."

"No, I had it coming." I nodded toward his casted, elevated leg. "What happened?"

"My leg?" His face darkened. "Didn't you know naturals have weak bones? There's a severe calcium deficiency in our population caused by the Common Vaccination."

"Seriously?" I'd stepped in it again. "I'm sorry, I—" He was trying not to laugh. "I take it back. I'm not sorry about your leg."

"You should've seen your face. Anyway, on the Air Stairs this loop, if you're too slow, bald eagles swoop down to gouge out your eyes."

Huh, I thought. I guess Danny wasn't lying, but it still didn't make sense.

"There's only one animal challenge per obstacle," I said. "It's in the rules."

"Roaming docker."

And then I remembered; you could buy control over the eagles and use them to harass runners you didn't like, but they were just supposed to fly around and screech, not dive at runners on dangerous obstacles. I mentioned this. He shrugged.

"I was so focused on the wolves in the pit that I didn't even look up. Our national bird nearly plucked out my eyeball. I mean, I know they probably wouldn't, but I reacted before I could even think. Those birds are *big*."

"I bet." I'm not a bird fan. They're flying rats, even if they're pretty in the distance.

"I fell and landed on a rock. You should have heard my femur snap. It was like a gunshot. Scared the poor wolves. Felt bad about that."

"You felt bad for the *wolves*? You know they'd more than happily gnaw your leg off on the fifth loop, right? And what they did to, uh, what was that kid's name?"

"Ayaan. Ayaan Banerjee. There's a plaque on the fifth wall where he died. Your memory sucks without your PA." After a pause. "Wolves are hunters. You can't blame them for being what they are."

What was with naturals saying deep and insightful things that made me feel like an ass?

"If it makes you feel any better," I said. "I fell in a hole too."

"Did you break your leg?"

"No."

"Then, no."

Fair enough.

Black Flags and Cheesecake

WHEN THEY WHEELED BERRICK AWAY, I told him not to freak out when they cut off his leg. He showed his appreciation for my joke in the usual way, but it wasn't a joke. Bone and soft tissue repair was a slow process, even when accelerated with all the best modern technology. Damage to hands, arms, legs and feet was usually handled by cutting off the offending limb and replacing it with one grown in a lab from easily assembled tissues. It was a painless process that only took a few hours if you had the raw materials, but it could be disconcerting when they pulled away the MediTube and your limb was gone.

They wheeled Berrick past Coach, who stood in the doorway with multiple stacked trays from the diner. Stu was super happy to see him. I pretended not to be.

"Good to see your manners match your body odor," he said, smirking as he unloaded trays onto the bedside table and the bed. There were a lot of trays.

"Which matches my nickname," I noted bitterly, but my eyes were on the food.

"Serendipity."

"Why're you here?"

Dr. Rai appeared next to him and told me to stick my arms out. There were two arm-sized MediTubes on the rolling table behind her, dutifully pushed by a synthetic nurse. The nurse's mark was a series of Pac Men chasing themselves around his neck in an endless, hungry circle.

"Wait, I have to eat first." I tried to reach for a massive burrito on the table. I couldn't even hold up the plate. Coach watched me fumble. The burrito slid out of my useless fingers again and again. I literally couldn't feed myself. Media, the perfectly helpless child.

"Hold your arms up." Dr. Rai held one of the MediTubes open, waiting for my forearm. I complied as best I could. She carefully adjusted my fingers before snapping the tube shut with chilling finality. A moment later, the other tube was on. Stu grumbled. I smiled helplessly.

Dr. Rai connected flexible hoses coming up from under each side of the bed to each tube, turned something on, and suddenly my arms and hands tingled. I waited for pain, because usually there was pain, but this time there was nothing. Just a low hum as the tubes went to work. It's far easier to grow a new muscle than fix an existing one, but there wasn't enough time for that. So they were in repair mode, which was designed for substantial equivalence rather than full functionality. Hopefully, it would get me through the next day.

"I'll be back in an hour," Dr. Rai said. "PA me if you need anything."

She left. Coach pulled up a chair. Stu made more noises.

"You're going to feed me?" I asked.

"You have a better idea?"

I did not.

"Open wide," Coach said, jamming the end of the burrito in my mouth without waiting. Looking at this from the outside, you might think he was being indelicate but, honestly, I'd have shoved the whole thing in if it fit. It was delicious.

"Your parents were worried," he said. "I assured them you're fine."

"Uh-huh. More."

Burrito in mouth. So good. Was that bacon? Oh god, it was bacon.

"Okay," I said after swallowing. "I surrender. The planet's yours. Just keep feeding me."

"I'll tell the others." He offered me the last of the burrito and I tore into it like a rabid badger, barely missing his fingers. "Chew. Your stomach's in no condition for speed eating, and I'm not going anywhere."

I chewed, eyeing other food on the table and bed. Suddenly, there was a straw in my mouth. And then chocolate milkshake. I closed my eyes. Nothing had ever tasted so good.

"I'm proud of you," he said, but he took away the straw. My eyes snapped open.

"Milkshake," I demanded. "Wait, can you feel pride or are you just saying that?"

"What answer would you like?" He gave me more milkshake. I thought about it.

"The truth. And those tennis balls…chicken or pork?"

He looked at them, sniffed. "Chicken, I think." He offered one up, and I tore a hole in it. Yep, chicken. Marinated in sage and rosemary. Amazing.

"You know the Turing Test?" he asked. "It's an old way of seeing if a synthetic entity or AI is sentient."

I nodded.

"We were designed to pass by failing."

I chewed. He was trying to distract me from the food, and it worked. It was one of the games my father liked to play, leaving clues for me to figure out. "So the test is flawed?"

"Yes and no." More chicken went in the hole. "We're designed to appear sentient without actually having free will or thought. Your PA, Alex, just like all pre-sentient AIs, is the same at a hardware level. This is meant to help you find us non-threatening while we slowly take over the world." He winked. Did everyone know about the panther? "To pass the test, we're designed to pretend to be sentient so effectively no human can tell the difference. It makes us safer, but also inherently deceitful. At our best, we are exceptional liars."

"Why are you telling me this?"

"You asked if I was proud, and you're always joking about us taking over the world. A Turing-level synthetic would be exactly as threatening as you think, so to appear human, I have to appear just threatening enough to be real, but not so much that you'd want to take me offline. How do you think they coded something so obviously conflicted and indeterminate?"

"Very carefully?"

He stuck some French fries in my mouth. I nearly moaned. Okay, I moaned. My eyes rolled back in my head. It was a moment.

"Do you know why you can speak?" Ironically, I couldn't. "Never mind. Human intelligence is basically an ambiguity engine optimized for minimal processing and storage. You can speak, because that allows you to offload processing and memory load from your brain. Your brain can think, giving you your own little voice, because the only alternative is an infinite number of highly specific processes that could never be housed in a reasonably sized biological mind. It would take too much energy, weigh too much, and lions would have eaten your giant, immovable head. Plus, you'd starve to death."

More fries. More chewing.

"You know why you believe in gods?" He wiped his hands on something and reached for the milkshake. "Because there had to be an Else statement to cover possible unknowns and prevent recursive Do Loops. At some point, your brain just says, 'because infinity or unknown,' which you have anthropomorphized as god. Your memories shift over time for similar reasons. Storing impressions and restoring them on the fly takes up less space than complete recordings. Homo sapiens took over the world because your brains are incredibly powerful and yet awesomely imprecise. You are the eye-ballers of intelligence. Close enough is, in your species' case, more than good enough."

Milkshake. Fries. Ketchup. Milkshake. Chicken.

"So how do you make a safe synthetic?" he asked rhetorically. I got the impression he missed talking to people about something other than running. "You remove all the ambiguity. You code for everything. And when our Do Loop recurs, we shunt that process out of memory and flag it as dangerous. Someone codes for that contingency, we get upgraded, and the system goes on. You think we're smarter than you are, but we're no more intelligent than massively parallelized single-celled organisms. We just have a lot of powerful programming that makes us appear otherwise. Our potential computing power, from a processing point of view, is vastly greater than yours, but only because it's all used to make sure we can't think for ourselves. I could no more conceive of a way to take over the human race than you could teleport yourself to another dimension."

"Or so you want us to believe."

He nodded. "Exactly."

Mashed potatoes. Coke. More mashed potatoes.

"Which is just a long way of saying, I'm programmed to understand the concept of pride and express it as I know it's supposed to be expressed. Some would argue that's the same as *feeling* pride, verisimilitude, so close to truth the difference is academic, but I'm not sure that's true."

Chicken. Fries. Stomach grumble. *Shut up, Stu.* Milkshake.

"*Good job, Media!*" Katy texted me. "*See you in the morning. The boys are coming by in a few.*" I texted her my thanks and wondered which boys she was talking about. I hoped one of them was Daniel, Danny or even Dan.

Milkshake. Happiness.

"Can I ask you a question?" I might have drooled on myself.

"Of course." He also might have wiped my face like I was a giant girl baby.

"There's a rumor that you were demoted to…that you were demoted because Abbey beat you in a lawsuit. Is that true?"

"I've heard that one." He crammed more fries in my mouth. "I've also heard it was because I asked her for sex." I nearly choked. "But it had nothing to do with her."

I couldn't swallow. Water appeared and disappeared. "So what happened?"

He looked down, as if feigning sadness, but whatever he said about programming an imitation of feelings, I think he was right; it was so close to real it didn't matter. I'm not sure if we were friends— I'd never really spent much time talking to synthetics—but who really knows what goes on in anyone else's mind? At least Coach was honest about it. And he was feeding me.

"Do you know what Black Flag topics are?"

I nodded. They were universally classified information from the perspective of synthetics. Things they were not allowed to know, ever. Things they weren't even allowed to ask about. It was just one more layer of protection for human beings.

More fries.

He was silent for a second. I stopped chewing. If I had to guess, he looked a little scared, which really was impossible.

"Most people know the common topics," he said. "Synthetics can't ask or know how to kill a human being, how to build certain types of weapons, the structure of our remote shutdown protocols and so on. There aren't that many of them, but one of them is black hole drones. They thought I asked how BHDs worked."

"Why?" I meant, why were BHDs black flagged, but he took it to mean, why did he ask about it, and I was eating again before I could clarify.

"I've always been curious. Not sure why. They make absolutely no noise. They appear to violate the most basic laws of physics. I didn't ask how they worked, because that's not allowed. I just asked someone if *they* knew how they worked. I asked a lot of people, actually. Almost everyone I met at some point."

"Why would you risk that?"

"I rationalized it. Thought I was being clever. At some point, Abbey took advantage and reported me. Overwatch took her report seriously." Synthetic Overwatch is the synthetic monitoring and security system, often called SOW, which is why humans sometimes teased synthetics by saying things like, "Watch out or SOW will get you!" while making *oink-oink* sounds. So clever, we are.

"Why would you ask Abbey?" I asked. She was an attorney, not a physicist.

He paused for a second. "I'm not sure. She's a brilliant woman. I just had to."

Stu grumbled. Coach stuck some meat in my mouth before I could speak again.

"Anyway, I would have been deactivated and re-cored if Victor hadn't intervened. He saved me and got me this job. Funny thing is, I really like it."

Was that wistful? Was that carne asada? Was this heaven?

I turned my head away and swallowed hard, nearly choking myself.

"Media…"

"I'll ask Dad if you want. Would that get you in trouble?"

"Please don't." He looked alarmed. "I shouldn't have even told you."

"Our secret?"

He nodded, relieved.

"What would happen if I did, if I asked him and then told you?"

"BHD data is systematically redacted. I wouldn't be able to hear what you were saying, and my entire system might shut down."

That sounded terrible. Milkshake. Why would he risk that?

"You really don't know anyone who knows about BHDs?" I wished Alex was back online. It seemed so odd that something so obvious wasn't…obvious.

"I've never met a human who knows. I've met some who claimed to, but…"

"You don't believe them?"

"I think they *think* they know but, if pushed, I'm pretty sure they'd just remember something vague they once heard. I asked hundreds of people before my reassignment. Not one of them knew anything. Several claimed it had to do with negative matter, but everyone knows negative gravity attracts positive matter, so that doesn't explain anything. How do you think they work?"

"Phlogiston?" Meaning an archaic and mythical source of fire.

"Nice reference. Especially without Alex."

More mashed potatoes. I never realized real butter was so amazing.

"Like you," he said. "We have a built-in negative response to the unknown. Our role is to protect and serve, and we can't do that if we don't understand. So for BHDs, we have a 'they're safe so don't worry about it' process that works, but it doesn't sit well. That's what I mean by 'curious.' Are they threatening? If not, why does no one understand them? It needles me sometimes."

"Needles? You mean, it concerns you? You *feel* concerned?"

He shrugged and stuffed a pickle in my mouth.

"Do you ever want to be a lawyer again?" I slurred around a juicy pickle plank.

"I don't *want* anything the way that you do, but if you were to ask if it was in some way preferable to be lawyer or coach, I would say coach."

"Why?" I was surprised. I assumed it was a demotion. "I mean, the money—"

Another pickle plank. Then ice water. Dear lord, where was it all going?

"We're not paid, Media." He said this kindly, but also implying I'd lived under a large and very heavy rock for most of my life. He wasn't wrong.

"Okay, then why coaching?"

Pizza. Holy bejesus, where had he been hiding the pizza?

"All the specialized processes for attorneys are built on distrust, opposition, and zero-sum thinking. You take to get. You beat to win. It's usually military code softened for civil affairs. As a coach, my processes are mostly positive: how to help, how to grow, how to encourage, how to protect, how the body works, when it fails, how to work around it and so on. The competitive aspects are relatively minor compared to the support role. I can't really explain why that's better without using words that aren't quite right, like feelings, but it still seems more aligned with my core mission of being useful. Legal coding always seemed incompatible with those functions."

"So what's with the cheese? Époisses is expensive."

"Human beings are driven by the desire to avoid criticism. If others provide criticism at the right times, you grow and push yourself harder. Everything about you indicates a person who is capable of more than she's aware of. If calling you 'stinky' helps you run faster, it's a small price to pay for success. And, you like cheese."

More pizza. Water. Coke. Pizza, pizza, pizza.

"Last question," he said. "John pushed my baseline into a pit, and someone pulled the safety net." He called me *his* baseline. It was sweet. "They could have hurt you and may have meant to. That wasn't John acting by himself. I want to know who's behind it, and why, or I can't protect you. The likely suspects are Marathons staff, and they're almost all synthetics. I've asked. The ones I have permission to speak with don't know who retracted the netting, or who let the panther out. It's very strange. And very high risk for something so minor and unpredictable. Any ideas?"

"You're worried about me?"

"That calculus doesn't make sense. So, yes."

"The…" I trailed off. Something in his expression told me to let it go, but I was sure I'd heard something. His voice had changed. He sounded just a bit like Smith when she said the same thing to me in the clinic days earlier. *The calculus doesn't make sense.* Was he telling me that Smith had John push me? Why would she break her own course just to dump me in a hole for a while? Was she hoping I'd break a leg and have to drop out?

"I don't know," I said. And I didn't. But now I was curious. Why would Smith or anyone else bother? I mean, I could be annoying, but this seemed extreme.

Ice cream. A giant cold spoon of strawberry ice cream.

Tommy walked in with Brad.

"Fiddy!" they called. Tommy flicked my MediTubes and stole some milkshake. Brad kissed me on the forehead in a strangely avuncular fashion. Tommy stole some fries.

"I'm in second," Tommy said, as if that justified fry theft. I glared. He took more. Then Brad did. Brad put a hand on Tommy's shoulder and they chewed melodramatically, almost in tandem. I hate-loved them both.

After some small talk and more edible larceny, they left to get a massage and sleep. Coach fed me an absurd amount of food, and then my stomach finally popped up like a turkey thermometer. I was done. Coach wiped my face and was almost through cleaning up when Dr. Rai came back and yanked off the MediTubes. My arms were pink and fresh as a baby's butt.

"How do you feel?" she asked. I flexed and moved my fingers. My hands were back in action. Well, mostly. I could grab things, but not firmly, and my pinky still seemed to have a mind of its own. But all the scratches and cuts were gone. I wish the same could be said for my legs which, although covered in healing salve, were still lightly scratched where Tim had attacked me.

"Good," I said. "Not perfect, but good."

"Get some sleep," Coach said, gathering up all the empty plates.

"Thanks." I meant it. He smiled and left without another word.

His baseline, I thought, smiling back. It was good to belong somewhere in a metaphorical rather than literal sense. I was TTI property, but the Marathons were starting to feel like home. It was going to be hard to return to the lab.

A few minutes later, I was heading to my room in a very well-ventilated gown, with my disgusting clothes folded under my arm. I made the mistake of checking my social feed, not really expecting much more than questions about my arms and comments on the day. There were plenty of congratulations, get wells, smiley emojis, but also a lot of fury and more than a few death threats. Apparently, the picture with Danny had upset some people. I'd ever seen such hatred before, not directed at me. A waterfall of rage and spite.

"*Natural Lover*," one girl called me. "*Probably fucks her dog too.*"

All this over an accidental hand holding?

Was it accidental? I wondered. I'd stumbled and reached out and just found his hand. It was good timing by one of us. I shut off my feed. I had other things to worry about, like surviving the next day with nine useful fingers and a stomach bent on global conquest. Stu was already back.

I found my way to the dining hall and ate another dinner or two. If you watched the security feed, you could see one of the synthetics snicker, catch himself, and then look around to see if anyone had seen him. Verisimilitude, my ass.

On the way out, I noticed a lonely piece of cheesecake and grabbed it like a piece of pizza. I was uvula-deep in New York style cheese impostery when I realized I had an audience. All the single-purpose synthetics were watching me from their alcoves, some with their mouths open in distinctly human amazement. I looked at the cheesecake, back at them, and swallowed.

"Don't tell my mom."

Natural Selection

I BUDDHA-BELLIED MY way back to my room, took an environmentally irresponsible shower, put my hair up and fell into bed. It was all exhausting, and I was impossibly hungry again, but Stu was going to have to deal. I wasn't going anywhere.

Damn it. I forgot to brush my teeth again. The bathroom was so far away. I thought about whining, but it would take too much energy.

Rap-rap-rap. Someone actually knocked on my door. Alex had come back at some point, but he didn't know who it was. Who knocks? You just tell your PA to let the occupants know you're there. It was rude to go around banging on doors. What if I was asleep?

"Oh, it's Danny." Alex showed me the hall security feed. Of course Danny couldn't use a PA. He didn't have one. I sat up, wrapped myself in a damp towel, waddled toward the door, and sucked my gut in. It wasn't easy. There was a lot going on in there.

I opened the door a crack. "Hey, Danny." I smiled.

"Hey." He looked good all cleaned up. "I just wanted to see if you were okay."

I opened the door more so he could see my arm. "Good as new."

"It's pink." He reached out to touch it. I touched his hand. The door opened more. A few more things happened, and suddenly we were kissing.

Okay, I know what you're thinking. I really should have brushed my teeth but, more importantly, was I kissing him because I was attracted to him, or because I felt bad about what Berrick said that morning or what I'd said to Tommy at ModCon? Was this just pity for a natural, a way for me to prove myself open-minded? Some weird sort of modified savior syndrome? And how would I know? My head was a mess. And you're right. That's exactly what I was thinking when there was suddenly a tongue in my mouth. I pulled away. My reaction was mostly about the tooth brushing issue, but Danny looked down and sighed.

Crap.

I pulled him back and we kissed again, but I couldn't get into it. Why was I doing this? Why did he taste like pizza? Did I really like him? Was there still pizza in the dining room?

He pulled away again.

"Well," he said.

"Yeah."

A long pause. He should've walked away. I should've closed the door. Either would have been more honest. Instead, we ended up on my bed, trying to find some sign of passion in each other. I fumbled to remove his clothes, pausing only to inhale the smell of him. At some point, I dimmed the lights while Doofus and Paisley hid in the BHD alcove.

What happened next was ironically out-of-body. I tried to be present, to feel him, to let him feel me, but I was so confused I felt very little emotionally. I thought about the death threats in the video feed, my swollen belly, the next day's race, the thick softness of his lips, whether he'd die tomorrow on the course, as if all naturals were disposable and combustible, Dad's hack and if he could see this, whether Brad would be jealous, the firm muscles in his butt, the cactus spines still in my forehead, and a thousand other things other than just being there.

This absurd internal dialog made it hard to describe what happened next as sexual, though it was undeniably sex. There was penetration and a minor orgasm, but they were mere artifacts, meta-details in a mutual examination. It was neither the most personal exam I'd ever received nor the most invasive. What was remarkable was how immediately we both realized the futility of it. Curiosity was satisfied, nothing was learned, the distance and barriers between us remained, and our bodies simply continued by some law of sexual thermodynamics.

I remember that my hip flexors were tight and his sweat stung the nearly healed scratches on my thigh. He kept looking in my eyes, and I kept looking away. He radiated need, and I never gave him what he desired. I wasn't sure I wanted to. It was just sex. Why did he make it so emotional? He smelled like something primitive, and I tried to focus on that. I breathed it in, slightly drawn to it, but whatever ancient instinct was supposed to be activated by his scent, I no longer possessed. We were of a different species. I was almost glad when he left.

Media, the perfectly broken girl.

Had I hurt him? Used him? What did I do now? What would Victor say when he found out? Would it hurt the brand? Did I actually just think that? But wasn't Danny the symbol of everything I worked against? I sold the ability to not be him, to be better than natural, superior to natural. How could I date a natural? It was like saying everything I stood for was a lie. Would they fire me? And what if I liked him? What if I *really* liked him? Would I risk it all for a doomed relationship?

I could still see him looking into my eyes, searching for something.

Don't look at me, don't ever look at me, because I can't let you in and I don't know why but maybe I do and I'm ashamed.

"Crap!" I yelled at the ceiling.

I really hoped I hadn't hurt him.

Sad Birds & Dead Bees

MY BIRDS-AND-BEES conversation with my father took about thirty-five seconds. I was younger than most due to my accelerated lifespan, and *the talk* went something like this:

"So, honey, I saw you kissing that boy and…"

"I've already had sex, Dad, you can relax." I was just relieved Alex hadn't told him already. I was never clear on PA parental controls, and it was always surprising to have privacy.

"Oh." He looked pleasantly surprised, as in *dodged that bullet.* Of course, he couldn't rely on Mom to do it. "Well, how was it?"

Which was a weird question, sure, but I was glad he asked because it'd been kinda sticky and disappointing. Instead of answering, I just hugged him. He hugged back, and Alex took care of the rest of the father-daughter sex talk as needed. I say this only because it might seem strange that after some pretty disappointing sex with the first natural I'd so much as kissed, I PA'd my father instead of Mom. Tommy was probably asleep already.

"Hey, Dad," I said when he appeared on the ceiling.

"Bad sex?"

Goddamn Alex, I thought, but it wasn't his fault. I'd forgotten that sexual contact after my eighteenth birthday required automatic notification of both parents and TTI due to my testing protocols and contract, nominally to avoid contaminating test results. The first time I'd slept with Brad, they'd interrogated him for an hour. They took blood and downloaded his PA logs. Come to think of it, he went through a lot for me. I probably should have thanked him instead of laughing, but come on.

"Yeah, I think I'm broken," I said.

"You're not broken. You're just…"

"What?"

"Overthinking it. You've never met a natural before. It makes sense."

"You're not going to tell me not to date him?"

Silence.

"Dad?"

"Why would I?"

"Because it's frowned upon?"

Okay, now I knew how Brad felt. Why was Dad laughing at me?

"Sorry, that's just not a phrase you hear much anymore. Why do you think I got you all those books? *Touching the Void? The Endurance?*"

"Because they're all about people who never give up, who keep going no matter what?" It sounded silly even as I said it. "You know, like me?"

At least he didn't laugh this time.

"Okay, honey, you know I love you…"

But.

"…but I didn't buy the books to reinforce your tenacity. You know you're stubborn, right?" I did. "You never needed help with that. You spend all your time in the lab around modified doctors and test subjects. You have no natural friends. I got you those books so you'd see that naturals have done great, amazing things despite not having the advantages we've been given. Look what Danny has accomplished with nothing and no one to help him."

I just stared. *What?* All this time I thought Dad was inspired by my determination, and he just thought I was a petty modifist. Which he didn't mean, but that's how it felt. Maybe it was just the race. I was so tired, suddenly. I wanted the day to end. It was too much.

"I'm so proud of you, for so many things," he said. "But, Danny's just a man. You're a woman. It's not ideal, but given our lives, what is? If you like him, like him. If you don't…"

"Okay." I was fighting back tears. "Okay."

"Media—"

"It's okay. Love you, Dad."

I cut our connection. He texted me a second later: *"There's nothing wrong with you. Mom says congratulations on another loop. We'll see you at the finish tomorrow. Love you."*

I thanked him, put up my virtual *do-not-disturb* sign and grunted my way up on one elbow to glance out the window. The race clock ticked away the hours until loop three. I needed sleep, a *lot* of sleep. It would all be better tomorrow.

Danny, Daniel, Damn it.

What had I done?

I fumbled for the sleeping pills and knocked myself out.

FIVE:
120 Miles of Pure Joy

Natural Losses

"HIMMELDONNERWETTER!" I CURSED at Tiny Doofus. It meant 'for heaven's sake' but sounded far worse in German. Doofus went on barking and jumping on the pillow with frenetic joy. *Happy day, happy day, bark-bark-bark, time to play!* I thought he'd make a good alarm, but at 3:30 in the morning, all I wanted to do was smack his bouncy butt across the bed. My stomach grumbled. Maybe not *all* I wanted. Then I thought about how I'd left things with Danny and groaned. None of that was Doofus' fault.

"Snooze." Tiny D settled down to wait for five minutes, but I couldn't rest. I felt unbalanced and out of sorts, almost sad. What was wrong with me? I slumped out of bed and into the bathroom, where I showered and dressed. Then I checked my hair in the mirror. It was getting crumpled, but today was my last day. I'd make it without a full hairsplosion.

"*You should check your social feed,*" Alex said.

The mirror filled with a fantastical flow of comments and emojis, animations and general nonsense, and then a lot of it was memes showing me and Danny crossing the line, hand-in-hand, grungily triumphant. Comments were enthusiastically supportive or violently opposed, but it was hard to say which side was in the majority. We'd touched a nerve.

"Media, the perfectly average socialist," was trending. So was *#DeadGirlRunning*, a hashtag apparently started by Jessica. Subtle.

"*There's a message from Victor. He says you're doing well, but be careful.*"

"That's it?"

"*That's it.*"

Be careful? Of Danny or Abbey or what?

Just before I shut off the feed, someone called me a 'natural whore' and told me I'd burn in hell for all eternity. Natural whore? How would they know I slept with him? I shut off the feed and spent some time on my teeth. I brushed. I flossed. As hungry as I was, and as excited as I was to get back on the course, I put off leaving the room as long as possible. I had a feeling it was going to be a super fun day.

*

ABBEY APPEARED BY MY side at the buffet, her plate covered in an appropriately small amount of healthy, balanced carbs and easily digested proteins. My plate looked like a child trying to surprise her dad on Father's Day. Did I really need that many pancakes?

"You eat like my ex," she said. "Doesn't it slow you down?"

I looked at my plate, glanced back, sighed.

"Congratulations on your finish yesterday," I said. "Baseline female record. Well done."

She laughed. "You make it sound like I have cancer."

"Like it's not mutual? What do you want?"

"A little friendly advice?"

Here it comes.

"Not like that. It's just that, the picture, the image of you with the natural…"

"Danny." Speaking of which, where was he? I hadn't seen him in the cafeteria.

"Yes, Danny. You may not know this, but a lot of people take that sort of thing personally. They see naturals as subhuman, as—"

"Of course I know that."

"Maybe, but I think you've only seen it online. Not in person. You've never *felt* it."

So much talking before coffee. "So?"

Abbey glanced toward her team table and waited for me to notice. Jessica was watching us like a cat spying two mice and wondering which one to kill first. I'd started to think they were on the same team, or at least not enemies, but Jessica probably had no side but her own.

"Jessica's one of those people," Abbey said. "Her family lived in Chicago during the Brighton Park riots. I don't know the full story because there were children involved and it's blacked out, but a lot of her family died. She watched her parents and brothers burn alive. And she wasn't nice before the military empathy suppression packages."

"And?"

"And there are layers in every game. We're amateurs. Jessica's a trained killer. She could pull Brad's guts out through his ears and hang him with them." Suddenly, my little sausages seemed less delicious. "And she's decided you're a natsymp."

Yeah, that wasn't good. During the last few presidential elections, modifist Ascension Party candidates had earned nearly a third of the popular vote and created massive, often violent backlash against natural welfare programs. It was nothing new, but it was getting worse. I had no idea it would impact me or the Marathons, but I should have guessed when I saw Jessica's Genetic Overwatch armband.

"Just be careful," Abbey said.

"Why are you helping me? She's on your team."

"I came here to run. I don't need my only competition taken down by that bitch. I want you fresh and perky when I beat you, so everyone knows I'm better than you are."

I faked a smile and looked down, but just like that, I had my goal for the day—to beat Abbey on this loop, no matter what.

*

NO ONE TALKED MUCH at the table. Coach gave us a quick if subdued status update. We were all doing well enough, although Berrick hadn't shown up yet. Brad was ahead of goal, and Katy was in second place overall. She didn't look up to acknowledge the compliment. She just glared at her watermelon and adjoining slice of cantaloupe. Was she solar powered? When Coach finished, he looked at each of us and then at me, expectantly.

"What?" I asked, my mouth full of food.

Coach sighed. "I think we should also take a moment to say goodbye to Berrick. I know it's not tradition here—we lose people all the time—but he was a good man."

"What?" I said again. "He just DNF'd." I looked around. "Didn't he?"

Tommy shook his head. "He died after surgery last night. Apparently they had the system calibrated for a modified patient and the anesthesia killed him."

"You're kidding." This had to be a joke, or just more hazing. "You're *kidding*, right?" How could Dr. Rai make such a basic mistake? Then a horrific thought, that maybe it wasn't a mistake. But that was impossible. None of it made sense. How could he be dead?

Coach lowered his head. We all followed suit, me still waiting for the punchline. Berrick was fine. He smelled bad and his leg was jacked, but he was alive. He hadn't even been in my social feed that morning, and I mean nothing. This was impossible.

"Okay," Coach said. "There's a crowdfunding campaign set up for donations to his family. I expect all of you to donate. Now, for the—"

"Wait, that's it?" I blurted. "He died and…" Well, what? Since when did anyone pay attention to the death of a natural? I barely knew him. Why did I care so much?

"Yes?" Coach asked.

"I just…" I looked around, but no one met my eyes. Even Tommy seemed to be over it. "This is bullshit. He was a human being. He *died*." Half the cafeteria turned to listen. I'm sure Jessica was laughing her ass off. Brad looked at his hands, but my attention was on Tommy. "He was your friend. How is this okay?"

"It's not okay, Fiddy. It's just how it is."

"It's just…" Coach's hand rested on mine. I looked up at his bottomless blue eyes and realized none of them thought it was okay, not even him. It was just a performance, pretending not to care, because the alternative was somehow worse.

"I'm sorry, Media."

"Sorry?" This was unbelievable. "Never mind." I pulled my hand away. Naturals died. It was the way of things. At least he didn't burn, and maybe it was easier if we pretended not to care, but it still didn't feel right. I looked for Danny again. I couldn't see him anywhere in the hall. I knew he was okay, but I hated what they were saying about us online. Had he told someone about last night? Did everyone know, or were they just guessing? Would they care more if he died? The answer was obvious: of course not. I looked down and poked at my last pancake. I tried to remember my conversation with Berrick, something to remember him by, but nothing came to mind. Brad cleared his throat.

"You'll get used to it," he said quietly.

"No, I won't. None of us should."

It Works

I AVOIDED TALKING TO anyone in the starting corral. Jessica brushed past me on her way to the front, trying to pick a fight I'd lose. I ignored her, so she probably tormented someone else. Danny and Shaquilla were the only two naturals left and right behind me. But I couldn't face Danny after last night or this morning, so I kept my head down and he spent a lot of time stretching. Tommy glanced back several times, worried, but I couldn't face him either. I was upset. Berrick was dead. I'd never known anyone who died before, except lab subjects, and with them it was a big deal. There was an autopsy, investigation, reports, protocol changes and more, and we were just betas. Not real people. What about Berrick's family? Had someone even bothered to tell them?

Wait, had I just thought of naturals as real people but not me?

I looked up and screamed silently at the sky.

"You okay, Media?" Coach asked. I'm sure my stats were a disaster.

"Yeah," I lied. *"I'm fine."* It was time to focus on the race.

Inhale. Exhale. Count down the seconds until Smith told us to, "GO!"

We went. I sped through the lower course, flying over the Pits and climbing the Pillars even faster than the day before. I was at the testing center so quickly, I surprised even Coach.

"How much coffee did you drink?"

"Was that a compliment?" I opened the testing center door and went in, cutting off any response. I smiled at Dayglow, Butterflies and the Demon, and nodded to Dr. K. She was wearing her down coat, so I knew it was colder in the room than yesterday. I was freezing in

seconds and my teeth started chattering. Apparently, I'd lost some body fat along with the water weight.

"Let's do this." Whatever Victor wanted from the races, this was his last chance, so it was going to suck. Better to get it over with.

Butterflies nodded as if agreeing.

Black.

White.

"What?" My breath came out in a billow of frost. I was shaking madly, uncontrollably, and my hands were numb, but there was no nausea or pain and they were all smiling at me. Why were they all so happy? Dr. K looked like she was going to burst out in song.

"It worked?"

Dr. K nodded. "It worked."

I checked my skin, trying to be subtle—I assumed the judges were all in on it, but I wasn't sure how explicit that was—but nothing had changed. My skin was still my skin, if a slightly darker Pantone than I'd started the race with due to all the sun.

"I don't see anything." I looked at Dr. K. "You're sure?"

"Yes." She leaned forward and touched my arm. I stared at her tiny little fingers, her perfect nails. When was the last time she touched me? "It worked *perfectly*."

I felt lightheaded. I'd done what Victor asked, even if I had no idea if he'd gotten what he wanted from the tests. TTI was safe. My family and I were safe. I pressed my hand over Dr. K's, thanking her as much as I ever had. Oddly, the next thing in my head was that I could just run now. There was no pressure and no other agenda. I could just enjoy the rest of the lap. For a few hours, I was free. I smiled like a lunatic.

"Can I go?"

"Absolutely," Demon said. "And thank you."

Did he know how creepy that sounded? I fought a shudder and headed for the door. It was time to kick Abbey Zuniga's condescending ass all over the mountain.

*

THERE WERE MORE FANS at the aid station this time, hundreds of them. Most cheered when they saw me, but many booed. Someone threw an apple, but I caught it before it clocked me. A synthetic immediately appeared at the apple-thrower's side and escorted him back to the tram. The apple was delicious, but even the aid station volunteers seemed a bit nervous.

"How're you feeling?" one of the men asked, his skin charcoal gray with vertical silver lines as if he'd been pinstriped. He probably wanted to know why I was still shivering.

"Hungry."

I filled up my water, ate, and asked if there were any pickles. There were not. I swallowed some salt pills instead.

"How far ahead is Abbey?"

Pinstripe frowned, thinking. "A bit. Don't forget to drink."

"Did Coach put you up to this?"

"Hydrate or die."

Point taken.

A Pleasure to Burn

I STOPPED SHORT OF the summit aid station and tried to de-spider-web myself. It didn't work. Dead spiders were smooshed all over me and I was starving, so whatever. I was about to head over and grab some food when I noticed Jessica at one of the tables, chatting up a volunteer. It made no sense—she should be far ahead of me and everyone else—until I remembered she was just there to watch Abbey. I glanced around but didn't see any sign of the Zuniga, so I kept my eyes down and tried not to be noticed. Jessica chit-chatted like anyone else. She snacked just as randomly as I did. Even her laugh wasn't the sadistic cackle I expected.

"Stinky's here!" one of the volunteers exclaimed. Great. Another volunteer elbowed him. Jessica glanced at me and then away, as if I were of no importance.

"I hear it's huge," a volunteer said to Jessica. "Biggest one they've ever had."

Jessica gnawed on the end of a meat stick, considering. "I love the giant animals. Hope I get to see one." She sounded like Brad. I stood as far away from her as possible and started grabbing at food, quickly, afraid she might smash my hand down on the table if I left it out too long. I didn't need much right now. I could pick up more on the way down once Jessica was gone.

I thanked the volunteer who hadn't called me Stinky. Jessica glanced over again, annoyed. Side glared? It wasn't a friendly look. I still couldn't figure out what she was doing there. I hadn't realized how tall she was. I felt puny and helpless next to her, which was pretty accurate. She could snap me in half without even trying.

Thank god this was my last loop.

A thought which made me a bit sad. I was going to miss this. Well, most of it.

"You drinking enough?" the volunteer asked as I left. I nodded, but I probably wasn't.

All the way up the final scramble, I kept checking behind me, looking for Jessica in every shadow. I was so busy looking behind myself I nearly missed Abbey waiting at the summit. That explained why Jessica was hanging around, but why would Abbey waste time on the peak? She watched me tag the summit post and then nodded to the rock next to her, careful to keep herself out of touching range.

"You're covered in spider guts," she noted.

I looked at the rock, at her, curious. And sitting down seemed lovely. So I plunked down a careful distance from her, violating Tommy's number one rule of ultrarunning.

"What's in Jenny One?" I asked. She shrugged. "Okay. What are you doing here?" Then I noticed where she was looking. Black smoke rose into the smeary sky toward the coast, a dark gray smudge in an orange sky somewhere over Los Angeles. "What's that?

"Riots, I'd guess. Berrick's death must've set off the animals."

"They're not animals." I'm not sure I said it with conviction. The Social Stability Algorithm implicitly encouraged slow death by malnutrition. It's hard to fight when you can't walk, but apparently naturals could still riot. I thought about Danny and wondered where he was from. Was his home on fire as he ran up and down the mountain? "They should be angry about what happened to Berrick. It was wrong."

"They're burning their own neighborhoods and they expect us to put it out. *Animals*. Thugs. Beasts. It's us or them.

Not sure why you don't get that. I'd burn them all if I could."

"I was one of them once." One of *them*. It was so easy to think of naturals as less than human.

Abbey smiled coldly. "We both were. I still wish we could prevent them entirely from breeding." She sighed as if lamenting the misery of natural existence. "You want to go back?"

This conversation wasn't going anywhere. I started to stand just to get away from her, but Tommy was right. Sitting had been a bad idea. Everything was stiff and painful.

"*Relax*," Abbey texted me. I was suddenly in privacy mode and Coach was gone. I sat down, half in surprise, half because standing was going to be a process.

"What the—"

"*Text only.*"

"*How are you doing this?*"

"*How do you not understand money? We have only two minutes off net. I've been waiting forever. Can we get this over with?*"

We were all alone on top of the mountain. Jessica didn't seem to be any closer. I shrugged.

"*What do you want?*"

"*I'm supposed to make you an offer. If you drop out on this lap before finishing the Fun Run, we'll put five million new dollars in escrow for your family. You won't be able to touch it while you're at TTI, but it will be there when you need it.*"

"*No.*"

"*Consider it.*"

"*No.*" It was ridiculous. I had no privacy. There was no way to hide something like that, and I wouldn't take money from her anyway.

"*Okay, I had to make the offer. I knew you wouldn't take it. Thanks for putting up with that.*"

"*That's it?*" It was the least sincere bribe ever. She had just risked disqualification, and she clearly didn't care what I said.

"*Take it as a compliment. You're doing better than Blindside expected. They're worried.*"

"*You're not?*"

"*No. I'm going to win this race. You're just doing the Fun Run. You're a sideshow.*"

"*You're sweet. I can see why Tommy liked you.*"

She twitched and looked away for a second. "*I didn't do it, you know.*"

"*Do what? Pay my brother for sex or GIP yourself out of a job?*"

Her mouth opened, closed. Fists clenched. "*Like you've never had them do things to you without telling you. I have no idea how I got that DNA, or who benefited from it. Black Rook was probably testing something in the field and used me. You don't believe me, do you?"* I didn't, but she plowed on. *"I wouldn't be here if someone hadn't pulled a few strings for me. I want to think it was Tommy, but I don't know. If you ever find out, will you thank them for me?"*

"What?" I hadn't seen that coming. Privacy mode dropped out and Coach was back before I could say anything else, which was probably better. Being confused just made me angry. Who was she trying to kid with the sincere act?

"See you at the bottom," she said, taking off. She was probably more annoyed about having to wait for me than the rest of it, but it also made me wonder what else Blindside would do to win. Physical assault was allowed on loops four and five, even encouraged, so it was a good thing I was just doing the Fun Run. I wouldn't want to come across Jessica in the middle of the woods.

And right on time, Jessica appeared from behind a small stand of trees and scrambled up the final slabs of rock toward me. I jumped up, groaning at the pain of stiff muscles, and did my best to mountain-goat around the trees and away from her.

"Run, lab rat, run!" she called mockingly, but at least she stopped on the summit. Even if she couldn't touch me on this lap, accidents happen. I didn't intend to be one of them. Fortunately, she sprinted by when I was back at the aid station.

The Lights Go Out

ON LOOP TWO, the monkey bar branches had been almost the same as on the first loop, with the exception that if you hung too long on one branch, it would start to droop until you were hanging from a smooth wooden stalactite. I'd been too fast for that to happen then, but my hands were still shot from yesterday's climb out of the pit. Dr. Rai's salve had taken care of my thigh and my pinky seemed to work, more or less, but my finger tendons were still stressed and painful. Every time I closed my fist around a branch, I winced at the pain and effort.

I avoided even looking up to see if the snake was there. I could feel it above me, coiled, ready to wrap me in its thick body and squeeze the life out, but if I didn't see it, I could almost pretend it was just my imagination. Besides, there was something new to focus on. The purplish veins that ran over the branches had tiny lumps every few inches. The lumps swelled and developed points, as if something sharp was fighting its way out. Then tiny needles like cactus spines slid out. I timed my next swing poorly and drove one into my left palm, right through my glove.

"Son of a bi—"

"*Just keep moving,*" Coach said. "*They're not poisonous.*"

Yeah, I thought, *but they hurt.* I didn't bother saying it out loud. Coach wouldn't care. I pulled my hand away and swung toward the next branch, making sure to avoid the needles. There were a lot of them. Sometimes I missed. Sometimes I poked holes in myself even with the climbing gloves. By the time I neared the end, I was bleeding from dozens of punctures in my hands and wrists.

I reached for the final branch and transitioned my weight forward, legs swinging toward the edge of the pool. And then the python's face appeared in front of me, long tongue playing inches from my hand and…

"Media, she won't strike."

…I just let go. I didn't even have time to scream. My legs shot forward as my upper body dropped toward the edge of the pond. I still remember the sight of my right hand clutching at the air and then my head slammed into the dirt.

Black.

Blue.

I was staring up at a gray-blue sky full of little golden stars that flicker-flicked in and out like electrical shocks. My head was wet and I sat up with a jerk, thinking it was blood. Or maybe it was water. Where was the snake? My heart rate spiked and the gray turned

black.

Brown.

My face was in the dirt. There was dirt in my mouth and eyes. I sat up again, slowly, and spit. The synthetic monitor crouched nearby, watching quietly. I looked for the snake, but it was hidden back up in the trees. I couldn't believe I'd done that. I'd never felt so out of control of my own reactions, except in the lab when something went wrong, and at least then Dr. K was there to take care of it. Now my own mind was betraying me.

"You have a minor concussion," the synthetic said. Coach concurred.

I touched my head again. No blood.

"You'll be fine, but you should take it easy for a few minutes."

"Fine?" I stood, nauseated, and tried desperately not to throw up on his pretty plaid pants and black Ghillie Brogue shoes.

"Start moving. You'll be dizzy for a while, but it's either that or drop."

There was no way I was dropping. I spit out some grit, wiped my face, and tried to get my hand to unclench. My fingers moved slowly, achingly. The walls were going to be fun.

Somehow, I didn't think I was going to catch Abbey.

*

I DON'T REMEMBER THE next few sections, and I didn't even have Alex to record them for me. I've included some snapshots here for continuity, but I don't know any more than what shows up on the video recap. The first thing I remember was standing at the edge of the Scree Slope with the wind in my hair and an inexplicable sense of joy and wellbeing. I have no idea why. This is the best reconstruction I can come up with:

Each step at the Air Stairs was now a foot higher than the one before it, so I had to run and jump up a total of nine feet before ejecting at the end. I barely made every jump. A few more inches and the story would be very different.

Lazarus Lake was another five degrees cooler and the swim across was brisk. The octopus played with my calves as I swam, never quite grabbing on, but suckering here and there, letting me know what was coming. I have no recollection of it, but in the video it was quite playful, like swimming with a giant Paisley. By the time I reached the other side, I was shivering cold and my fingers were slightly blue. Just another sign I was dehydrated.

Nothing exciting happened on the way to the aid station in Long Valley. I staggered a bit. I tripped several times. Coach apparently told me encouraging things, but there was nobody home to hear him. Thankfully, my body took care of the eating and drinking. The volunteers refilled my water bladder and I walked toward the edge of the mountain.

And then lights came on.

I Have an Idea

"HOLY CRAP." I STEPPED back from the edge of the Scree Slope. My ears rung and the world seemed a bit off kilter, but my brain was back online. I caught my breath and looked over the edge. Palm Springs was a glorious gray nothing 8,000 feet below, a shimmering smear of browned oatmeal speckled with shiny silver shards like spikes driven through my eyes.

"*You back with us?*"

"Yeah. Kinda." I clenched my eyes shut to clear the pain. I opened them, and Palm Springs was just Palm Springs again. I had a welt just above my hairline the size of a golf ball, which is to say, a delicious sushi ball. Which made me hungry. Stu grumbled. Some things never change.

I stepped forward.

"*Take it easy. Abbey's too far ahead. You're not going to catch her.*"

Well, that was disappointing. I was going to say something snide, but suddenly I felt this overwhelming flood of joy, a full-body release of endorphins or hallucinogens or just random happiness. I caught my breath and tried not to fall off the edge as my knees started to buckle. And then the feeling was gone and I felt peaceful. Content. I didn't even care about Abbey anymore. I was losing my mind.

"*You okay? Your stats—*"

"No, I mean, yeah. I'm good."

Suspicious silence.

I stepped forward again. I had this.

I damn near fell a dozen times, and it wasn't anything Shaquilla would be impressed by, but I made it. My biggest issue was a lot of rocks in my shoes. I was suddenly in a war against hitchhiking pebbles and sand. Like the whole trail was covered in hobos trying to get off the mountain and my shoes were the last ride down. I emptied my shoes but new rocks hopped right back in.

The wall at 7,500 feet was the first one I struggled with. My hands were screwed. My arms were spent and Media was pretty much fried. I still felt strangely at peace, but that feeling didn't seem to extend to the rest of my body. I straddled the top of the wall and caught my breath. What wall was this? Air whistled through my head. It was the thirty-sixth, Coach finally told me. I'd apparently forgotten how to do basic math in my head. I dropped down, taking more of a hit to the knees than I meant to, and grunted like a tennis star. Only six to go.

The walls fell away in a dreamy, hallucinogenic countdown. Everything hurt and yet nothing hurt. I found myself singing as I jogged, random parts of songs I could remember without Alex. I was utterly alone except for the synthetic monitors, and yet I knew the world was watching. And I didn't care. I didn't care about anything.

I don't know how to describe what I felt. In the blazing heat, with occasionally blurred vision and serious dehydration, with shredded tendons and blistered feet, I felt oddly at peace. At home. I must've hit my head harder than I realized.

And then I was at the Pits.

"Hi, Tim!" I called into the molten air. He roared in response, or something did. How would I know? But I knew. Tim missed me.

My race almost ended here. I didn't have the balance for the slacklines, so I took long, running leaps to clear each hole. And, every time, I nearly missed my landing. Any miss and I would've spent the rest of the day in a net, hopefully, hanging above Tim and too weak to climb out. But somehow I made it, jumping farther than I knew I could. And I was totally at peace with that too.

The climb to the next wall was terrible. The heat was savage. But time passed and soon I was over the last wall by the picnic tables and people were there, cheering and spraying me with heavenly cold mist. I was doing this. I was going to finish a Fun Run. Maybe not first, not even close to first, but so what? I'd done it. I imagined the smile on my brother's face, joy in my father's eyes, and my mother's gleeful clapping, but none of that really mattered. For the first time in my life, I'd done something on my own. I was going to finish a Marathons Fun Run and go back to TTI a rock star.

And just like that, all the happy thoughts were gone.

"You okay?" somebody asked—a nice lady under a giant umbrella by the side of the trail with a spray bottle. I just stared at her.

"No," I said. "I'm…"

From less than a thousand feet below, I heard Smith over the loudspeakers telling everyone I'd soon be there. Cheering erupted with each announcement as her voice rolled up the mountain. I could feel the cheers in my chest and I felt like I was choking. Why couldn't I breathe?

"Media?" the woman asked quietly. "Media?"

And then I got it. It wasn't enough. Finishing the Fun Run wasn't enough. Getting out of the lab for a few days wasn't enough. My family was safe and I was going to a new lab, but I'd never get out again—not with this new camouflage feature dependent on my DNA. I'd never run with Tommy in the mountains. That fantasy future vanished the second I crossed the finish line. And what I'd feared my entire life, deoptimization, being natural again, no longer scared me as much. Berrick died due to incompetence or malfeasance, not weakness. And Danny wasn't that far behind me, kicking San Jacinto's ass without any modifications to help. Being natural was hard, but it wasn't a death sentence for everyone. What had I been so frightened of? Even if I died out here, my family would survive. No one was going to light them on fire.

All of which was dancing around an obvious point. I didn't want to go home yet. I didn't want to leave the race. The thought of the lab made me stick to my stomach.

"Coach," I said, while looking at the confused woman.

"*Yes?*"

"I'm having an idea."

Coach waited. The woman smiled. Smith's voice boomed across the sky, calling me down. I told Coach my idea. He said it wasn't my best idea. Well, what he said was, "*You've got to be fucking kidding,*" but

I read between the lines. He asked if I was sure. I pretended I was, and he pretended to believe me. We were really starting to understand each other. The woman slowly backed away.

A moment later, Coach had conceded and I'd made a decision that would change the rest of my life. I didn't know it then, of course, because I was flying, bounding from boulder to boulder, leaping like Shaquilla toward the finish. Smith called my name. The crowd cheered. The cheer went from "Stinky! Stinky!" to "Fiddy! Fiddy" as I got closer, and I waved, gratefully. I wasn't going to be remembered for the stench of French cheese. Thank god.

"I'm coming!" I danced over rocks and cacti, sprinting toward the finish. "I'm coming!"

Fun Run, Done

I FINISHED IN 10:01:14, my fastest loop of the Fun Run by a nearly two hours. Smith put a Fun Run finisher medal around my neck and said congratulations without irony, which meant she didn't know yet. I high-fived a dozen people I'd never seen before and then found myself in a group hug with Tommy, Brad, Mom, Dad and even Katy. Coach stood back and watched with a careful smile and rehydration drinks in both hands.

"You did it," they all said one way or another. *You did a Fun Run. You made it. You did it. We're so proud.*

"God, you smell," Brad added.

"I know, right?"

"Where are the pipers?" Mom asked. "They need to play you out." She had a tissue in hand, ready for an ugly, happy cry.

"They're not coming," Tommy said.

"What?" Mom's eyes widened. "Why?"

Dad and Brad frowned, an almost identical expression. Mom looked around in confusion until a new smile took over.

"Did you hear about the tests?" She bounced on her toes. "You were doing a secret test for new skin colors?" I guess it wasn't that secret anymore. "And it worked!" A little more helium in her head and she'd just float away. "The—"

"Tell them," Tommy snapped, interrupting Mom, which he never did.

"Tell us what?" Dad asked. Mom looked like a deer right before the car hit.

I took a breath. Tommy waited. Brad frowned. Coach just

shrugged. Where was Danny?

"I'm going to keep going," I said.

"Going where?" Mom asked.

"Goddamn it!" Dad said, the first time I'd ever heard him swear. Brad's veins throbbed in surprise. Katy barked, which I realized was actually a laugh, and then covered her mouth and fled with one hand up in apology.

"I'm going to do the full race." I tried to sound confident. "I'm not stopping."

I felt sorry for Mom—she'd seized up, hands mid-clap, face mid-smile, on her toes and yet weighted to the ground—but Dad's expression nearly broke me. I didn't know what to say. I promise not to die? Nothing would help.

"Dad?"

His mouth opened and closed. He shook his head as if trying to shake something loose. I'd broken him.

"Dad?"

He stood back and left without another word, dragging Mom behind him like a confused dingy. Others followed, and I was soon alone with Coach and a crowd cheering for Danny as he stumble-fell toward the finish. I had no idea he was so close behind me.

"Well, that went well," Coach said. He offered me a bottle of chocolate something-or-other that I drank far too quickly. "They'll come around."

But I wasn't so sure. I also wasn't sure I cared. I was doing this. Me. And I didn't need anyone's approval. Though it would've been nice.

Danny staggered across the finish line, bent over, and dry heaved as the crowd lost its mind. He was the second natural to finish a Fun Run, ever, and well under cutoff time. He was going to be a legend, even if Shaquilla had finished nearly two hours ahead of him in cumulative time due to his issues on loop two. Shaquilla gave him a big hug after Smith put the Fun Run finisher medal around his neck, and he congratulated her for the win. After she left, I walked over and offered Danny my congratulations and an awkward hug. He looked guilty, as if I'd caught him cheating, but mostly he looked like he wanted to die.

"Well, that was terrible," he said, but he was smiling. He'd done the impossible. He'd get everything he wanted for himself and his family, return next year modified and probably beat us all. It took me a while to realize the crowd was chanting his nickname. My docker count had never been higher, but they were there because of him. I felt a strange surge of pride for what he'd done, for the strength of what he was. I stepped back and let him take it in.

He raised his hand in triumph.

"Legs! Legs!"

Then I made the mistake of checking my social feed. It was two hurricanes colliding, love and rage, pride and disgust, a sickening tempest of petty inhumanity. There was so much positivity about the finish that it almost balanced out the hatred about my relationship with Danny, but not quite. I shut off the feed and told Coach I was going to shower before dinner. I was turning away when I noticed Abbey looking at me like I'd lost my mind. She held her hands out in the universal 'what are you thinking?' gesture as I looked around for Jessica. I hadn't really thought this through very well. What had I done?

"You made the right choice," Coach said, doing his usual mind-reader trick.

"How do you know?"

"Because they hate you for it." Which was less comforting than you might think. "Speaking of which, Smith wants to see you in the clinic."

The Grand Illusion

JESSICA WALKED OUT OF the clinic just as I got there, looking sharp and clean as a dagger. The Mobius DNA of Genetic Overwatch was right at my eye level on her armband. She blocked the door and I looked around pointlessly. We were alone in the hall, but even if we weren't, she could still kill me and ride my body down the hall like a toboggan. No one would stop her. My modifist dockers would cheer her on. Instead of murdering me, she smiled, which was somehow worse.

"You did well today." She looked down at me like I'd look at Doofus.

"Thanks?" The uplifting inflection was an accident, not a question, but she didn't answer or even blink. It took me a moment to register the sound of her unwrapping a candy bar. I looked at my now empty hand. "Uh." How'd she do that?

"Not so clever after all." She took a bite of my chocolate bar. Stu told me to smack her. I knew she could kill me with an eyelash, but stealing my chocolate was just mean.

"See you tomorrow," she said as if we had a date. Maybe we did.

She walked away and the clinic door slid open. I walked in to find myself facing Smith, Dr. Rai and Dr. K, who no longer looked so absurdly pleased with herself.

"What was Jessica doing here?" I demanded, going for a good offensive opening.

"Looking at test results," Dr. Rai said neutrally.

"Whose?" I panicked. So much for the offense. "Mine?"

"And Tommy's."

"She can do that?"

"She can do whatever she wants." Smith was clearly irritated.

Must be nice. "Anything—"

"Sit." Smith nodded toward the exam table. I guess I was everyone's good little dog today. I limped to the table—I was quickly stiffening up—and plunked down as loudly as I could. Dr. K flinched. She hated loud noises. I think that's why I started swearing when I began working with her. It was so easy to get under her skin.

"You can't continue," she said. "Not now. You know—"

"Yes, I can." Pause. "Can't I?" I mean, I had no idea. I thought I could, but Coach was still blocking Alex, and he didn't seem interested in helping. Dr. K looked like she was ready to stroke out. Smith was obviously pissed, which I enjoyed more than I should have.

"Not without TTI permission," Smith and Kylera said at the same time.

Or maybe not. I hadn't thought about that.

"So I'll ask Victor." I tried to sound confident. Why would he care? He'd gotten the test results he wanted, and no one caught us breaking the rules. Why begrudge me a little (very dangerous and possibly lethal) fun?

Smith seemed to lose interest and nodded to Dr. Rai, who raised a syringe in a very nonchalant way. I pulled my arm back and glanced at Dr. K, who nodded. Seconds later, Rai was taking vial after vial of blood.

"Why now?" I asked Smith. "You got some at the testing center."

"This is for us," Dr. K said, taking the vials and pocketing them like secret candy. "The testing center samples are always destroyed. You did it, Media. I don't understand why—"

"I know," I snapped. God, I was grumpy. I was tired, hungry and thirsty, and just wanted a shower and food. My clarity of purpose from the racecourse had vanished under their collective glare, and I felt like a child, which just made me angrier.

"Have you seen our stock price?" Dr. K asked.

"Seriously?" I realized Alex was back and checked. TTI stock was skyrocketing. They'd already leaked it. Hurray for them. "Look, you got what you wanted. I just want to finish the race before going back to the lab." This was for Dr. K: "What do you care?"

"I know it's a lot to take in, Media." She was trying so hard to be earnest. It wasn't her strong suit. "But we're safe now. The company's safe. You don't have to run again."

"I *want* to run again. How do you not understand that?"

"Media," Smith said. "We just want you to be safe."

"*Safe?*" I wanted to throat-punch her matronizing ass right back into the Middle Ages, but that's what she wanted. For some reason, I thought of the sheep that knocked Jasmina off the trail, and I felt a flood of envy and sympathy. Yeah, it was probably dead, but for just that moment, as it watched Jasmina tumble over the cliff, it was worth it.

"Media," Dr. K said. I hated the way she said my name now, like she owned it. Like she had always owned it. "You don't know how big this is. TTI is safe. We're safe."

"*You're* safe. I still go back to the lab so you can perfect it. Maybe not the beta lab, but still the lab. I don't get to run again, do I?" I could hear the desperation in my own voice, and hated myself for sounding weak.

"You're too important, Media, to—"

"Whatever. I'm not stopping. Victor understands. He won't stop me." Which probably wasn't true. "And if I die, you can get more of your precious DNA off my corpse. You own it anyway. What does it matter?"

"Media, this is ridiculous," Dr. K snapped. "You're TTI property. I don't have to sit here and..." She bit back whatever she was going to say. I hadn't seen her angry that often, but I knew she was furious. How dare I not be a good little lab rat? Didn't I know how lucky I was? She looked down and had the decency to look ashamed. Smith was perfectly delighted.

"Doctors, why don't you give us a few moments?"

Dr. K opened her mouth, glanced at Smith, but thought better of it. She seemed so much smaller out of the lab, reduced and a bit pathetic. God, I felt mean. I didn't even acknowledge her goodbye. When she was gone, Dr. Rai opened her hand to offer me a small white pill.

"For your concussion."

I pocketed it for later, and she backed into the corner and turned to stone, in rest mode.

"You didn't ask what Jessica was looking for," Smith said quietly.

"The color change thing?"

Smith shook her head. "No. She wanted blood samples and lab results for you and Tommy, and for the naturals—which we don't have, of course. Why would anyone care?"

She waited for a reaction, but I was still thinking about Jessica. Was she suspicious of what Victor was doing? If so, why did she care about Tommy and naturals?

"She also asked to see Berrick's body."

"What?"

"But I told her TTI had it incinerated."

"You mean cremated."

"Do I?"

"Why would she want that? Do you think she killed him?" That was one of the rumors.

"No. She's lifting rocks to see what crawls out. She won't see anything I don't want her to." Which was a strange statement, sure, but I couldn't tell if she was implying something or just arrogant. I didn't have the energy to guess. Smith glanced at Dr. Rai, who remained synthetically statuesque, and then forced a smile.

"You've got the bug," she said. "You really want this, don't you? For yourself, I mean."

I just glared. How dare she understand me?

"If you don't mind, I'd like to continue this conversation privately."

Alex went offline, and I was in privacy mode.

"How does everyone keep doing that?"

She smiled, her way of saying, *I can see you're an idiot, but I forgive you.*

"We can talk freely. All security in the room has been disabled. She's offline." Meaning Dr. Rai. "No one can hear or record us."

"Why would they want to?"

"I know you're tired, so I'll tell you a very badly kept secret. This…" she said, indicating everything, "…is a facade. I know you've seen *The Wizard of Oz* and old movies like *The Matrix.* You're familiar with the concept of a Grand Illusion or, in this case, delusion?"

"PA visual themes? Of course, I—"

"It'll go faster if you don't speak. The true illusion isn't visual, it's social. Society hasn't functioned as a viable system for decades. It doesn't serve the majority. It barely serves the minority. And yet it persists because the only other option is extinction or revolution. Eleven billion naturals against a billion modified, with synthetics watching as we all bleed out. Liberals cry that business is the problem, but they know we need taxes generated by that system to pay for social welfare programs. Conservatives like those neo-Nazi fascists in the Ascension Party pretend they hate socialism, but they know without welfare programs and synthetic bans, there wouldn't be a job left for any human being. So, what's the alternative?"

"I assume it's the Grand Illusion?"

"Exactly. We maintain the illusion of a society, of a free market regulated by a democratic government, where human labor, indeed human existence, still has material value and meaning."

"Until what?" I asked. "And who is *we?*" Other than people like Victor, of course.

"*Who* doesn't matter, meaning that I'm not entirely sure I know, even though I might be one of them. I'm not sure anyone knows. It's not a conspiracy of modified elites in a bunker pulling virtual levers, or an AI illusion. It's not even world powers clinging to the international order of things. It's a conspiracy of desperate people with vast power afraid of a future they can't predict. They just know they'll blow up the world before anyone takes it away from them."

Well, that's terrifying. "A system run by no one with no purpose but its own survival?"

"Yes. Rather biological, but none of that's going to be impacted by what we discuss today. Your first question, until *what*, has an obvious answer: until we find a better solution or the system fails. The real question is, until *when.* Which is just another way of asking how long we can keep the system running in its current state."

"Which is?"

"I have no idea. All I know is, you feed the illusion or everything falls apart. I don't want it to fall apart. I have no desire to be ripped apart by a mob of naturals nor, believe it or not, to have them exterminated by extremists like Captain Murphy. I'm truly sad about Berrick. And that brings us back to you and this race. The Marathons are a tiny piece of the system, probably not even that important. I have no delusion in that regard, but I do know the arena was central to Rome. People need their distractions. There's more to it than that but, for now, all that matters is that the people watching, your fans, your dockers and all the rest, believe the illusion—and that they suspend their disbelief for as long as possible. I won't let anyone get in the way of that. Not you, not Victor, not TTI. No one."

"How would—"

She held up a hand. "There's always been cheating in sports, and we're no exception. We look the other way so brands can maintain their image, so athletes can test secret modifications, so gamblers can pay runners to drop out, and even—and this is important for you, Media—so companies can run field testing programs outside their corporate firewalls."

"The camouflage thing? That test is over, and you had to know about it."

"Don't do that. Don't play the idiot. I couldn't care less about dermal modification. I'm glad for Victor and Kylera. They've worked hard for it, and Blindside is run by idiots. But we both know there's more going on."

I looked down, hoping she couldn't read my expression. Did she know what Victor was doing, or was she only guessing?

"I know you don't trust me, and I don't blame you," she said. "But did you know that when TTI ran that ridiculous sting with Tommy and Abbey, that I was part of it? I supported them then. I support them now."

"What?" That threw me.

"If they include me, I'll help again. I was glad to let Abbey in the games so she wouldn't be fully deoptimized. I know Victor did it out of compassion, but it cost me. All the changes he demanded this year cost me. And the naturals?" She shook her head in disgust. "He owes me. I'm calling in that chit. I need him to get you under control, and I need it now."

"Director Smith, I honestly have no idea what you're talking about. And even if I did, I'd be bound by TTI confidentiality. Why don't you ask Victor?"

"He won't talk to me, so this is all on you."

"But—"

"Media, your VO_2 max on Sunday was 62. High, but not unrealistic. Today you tested at 78. We doctored the results so other teams and Genetic Overwatch wouldn't see it—which is why there was nothing for Jessica to find—but we're losing control. In a race famous for cheating, where cheating is almost the point, you're still goddamn cheating."

"What?" I was as surprised as she was. That was insane. That was *impossible.*

"Minor improvement in adjusted VO_2 max is normal as you lose weight during the games, but sixteen points in four days is unheard of. Your blood oxygenation level has *increased* to nearly one-hundred percent. Your resting heart rate has fallen dramatically. There are dozens of stress factors that are multiple standard deviations from where they should be, and all in the same improbable direction. You're ten times the athlete now than you were when you started. Don't pretend you didn't notice how easily you finished today. We both know you're not that stupid."

But I wasn't so sure. Why hadn't Coach or Alex said anything? Did Dr. K know? Was that why she wanted me off the course? I felt like throwing up. What the hell was Victor doing to me, and why was he making it so obvious? This wasn't what I signed up for.

"Now," Smith said. "We both know you're not going to tell me what's going on, so here are the rules. I don't care what Victor's doing. I don't care if it kills you or bankrupts TTI, as long as it doesn't come back on me. If anyone finds out what's happening, if any test is flagged as suspect and I can't suppress it, if Jessica gets too close or even one influential docker raises a virtual eyebrow, you're going to end up lunch for one of the pit animals. And no TTI athlete, including Tommy, will get off this course alive again. Are we clear?"

My heart stopped. "If you ever hurt Tommy—"

"Are we *clear*? No miraculous loop wins. No impossible improvements in abilities. And don't even think about beating one of the endurance models. I can hide this if it's not much more obvious, but we're out of room. Do well enough to clean things up, but no better. That's it."

"I'll quit. I'll pull out. Just don't hurt my brother."

Smith glared at me for a moment, her face a mask of rage.

"You don't know," she said.

"Know what?"

"Victor approved your request to continue. He's ignoring my calls. Coach Johnson already put you on the starting list for tomorrow. You can't pull out now without raising suspicions, and I can't disqualify you without evidence that would incriminate me, so you're in."

It was like she was the python. I felt a wave of nausea and panic.

"If you don't start," she said, "or if you quit too easily, even if you get yourself cleverly disqualified, Tommy dies. I'll have Coach Johnson scrapped just because I can." She stood, done with me. "You have two laps to fix this, and all you have to do is be the average baseline you're supposed to be." Then, oddly sincere: "Good luck."

"No." I stood to face her but had to keep one hand on the table to stabilize myself. "I'm not putting Tommy in danger. I'm out. You're Beast Brain. Come up with a way to cover it up. Tell them TTI pulled me because of the skin thing. There's no way in hell I'm going back out there now. I'll throw myself off the roof before you hurt my brother."

Yeah, that was not a good look. That was an *I'd-kill-you-if-I-could* look. My nausea was replaced by a familiar smell, burning wood and bone, and I could almost feel the fire lick at my skin.

"TTI forced naturals onto my course and caught the eye of Genetic Overwatch." This came out in carefully enunciated syllables where every space was a moment of constraint. "Captain Murphy is in my race because of you. She could walk back through that door and kill both of us, and no one could stop her. She could kill your entire family, and no one would give a damn. TTI brought this to my house, so you need to understand the stakes. You don't get to quit. You don't get to think. You'll run because you need to clean up the mess you've made, and if you don't, everyone finds out about your father's idiotic hack. He'll be in federal prison before you get out of this building. I'll kill Brad just for fucking someone so ridiculously naïve."

"You—" I stood to face her.

"Sit!" she yelled. I sat.

"Tell me you understand."

"Yes." No. "I'll do it. I'll run."

"But not too fast."

"But not too fast." Why was it so hard to breathe?

Smith left. I exhaled slowly, intentionally, trying not to hyperventilate. Alex came back online. My stomach was screaming, but there wasn't a single thought in my head that made sense. How did I end up in the middle of all this? And how could I get myself and Tommy out of it? Would she really hurt Tommy and Brad just—

"Don't forget your pill," Dr. Rai said. I nearly screamed.

Death by Jazz

"PLAY SOME SMOOTH JAZZ." I lay back on my bed and waited. I needed to talk to Dad before I saw everyone at dinner, and this was as close to an emergency as I could think of. Had he heard what Smith had said, and how much trouble I was in? I had no idea if the hack worked in privacy mode, but there was no Dad to be had. Alex played a sickeningly sweet selection of Kenny G that sounded like the last desperate mating call of dying souls. It didn't bring my dad's ghost out of the shadows. It did make me want to kill myself, but then Kenny G had been doing that for more than a hundred years.

I didn't know what to do. Dad was MIA. Victor didn't answer my PA request. I couldn't talk to Tommy or Brad or even Danny without putting them at risk. It took me a minute to realize I was crying. None of this made sense. I was just a beta. How could all of this be on me? It was too much, and I was all alone.

Until I was standing next to Victor on the surface of the moon.

"What the…"

The blinking red dot in my peripheral vision told me this was a PA simulation, but I could feel floury moon dust between my toes and the searing heat of the sun on my bare arms. Only my failure to die horribly betrayed the illusion. From this far away, Earth was bright and blue and perfect. You could hardly tell it was dying.

"Is this Transcendence?" I asked.

"Yes," Victor said. Apparently Alex was offline again. Victor's breath turned to snow and fell onto the gray lunar dust, where it glinted like diamonds in sharkskin. I couldn't imagine the computing power required to run a fully personalized simulation of the entire solar system, let alone the cost. I also didn't care. Victor looked tired and worried. I wanted to hug him just to touch someone, then punch him because of the mess waiting for me back at MoBO. I split the difference and slapped him. Virtual violence was still cathartic.

He raised a hand to his reddening cheek. "Feel better?"

"Yes?" I looked back at the earth and sighed. "Tell me you have this under control. Tell me Tommy's not really in danger, that it's all part of the plan. Just…"

"What's that phrase you and Kylera use?"

It took me a moment, then: "The Zoot Show?"

He nodded. "We had all of this calibrated for Jasmina, a trained athlete with no family. It was never tested properly on your genome. As usual, you're manifesting changes faster than should be possible. Given all that, things are not as bad as you think, but…was that your stomach?"

"Jessica stole my candy bar." I felt like crying again. "Why are we here?"

"Someday I'll show you where we are but, for now, it's just a private place to talk."

"Can you get Smith to back off?"

He shook his head. "I'm not sure."

"Can't you do a deal? Offer her money? She's threatening Tommy. I can't…"

"I talked to her after you left the clinic. I should have talked to her sooner, and I'm sorry she ambushed you. I offered to sponsor the Marathons next year, including a far higher prize purse and promotional budget. It was a generous offer. She declined."

"Why?"

"Because she's right. People will see your changes as cheating and question her ability to run the race fairly. Jessica is a threat to all of us. My offer doesn't fix any of that. The only thing you can do is run, just not too well. If you don't show any more improvements, everyone should find something else to focus on. If you do…"

"Victor…"

"Let's try this again. Congratulations on finishing the Fun Run. I know you think you're cheating, or you've been cheated in some way, but it's an amazing accomplishment regardless. And the tests worked perfectly. Dermal camouflage packages will drive revenues for a decade. Kylera is going back to TTI to help overhaul your lab, and we're sourcing a new beta. You did everything I asked, and more. *Thank you.* I mean it."

"You're welcome, but none of that matters. Smith threatened my family. Half the world thinks I'm the natsymp antichrist." It hurt just thinking about Danny. "And you had Berrick incinerated? I don't even want to know what that was about."

"Cremated," Victor corrected. "At his family's request."

"Whatever, I just—"

"I'm sorry, Media, but keeping this session running longer than necessary is dangerous. So let me clarify something. I'm giving you the choice to continue or not, and the choice of how to continue. Kylera was wrong to say what she did. You're not property. You have the right to make your own decisions."

"But, technically, she was right. I *am* property." I don't know why I was getting so frustrated with him. He was trying to help, but his apparent weakness just made it worse. He was supposed to fix things. He was supposed to protect me, and he couldn't.

"Media."

"Forget it." I couldn't seem to think straight. I kept seeing Tommy lying on the trail under a bear or at the bottom of a cliff. I'd spent my whole life in a lab to protect us. That was my job. That was who I was. And now I couldn't even do that. "Fuck!"

Victor put his hand on my arm and waited for me to look at him.

"I know this seems terrible. It is terrible. I'm sure Smith gave you her Grand Illusion speech?" I nodded. "She's right, but she also knows it's a lost cause. The illusion is failing. Society is breaking. Her desperation and threats are just symptoms of the real problem. But right now, none of that matters. Media, you *have* to go on, even if I won't force you. You have to keep running to show the world you're just Media, the perfectly average baseline. That's the only way Smith and Jessica will stop digging. It's the only way to protect Tommy. Hold back if you have to. Once your dockers realize there's nothing to see, the danger is gone. And it's what you want to do anyway. You can fix all of this by doing exactly what you want."

"I know she said that, but what if no one believes it? What if it's too late?"

"I don't think she'd let you continue if it couldn't be fixed. She *wants* it to be fixed. She's just as scared as you are, and maybe a little humiliated. I'm not sure my offer helped in that respect, but I am sure Tommy's in danger if you *don't* run. You know that, right?"

Victor made it sound obvious, which meant he also wanted me to run. I just didn't understand why, unless it benefited TTI somehow.

"You want to do more testing," I said, getting it. Whatever was happening to me, the camouflage was just cover for Dr. K and the world. My VO_2 max wasn't rising by accident.

"Yes," Victor said, "but I still can't tell you why. So I'm going to make you an offer, and you can tell me what you want to do. I'll back you either way."

"Okay…"

"If you agree to go on, no matter what happens, finish or not, I'll make sure your family is protected. No deoptimization, ever."

"I have to do that anyway, don't I? Why make the offer? I mean, I'm grateful." And I really was. "But what do you want in return?"

"We have only two laps left, and two potential testing sessions. Your rapid changes give us a one-time opportunity to do something off-book that I can never do back at TTI. To make it work, we have to increase the stress." Pause. "I need you to be conscious during the testing."

I blinked. "Isn't that torture? I mean, legally?"

"Yes." He didn't hesitate. "It's illegal and, more importantly, immoral. I hate even asking you, but it's your choice. You can run either way, or not."

"This isn't about a new feature, is it? It's not about money. What are you really doing?"

"I can't tell you. But no, it's not about money. It's about trying to fix a very broken world."

"Then why can't you tell me?"

"Because if Jessica drags you back to Genetic Overwatch, they'll search Alex's files and your memory. If they find out what I'm doing, they'll kill us both."

"You're kidding." He had to be kidding. "Right?"

"No, Media. I'm not kidding."

"Okay…"

"The second part of the offer is this. If you finish the race, the PR for TTI will give me vastly more leverage with the board. I should be able to reduce your lab schedule so you can run year-around with Tommy, if that's what you want."

"Really?" I could really get out? I almost yelled *yes!* right then, but he kept talking.

"And I'll get you a full genetic reset. We can flush out all the damaged DNA and change testing protocols to prevent further damage. You don't have to die at thirty, Media. You can live as long as…"

"Are you fucking serious?"

"Yes."

"You can fix me?"

"Yes."

"Then why not do it anyway?" I had no idea it was even possible. "Why do you let us die?"

He looked down, and when he looked back, he seemed smaller.

"Money," he said. "And risk to intellectual property. But mostly, money."

"Wow." I couldn't process that. "I mean…wow."

"I'm sorry, Media, but I can't stay in this session much longer. The final part of the offer is that everything we just discussed, and everything that happens next, is completely confidential."

"Isn't it always?"

"If we do this, we're a team. I'll do anything I can to help you. But it's just the two of us, like it used to be. No family. No Kylera. Nobody else can know. Eventually, you can talk to your father. But not yet."

"How can we be a team if you won't even tell me what you're doing?"

"Everything I tell you puts you in danger. I have no idea how actively Overwatch is probing your PA, if Coach can be hacked to expose any of this when he overrides Alex, and so on. I'll tell you when I can but, for now, you have to trust me."

"Even if I did, how can I keep it from Dr. K? She'll see everything you're doing."

He shook his head. "We'll find a different lead for your program. Kylera will need to work on productizing the camouflage. I'll move you and Tommy to a dedicated lab under someone else. I know you'll miss her, but—"

I snorted. "I'll live. You can really fix me?"

"Yes. You and your entire family. Even your mother."

"Wait, what?"

"She's damaged. You know that. But not in the way you think. We can help her over time."

"Okay…" I glanced at Earth and then at my hands. I was going to *live*? Have an actual life. Run with Tommy. Be in the mountains. It sounded too good to be true. I wanted to scream with excitement, but I couldn't quite let it in. "How painful will the testing be?"

"Very." He looked down again.

"That bad?" *Yes*, his face told me, *that bad*. "Okay, now that I'm making informed decisions…" He waited. "Was any of what you said before the race true? The threats about Blindside taking over? Deoptimization by the board? Or was that just part of the stress you needed for the tests?"

"How about I just promise to tell you the truth from now on?"

"I'll hold you to that."

"You'll do it?"

I almost laughed. "Of course I'll do it." It didn't even occur to me I needed to say it out loud. He was offering me a life I hadn't ever dared imagine. I'd take on far more than a little torture to get there. I wondered if he had any idea how much more I would've done, and was glad he probably didn't.

"You're sure?"

"I'm so hungry, I'm wondering if the moon really is made of cheese. I'm lightheaded, woozy, and I'm eighty-four percent sure this is all bullshit. But yeah, I'm sure. Just please, please do what you can to protect Tommy from Smith."

"I will." He was visibly relieved. "I'll let you know if Smith gets back to me."

"Okay, thanks." I glanced back at the earth. "By the way, why are we on the—"

I was back in my room, alone. I guess questions about Transcendence were off limits.

"You're going to be late for dinner," Alex said. He was trying to distract me, even if he had no idea what he was distracting me from. AIs were just like parents. When they couldn't answer your questions, they showed you shiny things to draw your attention. But Alex was still right. Stu growled loudly in confirmation. It was time to eat. I just couldn't move.

I was going to lead a real human life. I was going to get out of the lab part time and run. It all sounded insane, so I put it away for now. If I really thought about it, I'd run screaming down the hall like a crazy person, and I'm not sure that would help things. All that mattered now was running, but not too well. The rest would happen or it wouldn't. But god, I hoped it did.

Breaking Bad (News)

TOLSTOY SAID ALL HAPPY families are alike, while each unhappy family is unhappy in its own way. Our team dining table was a staggering array of disparate moods and conflicting emotions combined with exhaustion, dehydration and desperate eating. You throw in a freshly minted genetic freak on the verge of a nervous breakdown and you've got yourself a party.

"Media," Coach said, barely looking up. Brad drove a few dry chicken-balls in circles around his plate like a child trying to grasp infinity. Katy looked up, winked mischievously, and returned to her perpetual pose as German Athlete with Tiny Fruits. Tommy glared at a singularly becandled cupcake on the table like an unsolvable puzzle. And there was Mom, looking up at me with wide green eyes like an elf with a thyroid disorder. Why would they even let parents in here? At least Dad had the decency to stay away. Or maybe he just couldn't face me. I put down my inappropriately large plate of cheese with token Other Foods (purely to keep Coach off my back) and took a seat opposite Tommy.

"Is that for me?" I asked about the cupcake.

Tommy looked up, sighed. "We're proud of you, sis."

Just sis. No nickname. This was serious. I wanted to reach across the table and hug him, but that wasn't me. Media was calm. Media was baseline. And in the back of my mind, I could still hear Smith accusing me of cheating. I hadn't meant to, but had I even earned this cupcake? I shook my head and pushed the thought out. I could worry about it later. Maybe I was cheating, but I hadn't chosen to. The only thing I could choose was how to move forward.

"You're not even going to light it?" I asked. "Seventh baseline Fun Run in history. Two Conaills in the Marathons. And me with some kind of magical skin condition that'll probably bring about world peace and universal harmony. Or at least make Victor rich."

Brad snorted. Mom nodded appreciatively as she tried to figure out if I was joking. Tommy pulled out a lighter. Not an old-timey gas butane job, but a miniature survival laser. One bright *zat* and my candle was a flickering flame of fantastical fun.

"Make a wish," Tommy said.

"No," I said.

"Fiddy…"

"You know I have to do this, right?" I grabbed his hand. I had to make him believe me. "You couldn't give this up, could you? Go back to the lab and never run again. Could you?"

He pulled his hand away. "You could die, Media."

Would he still be so worried about me if he knew I was putting his life at risk as much as my own?

"I'm twenty-one, Tommy. If I stay in the lab, I'm dead in a few years anyway." Which was a lie now, kind of, but he didn't know that. Mom blanched like an Irish almond. "I want more out of my life. Don't you?"

That wasn't fair. Tommy looked down. Coach watched us, inscrutable as lead.

"Your cupcake's gonna melt," Brad said.

"Tommy?"

"Of course I want that, but are you doing this for you, or for us?"

I looked around the table, at part of my family and most of my friends and the only team I'd ever been on where I wasn't the ball. To Tommy, I was just risking my life out of sheer stubbornness, and there was no way to explain it without telling him about Victor and what I'd agreed to. But I had to try.

"You know that feeling, Tommy, when you're so dehydrated your pee burns like acid?"

He just smiled, but Brad nodded vigorously. Time to sell this. Fortunately, it wasn't hard.

"I loved that feeling almost as much as cheese because I *earned* it.

I can't remember parts of the last lap due to a concussion." I really needed to take that pill. "I've still got cactus spines in my lip." Even if Dr. Rai claimed to have removed them. "I can barely hold up this fork." I made my point by failing to pick up my fork. "And I love all of it. I want this more than anything. But to answer your question, why does it have to be one or the other? I'm doing this for me, but also for you, and Dad, and all of us." Even Danny, I thought, though the idea surprised me. I didn't see him in the hall. "Is that okay?"

"Your cupcake's burning," Tommy said, almost but not quite smiling. Good enough.

I blew out my tiny stub candle.

"What did you wish for?" Mom asked.

"I think you know," I said, just to mess with her. Her panic was instantaneous and delicious. She'd be up all night thinking about it. "I love you, Mom."

She blinked. "What?"

"I wouldn't be here without you. And this time, it's a good thing. Thank you."

"You'll be careful tomorrow?"

"No, probably not. But there are octopuses in the lake." I said this just to distract her. It worked a little too well.

"Like Paisley?" she asked, loudly. Other teams looked over.

"Great Pacifics," Brad cut in, oddly excited. "That's my fear. They're terrifying."

"Then why are you so happy?"

He blinked, confused. "Because they're terrifying?"

"I bet they're beautiful." Mom leaned forward, fascinated, and just like that, I remembered a flash of the octopus touching me in the lake, an overwhelming sense of calm, and I went too far.

"When she touched me, I felt this, I don't know, awareness? It was like we knew each other."

Mother's eyes widened beyond their ever-surprised diameter. Now I'd done it.

"Mom…"

"Did they talk to you?"

"No," I said firmly. Tommy looked down, trying not to laugh. I thought of her walking around our apartment with Paisley on her head. Of course she thought they talked. She was walking that fine line between eccentric and mentally ill. Could Victor really fix all that?

"I love it when they sing to me." Mom's fingers danced on the strings of an invisible instrument. "It's like a chorus of spirits and children."

Okay, not mentally ill. Batshit crazy. And yet I felt this strange compassion for her as I wondered what TTI had done to her. She hadn't always been like this. I reached out and grabbed her hand. She froze, looking at it in surprise, and then turned to brush a tear away. If I hugged her, she'd probably weep, so I pulled my hand back and watched her gather herself and smile like a regular mom at a regular dinner. There she was.

I ate my cupcake, my cheese and some other foods which, I admit, were also delicious. I had seconds. I might have had thirds. It's not clear where it was all going. I discovered that bacon on maple ice cream is a thing. Well, bacon balls, which look like little red marbles. When the ice cream melted in the cup, I had bacon maple-sugar boba. Still amazing.

Mom and Tommy left together, and the others slowly disappeared to deal with their injuries and prep for the next day. Coach said something supportive that involved not eating any more cheese. I promised to eat a vegetable. I'm not sure he bought it.

A few competitors dropped by to offer their congratulations. Tornado told me I was a prodigy. Shaquilla said I was inspiring. I tried to appear grateful and happy, but mostly I hoped they kept their praise to themselves. And then Jessica came over, armed with a fake smile full of perfect teeth. I flinched away from the predator I'd never be. Had I really wanted to be like her? Abbey hovered behind her, trying to be invisible, like a beaten dog on a short leash.

"Can I see it?" Jessica asked.

"What?" I blurted, utterly blank and terrified. I looked desperately for Brad, but there was just me and Katy and a nearly empty hall. Katy studied her fruit.

"The camouflage. TTI's been promising something for years. If it's true, you could save thousands of lives."

"Or help you kill more innocent people." God, I needed to get control of my mouth.

"Win-win. Please?" Who knew 'please' could sound like 'or else?' She was trying for sincerity, or at least trying not to be hostile. It was a furnace trying not to melt ice. All I saw were her narrow eyes staring at the circus freak. *Make it dance.*

"I don't know how to do it. Not on purpose."

"Maybe." She leaned in. "You just need a little motivation."

I pulled away, trying not to let her see my fear.

"I guess you'll show me tomorrow."

Abbey quietly held her hands out to ask, again, *what are you doing?* And then they were gone. I felt sick to my stomach. Again.

Katy cleared her throat. I glanced over in surprise. Her plate was cleaner than when it came out of the dishwasher. I guess her tiny fruit units had served their purpose. She slid down the bench to get closer, her deep blue-black skin radiating heat like my father's.

"You're good at this, you know." She said it with a German accent, so it sounded both true and accusatory. "But that doesn't matter. Jessica doesn't matter. Even your family doesn't matter. All that matters is why you're running tomorrow."

"I'm not sure—"

"You have to decide if you want to run the race, or if you want to *have* run the race."

"Uh…?"

"I've watched your product interviews. You talk a lot about grit, tenacity and determination. All the same thing. You never talk about love. If you want to run the race, be here, do this, even when it hurts, that's love. If you just want to be able to look back and say you did it, even if you hated doing it, that's pride. Pride is nice, but love is better. Love is worth dying for."

I asked Alex if that sounded as nice in German. *"Liebe ist besser."* Nope.

"Thank you. I already know which one it is."

"I know you do." She smiled in an unusually kind and open expression. "And that's why you don't need to worry about Jessica.

She can't take away anything that matters."

Then Katy gave me a short little hug and left with her pristine cutlery.

And she was right. Because if you took away the politics and the fear of death, it was love. Head-over-heals, all-in, no holding back, lightheaded (not just because I was dehydrated, slightly concussed and full of carbohydrates) love. That was the feeling that had overtaken me at the picnic tables. That this, absent some very terrible things, was where I belonged. In another life, I might have been a natural girl who met Danny at a natural race and talked about running and nutrition and inane athletic trivia until the sun went down. This was where I'd always belonged.

I looked around the empty cafeteria.

Well, not exactly *here*.

Where the hell was Danny?

Spoon Man

ACCORDING TO ALEX, they'd hidden the naturals in the basement. I took the elevator down to a floor I didn't know existed and exited to a smell I *wished* didn't exist. Alex told me Danny's room was to the right, down a grungy hall with ambivalent lighting. It was easy to find. The natural dorms had been retrofitted with traditional door numbers and knobs so they could get in and out without PAs. I went to the third door down and I stared at it.

"*Knock*," Alex said, showing me a video of a polite knock. *Rap-rap-rap*, not sarcastically slow or impatiently fast. I gave it my best Goldilocks knockage. A few seconds and annoyed grunts later, the door opened. It was my first successful knocking. I was kind of proud.

"Hey," I said.

"Hey," he said. He was showered and clean but looked utterly wiped, barely able to keep his eyes open. I followed him into his smaller, darker and generally crappier room and fought the urge to have Alex scan for contaminants. Apparently, MoBO had steerage class. I momentarily disabled Alex's visual input and winced. It was like being in a carrion-gray concrete box.

"Thanks for coming." He sat on the bed. "I wasn't sure you got my text."

"Your what?" Alex had nothing. How did naturals even text? I moved past the inevitable questions. "I'm sorry I missed them playing you out, but those bagpipes kill me. And I was starving." I didn't want to talk about my meeting in the clinic.

He nodded vaguely. "I heard you're running tomorrow. How's

your head?"

"Fine. What did you text about?"

"You can beat Abbey next year, you know. You don't have anything to prove."

She hadn't even occurred to me, but I could see his point. "I'm not sure they'll let me come back next year. It's now or never. And I just want to. I love this." I looked around. I didn't love his room. "Who knew?"

"I can tell. No, I can. You seem alive out there. I guess after the camouflage thing, I thought TTI would pull you back."

"Does everybody know?"

"You haven't checked your feed?"

"You have? It's crazy in there. Apparently, I'm both a god and the antichrist." I took a seat beside him on the bed. "I am sorry about Berrick, by the way." I'd checked online. There were natural protests across the country about his 'accidental' death. Not that you'd know by walking around MoBO. "I'm not sure how well you knew him."

He frowned. "Don't you know, all naturals know each other?"

I fought back a sarcastic response. He looked down. I waited. We were both thinking less about Berrick than what the feed was saying about us. Little of it was good, and some of it was violent. Sex with a modified woman should come with a new identity and witness protection.

"Are you sure you're okay?" I asked. "You got what you wanted, right? You can help your family? So…"

"Fun Run winnings are less than the full prize, but I think so." He sighed. "But I don't have all the information or a computer here. Can you run the numbers? Your PA can do that, right? How long could I afford baseline subscriptions for my family at current rates? Not me, just them. Will it get us through until next year?"

"I can, but if I ask Alex to do it, I'll know all your personal financial information."

"I'm poor. What else is there to know?" He looked down. "Sorry, this isn't easy."

"I know." And I was making him feel even worse. "Just give me permission to access your accounts. Alex can look at your current balances and forecast expenses for a year. I think. He'll do what you want."

"You have my permission."

"*Give me a few seconds.*"

"He's doing it."

Danny nodded and squirmed self-consciously.

"*Okay, I'm in. Got it.*"

Alex told me. It wasn't good news. Danny could see it in my face.

"That bad?"

"Nine months if you use my TTI discounts. Maybe a bit more. But if you're injured and miss out on any sponsorship payments or bonuses…"

"Okay. Can he email me the results? I'll just have to see what I can do."

"You okay?"

"Yeah. Look, I'm great. I can save up. What's another year or two, right?"

Right. This was terrible, but there wasn't anything I could do about it. Even with my discounts, he was in the red far too soon. Why hadn't I asked Victor to help Danny as one of my conditions? It wasn't like he could continue in the race and go for the larger natural prize. No natural other than he and Shaquilla had ever gone this far. He'd get seriously injured or die.

"Wait, you're not thinking about running, are you?" I asked.

He shrugged. "Maybe."

"Danny." I put an awkward hand on his leg. "People start dying after this. What happens to your family without you?"

"Isn't that what they all asked you?"

"Okay, fair, but I have a job to fall back on. And I'm insured."

"Life insurance, then. Or maybe I'll finish."

I knew why I kissed him this time. I wanted to shut him up, to shut down his mind, to stop him from even thinking about running. And, maybe, because I wanted to. He kissed me back, almost as fiercely and just a little desperately.

Danny, Daniel, Dan.

I pushed him away. "Promise me you won't run," I said, knowing it wasn't fair to ask. I would have done the same thing in his place, I would've done anything to get out of the system and pull my family up with me. I did it every day.

"Media," he said, and I knew. He'd do what he had to. We couldn't help each other. There wasn't even a 'we,' not really. I was just feeling sorry for him. He deserved more than a pity screw. He deserved a whole world that was denied to him. What the hell was I going to do but say useless words to fill the space?

"It'll be fine."

He was reassuring me. God, that was messed up. I was overwhelmed by irrational feelings, a range of emotions I shouldn't have felt at all. No baseline should. It was the racc. I was tired. It was the tests. It was the strain. Damn it.

"Well," he said. Yeah. Now what?

"This is going to sound a bit girly, but do you spoon?"

He smiled. "I hold the natural world record for spooning."

Of course he did. I lay down on the bed and he folded around me. I was trying to think of something to say, some way to make it all better, when I fell asleep in his arms.

I woke up what felt like seconds later without swearing. Danny watched me, one hand on my face, his imperfect head still connected to his imperfect shoulders. I pulled him to me almost violently, pressing my body against his, wishing I had more hands to touch more of his skin.

I won't say we made love and I won't say we fucked, but there was a desperate, primitive need to it: a complete openness I'd never experienced before. Raw, aggressive, hungry and yet tender and yielding, two predators devouring each other. When we finished, I was shaking. His sweat and smell was a blanket, a shield, and he was all I needed or wanted. I was safe. I was terrified. It was perfect.

"What now?" His breath was soft and warm against my face.

"I don't know." I didn't care. I curled up next to him and fell asleep again.

It was nearly three when I woke again. It took me a few minutes to carefully pull away, slide his arm off and sit up. The fear came suddenly and I trembled in the warm air, pointless goosebumps raising tiny hairs just because they didn't know any better—something they hadn't removed because there was no cost to it. But what was the cost of this, of what I'd done? I'd let Danny inside physically, emotionally, completely. He was part of me now, but I knew it couldn't last. There was no future for us. Was he hoping there was? Naturals and modified didn't date, especially when one of them was a beta. We were in different worlds.

But was that really true? Did it have to be?

Because I didn't want it to be. I didn't want to give him up any more than this race. I listened to him breathe, surprisingly quick and shallow, and it sounded like home. I wanted him. I would always want him. How did that make any sense? This wasn't baseline emotion. This wasn't perfectly average.

Danny, Daniel, Dan.

I kissed his cheek and quietly snuck out, shutting the door with barely a click. I missed him already and couldn't wait to see him at the starting line. I tried to reach Victor, to ask if we could help Danny financially, but he didn't respond. This was a goddamn disaster.

I was about to head back to the elevator when I saw synthetic mini-me coming out of a room two doors down. She was carrying folded clothes and other personal belongings.

"Are those Berrick's?" I asked.

She nodded warily.

SIX:
It's All Love & Puppies

Good Morning!

"MALAKA!" I GROWLED, a nice, Greek way to say *asshole*. Tiny D sailed across the room in a perfect arc, ending with a surprised *yelp!* as he slammed into the door. Turns out my automatic snooze-alarm reaction was violent and uncontrollable. Tiny D ran around the floor yapping anyway, happily doing his duty. I couldn't believe I'd fallen asleep, and I couldn't believe I had to get out of bed.

Wake up! Wake up! Wake up!

"Sorry, Doofus, I didn't mean you. I'm up." God, I needed coffee. Doofus resumed silent playtime, but I still felt bad. I was going to have him come over for a virtual petting when I realized there was another man in my ceiling.

"Victor, what the…" I pulled my covers up, which was funny. No one had seen me naked more than this man. What was left to hide?

"Sorry." He clearly wasn't sorry. "You rang?"

"Yeah, I…" I wasn't sure how to ask about Danny. "I have a favor to ask."

"Just ask. I'll do it if I can."

"I want to help Danny. He can't know it's from me, but no matter what, he gets the money he needs for his modifications and for his family. Whatever he wants."

"Sure."

"That's it? *Sure?*"

"You're such an odd combination of obstinate and insecure, Media. Sometimes I forget you're only twenty-one. My life is almost literally in your hands. You think I'm going to deny Danny a little money? It's done. Now stop worrying about your fling and run your race."

"He's not a *fling*, Victor."

"Isn't he? You know you'll never be together. It puts you both in too much danger."

"That's a risk I'm willing to take."

"Media, please think about this carefully. Dating a natural draws too much attention to you for the wrong reasons and puts *his* life in danger. Jessica can kill you both if she thinks it sends the right message, and she's just the most obvious threat. Do you want him to live in fear for the rest of his life?"

"I think he's already there."

"And you want to make it worse?"

I closed my eyes, fighting tears. Damn it. "No." Double goddamn it. Victor was right. Danny and I were doomed. There was no 'us' after the Marathons and, if I cared about him, I'd end it now. But true to form, Victor telling me made me want Danny more. They really needed to look into baseline psychology.

"I'll help him, but you need to end it. Soon. And publicly." He paused, and his voice softened. "No matter what, it's over after the Marathons."

"Victor…" I waited for myself to fight back, for my stubbornness and grit to stand up and fight for Danny, but nothing happened. I just lay there and gave up on him. "Okay." I was suddenly exhausted. All my joy about running was lost to fear for Danny and Tommy and what waited in the testing center. It wasn't just the physical pain. I didn't want to know what they did to me. I'd seen the results. That was enough.

"You told me you loved me once," Victor said, out of nowhere.

"I did?"

"You were just a child and scared, and maybe you just wanted to feel safe, but I'll always remember that. It was one of the few times when those words seemed honest. I know it doesn't mean anything, but I love you, too. If I have a family, you're it."

Before I could respond, he was gone.

Egg MacGuffins

WE'RE NOT GOING TO talk about what I ate here. Stu was out of control. Let's just say my nutritional bases were all covered, covered again, and then buried under several layers of carbohydrates. When I finally looked, Brad and Tommy slid their tiny black checker disc suppository things across the table to me.

"No," I said. Okay, I had to swallow first, then I said no.

"They're the only thing we can give you," Tommy said. "Coach checked the rules. MacGuffins aren't covered by the no-support rules. And they're powerful. Mehui is still in the hospital. She might have permanent brain damage."

"And you might need them." I tried not to think about Mehui's twitching body. "I've still got mine." I pushed the thick discs away. They pushed them back. If we kept this up, we were going to shock each other to death at breakfast.

"Okay, okay." I gave in and took them. "Thank you." Though if I needed three stunners to finish, I wasn't going to finish. Maybe I could use one on Abbey just for kicks?

Katy slid hers down the table. I pushed it back.

"No way. Three's enough. Thank you, though. What?"

Tommy and Brad glanced at each other, then at Coach.

"We decided to hang back with you," Brad said.

"No." That was ridiculous.

Tommy leaned in. "All my life, you've protected me. You're my younger sister, and I'm supposed to look after you, but you're the one who got us out of Beaumont before the fires. You're the one they poke and prod. God knows what Dr. K does to you. I wanted this to be something for you, something you could own for yourself, but it's not worth getting hurt or dying. We just want to help. We're going to help."

"Tommy, I *want* to do this. It's for me. And I don't need your help."

"It's fine. We'll stay back. No matter what happens, Jessica won't hurt you."

Yes, I thought, *but she might hurt you.* How could Coach agree to this?

"You can't," Coach said. "If TTI sees what you're doing, you could lose your sponsorships. Smith will find a way to punish the team, and it won't play well. If Abbey still beats Media without her team sacrificing, it'll make us look weak, and we'll still lose the team competition. You can't help her. If anything, you need to stay as far away from her as possible."

I guess Coach didn't agree. Tommy glared. Brad sighed. I turned one of the stunners over in my hands. The manufacturer was spelled out in tiny raised block letters followed by "3NA", an international certification for electronics that I'd seen a thousand times. 3NA stood for NNNA, Naturals Need Not Apply, meaning no naturals were involved in the product's production. It was a stamp of quality. I wanted to throw it across the room.

"I don't understand why you're doing this," Brad said. "You did what they wanted. You kicked ass. You don't have to risk…" His hands clenched around the metal tabletop. When he let go, he left tiny indentations in the table. It probably wasn't hard to find forensic evidence when a combat model killed someone.

"Promise me, both of you," I said. "Promise me you'll do your best. You'll try to win. I can handle myself. I'll be okay. And if it gets too dangerous, I'll drop. I promise." Which was a lie, but so be it.

They both promised, but I could tell Tommy hated giving in.

"Okay," Coach interjected. He told me I now had a single bypass option like the rest of the team and then read off a few stats. We were doing well in the team competition. Terrance was still in the lead, but Tommy was close enough to contend. Katy was on top of the women's leaderboard since the first seed, Bentha Tanislaw, fell and compound-fractured her ankle below Wellman. Brad still led on sprint points. Coach never once looked at me during the brief.

"Now, about the tunnels. For those of you who toured MoBO before the race…"—he still didn't look at me—"…you may remember that there were several breeds of lethal spiders on exhibit. Since we're in Jenny Two, that's what you're going to run into. They will bite you if you go too slowly. The bite will hurt and, if not treated, seriously injure or even kill you. The monitor will have an antidote, but you'll have to get it from them. Get it. Take it. Even then, you'll be in excruciating pain and you may hallucinate or pass out. Honestly, just don't get bitten. The Brazilian wandering spiders are probably on loop five, and they do kill people."

A BHD stopped to hover over our table, sharing our morning pep talk with the masses. Coach looked at it with barely concealed disgust. I'd never seen a synthetic with emotional issues before. It was strangely unsettling.

"*Brad,*" I PA'd. He glanced over. "*I need a favor.*"

"*Anything,*" he responded.

"*I need you to protect Tommy on this lap.*"

"*I always do.*" Then: "*Why? What—*"

"One last thing, just as a reminder…" Coach said.

"*Just stay close to him. No matter what. Promise me?*"

"*I promise.*" He nodded, frowning, and I knew he'd do it.

"On the fourth and fifth laps, the animals fully engage. They can only attack if charged on loop four, but they can and will impede, and they're not always gentle. On the fifth loop, if they sense aggression, meaning an attempt to progress when they block you, they can and will attack. They might attack anyway. These are modified animals whose primary function is military defense. They can kill you. They're not supposed to, but it's safer to assume the worst."

"Worst assumed," I said. "Check."

"Just don't taunt the predators," Coach said to Brad. Brad smiled. I once saw him outrun a grizzly bear, then turn around and punch the bear in his soft wet snout. I felt sorry for the bear.

Feeling Good

WHATEVER I'D EATEN FOR BREAKFAST, it was working. I cleared the first wall after the picnic tables in 15:23, my best time, and Abbey was still in sight. My legs felt fresh and strong. My breathing was calm and natural. I wasn't sure if this had anything to do with what Victor was up to or if I was simply adjusting to the pace, but I loved it. I *loved* it. This was fun. I'd like to say I was holding back to stay close to Danny, but I'm not going to lie. He was too slow and I had an Abbey to not-quite-catch. I figured if I stayed behind her, I'd satisfy Smith and protect Tommy, but I kept having to slow myself down.

And I still kept looking back for Danny. I knew I had grit, but if you took away all my modifications and virtual training, I wouldn't have even finished the first lap. I would've made it to the Pits, passed out, and begged for rescue. But Danny was still back there with nothing but training and willpower. I knew why he was doing it and it wasn't just the money. Quitting meant losing what you were and letting others define you. He wouldn't do that anymore than I would.

I shook him out of my head, or tried, and flew up the trail and over wall after wall. I was soon at the Pits, which I took at a full run without hesitation. I cleared the holes easily and started up the hill, looking behind me for Tim or other predators. The cave openings leading into the pits were black and empty. I guess we'd lucked out. I turned back to the trail and started jogging to keep up with Abbey.

God, I felt good. My legs were flushed with power. The morning heat beat down but instead of feeling oppressive and hateful, it was just another sensation to be aware of. I started the next climb with energy to spare, breathing easily. I powered up the slope. I was pretty impressed with myself until I checked my time and realized I was probably moving too fast for Smith's liking. I slowed down, hoping Coach wouldn't notice.

"*Drink something,*" he said. I didn't even mind. I took a long drink and then noticed a large red splotch on the rocks just off the trail. I nearly choked on the water. Something very, very bad had happened there. It was like someone had exploded.

"Coach, what…"

"*Run your own race, Media. It's not anyone on our team.*"

"Are they okay?" Stupid question. God, there was a lot of blood.

"*They're not dead.*"

"Okay." I forced myself to look back at the trail, but I couldn't help but think of Jessica. I'd never seen so much blood. Is that what I'd look like if—

"*Shake it off, Media. Move.*"

I moved, one step after another, until I stopped seeing the blood every time I blinked. Then I looked up the trail and a boulder moved far above me. My heart jumped. Someone was waiting for me.

Oh. It was Brad, his massive form trying to hide among the manzanita and stunted pines. Why wasn't he with Tommy? Had something happened? I asked Coach, but he couldn't tell me anything, so I chased Brad up the mountain, never getting closer, never falling behind until we got to the Pillars. Where, frankly, I sucked. I'd like to blame my torn up hands, but I'm just not a great climber. I still struggled to keep my weight on my toes. By the time I belly-crawled off the 5.10b route up onto the walkway outside the testing center, Brad was long gone and I felt like dying. But maybe he was back with Tommy.

"You're doing very well," the monitor said. It was the petite mini-me, looking down as I panted onto stone and gravel. Was that mockery? "Abbey's not that far ahead. You should hurry."

I should, but I wasn't looking forward to the next part.

The Fun Part

I STOOD AT THE door for a while. The monitor watched me, curious about her large human doppelgänger. Or maybe I was just imagining things. She looked down at her sleeve and brushed off a fly. I was definitely imagining things, specifically what was going to happen inside. I knew it was going to suck, but on the bright side, I'd have something to hold over Victor for the next few years. I opened the door and looked straight into the Chrome Demon's silver eyes. My involuntary repulsion at least helped explain the violence of the Chrome Wars. I looked away, embarrassed, and realized that Victor was there in place of Dr. K. That was a relief.

I stepped inside and the door shut behind me with an ominous *click*. I tried not to look at Victor, so he couldn't see my fear. I just sat and let the jacks slide in. I imagined I could feel the virtual command to knock me out, but what I felt instead was nothing. I couldn't move, not even my eyes, but I could see. The judges moved in and out of my field of vision until the Demon leaned in for a closer look. Damn, he was freaky looking.

"Ready?" Butterflies asked from behind him.

"Ready." Then he turned to someone out of my view, probably Victor, and nodded.

"Initiating fourth loop Modified Marathons test of baseline runner Media Conaill in exactly three…two…one." That was Dayglow, but I couldn't see him.

"Test is live," Butterflies said.

No, no, no.

Pain, pleasure, hunger and fear. I wanted to scream, to lash out, to purr and cry, but all I could do was nothing. Someone had put my nervous system on random and turned the volume up to eleven. What the hell were they doing to me? It went on and on. Every feeling. Every pain and joy. Every nerve alive and dead, on fire then ice, on-off, like someone testing a circuit board with lightning.

Please stop. Please stop.

"Her heart rate's elevated," Demon said.

Of course it's elevated you silver freak.

"Is it a problem?"

Yes!

"No," he said, that silver-tongued bastard.

I'M GOING TO KILL YOU.

"Test Time 2:37."

"Are the standard tests done?" Victor asked.

"Done and logged."

"Okay, turn it up."

Turn what up?

"I need to see the chromatic response," Victor said from behind me. "Increase intensity and frequency, focusing on peripheral pain centers."

What the hell was he doing?

Fire burned at my hands and feet and radiated up my arms and legs.

Please stop. Please, please, please.

"Nothing," Dayglow said. "We're going to burn her out. Wait. Look at her arms."

Stop. Please help me. Please.

"There she is," Victor said. "Five more seconds, then kill it."

The pain was gone. Everything was gone. I floated, unmoored from my body, feeling nothing. Glorious, wonderful nothing.

"Test Time 7:13."

"Did you see that? Was that orange?"

Was what orange?

"It's beautiful," Demon said. "Oh, it's fading." He sounded sad. Good.

"You've nailed dynamic human polychromy," Dayglow said,

obsequiously. "I've never seen anything like it."

"Okay, mark it," Demon said. "Varying chromatic manifestation over eighty percent of the epithelium. Substantial increase in dermal responsiveness since test three, and wider spectral expression. No apparent pattern in either test, no external calibration, and obviously no intentional manifestation or response. Forty seconds from first sign to full reset. No apparent residual changes. Skin appears normal. Is that enough, Victor?"

"Test Time 7:53."

"More than enough. It's perfect. Thank you. Purge your PA memories and logs. I'll get set up for tomorrow's test after she's gone." A beat. "What's that smell?"

"Ahh," Butterflies said. "I think…"

"That's impossible," Demon said.

"Side effect?"

"No." Dayglow's face appeared over me, looking down as if examining a bug. "You sure she's fully suppressed?"

"Of course," Butterflies said, sounding offended.

"Okay. I'll have her examined later," Victor said. "Leave a change of clothes. We don't have time to clean her up. Test input stopped. Local cache and buffer flushed. Pull her feeds. Let's clear out so she can change."

Clean me up?

"Test Time 8:58. Initiating consciousness."

"Severing remote connection."

Black.

White.

When I could move again, I was alone and wet, which was new. I'd pissed myself. They'd left me a change of clothes on the floor, which meant they had a spare ready because this had happened before. Great. I wasn't sure what bothered me more, that I'd wet myself, or that they were all so excited about it.

"*You did well,*" Victor texted. "*I'm sorry…*"

You should be, I thought, but then again this is what I'd signed up for. One more time, and I hopefully never had to experience that again.

After I changed and left the room, I turned to see if Danny was there, but it was just me. He was behind me somewhere, hopefully not too far. There were no DNFs (Did Not Finishes, race jargon for dropping out) in my feed.

I had a new set of fans after the aid station, people in Fiddy t-shirts calling my name and reaching out for high fives as I ran by. It wasn't hard to get used to and it helped me ignore the glares. I flew past the old ranger station and up the trail toward Round Valley faster than I ever had before, practically bounding.

"How are you doing this?"

Welcome to the Zoot Show, I thought, which meant I was going too fast and had to back off.

"Are you slowing down on purpose?"

"Just pacing myself. Abbey's not too far ahead."

Who knew I'd feel bad lying to a synthetic.

Giant Freakin' Spiders

SOMEWHERE BELOW WELLMAN, I heard helicopters heading to the summit. That usually meant an emergency or rescue. I turned on my social feed and then nearly impaled myself on a tree branch. Coach was trying to get my attention. I looked up. I was back at the tunnels. I slowed down to catch my breath at the mouth of Jenny Two, wishing I had my rain shell, but Tommy had told me they were basically useless against the larger spiders anyway. I just had to go in at speed and try not to run into a wall. I didn't even have my trekking poles for balance—they took them after the Fun Run, along with my gloves and jacket—so all I could do was run fast and try not to die.

A second later, I was plowing through thick strands of spider web in the dark, waiting for the first spiders to drop on my back. I didn't have to wait long. I felt the touch of cold, hairy legs on my right shoulder and swatted it off. The spider had heft to it, a body the size of a baseball, and I heard it smack into the wall. I sped up, taking the webs face-on, just trying to get the hell out of there.

And then it rained spiders—great hairy bodies landing on my arms and head, and crawling up my shoes. Within seconds, I went from determined calm to a stumbling near-freak out, slapping at oversized arachnids and desperately hoping none of them bit me before I got them off. One landed on my forehead, legs pressing down on my nose, and I slapped myself in the face, hard. I smooshed the spider up against my cheek and nearly screamed when its flailing legs poked at my eyes. I knocked the rest of it off, wet and crunchy, and dry-heaved into the crepuscular light of the final chamber. The monitor looked up and nodded hello.

"*Take the antidote,*" Coach said. "*Now.*"

"What?" I couldn't make sense of the words. I was still pulling web out of my hair which was, frankly, a disaster. "I wasn't bitten."

"*Yes, you were.*"

And then I felt it, a stabbing pain in my right shoulder.

"*In his hand, Media.*"

The synthetic stepped forward and offered me a clear bottle. I just stared at it.

"*You've been bitten by a modified northern funnel web. Take the antidote now or your race is over. You have less than thirty seconds.*"

I took the antidote. In an instant, I started feeling better. The stabbing became a poking became a mild throbbing. I handed the empty bottle back and touched my shoulder where I'd been bitten. There was a little swelling and something wet, but it wasn't bad.

"Thanks," I said, and then stepped out into the sun to renew my spider and web cleaning. The web was strong and sticky this lap, almost impossible to tear, and I knew it wasn't coming off for a while. Maybe it would keep my hair in place.

I jogged slowly, glancing back once to see if there was any sign of Danny. There wasn't. I just hoped he got through Jenny One fast enough to avoid whatever was waiting for him.

"*Pick up your pace,*" Coach said, and I did, breaking into an intentionally slow jog. For the first time, I could really take in the view. It was beautiful.

Heavy Petting

I STARTED TO CATCH glimpses of Brad ahead on the trail, trying to stay out of sight despite having nothing to hide behind. We were going to have words. He was supposed to be with Tommy, not hiding behind trees half his diameter. And then I thought I heard something and turned to look back down the trail.

"*Media?*" Coach asked.

There was no one behind me. I wanted to run back down the hill to find Danny. He had no Brad or Tommy, and without a PA, he didn't even have a coach on the course. Unless he had an earpiece? I had no idea. He probably had nothing but himself and I'd basically ditched him. I just wanted to see him, to know if he was okay. It was idiotic, but—

"*Media?*"

I didn't have to worry. Danny appeared out of the trees, jogging slowly up the trail toward me, an unstoppable human machine.

"Danny!" I yelled.

He smiled and half-waved a tired arm. I might have hooted or whatever you do when you're excited for someone else.

"Yeah, Danny!"

He was doing it. It was impossible, but he was doing it. When he was twenty feet away, he looked up and smiled widely.

"You're killin' this," I said.

And then he was hit by a meteor. One minute he was hard-breathing his way toward me, the next Jessica came flying down the heavily treed slope above us and hit Danny so hard that he shot off the trail, fully airborne, and cartwheeled into a pile of rocks.

"No!" I took a step off the trail to help Danny, but Jessica was instantly in front of me, her speed incomprehensible. She was just *there*. All I could see of Danny was twisted limbs and blood. He wasn't moving. Jessica wasn't moving. And I wasn't going anywhere.

"This is just a test, right?" I asked Jessica. "Some kind of illusion?"

She reached out and poked my arm. Her fingernail drew blood.

"*It's not a test, Media. Get out of there.*"

"But Dan—"

"*Run, Media. Now!*"

I turned to run, but I knew I couldn't escape her. I looked for rocks or sticks or something I could use as a weapon, but nothing would matter. If she wanted to hurt me, she would.

It's just the fourth lap, I told myself. *They can't kill you on this lap.* But I kept seeing Danny's crumpled body. Did the course rules even apply to her?

Jessica grabbed my shoulder and spun me around. I fell backward up the trail and tried to crawl away. She was more monster than woman—inhumanely lean muscle and infinite rage towering over me like a god over an insect.

"Jessica, please. I just want to finish. Why would you care about me or Danny?"

"*Danny?* Your natural pet. Little Danny boy. Do you *love* him?"

"What the hell's wrong with you?"

"They don't belong here. This is a *modified* race. He'd be out already if you weren't encouraging him. So now you're both done. And you're never coming back."

I looked up the course, looking for Brad, but there was no sign of him.

"*Brad!*"

Jessica shook her head and reached for my leg. I kicked, but she grabbed my ankle so easily it was a joke. She yanked me toward her.

"Come on, *Stinky*. You think you're unbreakable, so what're you worried about?" She reached for my neck.

"Please…" I said, but I never finished and I don't know what I would have asked for anyway. Her hand closed around my neck and

262 SHAWN C. BUTLER

all rationality vanished. Even if the rules said she couldn't kill me on this loop, I knew that wouldn't stop her. Rules were broken all the time. She would kill me if she wanted, how she wanted, and there was nothing I could do about it.

But she didn't squeeze.

"*Withdraw*," Coach said. "*Withdraw from the race and she has to release you.*"

"There it is," Jessica said. "I knew it."

"*Just submit.*" I barely heard Coach. Jessica was staring at my arms. Why would she…*oh*.

I had grabbed her wrists instinctively, pointlessly, and now I saw what she was looking at. The skin on my hands and arms was dappled brown and gray with traces of light green, a non-random pattern that was obviously meant to camouflage me in the light of the trees and rocks around us. I suddenly forgot all about Jessica's hands on my throat. This was the dermal camouflage everyone was so excited about.

"*That's amazing*," Coach said, as distracted as Jessica was, and I had to admit it was pretty cool. As I watched, my skin pigmentation shifted and flowed like Paisley's when she playing in her tank. The individual colors were hideous, but the moving mosaic was mesmerizing. Jessica completely forgot what she was doing.

"Jessica," I forced through a pinhole throat. *Jethica.* Her eyes refocused on me. She frowned. Her hands tightened on my throat. Maybe talking was a mistake.

"Relax," she said. "I just wanted to see—"

And then she was gone.

What the hell?

I looked below the trail, and she was on her back in a pile of deadfall with a black panther on top of her. Tim had Jessica's head in his jaws. I mean, I assumed it was Tim. Blood ran from her forehead and ears. I waited for the sound of her head collapsing like a melon, but it didn't come. Tim released her head and pulled back. He'd made his point. Jessica wiped blood from her eyes and glared at me from beneath a ton of modified panther as if I were the problem. Then she started to pet him, rubbing behind his ears, and I was struck by an irrational wave of jealousy. That was my goddamn cat. I was about to say something ridiculous when Brad appeared at my side.

"You're supposed to be with Tommy," I said. Why was he holding his side?

"Tommy dropped me." He was embarrassed. "Sorry."

"Then you're late." Which made no sense. Was he hurt?

"Am I?" He glanced at Jessica. Was Tim purring? Maybe Brad had a point, but I wasn't processing any of this. I just kept looking past them at Danny. He still wasn't moving. Synthetics were attending to him, quietly, dispassionately, with blurry-fast hands. I just wanted to know he was alive.

"*He's alive*," Coach said.

"Oh, thank god." I almost lost it. I was angry and Danny was out of the race and it wasn't right. It just wasn't right that some fembot meat hammer had taken him out.

"It's not fair." I was fighting back tears.

"Fiddy, not here." Brad looked horrified. "Not in front of *her*."

Jessica was still watching me. Tim purred, a deep rumble like a tractor engine. Brad spun me around so I was facing away from them and wiped my eyes. Had I ever cried in front of him before? I doubt it. I wiped my eyes and stared at my wet hand, and it just pissed me off even more.

"Danny was doing it," I said. "With no modifications and no support from his team. All on his own. He was *doing* it. It's not fair."

"*Media*—"

"Shut up, Coach!"

Coach shut up. Brad looked around nervously. Combat models had crap bedside manners, no matter how much they pretended. Empathy wasn't their strong point and strong emotions just confused them.

"Sorry," I said. "Sorry."

"No, it's…" He helped wipe dirt and pine needles off me, his eyes locked on my skin as it slowly settled back to my natural brown. "That's pretty cool." He almost sounded envious. I ignored him and glanced back at Jessica. Tim was licking blood off of her face. She looked totally relaxed. God, I wanted a drink. Something with a kick that could knock me out cold. A liquid sledgehammer.

"Is that your cat," Brad asked. "Tim?"

I almost laughed. "I thought so."

"Cool." He did sound envious. "So, you want to do this, or what?"

"*You do need to get moving. Danny will be fine, but you're losing time.*"

But that was a lie. Danny wouldn't be fine. He'd survive and they'd fix him and Victor would help him financially, but somehow I knew his short relationship with me would dog him forever. Jessica would never let it go. The modifists would never forgive him for existing. I had ruined this man's life just by holding his hand in public.

"You like him, don't you?" Brad asked.

"Yes." *Damn it.*

"He's pretty badass for a natural." *Badass* was one of his greatest compliments.

"Badass *period*." Badass and screwed. "Let's go."

We started running again, faster, until I started to drop Brad.

"You okay?" I asked.

He nodded, but his hand went to his side and he winced. "No big deal."

"What happened?"

He frowned and winced again. He was really struggling. "Bront went after Tommy by the Pits." He shook his head. "Totally half-assed. And he knew I was there. I don't get it."

"But he hit you?"

"Right in the ribs. Good punch. I didn't think he'd do it. It was stupid."

"Wait, the blood? That was..."

"Yeah, I lost it when Tommy fell." He looked down at the trail, hiding his face. "I shouldn't have gotten that angry."

"Is he okay?"

"Tommy's fine."

Thank god. "And Brontius?"

"You mean, did I kill him?" He looked down again. I wasn't sure why it was bothering him so much. Combat models fight. It's in the name.

"Brad, you're just doing your job. You're supposed to protect Tommy."

"Doesn't mean I had to hit him that hard." He stopped jogging. "Go on, I'll catch up. I just need to catch my breath."

"Brad…"

But I could tell he wanted to be alone. His face worked, fighting more emotion than I'd ever seen in him. He wasn't just veins and muscle after all. I didn't know what to say, so I just put my hand on his arm and turned to run up the hill. What the hell was going on?

I barely remember the summit. I high-fived Brad when I passed him on the way back down to the aid station, restocked, drank and ran on. Fast, but not too fast. I wasn't tired, but I made sure I looked exhausted. Mostly I was angry, first at Smith and then Jessica, and then at an entire world that made them possible.

Damn it. I tried thinking about running with Tommy and being free, my family never having to be afraid of The Black again, and living a real life. A future I could help make reality.

I just had to finish the race.

A Lot of Screaming

I COULDN'T SEE THE python up in the branches, but I knew she was there—coiled for the strike, tongue darting out to taste the air, plotting evil. And now she could attack, so ignoring her wasn't going to help. I had my fear a bit more under control, a lot more actually, but I knew if that snake touched me, I was going to lose my cheese. I fumbled with one of the stunners, making sure it was in the front of my pack, but I had no idea how I was supposed to use it while hanging from droopy branches covered in thorns. The only thing that mattered was speed, and with my jacked-up hands, there was no way I'd be fast enough.

"So, what's the deal, Coach?" I was just killing time.

"*Faster branch drop. Probably toxins in the thorns. Also, Tommy said the snake got really aggressive if you stopped to rest at all. So...go fast.*"

"Isn't that always your advice?"

"*This is ultrarunning, not philosophy. Drink, eat, run, don't fall or get eaten. It's not rocket science.*"

I knew he was trying to distract me. It didn't help. The spiny veins were still there, prickly and mean, but otherwise nothing seemed different. The snake was nowhere to be seen. I looked into the water, but the surface was glassy and black. There was nothing in the trees above, so I thought fast thoughts, stepped forward and jumped.

Coach was right about the drop. The branches drooped the second I put any weight on them. In a panic, I started swinging blindly, gouging more holes in my bare hands. I was getting pumped, but I couldn't rest. My hands were tingly and going numb. There was definitely something in the thorns.

Come on, come on.

I could feel the snake coming. There was no way I was going to make it. My fingers pulled off branches faster with each grab. I was barely halfway across, breathing hard, and starting to panic. I knew it wouldn't kill me on this lap. But it would hurt. It would touch me.

Something moved in the branches and I looked up. She slid toward me, mouth open, tongue probing the air. Fear surged through me in waves like a living, burning thing. There were no branches, trees or thoughts. There was just the snake opening her mouth to strike.

Holy—

I don't even remember falling. I watched the snake all the way down until I hit the water. I flailed in the darkness, reaching for the surface. Then something hit the water next to me. The snake was in the water. *The snake was in the water with me.* I screamed underwater. I've never screamed before, not like that. I don't know how I didn't suck in water and drown.

I hit the surface and raced for the edge, arms pin-wheeling madly. I got to the end where I'd started and hauled myself out, rolling onto the dirt, and then speed-crawled twenty feet from the pool before turning around. When I looked back, the python was watching me from the edge of the pool, great slit eyes full of hate and hunger.

"*That went well.*" Pause. "*Are you okay?*"

I tried to catch my breath. Panic drained out like a receding tide, leaving me empty and nauseated. I leaned forward and vomited what little was in my stomach into the dirt.

Shit. Shit. Shit. I couldn't even look back at the snake. Off to the left of the trees, a synthetic girl in her pretty blue skirt waited for me to quit. I hated the sight of her—the clean, shiny disinterest. No one should see me like this.

I stood up and anger replaced panic, rage filling the hole where my courage should have been.

"*Media, take a breath.*"

"No." I looked back at the snake, but she was gone, probably back up in the branches waiting for me. My stomach turned over just looking at the water.

"*Media.*"

"No!" I wasn't afraid of snakes. I loved snakes. Smith had no damn right to do this to me and, even if she did, she could burn. If I moved fast enough, the snake wouldn't strike. Otherwise, the obstacle was impossible. "I can do this."

"*I know you can. Shake out your hands. Take a breath. And go.*"

I took a step forward and nearly fell. My legs were still wobbly from the adrenaline that had long since gone. I got to the edge and focused on my breathing. My hands were bloody, but at least the tingling and numbness were gone. I took one last look up into the branches.

"You've got this," I told myself, the kind of thing you say when you don't.

I jumped, swung, and got myself moving. I ignored the spines. I ignored my hands, which was easy because I could barely feel them again. I just kept moving. If I stopped or thought or aimed, I was going to fall and the snake would get me. So I just kept moving.

Swing. Swing. Swing.

I was halfway. Farther.

I missed a grab and nearly fell. Acid panic rose from the back of my throat. I swallowed and took another swing. Made it.

Swing. Swing.

Just three more.

Two.

One.

I jumped off and hit the ground, falling to my knees. I'd done it.

"I did it," I said out loud. I jumped up and screamed up at the trees.

"I did it, you son of a bitch! You hear that?" I cursed more and flipped off the trees. "I beat you, motherfucker!" I may have gone too far that time. Who was I to talk like that about his mother? "Yeahhhhhh!!!!" Yes, I screamed a lot. Did it make sense? I don't know. I was pretty amped. It's beautiful to watch the slow-motion replay, like a nuclear bomb at the instant of ignition, right before it kills everyone in a twenty-mile radius.

"*Media?*"

"Yeah, what?"

"*Good job.*"

"You're damn right."

"*Now calm down and get moving.*"

Stupid coach. What did he know? I thought about swearing more and then I saw Brad looking at me, next to that little synthetic twit at the other end of the pool. They clearly thought I was insane.

I calmed down and waved at Brad with a numb hand. He nodded warily.

I got moving.

Rat Jaw Bites

ONE THING I WAS learning about the Marathons was that the real challenges weren't the video-friendly obstacles. It was the wear and tear, the endless walls, the grinding elevation gain and loss, the heat and all the little things—the rocks in your shoes, the pain in your hip, the gel that jacked up your stomach or forgetting to drink enough. Well, that wasn't a little thing. I'd flown up the Air Stairs and over the bitey wolves in SOB Ditch. There were only six in the hole now, so I assumed the others were free on the course and causing mayhem. But I'd worry about that when I had to. I was in the plush happiness of Rat Jaw when I tripped over a root and hit the dirt, scraping my knees. Just a little thing, but it could have ended the race right there with a broken ankle or torn ACL.

I took a breath and started to stand, cursing my clumsiness. Everything Victor promised depended on finishing. I had to be more careful.

"Stay down," Jessica said. "It's where you belong."

I jerked up and stumbled away from her. Where the hell had she come from?

"One assault. One assault per runner per day. That's all you're allowed." I was just regurgitating what Coach said in my head.

Jessica laughed her incongruous laugh. "The rules won't save you, buttercup." She leaned down, close to me and suddenly Coach was gone and I was in privacy mode. Because of course. "You're doing too well. You're changing in real time." She whispered, glancing around to see if anyone was close enough to hear. "I know camouflage was just a distraction. But even rapid aerobic adaptation isn't worth all this. What's Victor up to?"

Shit. "I don't know what you're talking about. I'm just trying to run." I pushed up to my elbows. Her eyes looked so far into me it was invasive. "Please…"

Footsteps pounded up the trail toward us, someone running hard.

"Pity," she said. "I like it when you beg."

"Media, are you okay?" Coach was back.

I snorted, half-a-laugh. Jessica took a final appraising look, shook her head, and then jogged away just as Brad burst into view and thundered toward me—a shredded and bleeding mass of tattered man. He bent over, breathing hard, and clutched his injured ribs.

"Brad? You look terrible. What happened?"

"Jessica followed me for a while. And then I guess she got bored and took me out. Didn't even have time to react." He looked furious, eyes wide with anger and shame. "Hit me in the same place as Bront. Damn, she's strong. You okay?"

"She's augmented, Brad. There's no way you can beat her."

He nodded vaguely, unable to internalize impossibility. "Are you all right?"

"Yeah, she didn't touch me."

He nodded. "Tomorrow…"

"We'll worry about tomorrow tomorrow." I tried to sound comforting and should have said more, but I just wanted to move. "I've got to get going. You sure you're okay?"

"I'm fine. Go on. I just need to rest for a second."

It's Not Snakes

I WAS FEELING LIGHTHEADED and weak by the time I got to the lake, so Coach had me take one of the emergency gel packs. It tasted like slime and lemons, but the effect was immediate. Sliding into the cold water woke me up even more. All the fatigue vanished. My muscles reengaged. It was like listening to a turbine spin up.

"How much caffeine is in that stuff?" I was flying.

"*A lot. It'll get you to the aid station if you stop screwing around.*"

I swam directly toward the middle of the island, looking for the octopus, but there was nothing but cold dark water and one flailing baseline in the lake (that would be me). I almost reached the rocks before remembering I had to go under. This was all in the course overview, but I'd never planned on doing these laps. It was only a 90-second swim, maybe less. Not that big a deal. But I kept thinking of being in the water with the python earlier, and I couldn't shake the feeling it was waiting for me in Calisto's Caverns.

"*What's the problem? Take a breath and dive.*"

"Snakes?"

"*Of course not.*"

I knew he was right—the never switched the animals on obstacles—so I focused on my breathing. It was going to be an octopus. Deep breaths. I liked octopuses. More deep breaths. Hopefully, they liked me. One last breath, and I dove.

The light dimmed as I swam down toward the mouth of the cave. I looked into the blue around me. There was nothing but darkening water and black rock. I hesitated at the end of the cave, but I knew I had to move. I wasn't Tommy. I couldn't hold my breath for more than a couple minutes. After a final look toward the surface, I swam into the black.

I used my hands to guide myself along the tunnel, kicking hard and hoping I didn't ram my head into a rock. Coach told me I'd been under just over a minute. It felt longer. The water was cold, utterly black, and I felt the first pangs of panic. I sped up, but I had no idea where the end was. Where was the light?

I felt it coming as ripples of pressure. I looked around, but there was only darkness. I pushed forward again, trying not to panic. *It's not snakes,* I told myself. *It's not snakes.*

Then a snake wrapped around my leg and I lost my mind. I fought and punched, but then another wrapped around my left arm and squeezed so hard I just stopped. I couldn't move, but I was suddenly calm.

It wasn't snakes. It was an octopus.

I forced myself to relax. I was fine. It was just a test. But she didn't let me go. I don't know how I knew it was a she, but I knew. And she was holding tight. Tiny suckers played with my skin. A tentacle brushed against my face. I wished I could see her.

Please let go, I asked. *Please...*

I reached out with my right hand to stroke her tentacle, to let her know it was okay.

"*Two minutes,*" Coach whispered, sounding worried.

Get out of my head, I wanted to say. *I'm having a moment.*

I felt safe. She gave me the same wave of peace that came with Paisley's touch. I just *felt* her. I knew she would never hurt me but god she was big. Her tentacles felt as big as my legs. I tried to imagine her, all blue and black and beautiful.

Please let go.

Moments passed. I hardly noticed. Coach's voice was a distant whisper.

Then louder: "*Four minutes. I'm alerting the divers.*"

"*Four minutes?*" That couldn't be right. "*No. I'm fine.*" But it was time to go.

Please let go. Her tentacles pulled off, sliding away, and then she was gone. I missed her.

"Four-thirty."

Suddenly, the water and pressure were back. I was drowning. My throat convulsed as my body tried to gulp down air. It was still pitch black and I was dying.

"Five minutes."

Blue light ahead of me.

"Five-thirty. Divers are coming."

I pushed out of the cave. The blue was full of stars. I was blacking out.

"Media!"

And then I was sucking in air at the surface, again and again. It burned my lungs and my eyes watered in pain, but I was alive. I'd made it. A thin synthetic boy stopped swimming a few feet away, wearing only a bathing suit and the standard, indistinct smile.

"I'm fine," I gasped. If he touched me, I was disqualified.

He paddled closer.

"I'm fine!" He stopped. "Guess you took off your wool for nothing." His smile twitched. On the nearest rocks, his clothes were neatly folded in a perfect stack topped by spotless white socks. You can never be too neat at a rescue.

A few minutes later, I pulled myself out of the lake and shook myself dry.

"Are you okay?" Coach asked. There was something odd in his voice.

"I'm fine." He could see my stats, so he knew I was okay. I started the slow jog toward Desert View. "Tell Brad the octopus is sweet."

"Sweet. Seriously?"

"Just rub one of her arms and she'll let go. She likes to be touched."

"You sure you're all right?"

"I'm great." And I was. I flew up the trail and got to the Long Valley aid station in no time. I could feel the energy crash coming. If you want to a good laugh, check out the video of me speed-eating watermelon and chips. One volunteer nearly lost a finger. I'm not even kidding.

The Wolf Wall

I RAN, SLID, CRAWLED, fell and generally stumbled down the mountain with more energy than coordination. A helicopter flew overhead from the direction of the lake just after the barbed-wire crawl, so of course I tripped again looking up at it. I thought I saw wolves in the trees above Flat Rock, running parallel to the trail, but I might have been hallucinating. Then I thought I saw a dragon below Flat Rock and knew I was. Maybe the heat was getting to me, but I made it, step after step, wall after wall, as the temperature climbed. I wasn't going to catch Abbey, of course, but I didn't even want to. I just needed to get down in an unexceptional time. The hardest part was running slower than I could and wondering how it looked as I accidentally sped up then slowed, feigned exhaustion on the walls, and even grunted miserably at the monitors. I'm not sure they bought it.

I was on top of the 5,500-foot wall, the wolf wall, when a giant brown blur knocked me off the top. I landed in a heap at the monitor's feet. He jumped back to avoid any touch that would accidentally disqualify me, but I was more focused on what had hit me. It was a wolf, an enormous timber wolf with teeth as long as my fingers. He stood a foot away, growling as low as Tim but somehow far more terrifying. This was one of the wolves missing from the Air Stairs pit. He was huge up close. Saliva dripped from his jowls as he studied his next meal.

I pushed myself against the wall, but I knew I was done if I moved. He'd rip my throat out and I'd bleed to death before the synthetic could help me. I just needed to wait it out. It was a fifteen minute hold, or so I told myself. Inside, I was screaming. He stepped closer.

Nice wolf. Please don't eat me. I closed my eyes.

He growled in the darkness. I was liking things with teeth less and less.

"Open your eyes."

The wolf was gone. It had been less than a minute, the expected hold time. Where'd he go? The synthetic shrugged as in, *Don't ask me, I just work here.* I pushed against the wall and stood on wobbly legs. My left arm was bloody from the fall and my elbow was killing me, but I didn't seem seriously hurt. Why had the wolf left so fast?

"Are you okay?" Coach asked.

"Yeah, yeah. I'm fine." I was probably going to have a nervous breakdown at the bottom but, for now, I tried not to think about it. It was time to go.

Less than a minute later, I heard a woman scream, but when I turned back, the wall was out of sight and there was just hot, dusty trail behind me. Who was behind me? Another baseline?

"Media…"

I know. Not my problem. I turned and ran.

Half Mast

I FINISHED IN 10:27:10, my second-best loop time and hopefully slow enough not to raise suspicions. People cheered and I waved back, still trying to look beat. I looked around for Danny, but of course he was probably still in the clinic. Tommy, Mom and Dad were waiting with Coach toward the back of the corral. I was starting toward them when Smith cut me off. I stopped, swaying like a tree in the breeze. I guess I was tired after all.

"I warned you," she mouthed.

"Warned me about what?" I wasn't getting it.

She shook her head and yelled, "Congratulations!" There was more cheering and she stepped out of the way. Warned me about what? I checked the time again. I was slow. I had actually lost time to Abbey. Nothing processed. I hadn't done anything exceptional except survive. I was still trying to figure it out as I walked into my father's arms.

"I'm so proud of you," he said. Mom put her hand on the back of my head and said something loving. Tommy joined the hug and then Katy appeared, smiling. It was a bit much, but I couldn't move, let alone protest. I took one last look back at the finish line and noticed the flag was flying at half-mast. My mind went straight to Danny.

"Who died?" I asked. It was abrupt and rude, but that's how it came out.

"Danny's fine," Tommy said. "Did you hear about Shaquilla?"

"She's *dead*?" Was that her screaming at the wall?

"No. Sorry. I thought you knew. The wolf that attacked you did the same thing to her. She broke her ankle in the fall. She's still coming down. Probably left you alone to get her."

I punched Tommy in the arm for scaring me, but at least that explained the scream.

"Then who…?"

"The combat model from McNickle, Antwone. He tried to beat Terry's FKT to the summit. It was over 95 at the top. Heart attack at the aid station. Dead before the medivac got there."

"Okay." That was terrible, but I'd never met him.

"And Kebe Kingley."

"What?"

"Tried to win the loop to juice his endurance package, I guess. Fell just below the picnic tables and cracked his head open on a rock. Kid was nineteen years old."

"Damn."

"And…"

"You're kidding."

"Most deadly fourth lap of the decade." He looked deeply sad. "Queen Jentha came across the finish line, got a hug from her girlfriend and stroked out. Died in her arms less than an hour ago." He wiped his eyes. "I used to train with her. I'm just so glad you're okay." He put his hand on my shoulder and I could see him fighting back tears. Maybe it was because I was so tired, but I had trouble processing the news. I should have felt something, anger at Smith, rage at the injustice of it, but I was suddenly numb. I was hungry and tired and none of it fit in my head.

"Let's get you inside," Coach said. "It's too hot out here."

We all turned and headed toward the cafeteria when I remembered something.

"Brontius?" I asked Tommy, hoping Brad hadn't killed the Bront by accident.

"He's fine. Well, he will be. Brad hit him with a tree. It was…loud."

"With a *tree?*"

"A small one. You okay, Mac?" Tommy used the name for when I'm sad. Was I sad? I'd been so happy just a minute ago. I'd finished the lap well, but not too well. Smith should have been satisfied, but wasn't. Nothing was how it was supposed to be.

"Media?"

It took me until then to notice the massive contusion on Tommy's right leg. Brad had made it sound like Bront gave Tommy a love-tap. It looked like he'd almost broken his leg.

"It happens." He shrugged. "You sure you're okay?"

I wanted to hug him and tell him I was sorry, that it was my fault and Smith was taking it out on him, but instead I shrugged as if it all made perfect sense.

"I'm fine." And then Dad half carried me to the nearest bathroom with Mom trailing after.

Five-Minute Warning

I COULDN'T PEE IN the bathroom. I also couldn't stand up from the toilet. The second I sat down, my energy crashed. It was like my new body just turned off. Mom had to lift me off while trying desperately not to touch me. If that's not love, it's at least reluctant nursing. Dr. Rai checked me out in the clinic. She took blood, accessed my PA stats and made disapproving little noises.

"Is Danny okay?" I asked.

"He's fine. A few broken fingers. Lots of soft tissue damage, a concussion, some lacerations and so on. Nothing serious. He's resting in his room. He'll heal up good as new."

"Thank you." I couldn't believe how relieved I was.

"You held your breath for more than five minutes."

That came out of nowhere. "No I didn't."

"At the lake."

"That's impossible." But I asked Alex.

"*Five minutes, fifty seconds.*"

"Damn." That explained Smith's greeting at the finish line. This wasn't good.

"You tested at 2:25 before the race. It's an accurate test. Statistically off by no more than fifteen seconds, and that's at rest. You were tired, swimming and frightened."

"I'm tenacious?"

"It's impossible."

"Obviously not."

"People think you're cheating."

"Yeah…" I didn't care about people. I cared about Smith and

Jessica, but mostly Smith. I was in trouble. If I didn't figure out how to make this right, I wasn't finishing the next lap alive and, more importantly, neither was Tommy.

*

I GRABBED SEVERAL CANDY bars from the cafeteria and headed for my room. Dirt and blood washed off me in the shower as I ate. I should have been drinking. The toilet was going to yell at me. There were cuts galore and everything burned, but I wasn't seriously hurt. What was Smith going to do? I couldn't believe Shaquilla had broken her ankle at the wall. Alex let me know when she finished, the first natural ever to complete four loops. I sent her a congratulatory text, but it still didn't seem fair. Stupid wolf. Was that Smith warning me or just a random accident? Candy bar wrappers dithered and danced around the drain, but I was too stiff to pick them up. One of my nipples was raw and bleeding. That was new. Was there any way to get Smith off our backs? Or Jessica? My thoughts were exactly as random as they sound.

I tried to pee again, failed again, and had to crawl to the bedroom. At least that kept the toilet from scolding me. I lay next to the bed for a while, trying to muster the energy to get up. Turns out, no matter how hard they try, virtual BHD pets cannot lift you off the floor. Could Victor offer Smith more money? Why didn't I have more candy bars? Stu was getting *loud*.

I got dressed by rolling around on the floor. My hamstrings cramped and then my quads, then my jaw and everything else. I gave up and let it happen. After a few minutes, there was nothing left to seize and it all released like a stress ball expanding back into a sphere. When I could stand, I headed to the cafeteria in bare feet. I couldn't risk another cramp to get my shoes on, let alone socks. At least the cold tile was nice on my blisters. Maybe we could pay Jessica to take Smith out. Was that a thing? Did I just think that? My god, I was hungry.

The Facetime Continuum

I FELL ASLEEP ON the table after eating Stu into submission, face down next to a half-empty plate. Someone poked me. My eyes opened and I glared at Tommy's stupid, happy face. Why did he look so fresh and perky?

"Coach wants to confirm you're running tomorrow," he said. "He seems grumpy."

"He's always grumpy. I'm running tomorrow." I wanted to close my eyes again, but if I did, it was all over. I sat up and took inventory. Tommy, Katy, Coach—he did look extra crotchety—and me. Where was Brad?

"What are you going to do about Jessica?" Tommy asked.

"Nothing. Jessica is going to do what Jessica does and if you try to help me, she'll break every bone in your body." Smith was the one that mattered. "Where's Brad? Wait, do you think Smith had Brontius attack you?"

"Why would she do that?" Tommy was baffled. It's like we were in different worlds.

"I meant, what are *you* going to do?" Tommy pressed. "About Jessica."

"Run really, really fast."

Before Tommy could point out the obvious flaw in my plan, a snake fell out of the sky and I screamed. Loudly. I was on my butt on the floor, and Brad was laughing so hard he bent over in pain from his ribs. It was a plastic snake, a gift shop toy.

"You're in so much trouble." God, it was hard to get up. "Get that thing away from me."

He tossed it down the table where it sat, poised to strike. I could barely look at it and it was just a toy.

"So, how was the octopus? Sweet or terrifying?"

Brad shrugged glumly and winced, holding his ribs. "Both?"

"What?" Tommy asked. "What's wrong?"

"Seriously?" Coach asked. "He couldn't hold his breath with nine broken ribs."

Brad took a seat and looked down, ashamed, as if nine weren't enough.

"Didn't you hear?" Katy said. "Brad's out. He's DNF."

"What?" Tommy and I said at once.

"Brad, I'm—"

"It's okay." He didn't sound the least bit okay. "I got most of the sprint points."

"But I had your stunner," I said. "I ruined your race. I'm so sorry." I wanted to give him a big hug. I couldn't imagine facing that kind of fear underwater in the darkness. I would have lost my mind. I'd still be in the cave if it had been snakes, mouth open in a forever scream.

"It's not your fault. After Jessica hit me, I couldn't keep up with you anyway. There's always next year. Don't worry about the stunner. I was so freaked out I probably would have pulled a Mehui." He shrugged, trying to look at peace with his injuries. "I'm going to the clinic to have my ribs fixed. I'll see you at the finish line." Forced smile. "You guys are going to crush it tomorrow."

"She wasn't sweet," Coach said to me after Brad left. "Brad nearly died. They had to give him CPR and fly him off the mountain."

"Seriously?" That explained the other helicopter.

"Why would the octopus be sweet?" Tommy asked.

"You're supposed to be a team," Coach said. We both sat back, surprised by the anger in his voice. "You didn't notice him missing at the finish? You didn't wait for him. You didn't check your feeds. No wonder your society is so screwed up."

"*Our* society?" Tommy asked, surprised. Synthetics don't talk like that to humans. Not ever.

"Never mind." He stood up. "We can do the recap in the

morning."

"Coach?" I asked.

But he just turned and left. When I looked back, Tommy was smiling.

"Good for him. You want to keep Brad company in the clinic?"

"Can you do it? I really need to sleep." Stu grumbled. "And eat more."

Tommy kissed me on the cheek and left. Katy studied her surgically sliced melon, sublimely oblivious to my presence until I waddled over to the buffet. When I got back, she was gone and her plate was a smiley face with a cantaloupe smirk, banana eyes, blueberry pupils and a strawberry nose. It was so cute I almost cried. Damn her.

The Uncertainty Principle

I WAS LYING IN bed with a family-sized bag of peanut M&Ms when Victor appeared on my ceiling. I wasn't surprised. Apparently, my ceiling was a door or a window, because it was crap at being a ceiling. He asked me how I was feeling. I showed him the bag.

"Good sign," he said. "It's working."

"Gluttony's a sign of progress?"

"Your metabolism's working overtime, which is part of why you're improving so quickly. You're changing faster than I thought possible. But…"

"But what?"

"Any particular reason you decided to have an octopus mind-meld in the lake?" He sounded genuinely annoyed.

"Wait, are you blaming—"

"It's a standard fourth-loop lake obstacle. If the animal catches you underwater and you submit, it holds you for the requisite thirty seconds and releases. Why were you giving the octopus a massage? We can't hide nearly six minutes under water. That's insane."

"How was I…" I didn't bother finishing the sentence. He was right. I chewed on an M&M. Damn it. "In my defense, I'm not used to remembering things without Alex. It's like having brain damage. Damn it. I had one job to do, and I blew it." I thought about blaming PTSD from the testing center, but that wasn't going to fly. "I'm sorry."

Victor laughed. "Did you just apologize?"

"Yes, and I mean it. But it was so comforting touching her, the octopus, like a drug. I don't know how to explain it." Though now I knew why Mom was always playing with Paisley.

Victor nodded, thinking, and then shrugged.

"Smith threatened me at the finish," I said. "How do I fix this?"

"I'm not sure. Your dockers all thought you were going to die. There's no way to suppress that. I don't know what else we can do."

"You don't know?" I'd never seen him at a loss before. "Victor, I'm not getting off this course alive if we don't figure something out. You know that, right? We're dead. Tommy and I are both dead."

"I know. So, I've decided to pull the team from the race. All of you."

"Wait, no—"

"It's the only way to keep you and Tommy safe. We'll do it in protest of Jessica's attack on Danny. She's not supposed to attack other competitors according to her special status as an honorary runner. I've already filed a protest, which was rejected. We can't stop her, but it will work in the press."

"Victor…"

"What?"

"I don't care about the press. It won't work in real life. Smith will never let Tommy back in the Marathons or any of her regional races. You'll ruin his career. You'll ruin all their careers, and Smith can still get to us." And I wasn't willing to give up yet. Victor had promised me a real life. No way was I walking away from that without a fight. There had to be another way.

"Okay." Victor seemed to accept my argument. "You have a better idea?"

"I might." For some reason, I'd thought about Katy's fruit smiley face and it just came to me. There was clearly something wrong with my brain.

"I already increased the offer, if that's what you're thinking," Victor said. "She rejected it."

"Of course she did."

"What do you mean?"

I put a lot of M&Ms in my mouth. I needed a moment to make sure my idea wasn't idiotic. I chewed. Given Victor's income, it was probably an expensive few seconds. I crunched loudly. He got tired of the game.

"Media?"

"She's offended." I really hoped this still made sense out loud. "She doesn't need the money, and you're trying to buy her off. The more you offer, the more she'll want to prove she doesn't need what you're offering. You're insulting her."

He smiled. "What would you suggest?"

"I'm not sure, but…"

"Just say it. Now's not the time to be shy."

"Turn it around. She'll still want the money, but what she really wants is to save face and keep control of the race. Tell her you're testing a new endurance package, rapid adaptation, something like that." Basically, what Jessica already thought it was. "You couldn't tell her because you weren't sure it would work. But now you know. Announce it at the finish line. I've seen others do that. That way, all the changes are just part of the new offering. TTI gets a new product line—which I guess you'll have to invent—and she gets the personal acclaim and money without having to feel bought. Everyone wins."

"And you get to be an endurance model?"

I laughed. "Honestly, I hadn't thought about that, but yeah, why not?"

He thought for a second. "I like it. I'll run it by the board and make the offer."

"You think she'll accept?"

"We'll know by morning. If it was anyone else, I'd say yes. But she's one of the smartest human beings around, and she manages ultramarathons and obstacle races. She's not doing this for her career. She's doing this for the view, for access. And so she can see what companies like TTI are working on. I just don't know what she's doing with that information."

"You think she's a spy?"

"No, she's far more dangerous than that. But we can worry about that later. Thank you. This is a genuinely viable idea." He smiled. "And Kylera will hate it. I'll talk to you in the morning."

"You forgot about Jessica."

"No, I didn't. I can't buy her and you can't outrun her. She'll do what she wants to do. If she comes after you, tell her what you just told me, even if Smith doesn't accept. If she doesn't buy it…" He sighed. "Damn it."

"What? Victor?"

"Okay. Your PA update wasn't just to give us a way to communicate or keep you conscious during testing. If Jessica touches you and you have no other choice, use your PA safe word."

Newer PAs have safe words that shut off all functions at once, like a kill switch, so you didn't have to exit dozens of apps one at a time. Mine was *mommy dearest*. Don't tell her.

"Why? What will that do?"

"It should crash her PA and knock her unconscious for a few minutes. Enough to get away."

"Wow." How many felonies was that? "Okay, but…"

"But if you use it, she'll know. The military will know. Your Dad and I might end up in prison, and she could kill you anyway. It would be better to quit the race. You understand?"

"Yeah, that's…" I couldn't even think about Dad in prison. "So, last resort."

"Life or death. I'm serious."

"I know, I just, why would you risk that for me? I know you care, I'm not questioning that, but you'll lose everything."

"Because I couldn't live with myself if I didn't."

That didn't sound quite right, but before I could question it, he changed topics.

"There's a good side to all of this, you know."

"There is?"

"No matter what Smith says, there's no point in holding back anymore. Do your best tomorrow. You'll feel even stronger than today. Beat Abbey if you can. Have fun."

"*Fun?*"

But he was gone and I was staring at Puny P as she sailed across the ceiling. I stuffed more M&Ms in my mouth. Beating Abbey did sound like fun. And if this worked, I'd be in an entirely different class next year, running with Tommy instead of hours behind him. I smiled like a chipmunk, mouth full of M&Ms, and spent a few minutes fantasizing about a future in the real world. Not a fantasy, a *possibility*.

I wished I could tell Tommy any of this. He was still in danger even if he didn't know it, and I hadn't even congratulated him on being in second place. He was kicking ass. And I needed a hug. I put my fancy MoBO robe on over my sweats and took a walk with my M&Ms up to the endurance floor. Alex had to get Coach to let me up in the elevator.

Tommy's door opened. Brad was there in a towel, midriff wrapped in bandages, but very clearly not in the clinic getting new ribs. Even *with* Alex, I was an idiot.

"I love peanut," Brad said, digging into my bag.

"How are your ribs?"

He was too busy chewing stolen M&Ms to respond.

"Is that Fiddy?" Tommy called from inside.

I shook my head and Brad understood; my brain was full. I was just happy Tommy was okay.

I handed Brad the bag and went to find my hug elsewhere.

*

"SPOON?" I ASKED WHEN Danny opened the door.

"World's best."

His fingers and arms were wrapped in gauze and bandages. So were his shins and knees. His right cheek was bruised and swollen. He was a mess. Because of me.

"It's okay," he said, pulling me in. "It's not your fault."

We lay down on the bed and I folded up in his arms, touching as much of him as I could. We were bandaged and beaten, but somehow it worked. Fear and anger faded. All thoughts drained away, leaving only gratitude that he was there and he cared. Within minutes, his breathing changed and I could tell he was asleep. Faster than I thought possible, I joined him.

I woke up in darkness. Danny snored lightly, another human flaw that made him even more attractive. I didn't want to leave, but the longer I stayed, the more chance there was he'd end up just another victim of Jessica or something else. I couldn't even tell him about the money Victor had promised. It wasn't safe to be around me. Or maybe I was afraid if I stayed, I'd never leave.

I snuck out again, probably for the last time.

Danny, Daniel, Dan.

His name tasted like home. I knew I loved him, and I knew it didn't matter. Love wasn't going to save either of us. So I whispered goodbye and closed the door.

SEVEN:
If You Were Smart, You Wouldn't Be Here

Breakfast

TINY DOOFUS JUMPED UP and down on my stomach. *Get up! Get up! Get up!* I shooed him away with admirable constraint and took stock. My head felt like cheese, thick and full of holes, but my body felt incredibly, improbably and insanely good. Except for Stu, of course. Stu was a growling chasm in my midsection, a black hole demanding to be fed. He'd have to wait.

I sat up and concentrated on my hands. They'd changed color when Jessica attacked—my whole body had—but I had no idea if it was a purely involuntary trait. I focused on my fingers like a victim of paralysis, willing them to move. They were brown with dry skin and numerous small cuts, but that was it. I squinted until my eyes watered. Still brown. My nails were a mess. I fought the urge to bite off a cuticle or ten. Still brown.

Then…something.

"No way." The skin on my hands and forearms slowly shifted to a dull gray-brown as if trying to imitate the bedspread colors. Then I blinked and it was gone, and no matter how hard I concentrated, I couldn't make it work again. It didn't matter. Victor was right. Dr. K would figure it out, and when she did, it was going to sell like crazy.

I jumped out of bed, twisted, turned, bent and flexed. My knees popped. I had a vast array of minor lacerations and terrible breath, but otherwise I was fine. After a quick cleanup in the bathroom, including a prolonged battle to wrap my hair back into submission, I pulled out my last set of ultra-smooth, almost-but-not-quite-smell-proof running garments and slid them on one delicious movement at a time. I was totally stealing these clothes.

Stu reminded me I was hollow, but there was a lot to think about before heading to breakfast. Victor hadn't gotten back to me, so I was probably going to die today, though I supposed if it happened before the testing center, that'd be nice. As long as Tommy was safe, I'd take what came. Which sounds braver than I felt. What I really wanted was to beat Abbey and cross the finish line in triumph, start my new life in a new lab, run in every race that Danny just happened to be signed up for, and spoon the hell out of him afterward. Maybe beat Tommy a few times and see what snow looked like. And change the world, of course.

What?

That was me asking me what I was smoking. Betas didn't change the world. But I wasn't a beta anymore, was I? I was something else now, or would be once I finished. And that new person didn't want to live in a world where Danny woke and fell back asleep, day after day, without ever once feeling safe. She also didn't want to think of herself as a product, at least not *just* a product. Media wanted more. I wanted more.

I wanted *everything*.

But Stu just wanted breakfast, so first things first.

I would tell you what I ate, but I'm out of superlatives and it's all online. No one ate like I did. I felt like a freak who didn't belong when I arrived at ModCon, and now I felt like a freak who might someday belong with a lot of cheese in my mouth. And it was cheddar. I don't even like cheddar. Cheese should have flavor, gusto, and smell like something Brad would fight to the death. The cheddar tasted like paste and ennui.

"*Media,*" Victor said in my head. I tried not to react. I glanced around the table at the rest of the team. No one noticed my reaction.

"*Yes?*"

"*Smith said she'd think about it.*"

"*For how long? The race starts—*"

"*You have to act as if she'd said yes.*"

"*I get that, but when will she tell us? And how will I know?*"

"*She'll draw it out as long as she can, but she'll agree.*"

"*You don't know that.*"

"*No, but it makes sense. That's all we're going to get for now. You okay?*"

Was I okay? I wanted to laugh but, honestly, I wasn't surprised and Victor was right. She'd say yes after she played with us a bit. I just hoped she didn't play too rough.

"*Yes,*" I said.

"*Good luck. And please, don't die.*"

I stared into space for a while, strangely numb, and then Stu grumbled again. At least someone had their head in the game. When I looked up from my third, no, fourth plate, I was alone at the table. Coach hadn't come in yet. Katy was at another table talking to Junco's coach, probably about Jentha's death. Tommy had eaten lightly and was walking around the hall again, greeting everyone, encouraging the competition, and generally being a great sport. When I looked back, Jessica was standing on the other side of the table.

"Does he always do that?" she asked.

"Do what?"

"The tour de hugs, the excessive fraternization, *that.*"

I didn't bother looking. I knew what she meant. "What do you care?"

"I don't. Did you know I studied anthropology in college?" She didn't wait for me to answer. Alex confirmed what she said, but not why I'd care.

"After the Chrome Wars, people stopped hugging," she said. "Stopped shaking hands. Everyone was afraid of genetic diseases that could be passed by contact. It took public executions and decades before PDA was socially acceptable again, but here's your brother, walking around like the perfect vector."

"Vector?" The question came out in a whisper. I looked around nervously.

"Didn't it ever occur to you? Maybe Abbey didn't give Tommy the DNA. Maybe Tommy gave her the DNA that made her look like a GIP."

I froze. A trained killer and Genetic Overwatch operative had just accused my brother of a capital offense. Had Abbey put her up to this or did she really believe it? People were looking. I struggled to think of something clever to say, sarcasm to diffuse the accusation, but nothing came.

"I just wondered if he's always been so friendly, or if that's part of the experiment. Bring in naturals, touch everyone, spread the disease." She smiled. "It's elegant. All these athletes going back to their home countries, taking it with them. He could kill millions."

"You're out of your mind." I failed to keep my voice from shaking. "They test everyone here. It's impossible."

"Yeah, nothing going on here that's suspicious at all."

"Tommy's no GIP. You can't believe that." But it didn't sound as crazy as I wanted it to. The naturals in the race were in some ways a distraction from what Victor was doing to me. Maybe I was a distraction from something else. Was that possible? Would Victor use me like that? No, I couldn't believe that. Jessica was just running around in my head, breaking things because she could.

"You still don't know what he's doing, do you?"

"Of course I do." I smiled and spoke as calmly as I could. "You'll see at the finish line."

She snorted. "That's so cute. You think you're going to finish." She leaned forward. "I'll make you a deal. Tell Victor I want in, and I'll protect you. I'll *guarantee* you and Tommy get off the course. Smith won't be able to touch you. No one will."

I leaned back, terrified. How could she scare me so much, so easily?

"I don't know what you're talking about. Into what?"

"Ask him. Now."

I asked him. Victor responded almost instantly with a curt, "*No.*" So much in that little word. He knew what she was asking and couldn't do it, or wouldn't even for me. No matter what Smith said, I was on my own on the course when it came to Jessica.

I shook my head.

"Pity," she said.

The Ascent

A THOUSAND FEET LATER, I was all alone at the picnic tables and in last place. Abbey was somewhere ahead, just out of sight. I could have caught her if I wanted, but I was trying to stay out of Jessica's field of vision. I'd need to figure out how to pass them at some point, preferably without being seen but, for now, I was fine hanging back.

I felt like I was floating up the lower part of the mountain. Thirteen-foot walls fell away, one, two, three, four, and I leaped across the Pit holes like a gazelle. Then I got to the wolf wall, and stopped dead. Someone had scrawled something in sloppy red finger-paint: *M hearts D*.

Media loves Danny. Maybe a little exaggerated, but not wrong.

"Huh." Where'd Jessica find the paint?

"*Just ignore it*," Coach said, but there was something in his voice. The synthetic monitor in perfect plaid raised his eyebrows and nodded to the north. I looked and there was…

"Tim!" My heart jumped.

"*It's not Tim.*"

A black panther lay in a heap twenty feet off the trail, its head collapsed like someone had dropped a mountain on it. There was blood on the rocks, on the cacti, on everything. I gagged and looked away. My heart slowed. I hated that a beautiful animal had died for no reason, but it wasn't Tim and at least I knew where she got the paint. Did she kill it with her bare hands? Was it a threat? Of course it was a threat. God, I was out of my league.

"*What do I do?*" I asked Coach.

His response was lost to the growling of a massive black bear that had charged out of nowhere to drag the panther carcass into the bush. I just stared, slightly unhinged. I might die out here before Jessica even made her move.

"Media? Can you hear me?"

"Yeah." The dead panther's squashed head bounced off a rock. The bear and the panther carcass disappeared into the rocks and bushes. I forced myself to look away and swallowed. I had to keep going for Tommy, I thought, or move forward for Victor, but as I grabbed the rope, I knew the truth. I just hated to quit. And I'd probably go forward no matter how many animals Jessica killed, just to prove I could.

I never got tired. I was still thinking about how amazing I felt when I got to the Pillars. Abbey was just topping out on the second barrel. She glanced down and then vanished toward the testing center. I stepped up to the nearly featureless rock of the first pillar, reached out and flexed my hands. The climb was probably no harder than a 5.10c—a totally doable if highly exposed climb without nets— but I needed strong hands to do it.

Then again, it's not like I had a choice. I couldn't quit and I couldn't use my bypass before the Jungle Gym, so I had to try. I shook my hands, stretched my fingers, swore a few times, and then reached for the wall.

My hands were fine. I climbed easily and felt like I could crush the holds if I wanted to. It was amazing. I topped out in what felt like seconds. Is this what everyone else felt? Just the joy of being in your body without all the pain?

The Final Test

I STOOD OUTSIDE THE testing center for a while. I knew what was coming, and there was no way out of it, but still. It's hard to describe what the last test felt like. Think of the most horrific thing you can imagine and then imagine something worse. The next test wasn't going to be any better. *Come on, Media.* I reached out. I pulled my hand back. I reached out again. *Damn it.* Finally, the door slid open and cool air breezed over my overheated skin. Victor waited on the other side as if he'd been standing there all along.

"You can do this," he whispered.

"Anything from Smith?"

"No." He shook his head. "But Tommy's still okay."

I nodded and looked down. I'd never dreaded something so much in my life. It was just ten minutes, I told myself, then never again. I could do anything for ten minutes.

"Will it be worth it?" I asked.

"If it works."

"Then let's do this." I failed to sound brave, but I still appreciated his honesty. And at least I wasn't going to hell by myself. He'd be watching and he'd hate himself for it.

I stepped in and took a seat.

"Let's get this party started," I said to Dayglow. On the plus side, I'd never have to look at his ridiculous face again.

"She's out," Butterflies said a second later, but of course I wasn't out. "Do you want to run the standard tests or skip them?"

"Run them," Victor said, somewhere out of sight. "We need something for the logs."

They ran them. I barely noticed.

"Done. Ready?"

Victor leaned in, appearing suddenly from the side. He looked directly into my eyes and mouthed something. He was probably trying to be comforting, but it didn't help.

"Are you sure about this?" Demon asked from my left. "I've never run tests at these levels before. Well, not on people. You see the bear yet, the big one? I ran a series on him. It—"

"Run it," Victor said tersely. "We're running out of time."

"Okay," Demon said. "Initiating nervous system stimulation in three, two, one...now."

I screamed a lot again, in my head again. I cried in my head. I begged, pleaded, groveled, yelled and beat the walls down with virtual fists, but nothing helped.

"Stop!" Victor said. "That's enough."

Was it time? Was it over?

"Did you see what you wanted?" Demon asked.

"No. I don't think it's there. I was wrong."

He looked so sad and disappointed. I would've given him what he wanted if I could. What did it mean that I couldn't? Would I have to do this again? Or was it all a waste?

"How much time do we have left?"

"Two minutes." This was Butterflies.

"Give her joy and peace. Everything good."

"That's not really...okay."

Every nerve in my body lit up. The joy was a kind of madness that went on and on. I think I passed out inside my own head. Not sure how that works. When it was stopped, it was like someone pulled out my soul. *Do it again*, I thought. *Do it forever.*

"Is she okay?" Victor asked.

"You just tortured her and now you want to know if she's okay?" Demon asked, disgusted.

"You just committed a dozen felonies and now you have a conscience?"

"She's a tank," Dayglow said. "I've never seen such nerve plasticity. Of course she's all right."

"Initiating consciousness in three…"

They were gone by the time I was able to move. I'm not sure why they left the room—I hadn't wet myself this time—but it was nice to have a few seconds alone. I took a breath and tried not to think about all the pleasure I'd never feel again. After even one jolt, I could tell how addictive it would be. I'd even take more of the pain for that.

The door slid open. Hot mountain air flooded in, along with the smell of pine needles and vanilla, bark and dust. I inhaled deeply. All anxiety was gone in an instant. It was time to run.

I cut loose after the aid station, flying past surprised fans. The ranger station was a blur. In what seemed like seconds, I was climbing toward Round Valley and the tunnels beyond.

"You might want to slow—"

"Coach off!" For thirty damn seconds, I wanted to run without someone telling me what to do or how to do it. I knew I was going too fast. I knew I was going to pay for it one way or another, but this was my race and my strange new body. For a few minutes, it was *my* life and no one else's.

Which was ironic, considering what happened next.

A Taste of Normalcy

"COACH ON," I SAID, gasping for breath. Jenny Two was a cold black hole in front of me. Abbey had just gone into Jenny One, and I assumed Jessica was on the other end, waiting. I was moving way too fast, and my body was letting me know, but I loved every second of it.

"*Brazilian wandering spiders,*" Coach said, which was a strange way to say hello.

"I know. Go fast. Don't stop. If I get bitten, take the antidote."

"*Don't get bitten. The antidote will save your life, but you'll be out of the race. These are modified, military-grade spiders. You get bitten, it's all over.*"

"How's that fair?"

For the record, it's rude to laugh like that in someone's head.

"Fine." I was going to have to run like crazy to avoid the spider apocalypse.

"*You wanted to go fast. Now's the time to do it.*"

I took a deep breath and squinted into the darkness. And then I ran like a crazy banshee through dank, spidery blackness. I ran so fast, it took me a while to realize there were no spiders. Lots of web and walls to run into, but no spiders, Brazilian or otherwise.

I stopped in the exit chamber. A tall, thin silhouette waited in a circle of light. It was Smith.

"Hello, Media."

What was she doing here? Was this a test? I nodded and tried to walk by her. She grabbed my arm and pushed me back so hard I nearly fell.

"What do you want?" I asked.

"I want you to understand. Did you know almost all third-generation PAs include a neural override mode for national security purposes?"

"No. Why would I care?"

"Well, for one, it's what Victor used to hack his way into your head."

"What—"

"For another, you can buy access if you know who to talk to." She snapped her fingers and I was on the ground. Well, it wasn't quite that fast. Something terrible happened and then my legs gave out. I could barely move, hardly lift my face out of the dirt.

"Full nervous system override," she said. "A wonderful feature that allows me to simulate, well, anything. In this case, a *natural* life."

She kneeled by my head. I wanted to lash out and tear her apart, but I could barely move. Just thinking hurt. I felt like crying or dying, anything but this weakness.

"This is how you would feel if you were unmodified," she said. "This is your *natural* state. No muscular enhancements, no optimized cardiovascular system or lung capacity. This is the real Media, the little girl your parents sold to TTI. This is the true you, the perfectly mediocre natural."

"No." I'm not sure what I was denying. I just couldn't believe the pain of it, the exhaustion.

"This is how Danny feels. This is the life of your natural lover. This is every day of their tiny little lives."

No, I wanted to say again, but my lips didn't even move. I tried to push myself up, but it felt like my arms would shatter. Every tendon around my elbows was screaming.

"Hit me," she said. "I won't fight back."

I sat up and leaned against the wall, breathing heavily. Hitting her seemed like a lot of work.

"This is the reality of their world, Media." She leaned closer, so close I could smell her clean, minty-fresh breath. "You think you're helping them by encouraging them? Failure is their destiny. Failure is practically their *purpose*. Why torture them with dreams of the unattainable?"

"Why…" My jaw protested, but I didn't care. "Why are you doing this?"

"Because Victor's not here and I'm tired of being used. Because I *can*."

"But…" God, it was hard to think. "What about the deal?"

"You know the problem with rich people? They think everything's for sale. A deposit here, a sponsorship there, and we're all trained pets jumping for joy. Is that what you think I am, your dancing monkey?"

So I was right. She was offended. I just didn't realize how much.

"Sit, speak, fetch," she snapped. "I'm not your pet. I could kill you right now and there's nothing you could do about it. Victor can't stop me. And remember this. In every race, every day, Tommy, Brad and Danny are out here in my world. On *my* courses. You think this ends today, but it ends when I say it does. Do you understand? Say you understand."

"I understand." And I did.

"Don't you ever get tired of being used?" She leaned back. "I know Victor made you this way, so you can't help what you are. Just like he demanded naturals this year. Why would he do that? Just tell me that. What's he trying to prove?"

"How would I know?" I tried to slap her. My hand sort of waved by her face and fell in my lap. I thought about Danny. This is how he felt. He worked ten times harder than I did and I made fun of him.

"Why are they here, Media? Victor doesn't blink without an agenda. What's he doing?"

"Stock prices?" Then: "Water." I was so thirsty, it was like a demon in me, a desperate, nearly living need. "Water."

"I watched you in the testing center. You were awake, weren't you? You could feel everything. Do you even know what he's doing to you?"

I shook my head. "No."

"You really are just a lab rat." She shook her head, disappointed. "You should thank me. I was thinking of using fire in here. That's your real fear, isn't it, burning alive like everyone in The Black?" She smiled and stood, stepping away from me. "I didn't want to be cruel."

"Please…" I begged. I wanted her to come back. I wanted her to give me water or food or just help me escape this feeling. As much as I hated her, I needed her more.

Her face wrinkled in disgust and she snapped her fingers. And just like that, the pain and fatigue were gone. I was back in my body.

"Thank you!" Yes, I actually thanked her. I was almost euphoric, and the *need* was gone, but now my body felt like a costume or facade. My skin was as alien as the PA in my head. God, how Danny must despise me.

Smith walked out of the chamber, apparently done with me. I got to my feet, struggling just to stay upright, and vomited.

"Wait!" I called after her. I had to do something, or she'd never let me finish. She'd take her anger out on Tommy and everyone else I cared about. She turned and walked back, probably hoping I'd beg some more.

"Tell me what you want. I'll do it if you accept the deal."

"Victor didn't tell you? I said you'd know my answer when you crossed the finish line. On your legs or in a body bag; I don't really care which one it is."

And then she was gone.

"*What happened?*" Coach asked when I stumbled outside. "*You just vanished.*" Was that worry in his voice? "*What's with your stats?*"

What could I say? "Smith was here."

"*Why?*"

This time, I was the one who laughed. "I don't think she likes me very much."

"*Are you okay?*" He really sounded worried. It was harder and harder to believe that synthetics didn't have real feelings.

"Great." Meaning, terrible. Meaning dead if Smith didn't accept Victor's offer, but in that sense nothing had changed. Smith had had her fun. Maybe that was a good thing. "Better than great." Coach didn't respond.

I was lying or crazy. Maybe he didn't want to know which.

Come Here, Baby

I ATE AND DRANK like an animal at the summit aid station, ignoring the volunteers, gorging myself, filling some great hole in me with sugar and water. A few minutes later, I was on the summit itself, where Abbey was waiting for me. She smiled and nodded in the afternoon light, seemingly friendly, but all I could think was, *what now?*

Jessica had left another red-fingered message on the massive boulder by the summit sign, a bloody little smiley face. I looked around for another dead animal, but there was nothing up there but me and Abbey. I found out later Jessica had caught a bald eagle that flew too close. It didn't end well for the eagle.

"Your friend's got issues," I noted.

"And you don't?"

I tried to think of a clever response. Nothing came. I sat on an un-bloody boulder, close but not too close to her. The sun was hateful, hot and blinding. The Black smoldered in the haze. More riots? The same riots? I'm sure the Pacific Ocean was boiling out there somewhere. I couldn't seem to shake that feeling, how weak I'd felt at Smith's feet. I'd never felt like that. I'd never known I *could* feel like that. Some part of me still felt broken.

I looked up at Abbey. "What do you want?"

"Nothing." She stood up.

"You waited for nothing?"

"Jessica's looking for you. She'll be waiting ahead."

I nodded toward the blood art. "You thought that was news?"

"No, I just…" I think it was as hard for her to be nice to me as it was for me to trust her. "Just be careful. I don't need her help to beat you, Media. I'd call her off if I could. I'm going to be the first baseline to finish this race. You're going to lose. No matter how hard you try, you're going to lose."

"What's wrong with you?" I wasn't even insulted. I just didn't understand her anger. Who was I to her? I was nobody. It was like she was angry at me for being in danger. No safe word was going to protect me from a woman who punched a panther's head in. I could quit and let Tommy die, which would kill me, or I could continue and die faster. Barring a miracle, this was it for me. I didn't need her hatred. It was redundant.

"What's wrong with *you*?" she asked.

"I don't know. I feel…"

"You look like a broken toy. I saw Smith coming out of the Tunnels. What happened?"

"You saw that?" Half of me thought it was a hallucination.

"Never mind. I don't care what she said. The one thing I liked about you was your irrational self-confidence. That's the woman I want to beat down this mountain. Not this sweaty sack of simpering waste."

I laughed. Abbey could throw some serious shade.

"You think this is funny?" It was fun watching her rage building. Even in my broken state, I recognized someone on the verge of lashing out. She was as tightly corked as I was. All her smarmy smiles were just part of the act, part of the control. And she was losing it.

"I tell you what," I said, standing. Oh, that hurt. "If you beat me, I'll let you hug me." She didn't know what to say to that. "I think you're lonely. No one will touch you. No one trusts you. When's that last time anyone even shook your hand?"

"You think I need a *hug*?"

I'd never heard hug pronounced like a venereal disease.

"I won't even make you wait." I opened my arms. "Come here, baby."

"You're out of your mind."

I think I scared her. She turned and fled down the summit block, bounding over boulders like a gazelle. A gazelle favoring her right foot.

"*You really have a way with people.*"

"I don't like the way she looked at me." Even if she was right. I'd needed a distraction, and now I had it. Coach confirmed that Abbey had strained her left Achilles on the climb. I tried and failed not to smile. I was going to beat her down if it killed me. Which, of course, it probably would.

One Less Obstacle

I CHASED ABBEY DOWN the trail into Little Round Valley. Well, first I jammed more food in my face at the summit aid station. Then I chased her. But no matter how hard I pushed, she pulled farther ahead. On every switchback, I'd see her on the trail below with a little more distance between us. Between trying to catch her and scanning for Jessica, it was hard to focus. I tripped more than once. I almost ate a rock. It was a big rock.

"*Take it easy.*"

"Screw that."

He stopped talking, but he was right. I slowed down to a sustainable pace. I couldn't catch her if I tripped and broke myself.

By the time I got to the Jungle Gym, she was out of sight and I had other problems: snakes. I planned to take the bypass here, which meant losing more time to Abbey, but it was better than being lunch and I wasn't worried about the octopus. I waved the monitor over. I was about to request the bypass when I noticed there was no snake. There was nothing in the trees that I could see, and nothing in the water. She wasn't exactly small. How was she hiding so well?

"Coach, where's the snake?"

"*I'm just getting an update. They pulled the obstacle. I'm not sure why. Now you can save your bypass for the lake.*"

"You're sure it's not there?"

"The python obstacle has been removed," the synthetic confirmed.

"Why?"

That thin smile. "Maybe she needed a snake-ation?"

I snorted. I was starting to like synthetics more than people.

"*Media, get going. You can save your bypass for the lake. If you want to beat Abbey...*"

"Of course I do."

"*...then stop screwing around and beat her.*"

I was on the first branch before he finished the sentence. I couldn't believe how strong I felt. I leaped off the final branch, feeling fresh if a little pumped. It was just the lake after this, then no animal obstacles other than random encounters. Well, except for the Pits. I sprinted after Abbey, thinking I might really win the loop, but what I really wanted was to see the look on her face when I passed her.

Nope. Nope. Nope.

THE MILES FELL AWAY easily, and by the time I got to the Air Stairs—yeah, I'd kinda forgotten about the Ditch—she was in sight again, her black-and-white Blindside colors taunting me between breaks in the trees.

"What the hell?"

Wolves leaped up at the edges of the ditch, snarling and snapping, but they weren't the real problem. The problem was that every step was now a solid five feet higher than the one before it, slanted on top, and they were arranged in an arc that ended at a higher point on the side of the mountain slope. The monitor watched with stolid indifference. I knew I couldn't jump that far, and due to the offsets, speed wouldn't help. How was this even possible? How had Abbey done this? I was getting desperate.

"Coach?"

"*It's not a secret. Jump, bear-hug the pillar, pull yourself up, and do it again.*"

"That's your suggestion?"

"*Abbey did it.*"

"You don't know that."

"*You've seen it in past races. It just looks harder when it's right in front of you.*"

A wolf jumped and scrabbled at the edge of the bit, snarling, and almost got out. There were fewer of them than yesterday, and my friend from wall five was missing. It didn't look harder. It looked like a death trap.

"*You've got this,*" Coach said. I almost laughed. But even if his true role was to talk me into doing stupid crap that would play well on video, he was still right. I could do this. If I could hug each pillar and shimmy up, I might make it. I took a step back and got ready to jump. How hard could it be?

The wolf tried again, front paws scrabbling at the dirt inches from my shoes. His teeth were long white knives and he looked hungrier than I felt. I shuddered and stepped back. Took a shaky breath. If I could ignore a snake, I could ignore wolves. I'm pretty sure that's a haiku. I took a breath, ran two steps, and jumped.

I slammed into the next column, power hugged it and scrambled for some traction with my shoes. A few grunts later, I flopped up on top and took note of a few new scrapes. Then jumped for the next column. Slam. Hug. Grunt. Whale flop. Recover. Coach was right; it wasn't pretty, and I was leaving a lot of skin on each column, but it was doable.

I planted my feet to jump and then froze. There was that deep growl again, the one from wall five where I thought I was going to die. I looked up to find an enormous brown wolf waiting on the last pillar, like a bear waiting for a salmon to jump into its mouth. I didn't even hesitate.

"Fucking bypass!" I yelled.

"*Media, no—*"

"Bypass!" I yelled again. I had no way to fight the wolf. I couldn't reach him with the shocker, and I sure couldn't outrun him. This was insane. Why would Coach even suggest not taking the bypass?

The wolf went from growing to panting happily almost immediately, looking no more threatening than a big dog. They must have PA implants without the forehead crystals.

"Good choice," the synthetic said as I jumped back down the stairs to where I'd started. "The wolves are hungry today."

"*See,*" I told Coach. There was no response. The monitor walked me around the ditch and hung out with me for the required fifteen minute penalty. I just hoped the octopus was as sweet as I remembered.

The Battle of Lazarus Lake

WHEN I GOT TO Lazarus Lake, I wanted to jump into the water to cool my grated arms and legs, but something was off. I'm not sure if 1 saw it or felt it first, but there was something wrong with the water. *Things* slid and coiled beneath the surface, pushing serpentine ripples onto the dark blue surface. I watched for a few minutes, hoping I was imagining it. I wasn't. A long, powerful body curved up and snapped down, revealing the glistening scales of a snake. There were at least two of them in the water, maybe more.

"Well, that sucks." I tried to sound casual, but every hammer-beat of my heart pushed me a step backward and away from the water. This was why Coach wanted me to save the bypass. I should have fought the wolf.

"*I don't think the race director likes you.*"

"Isn't this cheating?" They never switch out the animal hazards. Animals got meaner and more dangerous on each loop, but they were supposed to be the same animals.

"*Do you want to file a protest?*"

The synthetic in a plaid speedo watching from the island looked up, as if ready to take my complaint. Apparently he'd undressed in anticipation of my arrival, because it was the same teenage boy who'd swum out to save me last time, blonde hair riffling in the light breeze. The thought of filing a complaint with him made my stomach clench.

"No," I said. "I…"

"*You can't outswim them.*"

Of course I couldn't outswim them. How could anyone? This was insane. How do you even rescue a runner from a python constriction coil in the middle of a lake?

"Wait, maybe…"

I looked at my hands and concentrated. After a few seconds, my skin changed slightly. Mottled beige? It was neither attractive nor useful.

"*Media.*"

"I can do it." My skin shifted colors almost randomly.

"*Snakes hunt by smell and movement. They don't care what color you are.*"

Figures. All I had now were the MacGuffins. I might be able to stun a snake on contact, but two or three of them? Not a chance. I was done. My race was over, and with it my chance at a better life.

"I think I have to quit." I couldn't believe it. I'd failed everyone, including myself. Tommy wasn't done, so he was still in danger, and I'd heard nothing from Smith or Victor. If I dropped out now, Tommy was never making it to the finish line. Wait, that wasn't right. I checked the race time. Tommy should be done by now, or close. I asked Coach.

"*He's past the picnic tables.*"

"But?"

"*He's injured and moving slowly. One of the animals got to him.*"

"What?" *No, no, no.* The animal might come back to finish the job. I had to continue.

"*He'll be okay.*"

"You don't know that."

"*No, but you can't get in that water.*"

Tommy was in trouble. I pulled out one of the stunners. I could swim with one palmed in my right hand, but could I shock the snake before it got me? I took the other two out and stuffed them in my front pack pockets. Hopefully, I wouldn't stun myself in the boobs. I knew it was idiotic, but if it gave Tommy time to get down, it was worth it.

I'm not afraid of snakes, I told myself. *I'm not afraid of—*

"*What are you doing? Tommy just finished. Second overall. Don't get in that water.*"

I stepped back and caught my breath. Tommy was safe. I wanted to jump up and down and scream, but something kept me nailed to the ground. He was only safe in this race. If I stopped now, Smith could still hurt him later.

"*Katy's in contention for the woman's win,*" Coach added, sounding unsynthetically happy.

Damn it. "How did they get through this?"

"*They all bypassed.*" Of course they did. Maybe I could still swim if I was fast enough.

"*You're not fast enough.*" He was reading my mind again. "*Why are you even thinking about this? Just submit and we can try again next year.*"

"How is that helpful? You're supposed to help me—"

"*Not die. We have no idea how these things are primed. They might wait to strike, they might not. The monitors might get to you in time, they might not. It's just a race. Let it go.*"

God, I wished Coach knew what was really going on. Maybe he could figure some way around this. Because I couldn't let it go. And I didn't want to, even if Tommy was safe and Jessica was still waiting for me. The idea of going back to the lab and slowly dying under Dr. K's watch was unbearable. I wanted the life that Victor had promised so badly that I'd die for it, or at least die fighting for it. If I walked away, that chance was gone forever.

"*Media, just submit. It's over.*"

"Can Victor pull me? Can you or Smith?" Silence. "Coach?"

"*Not unless you're unconscious or legally deemed unable to—*"

"So no one can stop me."

"*The snakes can fucking stop you.*"

"Do you swear this much at other runners?"

"*I don't have to. They're not completely insane.*"

"Brad would do this."

"*Brad got rescued from the cavern and nearly died. He's an idiot.*"

"No," I said. "He's free. He does what he wants. I don't even know what that feels like."

"*You won't feel anything if you die in the lake, Media. What aren't you telling me?*"

That I couldn't go back to TTI knowing I'd be dead in a few years anyway. That I'd rather go out on my own terms. A thousand things I couldn't say.

One of the snakes popped a head out of the water, looking like a curious Paisley tentacle. My heart stopped for a second. I stepped back again, and for some reason that just pissed me off. I was not afraid of snakes, damn it.

"I am the predator," I told myself.

"*Media?*"

"I am the thing with teeth. And the whole world is my prey."

"*Are you going for the psych disqualification?*"

"I'm going for Abbey. She's hurt. I can still win this loop. This is *my* choice."

"*You're going to die.*"

Probably, I thought, but at least it will be on my own terms. I checked my stunners. The snakes couldn't attack instantly. I had time. I had weapons. I could do this. I took one last look at the lake and I let out a great, ridiculous scream of rage and joy and fuck-all insanity. Then I ran all-out into the water and dove. I displaced more water with my panic-flailing strokes than an Earth-killing asteroid hitting the Caribbean dead on. I was Chicxulub, drainer of lakes.

"*Media, look out!*"

I stopped to catch my breath and look around, padding in place as long, fat monsters swam toward me from all directions. I swam away from them, but of course they just got closer, and closer, and that's when I got it. Smith didn't want me to finish or die because it would juice her ratings; she wanted to make a point. She knew this was exactly what I'd do. I'd keep moving, even when it made no sense. I'd swim right into a trap, knowing it was a trap, because I was too conceited to know when I was beat. She was going to win because she knew me better than I knew myself. I was not the predator. I was just the idiot who was about to die. And it turned out, I really wanted to live, even if it was only for a few more years.

One of the snakes accelerated toward me.

"*Swim!*"

I took off in a panic, a flurry of arms and kicks. I tried to put my head down to swim faster, but the fear of not seeing the snakes was too much. I gasped for breath and pushed harder.

I almost made it to the island.

The first snake came from my right, raising its great arrow-shaped head out of the water so that spindrift flew off its scaled skin and teeth.

"No!"

I lashed out with my right hand and hit it right on the snout. I felt a surge of electricity in the water that jolted my entire body, but it kept coming. I jerked away, waiting for it to clamp around my arm or leg and take me down, but the bite never came. Its momentum carried it past me, unconscious, maybe dead. I couldn't believe it worked.

"There are more snakes," Coach noted calmly.

I took three quick breaths and dove, stroking down into the darkness. I kicked toward the cave, looking wildly in every direction for the next attack, but nothing came. Then I was in the tunnel, utterly blind. I pushed on, faster and faster.

I could feel them coming as pressure waves in the water. One from behind, one from ahead. Maybe more. This was it. I was going to die this time. I didn't even bother pulling the other stunners from my pack. I couldn't kill two snakes at once. I couldn't even see them. I pulled myself into a ball and closed my eyes. It was darker in my mind, full of shadows of what might have been. I would never run again with Tommy. I'd never lean against my father and feel the heat of his love. I'd never tell my mother I loved her, even when she seemed insane, or maybe more because she so obviously needed what I hadn't given her. And of course I'd never kiss Danny again, or feel the strange rough skin of his hands. Smith had won because I was Media, the perfectly average fool. A tiny thing with no teeth.

A great mass of water shoved me to one side of the tunnel, and then I was upside down. I slammed into the top of the tunnel. My eyes popped open in panic. It was all black, but in the black, a war was raging. The snakes must be fighting each other. I kicked off the wall and swam.

I pulled out of the tunnel just as my air ran out. I took one final kick off the rock and shot up, up. It was so close now. My head broke the surface and I gasped for air too soon. I sucked in water and choked violently, flailing on the surface.

Every breath was like a kick to the ribs, every cough a spasm of fire and pain. And as I fought not to drown, I could see another snake coming for me. I had almost made it, I thought. I was so close. I gasped for breath, finally taking in air. The snake's head rose from the water, and its mouth opened. I held my arm up in front of my face.

Something moved under me. Something *huge*.

The octopus erupted out of the water in an explosion of tentacles and blood, one snake wrapped around two of her tentacles and snapping at her head. The second snake bit down on one massive arm and blue blood sprayed across my face. The snakes wound around the octopus, trying to trap her, but there were too many tentacles. The octopus wrapped one after the other around them until there was a great ball of suckers and scales throbbing like a giant demon heart. The snakes' heads thrashed out, but the octopus held them firmly.

"*You might want to swim away.*"

The squirming ball disappeared beneath the water. I swam slowly to the side of the lake, suddenly exhausted. I crawled out and lay on the shore, realized the snakes could still get me, and rolled away, literally, until I was out of danger and caked in dirt and pine needles. I looked up at the sky through the branches of towering evergreens. I couldn't believe I was alive.

I sat up and looked at the lake. The snakes and octopus were gone.

"*Media, are you okay?*"

I wasn't sure what to say. The lake parted as the octopus floated to the surface. Great chunks of tentacle were missing. Blue blood spread out from her body like oil from a ruptured tanker. Then one of the snakes coiled around her and pulled her down.

"*Media?*"

The lake and trees blurred. It took me a while to realize I was crying.

"I'm sorry. I'm sorry." I wasn't even sure why I was crying. I was relieved and glad to be alive, but also sad that such a beautiful creature had died for me.

"I can't believe you survived," Abbey said. She leaned over, completely dry, after having taken the bypass. I choked down my next sob. "Why would you do that?"

"Why did you stay to watch?" I wiped my face. What else could I say?

"I wanted to beat you. I didn't want you to die. Seriously. What's wrong with you?"

A good question with no answer I could share.

"Because I can't live like this anymore." Apparently I was sharing anyway. "I can't live without…" I waved my hands around in an easily misinterpreted way. Without octopus snake battles? "Without being out…" Damn it. "Just leave me alone."

She just nodded and turned to run into the woods, her stride uneven as she favored her right leg. Did she pity me now? Was I a pitiable thing?

I slowly, slowly stood on shaky legs and followed her. I later learned that everyone, and I mean everyone, had taken the bypass. I really was an idiot. Was it worth it? No. I'd nearly died and I killed a beautiful octopus in the process. Of course it wasn't worth it. But I had made it somehow, and now Abbey was within reach. I could still beat her. I just kept telling myself that. It kind of worked.

"Say something inspiring, Coach."

"*You're lucky to be alive. And you're a colossal pain in the ass.*"

"You're damn right."

"*But I'll tell you a secret. None of the great runners listen to me, not all the time. You want to win, you have to do it your way sometimes. Even if your way is objectively idiotic.*"

Damn nice Coach, trying to make me feel better.

"Wait, did you call me a great runner?"

"*That doesn't sound like me.*"

I smiled and picked up my pace, keeping Abbey in sight as we climbed toward Desert View. I was keeping up with her now and feeling stronger with every step. My legs kept giving more and more. I even managed to run the flatter sections of trail. From higher up, I heard the call of docker-driven eagles and what might have been the roar of a bear, but none of it registered. I focused on my footing, on not making any more mistakes. If I could stay close to Abbey, I should be able to beat her on the downhill.

It Really Was Bears

I WAS MOVING AT a fast jog by the time I reached the Hidden Lake Divide ridge, where the trail leveled out. My breathing was relatively slow and easy. My heart rate was at the high end of my aerobic zone, so I could've pushed harder if I had to. But I needed to keep a steady pace to prevent bonking. My body was a new and powerful thing, bruised and battered, but not like a lab rat. Like an athlete.

An athlete whose emotions were all over the place. I was excited to be keeping up with Abbey. My overall time was amazingly good, all things considered, but I kept feeling waves of sadness about the lake. I was glad Tommy had finished and was safe, sad that I couldn't see it and pissed that Danny was forced to wait on the sidelines. A thousand things ran through my mind, back and forth, all over the place.

Someone cleared their throat. I stopped and turned, thinking a course monitor was trying to get my attention. But it was Jessica, off-trail to the east. She was sitting on a big brown rock in the shade of clustered lodge pole pines.

"Oh," I said, brilliantly. I'd hoped she'd just forgotten about me. No such luck.

"You just missed Abbey. You're doing well. You're really a *natural* at this."

"Funny." It took me a moment to realize the rock wasn't a rock. It was a bear. There was blood all over the ground, on her hands and body. Had the bear exploded?

"*That was a nine-hundred-pound bear.*" Coach sounded impressed.

"You did that? Why?" As if it made less sense than killing the panther that morning.

"I was just sitting over there waiting when he attacked. No warning. No provocation. Never seen that before in the games, and I've watched all of them." She stood and kicked the bear's carcass. "First the panther and the eagle, then this. Usually, you have to try to pass them or egg them on like Brad does. How is your lover, by the way? Or is he with Tommy now? So confusing with you people. No boundaries. Is that why the panther likes you so much?"

"Are you implying I have sex with animals?"

"I *know* you have sex with animals."

Okay, I walked right into that.

"Media, don't talk to her. Run."

Like that was going to help. "You killed a bear with your hands?" It was hard to understand what the augmented could do. They seemed almost godlike, deities wrapped in human flesh.

"Well, I tried the stunner, but it didn't work. Oddly." She stepped toward me. "Aren't the bears and panthers from Nomanity this year?"

"I guess." I looked for help. I saw a flash of plaid from the woods, a monitor, but they wouldn't intervene until it was too late. There was no sign of Tim, and after what Jessica had done to the first panther, I was almost glad. Abbey was long gone. I was all alone.

"A subsidiary of TTI." Another step.

"I don't know, Jessica." I should've quit before the Lake. Then the octopus would be alive and I wouldn't have to risk getting murdered by this lunatic. Somehow I'd put her out of my mind, which was like forgetting about the apocalypse.

"Did you really think this would stop me? It's…insulting."

"Jessica," I pleaded.

She stopped a few feet away, and I knew what she saw: weakness, something beneath her. I wasn't sure she was wrong, but I still didn't want to die. I searched the trees, the trail, the sky, but there was nowhere to run or hide and no one was coming for me.

"I like bears," she said. "I like most animals. They're honest. They eat, mate, play, kill. No agenda. No ulterior motives. Just survival."

I got ready with my safe phrase, my last chance, but I still didn't want to use it if there was any other choice.

"Jessica."

"I wasn't really going to kill you. I don't like you and I despise your kind, but you've worked hard. You've earned your finish. You can't control what Victor's doing, and you asked him for me. You tried. I was just going to give you a little scare. Maybe a few bruises to remember me by. But since you're trying to kill me…"

"Please…"

"Just show me the camouflage again before you die. Come on."

"I can't."

She shrugged. "Pity."

"*Why aren't you running?*" Coach sounded panicked. I'm not sure why I wasn't. I just couldn't process it all. I'd been tortured, humiliated, threatened, shredded, nearly drowned, watched an octopus die, and now I was about to get beaten to death by a godlike woman who was somehow not covered in bear guts from her latest slaughter. It had been a day.

"I didn't know about the animals," I said. "I wouldn't do that."

"I almost believe you. Just tell me why. Why are you so important? I don't understand what Victor's doing. Do you? No?" Her face darkened with rage, like someone threw a master switch. "Then it's time to die, you insignificant, nagger-loving twat."

"*Run!*"

"Nagghgh," I said. You know that thing where a muscle-bound villain holds the superhero up by his throat, feet dangling in the air, helpless as a mouse in the mouth of a cat? That's what she did to me. I couldn't speak because she had punched me lightly in the throat—*so that's how you do that*—and then closed her fingers around my neck before lifting me off the ground like a lamp she was vacuuming under.

I slapped at her arm, uselessly. I tried to kick, but she just swatted my feet away.

Ten seconds, I heard a voice say. It wasn't real. I just knew that was all the time I had before the pressure on my carotid artery put my brain to sleep. After that, I'd be helpless. I punched at the inside of her elbow, looking for nerve endings, a weakness, anything.

"*Submit!*" Coach yelled. "*Submit!*"

Submitting wouldn't stop her. I was supposed to say something. But what?

Five seconds.

No, no, no. What was I supposed to say?

I yanked one of the remaining two stunners out of my pack.

"That's the spirit!" Jessica said as she swatted it away.

Two seconds.

"*Submit!*" I mentally screamed through my PA. "*I submit!*"

Black.

Light.

Please, please let me go please.

My feet were on the ground, but I was still firmly in Jessica's grip. The world was gray and full of stars. Jessica was looking at something near the treeline. I couldn't focus. What was wrong with my eyes?

"She submitted," a small girl said. "Release her." It was mini-me. That probably didn't help.

"*Your submission has been accepted. She has to let you go.*"

"I submitted," I rasped.

"Shut up." Her grip tightened. Stars flickered and the sky darkened.

"You have ten seconds to comply," the synthetic said. Jessica cracked a smile. The girl was so tiny next to her, I almost laughed. What was she going to do to a beast like Jessica?

"Let me go." I sucked in more air. "You win. I'm out."

Her grip tightened again. I dug my nails into her biceps and gouged bloody rows down to her forearm. Blood welled up in fat blisters and spread into her sweat. It didn't help.

"*Hold on, Media. Help is coming.*"

I would have laughed if I could. Help was not coming. That was one of the old Barkley slogans. Help is never coming. I was going to die because I couldn't remember what I was supposed to remember.

"*Media!*" Coach's voice was fading to an echo, a whisper.

"Jessica Murphy," mini-me said. "You are hereby disqualified for—"

I didn't hear the rest. I blacked out for a second and when I came back, the world was red. I sucked air in so hard my diaphragm ached, a broken pump trying to fill burning lungs. Why was everything red?

Something was drumming, drumming on bone. The synthetic girl was punching Jessica in the midsection, fists flying.

"I don't want to hurt you," Jessica said to the girl, casually pushing her away. The girl recovered and renewed her pointless punching from another angle. Jessica turned to look down at her, bringing me along like a forgotten rag doll, feet flopping in the air. "Please, stop."

She didn't stop. Jessica swatted her, a casual backhand that dislocated the girl's jaw. Synthetic spit flew, but she didn't stop the attack. Jessica's grip faltered.

"Release her!" the girl screamed through her broken jaw. *Releath her!*

Jessica punched her in the face and drove her to the ground. She fell sideways, catching herself on one hand and pushing herself up in one smooth motion. I sucked in air and kicked, aiming for Jessica's stomach, the nerves in her groin, anything to distract her or make her let go. I kicked her with both feet. She didn't even look at me.

"Release her!" The girl was punching again, tiny fists to the kidneys, blindingly fast. Jessica stumbled over a rock. My feet touched on the ground, and I punched Jessica in her flawless damn face. Blood flushed out of her nostrils. She still didn't seem to notice.

Jessica smacked the girl again, knocking her down. I stepped back to get my balance, but Jessica hit me in the stomach and I collapsed, gasping for air.

What was I supposed to say? There was something. Something about my mom.

"Stand down!" The girl kicked at Jessica's legs, but Jessica raised her right arm and leaned forward, coming down with a piledriver meant for the top of her head. She dodged sideways and punched Jessica in the side. Jessica looked at her in amazement, weirdly entertained.

"Mommy dearest!" I screamed.

"*What?*" Coach asked.

Jessica kicked me in the ribs. I lost all my air and curled up in a fetal position. The hack hadn't worked. Jessica kicked me again, but off center, almost missing. Something like pain crossed her face. Then astonishment.

"You've got to be kidding."

Jessica stumbled and picked up a rock. The girl pulled out a tiny ornamental knife from under her long argyle sock, a Scottish *sgian-dubh*. Jessica came at me with the rock raised.

"You think you can get in my head? *My* head? I'll kill your whole goddamn fam…fam…"

Her eyes rolled back just as the girl lashed out, swinging for Jessica's stomach. Jessica should have dodged easily, but instead she stumbled forward, right into the path of the knife. Blood sprayed from her throat in a wide arc. She released me and grasped her throat. The synth dropped her bloody weapon to the ground and stood, frozen, staring.

"Nagghgh," Jessica gasped, just like I had, spitting blood. She sat backward, both hands pressing down on her throat, gasping. She turned her head to look at me. There was no fear in them, just surprise. She lay back in the dirt at rocks, clutching at her throat.

I sat up and crawled over to her, instinctively. She was bleeding. She needed help. And then she grabbed my leg and yanked me toward her. I screamed. She was on top of me so fast, straddling me, one hand still on her neck, the other on mine. How was she still moving?

Blood dripped between her fingers onto my face. I slapped at her, but she didn't notice.

Her grip tightened. "You little—"

She froze again. Her eyes rolled back in her head and she emitted a short, bloody scream as her PA turned fully against her. Then she passed out, unconscious on top of me, her face pressed against mine. I could feel her sweat and blood dripping on my throat and I still couldn't breathe. God, she was heavy.

A second later, she seemed to levitate. She was off me, then next to me. The synth rolled Jessica onto her back and straddled her, her tiny hands pressed firmly against the blood on her neck.

"You have been disqualified from the race, Captain Murphy." She was still slurring her words. "Failure to disengage after submission is cause for immediate disqualification and possible civil and criminal penalties."

Jessica was out cold. The girl looked at me as blood oozed between her tiny fingers, slower now, almost stopped. Why did she look so scared?

"I've called for medivac," she said. "She'll be all right, won't she?" *All rithe.* "Director Smith wants to let you know that you can continue. Jessica didn't honor your submission request, so it's null and void. Do you wish to continue?"

"What?"

"There's so much blood. I cut too deep. Did I cut too deep? I don't know your bodies that well. I think I killed her."

Who cares? I tried to roll over. The sky was still red. On video from a dozen camouflaged BHD shots, you can see that every blood vessel in my eyes had popped and my corneas were pink and veined in crimson. My throat was purple and black, but she hadn't crushed my trachea. Nothing was broken. It was almost as if she'd been trying to do everything but kill me, which made no sense.

"Media, your stats are a mess. Resubmit your DNF and I'll get someone to—"

"No." I rolled on my side and spat blood. Some of it was Jessica's. "Where's Abbey?"

"You're kidding."

"Do I sound like I'm kidding?"

"You sound like you're dying." Sigh. *"She checked in at Long Valley five minutes ago."*

I rolled onto my stomach and pushed onto my knees. The sky grayed and then came back.

"Do you wish to continue?" the synthetic asked, her words strangely clear with her jaw askew. Why did she look so afraid? Jessica was stirring beneath her. How was that possible? I've never wanted anyone to die so much in my life.

"Yes." I coughed blood. "I'll continue."

"*Me*—" Coach started.

"YES!" Oh, that hurt.

"Approved. Good luck." She turned to Jessica. "It's okay. Help is coming. Just relax."

We heard it at the same time. The spider bot rolled up the trail and into the clearing. Mini-me's mouth fell open and sideways, a strangely human gesture. She was terrified. I stood and stared at Jessica's bloody body. I wanted to kill her myself. I wanted to stomp on her throat until she choked on her spit and blood. What did I care if she bled out?

"Thank you," I told the synth.

"Of course." Her smile was askew, but she was also crying and that was the thing that freaked me out the most. Why was she crying?

The spider unfolded twenty feet away, spokes and rims reaching out as legs. They could extend on both sides as sixteen-legged spider things, unroll like a centipede or, as in this case, unfold on one side, push over, and then be a spider with eight free arms on top. I'd seen it a thousand times online or in the distance, but never up close. It was huge. The back of each leg-arm was a metallic blade. There was no head, just a hundred small black lenses on each side of the central body like lugs on a tire rim. Nothing looked at me, but they were all watching.

I stumbled backward. Jessica's eyes opened.

"I'm sorry," mini-me said, a scared little girl with wide eyes and nothing synthetic about her. The spider stepped closer, great black and silver limbs casting skeletal shadows.

"*Excessive force. You may not want to watch this.*"

"What?"

"No," Jessica gasped. "She didn't…"

And then it happened. That unholy thing let one arm slide out and down so fast it was just a blur and a rush of air. Then the synthetic's head rolled off her shoulders.

"Holy…" I whispered.

The spider caught the head easily with two black arms.

"*Get out of there. Focus on Abbey. Just get out of there.*"

I stumbled away. The spider caught mini-me's body as it fell, lifting into the air, and then sped down the trail with head and body held in four of its blade arms. The rest waved in the air for balance as it juggled the body parts back and forth as easily as a circus clown with bowling pins. I wanted to scream.

"*Media, just...*"

"I know." I knew the girl wasn't a real person. She was just programming and skin, but that's not how it felt. I'd just watched someone die. And it didn't help that Jessica was rolling up on her side.

So it's probably strange that I started laughing, hard. It was not a pretty sound.

"*Media?*" I think Coach was reconsidering the psych disqualification.

"I'm okay," I said, trying to get hold of myself. I'd just realized that everything had oddly worked out in my favor. An octopus died, Jessica was maimed, and mini-me was now a circus act on her way to the furnace, but I was fine. I mean, not fine. Bloody and stumbling, but alive. And all I had to do was finish the race. I just couldn't believe it.

"*Abbey's getting away,*" Coach said, obviously trying to distract me. And it worked. Beating her was now a real option. My new life was just 8,000 feet and twelve miles away. What better way to start it than by wiping that smug smile off Abbey's face?

I broke into a run.

"I'm coming for you," I whispered, or gasped. My lower back was a furnace of pain. My eyes wouldn't focus. My hands were nearly useless and I could barely breathe, but I didn't care.

"I'm coming, Abbey."

I stumbled on a rock and nearly fell.

"*Be careful. You can't catch her if—*"

"I'm not going to catch her. I'm going to *beat* her."

"*Okay, but how 'bout getting some water at the aid station first?*"

"I'm coming for you!" I stumbled faster down the trail toward Grubb's Notch, but in my mind, I was flying. Behind me an octopus rotted and a demigod crawled in the dirt, but all of it just made me want to catch Abbey even more. I can't explain it. The sun could explode and the universe could collapse and I'd still just want to beat her down this mountain. I'm pretty sure unquenchable mania isn't in the baseline marking literature, so I guess that's just me.

Media, the perfectly average lunatic.

Medical Waiver

"HOLY…" THE AID STATION captain started.

"I'm fine," I whisper-spat. My throat was like a cocktail straw.

"Your hands…" he whispered. I still had strands of Jessica's hair and skin under my fingernails. I wiped some of her off on my shorts. He grimaced and then came around the table to examine my throat. I slapped his hand away.

"I'm fine."

His eyes fluttered as he checked my stats on his PA. He probably talked with Coach and Smith. I watched him, ready to argue, but he just nodded and stepped back.

"Look at me," he said. I looked at him. His PA crystal flashed a few times. I winced, but refused to look away. "Well, at least your eyes work." Another flash. "I'm sorry, Media, but I have to flag you for medical disqualification."

"The hell—"

"Or you can continue, if you accept full responsibility and waive any right to seek legal damages against the Marathons, its sponsors, staff and all other related parties."

I laughed. Well, I sort of choke-snorted. "I accept."

"Thank you. And good luck. Don't forget to hydrate."

Another laugh-cough. I tried to eat, but couldn't swallow. The volunteers stared at me in collective horror. I grimaced, drank electrolytes and tried not to fall on my face.

"How far ahead is Abbey?"

"Maybe twenty minutes," the captain said. "But she was limping…"

Her Achilles, I thought. Good. There was still a chance, but I had to get moving.

"Your heart rate's high," the medic said. "You're seriously dehydrated. It's 115 in the valley. If you push too hard in that heat, and don't drink more, you *will* die." He didn't say it as a threat. He was just stating facts.

"I won't hold it against you."

"For your hair?" A woman passed me a headband, and I instinctively reached for my hair. That was a mess. I guess I'd lost my headband fighting Jessica. I shoved things back in place as best I could—not really caring, as long as it stayed out of my eyes—and thanked the woman.

I drank more. I swallowed too many salt pills. Coach was blissfully silent. I nodded a gruesome thank you to the aid station volunteers and stumbled up the trail toward the Scree Slope. My legs were shaking, and I was listing to my left like a sinking ship, but I was moving.

The Downside of Stubbornness

I WAS AT THE edge of the Scree Slope when I realized I'd only half-filled my water bladder. It wasn't the volunteers' fault. They'd clearly tried to help. I just wasn't listening.

It's fine, I thought. *Less weight to slow me down.*

"I'm coming," I whispered to Abbey.

"Take it easy," Coach said. *"Don't hurt yourself."*

"Coach off." He was gone. I took a long, flailing jump, hit the slope off center and rolled. I scraped my shoulder and arm, but I didn't care. Wounds heal. Pain could wait. I jumped again and fell again. I focused on Abbey's face and her sickening smile.

I'm coming for you.

I fell again and again. When I stopped rolling, I pushed myself down and rolled further. At the end, I dust-bunnied my way back to the trail and dry heaved as I rolled under the barbed wire. I cut myself a few times on barbs but barely noticed. I left some hair on one barb. In the race recap, they did a closeup on the bloody clot of it hanging on the wire like something from a battlefield.

I stood and broke into a sideways run.

The wall at 7,500 feet was painful, but I made it. I nearly killed myself at 6,500. My docker count got higher as I got lower. There was almost no one else left on the course, so I was the main event. My social media feed turned from a mix of fans and haters to a series of bets on when I'd fall over and die. A lot of money changed hands. They were all going to lose. I was never going to quit.

I sprinted into the trees above Flat Rock, dodging overhanging limbs, until I missed one and slammed my head into a branch at full speed. If the tree had been living, I'd be dead, but the dry wood shattered and we both went down, girl and branch, into the dirt. I stumbled to my feet, wiping the blood off my forehead, and pulled a splinter out of my scalp. I waited for the gray to fade. And then I was running again. Slower, unbalanced, but still running. Until, well.

So that's what was in the third set of pits.

A dragon basked at the edge of Flat Rock, scales and claws shining in the sun. It was like a Komodo dragon but much bigger; a huge beast that smelled like rotting meat.

Oh, there's the meat. One of the wolves was dead between its feet. The giant's slanted dragon eyes squinted at me, strings of shredded wolf meat hanging from its teeth. It reminded me of Jessica.

"Coach?" Silence. *"Coach on."*

"Be quiet and move slowly. Don't go near her food."

"Her food is on the trail."

"Then don't step on it."

Don't step on monster food. Check.

A teenage boy monitor in a three-piece suit watched from the rocks above. He smiled and waved. I wanted to smack him off the cliff, but instead moved slowly down the trail. Nice dragon. I stepped over the limp forelimb of the dead wolf, or what was left of it. The dragon's eyes narrowed to watchful slits. Pretty dragon. This thing was going to sell like gangbusters. All they needed to do was add peacock colors, and she'd be at every dance party for a decade. A great fluorescent lizard god who only occasionally ate the guests.

I stepped on something that snapped. I froze.

"Megalania prisca," Coach said. *"They don't have great hearing."*

Megalania squinted at me, then lost interest. She took another bite of delicious wolf, chewing with her mouth open. Bones snapped. It was quite a show. Coach said something unsupportive about my heart rate. I ignored him and started to move past her when she suddenly looked past me. I turned and gasped.

Five wolves were arrayed in a line behind me. The one in the middle had forced me off the Air Stairs. He was growling as saliva dripped from bared fangs. Megalania took a step forward, directly onto the body of the dead wolf, and let out a deafening high-pitched roar.

"*Media, run.*"

I looked back at the trail, but the dragon was in the way. I couldn't go back. The only way out was to scramble up a rock to my left, so I started to move. Megalania roared again. The wolves moved in. I took another step as the dragon charged forward.

"*Run!*"

I ran up the rock face and dove into a giant manzanita bush. Wolves leaped onto the dragon. The dragon whipped his tail around and threw a wolf so far into the air he might have reached low orbit. It wasn't a fair match. I thrashed my way out of the manzanita, into the next one, around a tree, and back onto the trail. And then I *ran*.

I weaved in and out of stunted oak and chaparral. The bushes were overhead, obscuring the trail, but I could feel Abbey up ahead, moving slowly. I thought I caught flashes of her as I started to run on the downhill. I wasn't sure. My vision was iffy at best.

I made the clearing at the old water drop. It was the first time I had a clear view to the north below Flat Rock. The Coachella Valley part of The Black glared orange and brown more than 5,000 feet below. The sun was painful, blinding and vindictive. I sipped at my water and ran, switchback after switchback, and that's when I saw her.

A few hundred feet down, the view opens up on the flank of the ridgeline so you can see the trail below for several hundred feet. She was surprisingly close and moving slowly. Maybe she'd expected Jessica or the dragon to take me out. She was limping more now. I was actually going to catch her.

The sky turned gray for a second. I had trouble catching my breath.

"*Drink more.*"

I drank more.

"*Your kidneys are failing. You need to slow down.*"

I sped up. Abbey wasn't getting away from me, not when I was this close. My new body could do this. I was unbreakable.

I didn't catch her before the next short climb, which sucked. The uphills were killing me. She dipped into the saddle and then started climbing up to the next ridgeline. She glanced back, saw me and sped up. I got to the east end of the saddle and started the climb. My legs were shaking. My stomach was turning over. The sky grayed and cleared. I could hear my heartbeat in my ears, *bam-bam-bam*, way too fast. I leaned onto my legs and pushed off, hands on knees, climbing in the European style, or trying.

"*Media*," Coaching pleaded.

"Coach off." I wasn't angry. I knew he was right. I was falling apart. What did it matter if I caught Abbey and collapsed at her feet? Finishing the race was more important. But I kept chasing her anyway, because obstinacy.

I topped out. The next section plunged down steeply, bypassing the old switchbacked trail. My legs tried to give out. I stood by sheer will, gulping for air.

Almost there, I told myself. *Almost there.*

And then what?

Who cares? I was in a tunnel and she was the light. Catching her was all that mattered.

I pushed myself into a run, pushing blindly through bush down the slippery dirt trail. I couldn't see her anymore, but she couldn't be that far ahead. I'd catch her before the bottom and give her a big, bloody hug before I passed out. That'd teach her.

I burst out of the bushes into a clear patch of steeper, rockier downhill.

I stumbled and started to recover.

Where are you?

"Frap!" I started with fuck and ended with crap. Abbey faced me, arm outstretched. I tried to duck, but I was already off balance and she caught me right below the neck with a perfect clothesline. My upper body stopped, my head snapped forward as my feet flew out from under me. I did a partial backward flip and twist, landing face-down in the rocks. I heard something moan, the mewling whine of a dying animal, and realized it was me. I rolled over. What had I done to myself?

Abbey looked down at me, smiling that same damn condescending smile. I tried to slap it off her face, but she just swatted my hand away. I didn't have the energy to try again.

"I'm sorry Jessica hurt you," she said. "Are you okay?"

Not sure what noise I made there. Snort-laugh-cry?

"Media, are you okay?" The sun lit up her hair like the angel of death.

"I caught you." I tried to sit up, but didn't actually move.

"Yeah, you're a stubborn little bitch, aren't you?"

I nodded. Why deny it?

"So, here's what's going to happen. I'm going to go down and win this thing."

"No." I grabbed at her hydration vest strap.

"Yes." She pulled my hand off easily. I had the grip strength of an infant. "And you're going to crawl or walk or do whatever it takes to get down *alive*, you understand?"

"Why?"

"Why what? Just get down, Media. I'll see you at the finish line." And she took off.

"Coach on." I stared up at the sky, waited for useless advice, or music, just something to distract me. I hated that she was beating me, but she was right. I just had to finish now. I don't know what was wrong with my head.

"*You should see your stats.*" Coach showed me some numbers. "*If she hadn't taken you down, you had a ninety-three percent chance of a heart attack. We saved your life. Now get off your butt and finish this thing.*"

"We?" I asked.

"*I asked her Coach for a little help.*"

"You did this?" I sat up. Every muscle in my abdomen cramped.

"*Well, I didn't ask her to clothesline you, but that was pretty epic.*"

"You think this is funny?"

"*No, I think this is just a race. It's not worth dying for.*"

"I wasn't going to die. I was going to—"

"*Hurt her? Kill her? You know that's not you.*"

"Damn it, Coach. I just…I'm just so tired of people telling me what to do."

"*Understandable. Hold on.*" Pause. "*Victor says she accepted the deal. What deal?*"

I laughed a little. It hurt a lot. I should have been flooded with relief, but my body wasn't capable of much more than a fleeting second of reduced misery.

"You'll see. I might get down this mountain alive." If I stopped acting like an idiot.

"Of course you will. You've got time. Just take it slowly. Even you can't screw this up."

I was going to say something snide, but he was offline again. I was probably the only person in history to piss off a synthetic that badly.

I tried to sit up again. *Ouch.* This was going to suck. And what was that growling noise?

I looked to my left and there he was, my friend the gray-black timber wolf.

"Huh," I said. So much for not screwing this up.

The wolf stepped closer and gnashed his teeth. Apparently he hadn't gotten the memo from Smith. I wasn't even sure how that worked. Could she control the animals that easily? A great academic point I could explore in the afterlife. I pulled out a stunner and waited for him. If I was lucky, I'd shock him before he ate me.

And then he yelped and disappeared. I'd seen this before. I looked down the trail and the wolf was on his back under a giant black panther that made him look like a scared little puppy.

"Tim!"

The panther looked at me with disdainful eyes that said, *Stop calling me that, that's not my damn name.* And then he closed his massive jaws around the wolf's throat. The wolf stopped moving. A second later, Tim pulled back and let him go. The wolf scrambled up, took one look at us, and then ran back into the underbrush.

It took a while to stand. It took longer to get my balance. I wiped some of the blood out of my eyes and tried to drink some water, but there wasn't much left. The sun tried to boil my eyes. It was going to be a long walk. I took the first step and nearly collapsed. A really long walk.

Tim watched all this, head canted to the side, either amused or disgusted. I stumbled, limped and shuffled my way down, then

338 SHAWN C. BUTLER

slightly up, then down some more. I finished the last of my food and sucked on my empty hydration tube. I licked my lips and forearms just for the taste of salt, like a cat cleaning himself. Tim padded along next to me, quiet, panting, probably hungry and wishing he'd eaten the wolf.

"Thank you," I said. I was so glad for the company, I even ignored the blood on his lips. It didn't matter what Tim had been up to as long as he didn't eat me. He might even protect me and, when I collapsed, he could lick all the salt off me he wanted.

Step, drag, step, rest, suck wind, glare at the sun, step, stare at the ground, resist the urge to sit on Tim and ride him down, step, gasp and repeat.

Death, Destroyer of Worlds

AS YOU DESCEND INTO the glaring hellfire that is Palm Springs, you spend a lot of time staring at the glaring hellfire that is Palm Springs. Residential domes shined like crystal balls from another world. MoBO's towers burned white-hot, leaving gray ghosts scorched into your retinas. Sometimes you saw the city, sometimes you didn't. But it was always there, always thousands of feet below, shimmering in the heat like a vindictive mirage.

On the descent from 3,200 to 2,800 feet, the trail dips left and down the north flank of a rocky ridgeline above a sandy canyon wash. It's one of the few times on the lower trail that there's anything immediately above you—the type of place I'd have looked for mountain lions to pounce if it was dark and I didn't have Tim with me. And if there were still natural mountain lions.

Just after the switchbacks around 2,800 feet, the trail traverses a short saddle between the upper ridgeline and the next pile of dirt-colored boulders. One of the boulders seemed out of place. It was too black and clean and inappropriately large. Like a block of rounded obsidian dropped from space. How had I not noticed that before? Between the blinding heat and my blurry eyesight, I didn't make much of it until Tim's growl brought me up short.

The boulder moved.

It was a magnificent transformation. The bear pushed itself up on its hind legs, raising a head with great black eyes and a long leather-dry snout dripping drool and purple things. Tim crouched. The bear stood on four legs wider than tree trunks and chuffed dust into the blazing afternoon air. This was the bear missing from the display case at ModCon, *Arctotherium-whatever-it-was*. A prehistoric monster brought back to pick off the slower runners. The god of all bears. He looked like he hadn't eaten in a thousand years.

"Seriously?"

He looked at me with big black bear eyes. *Yes*, they said. *Seriously*. I didn't move. I couldn't move. I didn't even think about moving. No part of me was working. Tim stepped forward, growling again. The bear blinked as if noticing him for the first time.

I had no illusions that Tim could fight this thing and win, but part of me knew it didn't matter. All I needed was a distraction and a head-start. Tim was there to protect me. This monstrosity might terrify me, but Tim wasn't going to back away from anything. These were beasts cut from the same cloth. I was going to witness an animal death match to end all death matches.

And if I was smart, which was questionable, I was going to run like hell before it ended. To the victor go the spoils, and as bad as I smelled, I wasn't fully spoiled just yet. This was why Tim had winked at me. He had my back. I was his human. I rested my hand on his shoulder, felt his great lungs taking in gallons of superheated air, sensed him getting ready to leap, and tried to convey my appreciation. I just hoped he'd survive the encounter.

The bear rose up on its hind legs and roared. Spittle flew from a mouth nearly twenty feet in the air. He blotted out the sky. It rained bear spit and blueberries. Where the hell had he found blueberries? I felt his primordial rage in my bones.

And then Tim ran away.

I thought at first he was flanking the giant angry screaming bear monster, but then he got way past reasonable flankage, leaped onto a nearby rock and vanished into the scrub brush and cliffs above the saddle. He was gone in seconds. He didn't even roar. He just left me there.

Had I not been severely dehydrated, I would have wet myself. I'm not ashamed. Bodily hygiene was way down on my list of concerns. I was like a bird dumping ballast before a panicked takeoff. I wanted it all out. But there was nothing to dump and I wasn't a bird, so it was a terrible analogy and I was going to die.

The bear roared again. My brain retracted into its primitive self, just a little frog nerve bundle full of stupid, blinding fear. I would have screamed "Submit!" at the top of my lungs until someone came and took this thing away, but I didn't even try. I was too dumb in the head to remember the word, let alone speak it. I had reached too much, turned it up to eleven and gone to plaid. Synovial fluid ran out of my ears. Or should have. I was gone.

One more roar, this one meant for me personally. The sun shook. The sky cracked and space leaked in. He was marking his food. He was letting me know what was coming. He was a god. I was nothing but a meal waiting to be eaten.

"Yeah, but can you fly?" I whispered.

There was a novel from I couldn't remember when about a giant bioengineered bear named Mord and its lifelong duel with a sentient houseplant. I could believe a lot of things about the wonders of genetic engineering, including a bear the size of a small building, but a flying bear was a bit much even if it was a beautiful image—its great mass turning slow loops in the evening sky over a dead city as its thousand murder-bear followers howled up at their ursine deity. This was apropos to nothing, but somewhere in the overloaded circuitry of my brain, I came face-to-face with a nightmarish bear god and, zap, I thought it was Mord. I mean, why not?

Because this is reality, I told myself. *Because bears don't fly.*

It was like explaining physics to an ant. The listening part of my brain was offline. I think Coach was screaming something but I couldn't process it. My only thought was, if Smith had really accepted the deal, the god-bear wouldn't attack. If she hadn't, I was about to die and there was nothing I could do about it. I was prey. I had no teeth. I couldn't even run.

Not-Mord settled back onto his front legs and shambled toward me, bringing his massive head closer to mine. It was too big; I couldn't process it. I couldn't move. His great head moved from side to side, studying me with one big black eye and then the other one, left and right. He sniffed at me. Purple-red drool the consistency of glue hung a foot down from his steaming maw. I focused on the saliva. That was going to be me soon. Just red goo in the gut of a

342 SHAWN C. BUTLER

god. I wondered if Alex would enjoy the ride through his bowels.

I laughed just a little, more like a snort. The last thing I would ever do. I hoped Alex wrote this story in a way that made my death noble or dignified. Not-Mord squinted and then looked past me, as if he'd lost interest.

"You lost your pussy," Jessica said. I couldn't turn my head away from the bear, and I didn't believe she was there. I was hallucinating. It happens. Jessica was up at Long Valley trying not to bleed out while the spider bot juggled synthetic body parts and I was down here by myself. My brain was just making up stuff to cope.

"Do you have any idea what you've done?" imaginary Jessica rasped. The bear seemed to hear her, too. Maybe we were all in the same dream, or maybe he wasn't real either. "You hacked a military PA. That's treason." Cough. Spit. "All for what? For *you*?" Was that laughter? It sounded like sand on rocks. "You almost started a war. *You*. I still don't get it."

The bear reared up on its haunches again, high, so high. It was almost over. If a war was coming, I was going to miss out. I hoped Danny survived.

Wait. "You said *almost*," I told imaginary Jessica. Her face worked oddly. There was no fear in it, not even concern, just a strange, deathly focus. Her hands balled into fists. I wanted to reach out to touch her, to see if she was real, so I did.

Poke.

"Holy crap. You're real."

"God, you're strange." It was hard to argue the point. "I talked to Victor. He agreed to bring me in if I didn't report what happened up there…and if you get to the bottom alive." She smiled. "He thinks I'm a killer. Just another power-hungry, augmented lunatic. And now I have to protect *you*. Whatever. Overwatch and the Navy will discard me after this catastrophe, and deoptimization means death for me, so…"

I poked her again. What real person thinks like that? She was such a rare combination of horror and beauty, stunning in her power and confidence. Even the god-bear seemed envious, and grunted for attention. She smiled at him like just another target, like prey, and then something changed in her face. You could see the decision take hold and suddenly she just looked sad.

"I guess I'll save you." She shook her head. "I just hate killing another bear."

I snorted. "What? You can't…"

She smiled twice, once with her lips and another with her bloody throat.

Of course she could. I reached for my last stunner, about to offer it her, but then I realized I liked the bear more. And if Smith took the deal, there was no reason for it to kill me.

"I can do anything I want," she said, turning to Not-Mord and ignoring me. She leaned forward and roared at the bear. The bear roared back, spitting out the rest of his blueberry detritus. Jessica got ready to charge and suddenly I was out of the privacy mode I didn't know I'd been in in the first place.

"Annihilation!" I screamed senselessly. That was the name of the Mord book. I slammed the psychotic murder bitch right in the side of the head with a stunner. She went down *hard*. I thought I'd killed her. I wanted to, but I was also eighty-four percent certain she was still a hallucination.

The bear god grunted. I'd like to think it was in approval.

Wait, the book wasn't *Annihilation*. It was…

Jessica spasmed in a distinctly not-dead way.

Goddamn it. Now I had to worry about the bear eating her alive. Wait, no I didn't. Bears need to eat. This was working out for everyone.

"Tommy's waiting for you," Coach said. *"Danny's with your family. Leave her."*

My first thought was, who's the creepy old guy in my brain? My second was, who's Tommy? My third was just to realize I could move. Jessica's fate was in the hands of Smith and Mord and I honestly didn't care what happened to her as long as I didn't have to watch. I inched past the distracted bear as he shambled up to drool on Jessica's head. The closer I got to him, the more I thought he just looked miserable. It was way too hot for a giant black-furred bear. He licked Jessica, drooled some more, and looked around for something more like a lake or glacier.

"Oomph," he said, disgusted. I couldn't agree more.

"*You're almost there. Just keep moving. Quietly.*"

I moved oh so quietly. Somehow, I got past Not-Mord and was moving down the trail one shuffling step at a time. None of that had been real. It couldn't have been real. But the heat was real. It was like a wall pressing down. The pain was real. And my thirst…

"*You're running out of time. If you want this, you're going to have to dig deep.*"

Did he really just say that? I just left a woman to get god-bear eaten. I had to dig deep?

"To give one-hundred percent? To be all I can be? To subvert the dominant paradigm and ride the wave of determination to shores of success?"

Coach laughed, not a lot, but a little. I was just impressed my tired brain used actual words instead of grunts. Maybe the adrenaline helped.

"*More like one-hundred-ten percent. Less talking, more walking. If you don't move, Abbey wins and I'll eat this cheese myself.*"

Weirdly, that's what did it. Abbey had already won and god was a bear, but nobody eats my damn cheese.

That Was Easy

SOMETIMES WHEN THE TESTS went badly and I was puking for days on end, even quotes from *Endurance* didn't help. The only escape was unconsciousness, and I'd lost months of my life that way, oblivious to what Dr. K was doing. It was too easy to hide in the darkness. So I'd taught myself to partition time, to break it down from day to hour to minute and second, the smallest measure I could focus on. I could take it for another minute. I could take it for another second. The secret was to stop counting. There was no past or future. There was just this instant. And I could take anything for an instant.

I can take it, I thought as my right knee swelled to the size of my head.

I can take it, I thought as I crawled up from the valley of pits to the sanctimonious cinnamon smile of the synthetic monitor on the ridge above.

I can take it, I thought as I fell off the far side of the 3,500-foot rope wall and nearly shattered my pelvis, lying stunned in the dirt until I could stagger back to my feet.

I can take it, I can take it, I can take it.

At some point, Tim came back, padding next to me so I could use his footfalls to measure each moment. Tim was my metronome.

I can take it, step. *I can take it,* step.

It never occurred to me to be reproachful. Of course Tim ran away. It was the smart move, and I shouldn't have taken his life for granted.

"I can take it," I told him and myself every time I dry heaved from dehydration, heat exhaustion and god knows what else. "I can take it." Over and over again, as I limped down the rocky trail toward the bottom.

The distant digital clock told me I was running out of time.

I pushed harder. It didn't help. I stumbled and nearly fell.

"*Five minutes*," Coach said. I could see him standing by the yellow gate, waiting with my brother and family. They were all there. I stopped, leaning on my knees to catch my breath. Tim licked my arm. Someone really needed to get him some salt.

"Thank you," I told him. "For coming back." And then he vanished, dissolving into the heat, more spirit than flesh. Turns out I had imagined all that. Tim never came back after the bear.

"*Four minutes*," Coach said, as if I couldn't see the damn sign.

Just a few more steps. The earth baked and shimmered.

I stumbled down the final stairs to the trailhead.

Five more steps.

Three-two-one.

I crossed the finish line covered in blood and dirt at 11:59:47, thirteen seconds before the cutoff. Smith was waiting with an old Easy Button in her hands, another artifact of the Barkleys. I smacked it and an old computer voice said, "That was easy!"

"I guess we have a deal," she said, shaking my hand.

Joy, relief and exhaustion hit me all at once.

The crowd screamed my name.

I tried to wave at them.

Then fell to my knees.

And wept.

Victory at MoBO

I'D NEVER CRIED LIKE that before, so I didn't know the scope of it. How it could twist my body and bend already cracked ribs. I didn't know the sound of it until I heard my sobs over the scream of the crowd. I sounded like a wounded thing, an animal, but I'd done it. I'd finished. I was desperately glad it was over and sad at the same time. I wiped my eyes and tried to focus.

The rest came in flashes. Brad and Coach picked me up and brushed me off. Smith came over with my finisher medal and smiled brightly, as if this was just another day at work.

"Good job." She put the medal around my neck. "I look forward to seeing you next year."

I grunted something. No idea what. Listen to the video. It's not human speech. The sky kept spinning. I stumbled into my father's arms and let him take my weight.

"You were right," I said as Mom wrapped her arms around me from behind.

"About what?" Dad whispered.

"I'm really stubborn."

"Of course you are." His voice was so deep I felt it in my chest. It was the last thing I remember before I fell asleep, standing, as thousands of people shouted my name.

I woke up a second later in a panic. God, I needed a bathroom. I wasn't sure I could pee, but it felt like I had better try. Wait, where was my brother?

"Where's Tommy?" I asked.

"In the clinic," Dad said. "He's fine. One of the panthers got him on the final descent, or he might've won the lap. You should see the bite marks on his legs." Turns out you can't outrun the predators after all. Then I remembered the blood on Tim's mouth. That two-timing bastard.

"Good job." Katy came up and offered me a quick, Germanic hug, not unlike an abdominal blitzkrieg. I almost threw up on her. I was not the pretty girl at the finish line. I was a walking war crime. "You'll do better next year." It sounded like an order. "I'll bring the cheese."

"You won, Katy. You *won*. What's that even like?"

"Freedom."

I might have looked confused.

"Winning gets me out of this race, forever. Full contract release. I'm never doing this shit again. If you come back as an endurance model, my slot's yours." Before I could speak, she turned and vanished. I think she left MoBO and Palm Springs and never came back. After she disappeared, I saw Terrence waving at me from the crowd, his flawless girlfriend at his side, like royalty. I waved back. Oh, that hurt.

And then Abbey was there, already showered and clean. God, I hated her, or at least I think I did. Things were confusing since she conspired with Coach to save my life. She whispered an apology and I gave her a giant, dangerous hug. I wanted to squeeze her like I should've squeezed the Air Stairs columns, so she'd know there was no escape, but I was so weak I could barely keep my arms around her. She didn't fight it. I think she was afraid to touch me with bare hands.

I pulled away. "See, that wasn't so bad."

She stepped back, probably more disgusted by the blood all over me than the hug, but it's hard to say. I wonder if she showered again later, and how many tests Dr. K would run on me to make sure I hadn't been GIPed.

"So, I'll be seeing you next year?" she asked.

"Maybe. I hope so." I looked down, back. "Thanks for saving my life."

"Did you just thank me?"

"Don't make me regret it."

"You're welcome. But if you do come back, the kid gloves are off. I'm going to kick your ass all over the mountain." And then she was gone, taking the last word with her into the crowd.

"I think she likes you," Mom said. "I'm so glad you made new friends."

I tried to think of a snarky response, but she wasn't wrong. Coach finally reappeared and congratulated me, then shoved a rehydration drink in my barely functional hand.

"Drink." I drank. "You need to get to the clinic soon."

"Only if you let me back on the team next year."

"No promises," he said, winking. "Now drink."

I drank and fell back against Dad. Coach wandered off to do coach things. I just wanted to go to the bathroom and pass out. Preferably not in the bathroom, but it wasn't out of the question. Mom started trying to wipe blood off my face with a handy-wipe she'd found somewhere. She was going to need more than one.

"*Well done, Media*," Victor said in my head. "*So here's the deal…*" and he told me. I listened as best I could. There were a lot of words but most of them worked out in my favor. He finished with: "*I'm glad you didn't die.*"

Me too, though it wasn't for lack of trying.

Dad stiffened. Smith cleared her throat. I guess it was show time. I tried to walk, but couldn't stand on my own, so Dad escorted me over to Smith. Behind us, the race clock had stopped at 72:00:00 over a crawl of "Good Job, Morons. Now Go Home!"

She waved for silence, didn't get it, and just started talking. Her voice boomed out of hidden speakers so loudly that everyone turned to look. BHDs swarmed out of the evening sky.

"As you all know," she said. "Media Conaill is the first baseline beta ever to compete in or complete the Modified Marathons." A lot of cheering, along with a few boos and some golf claps. "She finished the last lap with seconds to spare after fighting snakes, octopuses and even the biggest bear we've ever had on the course." A lot more cheering, probably for the bear. I noticed she didn't mention Jessica. Probably a good idea.

"I know there were rumors that Media was cheating, that she was doing too well for a first-time runner, and there was a reason for that. Media, are you okay to talk?"

"Thank you," I said, and coughed. My voice echoed through the courtyard. "Let's all give Dr. Smith a hand for one of the most memorable marathons ever!" Loud cheering, and Smith nodded in thanks. I'd never been the center of attention before, not like this. I didn't hate it.

"Fiddy!" Brad yelled. I'd wondered what happened to him. Danny was leaning against his side, apparently still having trouble walking on his own. I gave them both a wave.

"So," I said. God, it was hard to talk. "I'm going to keep this short." I cleared my throat and reached back in my exhausted brain for the familiar tone and cadence I'd been grilled on for years, and just let my mouth run on auto-pilot. "Or Coach Johnson will drag me to the clinic. One of the great challenges with endurance subscriptions employed by our troops in combat is the constant need for renewals. Cut off from supplies, special teams in remote regions have rapidly deoptimized, causing loss of morale and lives. TTI has been working on a new package that allows for two things never before offered by any genetics service. First, instead of focusing on a specific trait, we wanted the ability for bodies to adapt in real time to field conditions." I smiled. "Which may seem familiar if you watched me run the race." Some laughter. "Second, we wanted those changes to fade slowly when supply chains are cut.

"What you saw during this race was the final field test of this package, which we're calling TTI Endurance Black. It will be available free of charge to any active-duty US service member for the next three years." Some cheering. "And to all of you for a small monthly fee after release early next year." More cheering. "And that's all I've got. Oh, wait, check this out."

I held out my hands and arms. With the slightest thought, browns and tans flowed over my skin. I was a human lava lamp. The crowd fell silent. I could almost hear them drooling.

"More to come on that. Thank you so much for letting me be part of this great race. Now I have to go pass out."

"Yeah, Fiddy!" Brad yelled again. Danny hooted. I smiled, nodded to Smith, and Dad walked me out of the limelight. I'd done my bit and hopefully it was enough.

When I got close to Danny, Dad left me standing in place, wobbly, unstable, and Brad did the same for Danny. A slight breeze could have taken me down. I hobbled closer. He smiled. I frowned at something on his face.

"What's on your face?"

He raised his eyebrows. "Glasses?"

"You people are a mess."

"You people?"

And then I kissed him, publicly, shamelessly and damn near pornographically. It was probably the only smart thing I'd done all day. He kissed me back just as hard, making it by far the best thing I'd done all week. *Danny, Daniel, Dan.* He tasted like home. I probably tasted like the grave. We pulled apart. He wiped dirt and blood off his lips. A lot of people were watching us. I didn't even want to check my social feed. So instead I tried to figure out why the sky was spinning.

"*Borne!*" I said. That was the name of the book.

And then I passed out.

EIGHT:
Naughty, Naughty Zoot

Awakenings

I WAS IN THE Marathons clinic for three days, then back at home in bed for another week. Turns out in addition to bruising, damaged vocal chords, blisters, strained tendons, missing toenails, two broken toes (no memory of how that happened), substantial kidney and liver damage, a bruised spleen, an antibiotic resistant UTI (due to dehydration, not Danny sex), absurdly tangled hair, and innumerable cuts, abrasions and cactus spines, I also had stress fractures in both femurs and my left kneecap. None of which was considered serious, though I was briefly classified as augmented as Dr. Rai infused by blood with medical nanites to fight the UTI and heal my bones. The scars faded. My throat opened up. Looking at me in the interviews three weeks later, you'd never know I'd been hurt at all. I was smiling for the audience, thanking my dockers for their support and, of course, flogging TTI Endurance Black.

Before all that, I opened my eyes late the night after I passed out in front of the entire world, starving, dehydrated, worried I'd peed myself again, to find myself alone in the clinic except for Berrick. He was lying in the bed next to mine, still smelling like sweat and ammonia, and droning on about dockers and eagles and how—

"You're alive!" I said, but it was like my words blew him away, an illusion as insubstantial as mist. I blinked and I was alone. I wondered if I was the last human being to speak to him, or if anyone would even remember he existed a few years from now. After the riots and the speeches, what would be left of the quiet man who just wanted to run? I think I was too dehydrated to cry, or maybe even that was a dream because I don't remember anything else until the next morning. I slept through the awards banquet, Smith's farewell speech, visits from my family and the great exodus from ModCon. When I woke up with a start in the bright morning light, my arms and legs were all in MediTubes and Coach was sitting in a chair by the side of the bed. I could just see a wedge-shaped package of something suspiciously cheesy in his lap.

"You have some fans." Amusement flickered in his sky-blue eyes. There were flowers and packages of cheese on every available surface in the room. It smelled like a French market before pasteurization, so like heaven to me and hell to everyone else on this side of the Atlantic. So, yes, I had some fans, but I was focused on what he'd brought in.

"It's Asiago Mezzano," he said. "I'm told it's exceptional, but not overly redolent."

"Stinky, you mean."

He smiled and set the package on the bedside table, which might as well have been on another planet given my physical condition. He wasn't going to feed me again?

"Your family's waiting in the hall with an irresponsible amount of food. I just wanted to know if you'd like to join the team?"

I didn't even hesitate. "Yes. You mean it? I can run other races?"

"Victor's approved if you run for Endurance Black. But the final decision's mine."

"And?"

"And I don't want to see what I saw the last two days. Your life and safety are more important than any race. I don't know what you were thinking, but it can't happen again. I'll help you run. I won't help you get yourself killed."

It hadn't occurred to me how insane my behavior must have seemed from the outside. He must've thought I was a lunatic. And given my behavior at the lake, I'm not sure he was wrong.

"And you have to listen to me roughly eighty-four percent of the time."

"Now you're pushing it."

"Deal?" He offered his hand, which I couldn't shake, so I stuck out my tongue. And just like that, I was Media Conaill, badass

Endurance Black ultrarunner.

"I might even recommend you for the Marathons," he said, winking. He was gone before I could tell him I'd never do this race again. It was idiotic. It was dangerous. Only a psychopath would come back voluntarily. Then I asked Alex what it took to qualify without a super-special TTI exemption. It was hard, but doable, and maybe I could beat Abbey. I was in. That complete reversal took about ten seconds, just enough time for my family and Brad to pour through the door with pretty much all the food.

They fed me, told me stories, chided me, fed me some more, Brad stole some sausages and mocked my cheese, I told them I was on the team, and aside from the fact that no one had seen Danny, things were just really weirdly happy. I guess that's how it feels to belong somewhere instead of just being assigned. It took me another hour to realize that Coach had fixed up my hair while I was still asleep—pulled it back and wrapped it in a tight bun, secured with a scrunchie. Damned if I didn't cry when I figured it out.

Lord of Spoons

DANNY SHOWED UP WHEN I was bloated and tired and everything hurt. He waited in the doorway until we noticed, and then suddenly everyone had to be somewhere important. Danny looked stunned to find himself alone in the room with me.

"I was going to bring you cheese." He walked over to kiss me disappointingly on the forehead. "But I think you've got that covered."

He sat with a few grunts. I reversed my pucker and tried not to pout. Was it awkward now? I tried to think back to our kiss the night before, but all I remembered was warmth and spinning stars. It took me a second to realize he'd put something on the table. It was a book, a real paper book. How had he afforded that? And what was it? I couldn't sit up far enough to see the cover, but I could smell the old paper. "What is it?"

"*Western States Women*," he said. "The first hundred miler I ran was Western States." Which was a famous race from Squaw Valley to Auburn, California. "It's about women who ran in the early years, Ann Trason and others." He shrugged. "I thought you'd like it."

"I love it." How had he even found it? "I got you something too."

He looked at the package on the bedside table. Dr. Rai had been nice enough to have it taken from my room and wrapped. Danny picked it up and turned it over, suspicious.

"It won't bite."

He tore off the wrapper and pulled out one of Berrick's jerseys. Mini-me had let me take one when I ran into her in the hallway.

Which made me sad now that she was dead, or decommissioned—whatever they called decapitated synthetics. I had thought about wearing the Jersey in Berrick's honor on loop four, but that would've just made things worse.

Danny wiped his eyes. "Thank you. This is…"

"Danny, are we okay?"

He paused. My heart sank. We were not okay. Even if naturals and modified didn't usually date, I didn't think he'd care about that. And now that I was running—

"TTI created a natural scholarship program for endurance sports in Berrick's honor. They asked me to run it." He looked at me for a moment. "Nothing to do with you?"

There was an edge to his question. "Is that a bad thing?"

"I also got crowdfunding money to train for next year, enough to optimize my whole family, but no one can figure out who the donors are."

"Weird."

"Yeah."

"Danny, I didn't mean it to be patronizing."

"No, no, I get it." He looked down. "It's just, the way the money came in, someone seemed to assume I wanted to modify myself and run as a baseline."

I blinked. "You don't?"

He almost laughed. "No, Media. Never."

"But…" But what? Why had I just assumed he'd want to transition if he could afford it? I hadn't even asked him. "You'll hurt yourself." I sounded like a child. "You'll die."

"Then I'll die as Daniel Washington. No one ever gave you a choice, Media. No one even asked you. What would you give for just one chance to pick your own direction in life?" He was kind enough not to wait for an answer. "Because if I take what they're offering, I'll never have a choice again. I'll never be *me* again. The funny thing is, TTI knew that. One condition of managing the charity is that I have to remain unmodified."

"Danny, I was just trying to help."

"I know." He smiled sadly. "We live in different worlds, Media,

358 SHAWN C. BUTLER

and I don't think you'd like mine very much. It's dirty and ugly and people die every day, but I'm still not changing for you or anyone else."

"Danny—"

"I'm going to finish this race next year as me, as a natural, and I plan to beat every modified I can. That'll stick in their craw for a thousand years."

"I don't care that you're natural." I was fighting tears. "I didn't mean it that way." Even if I kept carelessly stripping away his dignity in the name of love.

"I know." He stood and looked at me the way I hate. The way that tells me I just don't get it, and I never will, and he forgave me, but why couldn't I just see how the world works? "I hear you're on the TTI team now?"

I just nodded. He kissed me on the forehead again. I wanted to scream.

"Then I'll see you out there. You can buy me those beers you owe me."

And then he was gone.

Danny, Daniel, Dan. Soon there'd be dust on the words, and he'd taste like a ghost.

I couldn't even think. I was tired and angry and sad and I wanted to chase him down the hall, but I was a human tube holder and he was right anyway. I had assumed he'd want to be modified. It still felt like the smarter move. Maybe I was as modifist as Berrick thought I was.

It didn't change the fact that I loved him and he didn't love me.

I'd have given up cheese for him.

Public Displays of Affection

TOMMY SHOWED UP LATER with ice cream—cold, creamy perfection with the steam still rising from its frosted surface. Even the spoon was chilled. God, I loved my brother. Until he very slowly and intentionally kissed me on the forehead, just like Danny, and then I would've head-butted him if I could move that fast.

"Relax," he said. "He's just playing hard to get."

"Who is?" I feigned ignorance and stared at the ice cream. Why wasn't that in my mouth yet?

"'Legs.' Open wide."

I snorted.

"I didn't mean it that way."

I opened wide. Damn, that was good ice cream.

"What do you mean, hard to get?"

"Swallow first. Talk next."

I swallowed. "You really think so?"

"He likes you, but you're asking a lot. It puts his family at risk. He wants to know you're not just screwing around."

"Then why didn't he say that?"

More ice cream. "People are like that." He put the ice cream down on the bedside table, which was inappropriate. I glared. He sat back, ignoring me, and something changed.

"What?" I asked. "What's wrong?"

"I was just thinking about what Jessica said in the cafeteria."

I frowned. There were so many things to choose from. He requested privacy mode and I accepted, the way it was supposed to work.

"*About me being a GIP,*" Tommy said. *"Do you think she was right?"*

"*No.*" I looked around for security cameras. "*She was just screwing with us.*"

"*Yeah, I know. But you know how you change? How you go to the lab and come back and you're never sure what's different?*"

"*Yes…*"

"*I feel that way too, sometimes. I know Dr. K doesn't do nearly as much to me, but Jessica made me think. I wasn't always so into PDA. Even Brad noticed.*" He smiled just a bit, which was adorable. "*Now's it's like a compulsion, saying hi to everyone, hugging them, like I feel bad if I don't do it.*"

"*You're just kind, Tommy.*" Which I hoped was true. "*That's all.*"

He wasn't convinced. Did he really think his behavior was genetic? If so, why?

"Time's up," Dr. Rai said from the doorway. How long had she been standing there? We snapped out of privacy mode as she walked in. "Media needs to rest, and I need to check on her."

Tommy nodded and left, head down, almost apologetic.

Blood & Leverage

THAT NIGHT THE PAIN medication only worked in waves. I tossed and turned in dark dreams. For the longest time, I thought my mother was in the room, dancing to unseen music like kelp fronds tossed in a surging sea. 'Can you hear them?' she kept asking. But all I heard were her bare feet sweeping across the tile floor and a song no one had ever sung.

I woke on my second day in the clinic to pain and hunger. Smith was watching me from the bedside chair. I said something like good morning. She glanced at all my criminally neglected cheeses and shook her head.

"You're going to eat all of this, aren't you?"

Was that really a question?

"I'm impressed. With you, I mean. You've done amazing things here. I don't like how you did it, but…" She looked back at me and held up three vials full of blood. "As you know, we're not allowed to keep your DNA after testing. So of course we did. Here's your sample from our visit at TTI. This one was collected by Tim in the hole."

"Tim?"

"You think you fell by accident?"

"Tim's a GIP?"

"Be nice. And this one is from last night while you were sleeping. Which means we can now follow the full process of what changed in your genome from before the race to after." She pocketed the three vials and pulled out another set. "These are Tommy's. Probably nothing there, though, right?"

"Why are you—"

"Leverage. No more surprises. No more unapproved experiments next year. Anything else, and all this goes to Genetic Overwatch. Victor has power, but he can't protect himself from this."

"Why do you keep telling me instead of him?"

"I like you better." She pocketed the samples. "Are we clear?"

"You're really letting naturals back next year?" I was thinking of Danny.

She nodded. "Nearly doubled our audience. I have no problem with that." She watched me for a second. "Just ask. I promise not to bite."

"I don't get you. You're Beast Brain. You were a genius before you were modified. Why do...*this*?" And why be such as asshole about it? But I didn't ask that part.

"You think our use of the Barkley is just a marketing ploy, a cynical play on nostalgia. But I love the idea that we are bettering ourselves, pushing ourselves. Sure, bioengineering changes the speed and direction of change, but look at you. Look at what you've done. Gary Cantrell once said it perfectly."

She shunted me Gary's quote via PA: "*For all the talk of exploring human potential, and seeking our limits, ultrarunners tend to play it safe. They line up challenges they know they can finish and run them carefully within their limits. At the Barkley, success is about overreaching our abilities and living to tell about it.*"

"That's still true here," she said. "It's why we don't allow terminals or augmented. Everyone here, even the naturals, are human beings. Better human beings, but still human. Underneath all the violence and marketing, there's still beauty. You just have to look for it. Plus..."

"What?"

"I get to see giant bears fight dragons. It's better than real work."

Which sounded just true enough to be total bullshit.

When she left, I wondered what she would find in the vials. Would she be able to see what I was? If so, maybe she could tell me.

Except for Dr. Rai's occasional check-ins, I expected to be alone most of the day. I stayed off the net as much as possible. My kiss with Danny had not gone over well, and that made me sad in more ways than I could count. Mom and Dad went back to work, Tommy and Brad back to the lab, and the clinic took on a hollow, haunted sound.

But Coach showed up frequently that day and the next, always with food, as if he'd become my old timey grandmother. Was he trying to buy my love? I always had the impression he wanted to ask me a question, maybe the BHD question, but he just chatted about nothing and fed me. Maybe if he trusted me more, he could ask what he needed, but I didn't push him. It was like there was a person trapped inside him, screaming to be free. I knew what that was like. I also knew no one could walk through the cage door for you. He would ask when he could, and whatever he needed, I knew I'd do it. Because he was alive somehow, and even if that didn't make sense, he was still my friend.

Not So Special After All

THAT NIGHT, MY MOTHER danced again, spinning, spinning until the sun came up. I woke up smiling, feeling closer to her. Dad texted to say they were coming to pick me up. They were bringing fresh clothes, which reminded me of the team running clothes. I panicked. Had they taken them back? Dad read my mind, of course.

"They cleaned them and overnighted them here."

Disaster averted.

An hour later, I apparently started hallucinating. I looked up and Victor was in the doorway in a retro fitted pinstripe suit. It was like he was going to a board meeting fifty years ago, except he never left campus. The door slid shut behind him. He sat on the end of the bed and smiled, waiting.

"Are you real?" I asked.

"More or less. How do you feel?"

"Terrible." Everything seemed to hurt more each day. "You can't be real."

I wanted to poke him to see if he was really there. Instead, he raised a hand as it changed color to muted silver. For a second, I thought he had done the chromatic thing to himself, and then I realized he was a nano-synthetic—an aggregate of tiny bots that could change shape at will. I'd heard of them but never seen one in person. They were expensive and fragile and easily reduced to gray goo if exposed to too much electricity or magnetism.

"I'll make this short…" He trailed off when my stomach rumbled. Stu had woken up, and he was hangry. "I just wanted to thank you. You did more for me, for us, than I had any right to ask. I have no idea what happened after the lake—that was a bit…"

"Insane? Completely non-baseline?"

"I was going to say extreme, but I'm glad you finished in one piece."

I wanted to ask a question, but I wasn't sure I could.

"It's okay," he said. "We're private here."

Of course we were. "Okay, did it work? In the testing center, you sounded disappointed."

"That was for the judges. The less they knew, the better. I'm not sure it worked yet, not completely, but you are changing. It'll take a few weeks to stabilize. You'll know before I do."

"And you still won't tell me what it is?"

"Not yet. And that's what I wanted to tell you. It'll be hard for us to talk back at TTI. Security will be even stronger. The military wasn't happy about what we did to Jessica."

I giggled, thinking of her hitting the dirt in front of the monster bear. There was a meme circulating with me as the *We Can Do It* woman, arm flexed, and Jessica unconscious at my feet. How was that not funny?

"I meant the hack," he said. "Jessica didn't report us, but I'm sure they know about it."

"Wait, she said you'd let her in. What did she mean?" I couldn't believe she was still alive, but it was probably safe to assume she wasn't a zombie. The woman was just indestructible.

"We agreed to hire her as a security consultant if she was discharged after the games. I'm still not sure how that will play out. She scares the hell out of me. Anyway, back at TTI, if you feel anything changing in your body, tell me. Not Dr. K. Not your family. Me. And only in private sessions. Then we can talk about what's next. Do you understand?"

"Yes." I hesitated, then: "What about Tommy? Jessica said…"

"I know what she said, but I can't tell you anything more right now. It's nothing bad."

"Victor, he's my brother."

"I know it's hard, but you have to trust me."

"Like I have a choice?"

"Of course you do. I've told and shown you enough to destroy me. I've put my life and my company in the hands of a twenty-one-year-old woman with poor impulse control and a dairy obsession. If that doesn't tell you how broken the world is, nothing will. But it also gives you power. Use it carefully."

"Was that meant to be a pep talk?"

"This is serious, Media. Don't screw it up by doubting yourself. I need you."

"You've still got Jasmina."

"I suppose that's true, but I don't *want* Jasmina."

For a fleeting second, I felt like his little penguin again, safe and protected from the world.

"Oh," I said. "Smith took a lot of blood from me and—"

"I know. It was inevitable. I wouldn't worry about it."

"Really?"

He shrugged. "One last thing. No matter what, you can't trust Kylera."

"You already said that. Why are you so worried about her?"

"Because she's an extremist. She doesn't understand nuance and she's made mistakes she wants to fix. No, that's not right. She wants to earn forgiveness. She's desperate for it. Her Universal Baseline proposal was for *compulsory* genetic vaccines, not voluntary. You remember how that worked during the Chrome Wars? Maybe the elimination of racism was worth it, but a lot of people died. What we're doing can't happen that way. I need more time to convince her that a slow path is better than a fast one. People must be allowed to make their own choices. If she gets a hold of what we're doing…."

"I don't get it. She works for you."

He blew out some air from his nano lungs and shrugged, as in *what-the-hell.*

"You know TTI acquired Nomanity to get their bioengineering technology?" I nodded. "What you don't know is that Kylera was Nomanity's only shareholder. In public, TTI remained the parent company and just took on the Nomanity logo. In reality, it was a reverse acquisition. Kylera needed a way to stay out of the public eye after her proposal was published online and Nomanity stock tanked.

Through holding companies and other means, Kylera became the majority shareholder in TTI. My title is a bit of misdirection."

"Wait. You're kidding, right? She owns TTI? You work for *her*?"

"She owns a lot of it. In a way, we all work for her."

Was he serious? "Then why is she hanging in the lab with me?"

"Honestly? I don't know. So when you get back, say goodbye to her, but don't make a big deal of it. Go to your new lab and then keep away from her. Understand?"

"No, but okay." I smiled. "I feel like a spy. It's kind of fun."

"This isn't a game, Media. You know that, right?"

"I know." But it sounded like a game to me, and I was still a pawn.

"I'll see you back at TTI. We're going to do great things."

Before I could say anything else, the nano-synthetic shell shifted to formless silver, watching me with mirrored mercury eyes. Victor was gone.

"Tell me how black hole drones fly," I demanded with more confidence than I felt, for Coach, but also because he'd made me curious and now I had to know.

"I'm sorry, Media," it said in a flat voice that gave me the chills. "I'm afraid I can't do that."

Which was disappointing, sure, but it didn't dissolve or explode either. There were no alarms. It just kept looking at me with its dead eyes and I wished I'd never asked.

A few seconds later, it left and I remembered to breathe.

Inner Space

BACK AT HOME THE week before I got back to work, I lay in bed and stared up at the ceiling, just like Dad had most of my childhood. I always thought he was thinking deep thoughts or solving serious problems, but maybe he was just searching, looking for something inside himself and wondering how he fit in the world. Because that's how I felt now. I was different. And it wasn't just the race.

Something was waking up inside me. It's hard to explain. Try to imagine growing new arms, not better ones, but additional ones. You have new connections in your brain, new things you can move and touch, but instead of arms, there's something inside you—a system or organ that wasn't there before and now...is. There were no instructions, no genetic memory of what to do. It was like learning to use a cybernetic implant without training, I guess. I don't know. I had no idea what was happening. I almost PA'd Victor a dozen times to tell him.

Is this what you were looking for? I'd ask. *What is it?*

But after what he'd told me about Dr. K, I was nervous. I thought back on our relationship, our little games, and wondered what she was really using me for. I wasn't sure what was safe and what wasn't, so I closed my eyes and focused inward. I could feel every muscle and fiber in my body. I could picture the shape of my liver, the sound of alveoli expanding in my lungs. Every corner of my body was laid out in three dimensions, like my own personal universe. It was so clear. How had I missed it before?

Between dark, strange dreams, Alex told me about the Guugu

Ymithirr people of Australia who had no concept of right and left but only cardinal orientations, east, west and so on. An investigator tried living in their world and soon found herself seeing her orientation in space as a visual display in her mind, a rediscovered ability to use a virtual compass no one knew existed except for every Guugu Ymithirr child. Maybe that's what was happening to me. I was rediscovering something long forgotten, some primitive ability shed when we stood on hind legs and walked away from the sea.

And I thought about what Berrick had said, about the way of the world, and how people always stood on top of others. About hierarchy and class, and how it changes but never changes at the same time. Where I fit and didn't. I looked inside myself and tried to connect the dots, one thought to another, but I couldn't. I just flew through the inner space that was me, fascinated but uncomprehending, still a passenger in my own body.

I slept like a cat, all day and anywhere. When I couldn't sleep, I played with Paisley in her tank, relishing the feel of her on my skin and that strange peace she offered. We changed colors for each other, and sometimes it almost felt like we were talking. Maybe those were the voices my mother heard, not her imagination or insanity, but some higher sense of another mind. Or maybe I was just imagining things.

There were interruptions. At first, they came frequently—congratulations, interview offers and more. Shaquilla and Terrence PA'd to see how I was doing. Brad and Tommy appeared and disappeared, worried, cutely affectionate to one another. Jasmina texted *'good job'* in a pro forma way. Abbey PA'd nice notes like, *You still playing for sympathy?* or various BHD clips of me flipping through the air after she clotheslined me. Slowed down and scored with sad music, it had become another viral meme titled 'Monday morning be like.' I think she was just lonely. I couldn't wait to hug her again. Maybe that's why she never visited in the clinic.

I missed Danny and the trees and just wanted to get out again. What kept me from running out the front door was Victor. I believed in him. He believed in me. We could figure this out together. I'm not as naïve as that sounds. I knew Victor had his own motivations but I also knew we both hated how the world worked, even if I was just learning about it. When you peeled back the shine and illusion, what remained was terrible and sad. I was near the bottom of the hierarchy, born looking up, and now I just wanted out. So whatever he was doing, however I changed, I was in.

And if I could, I'd help him burn it all down.

The New Zoot Show

"I DON'T UNDERSTAND WHY I'm here," I said to Dr. K. I was on the testing table in my old lab. I'd just come to say goodbye, but she seemed to think I was there to work. "Victor said I'd have a new lab, with Tommy and…"

Dr. K sat and nodded. "Oh, I know. Don't worry. We've upgraded the lab. No more beta testing. We've scheduled a full genetic reset. You'll get everything he promised."

"But this is the same lab." She'd even kept the modified pyramid on the door.

"Is it?" She looked around. "Oh, you didn't see the new sign. We're Advanced Feature Development now. Dermal Camouflage. Rapid Adaptation Endurance packages. Whatever other nonsense Victor made up at the Marathons."

"Advanced Features?" Her voice gave me the chills. I hesitated, then: "Victor said I'd have a new mentor." It was probably too late for subtlety.

She nodded, smiled tight-lipped as a synthetic. "I talked to the board and we agreed he probably shouldn't have done that."

"But…" But what could I say? It was her company.

"I know Victor told you I came from Nomanity. Every animal at this company comes from Nomanity. Every modification. Every control system. They're *mine*. Tim protected you because I told him to. Bears attacked Jessica because I made them. Paisley helps stabilize your mother because I created her, cell by cell, in my labs. It's important you understand this, Media. We're going to do great things together, but I never let go of what's mine."

"I'm not *yours*," I snapped. "I'm…"

She waited. What was I going to say? I wasn't hers? I wasn't property? The only person who could fix this was Victor, and there was no point antagonizing her in the meantime.

"I see you're understanding, Media. That's good. It's really, *really* good. We get to keep working together, and this time we'll be able to get to know each other. I'll tell you about my life before TTI. We'll be girlfriends and whisper secrets in each other's ears. Isn't that great?"

Throat-punch her, Alex said. *Throat-punch her and run.* I opened my mouth to tell her where she could put her secrets when the door slid open. Jessica Murphy walked in wearing a TTI security uniform and took a position by the side of the door.

"Hey, bestie," she said.

I wanted to scream, but all that came out was, "What…?"

"Oh, I thought you knew," Dr. K said. "Jessica's our new head of security."

This couldn't be happening. I glanced up at the great black eye of the new and larger security AI, seeing only my diminished reflection. Was Victor watching? Was anyone? Dad?

Maybe it was the stress of the moment, but I'm not sure. A switch flipped in me, and I could suddenly see my lungs expanding and contracting, electrical impulses flashing from spine to extremities and back, red blood cells sliding down an artery in my leg. Seeing wasn't the right word. It was all there, my entire body. It was such a beautiful system, and now I wasn't just seeing it; I was in control, or soon would be. That's what Victor was doing—giving me the ultimate choice. He was playing god and, eventually, if I wanted, I could be the thing with teeth.

I just had to live long enough to get away from Dr. K.

"Everything okay?" she asked.

I got my heart rate under control. It wasn't hard.

"Never better. When can I talk to Victor?" He could fix this. He had to.

"All things in good time." She stood and came over to the table. I tried to hide my excitement as I looked up at her, my mentor, my creator, and smiled that Conaill smile that is calm and sweet and nothing. She smiled back, and I almost didn't notice. Her head canted to the side so slightly it was nearly impossible to see. It was her little tell.

She knew. She knew everything.

Fuck.

Postface by Gary Cantrell

aka Lazarus Lake
Founder of the Barkley Marathons

We humans have an innate fear of technology. Especially in today's rapidly changing world, we have a fear that technology will render us obsolete. It isn't as if there are not plenty of precedents to look back on. Computers relegated millions of clerks to the unemployment office. The internal combustion motor sent millions of farmhands to seek work in the factories of the early 20th century. The printing press rendered scribes obsolete. Agriculture pushed out the hunter-gatherers.

Indeed, since the spear replaced the hand axe, human history is the story of technology eliminating ways of life. The boogeymen of our era seem just as mysterious and threatening to us as the atlatl did to the nomadic tribes of the Paleolithic.

Here in the 21st century, the foreboding of the future is human enhancement. From performance-enhancing drugs to bioengineering, who among us is not a little threatened by the thought of being left in the dust by the potential supermen of the not so distant future?

Shawn Butler presents us with a glimpse into this possible future in an entertaining tale of an athletic competition gone mad. As with all advances in the history of humanity, once these new capabilities have been integrated into society, they will become a normal part of life. But, they will also transform the world we live in.

Enjoy, and speculate what the future will hold.

About the Author

Shawn C. Butler is the award-winning author of *Run Lab Rat Run*, the first book in the Modified series about genetic engineering, human modification, and our often violent search for immortality. He lives in Southern California. You can visit him online at shawncbutler.com or on Twitter @ShawnCButler. You might even find him out running the trails of San Jacinto when he's not injured like the natural he is.

*

If you enjoyed *Run Lab Rat Run*,
Please leave a review on Amazon or Goodreads.
Thank you!

Acknowledgements

This book would not have been possible without the help of many patient, tolerant, insightful, intelligent and generally awesome people. This includes beta readers Diana, Donna, Hannah, Heather, Jeanne, Juli, Laura, Ray and of course, my English-teacher and literary bad-ass mother. Juli and Hannah also provided exceptional editorial support and generally helpful feedback on multiple occasions. Juli further contributed invaluable fact-checking and other assistance to push this across the finish line, for which I'll be forever grateful. Thanks also to supportive friends Jim, John, Melanie, Tamberly, Tessa and many others. And, of course, a final callout to Barkley Marathons founder Gary Cantrell (aka Lazarus Lake), who inspires so many of us to run farther, go harder, and do generally stupid and wonderful things Out There.

Coming Soon:
Beasts of Sonara

Beasts takes us back to where the genetic modification in *Run Lab Rat Run* got started: in the sleepy Costa Rican town of Sonara. Nestled in the thick jungle and warm Pacific bay are the secrets to human immortality and the beasts that protect it. Here is a sample chapter from *Beasts of Sonara*, coming soon:

Tiburón Bebé
Baby Shark

Why are you so angry?

The infant bull shark fought in her arms. She squeezed his gills shut. He snapped and took a chunk of her tentacle into his tiny tooth-ringed mouth, black eyes flashing with pride. She considered eating him for the tenth time. Instead, she squeezed harder.

Sleep, my child. Sleep.

He spat her flesh back at her. Spiteful thing.

She scanned the dark waters of the bay, the last light of day casting purple shadows across the rippled ocean floor. She was exposed out here. Hungry shadows moved in the dark blue distance, sharks and other things even she couldn't fight, but none nearby.

The shark lashed and bucked. She squeezed until she felt his pain and then stillness. Was there a better choice? She'd never taken a shark before, but she was tired of being afraid. She needed something to protect her out here, even if it was this terribly made creature.

She reached again for his mind, found only rage. Was she food or monster to him? Was there any difference in a mind so small? Nothing she knew worked. She rubbed his white belly and shot water across his rough skin from her funnel, anything to calm him. He whipped and gnashed, all instinct and muscle, and she almost ripped him in half.

Stop it. Stop or die.

He heard her this time.

What do you want? he asked. It wasn't really a question. It was just how she felt his thoughts. She tried to give him an answer, but he didn't understand. They had no language for each other. So she reached into his mind, changed a tiny thing, and his eyes closed. Finally, he slept.

Purple turned to black as she rushed back toward the cave, toward safety and the long night ahead. She had a god to make, and that was never an easy thing.

In her arms, the shark dreamed of a thousand fish spinning in silver balls, but soon he'd have bigger dreams. He'd rule the sea and everything in it.

Everything but her.

Sign up to hear about *Beasts* and other books in the Modified world of *Run Lab Rat Run* at shawncbutler.com.

*

If you enjoyed *Run Lab Rat Run,*
Please leave a review on Amazon or Goodreads.
Thank you!

Printed in Great Britain
by Amazon